Remember My Name

Chase Potter

CHASE POTTER BOOKS
www.chasepotter.com

Remember My Name
Copyright © 2015 Chase Potter

This is a work of fiction. Names, characters, businesses, places, events and incidents are either the products of the author's imagination or used in a fictitious manner. Any resemblance to actual persons, living or dead, or actual events is purely coincidental.

ISBN-10: 0692376682
ISBN-13: 978-0692376683

For my brother.

ACKNOWLEDGEMENTS

So many people have helped me along the way, but first I'd like to thank all of my readers. Your encouragement and criticism have helped shape me as a writer, and this book wouldn't have been the same without your help. Thanks for sticking with me!

For feedback and contributions to this novel, I would also like to thank Brian Gumm, Nick Pageant, Meran Kreibich, Joseph Prout, Sunne Manello, and my husband, Mitchell.

Chapter One

Jackson

"Is that all you want?" His words hang thick in the air like the day's humidity – similarly coming on strong and definitely contributing to the perspiration under my arms.

"Yeah, that's it," I manage, ignoring my discomfort at being the focus of his piercing brown eyes. From the moment I entered the store, I haven't been able to look anywhere else.

He picks out the air hose connector from the shelf and sets it into my open hand, the tips of his fingers making the briefest contact with my palm. I glance up at him, letting my gaze linger there only a moment before I look away.

Following him back to the front of the hardware store, I wonder who he is. Northfield isn't that big, and he seems about my age, but I've never seen him before. He has a decent build, and he might even work out. It's hard to really tell, because his weathered t-shirt is a size too big and hangs off his shoulders. Splotchy grease stains cover the fabric, making it look like a dirty leopard print. Engine grease, not fast food grease.

He rings me up at the till. "Four seventy-five," he says, watching as I dig out the wallet from my back pocket. "Cash or credit?"

If the idea weren't completely crazy, I'd think that the extra looks I'm sending his way are almost being reciprocated. But they definitely can't be. That would be just a bit too brazen for this town, regardless of who this guy is.

"Um, cash," I say, sliding a twenty across the counter.

He makes half an effort at a smile as he gives me the change and points a glance at my purchase. "You working on some kind of project?"

Suddenly the blue shirt with the white lettering feels tight across my chest. "Redoing the roof. This is for the air nailer." I could elaborate, but I don't know what else I'd say. Unable to withstand his expectant gaze any longer, I look away. "See you."

"Later," he says, the hint of something I don't recognize filtering into his voice.

The door chimes behind me as I step out onto the sidewalk and squint into the sun. Rounding the corner, I let out a long breath. I've never met a guy like that before. I get myself in trouble sometimes, letting my eyes stray or saying something I shouldn't. But for some reason, I feel like part of him was right there with me. He wasn't exactly checking me out, at least not like I was doing to him, but there was something there.

I shouldn't get my hopes up, because it always gets thrown in my face. Sometimes literally, like last winter when the thing getting "thrown in my face" was a fist.

But that guy... he didn't seem to mind. Could he really be like me? If not, what else could it have been?

I'm halfway down the block when a voice calls after me. "Hey, wait up."

I turn as he slows to a walk. Eager smile, inquisitive eyes. It takes me a moment to remember to move my mouth. "Can I help you with something?"

Holding his hand out, he reveals a pair of aviators in his palm. *My* aviators. "You forgot these."

I pause, making him wait several seconds before I finally take the sunglasses. "Thanks."

"I'm Matt," he says quickly. Fingers drifting up, he brushes shaggy black hair out of his eyes. Is he nervous?

I hesitate before giving him my name as well. "Jackson."

"You live here in Northfield?"

I nod. "A few miles out."

He brightens, but at what, I have no clue. "Cool."

What's he waiting for? Silence wedges itself between us, beginning to threaten awkwardness when he asks, "You need help on that roof?"

"You're serious?"

Redness hits his face like a crimson sunrise. "I'm pretty handy, and that hardware place doesn't give me many hours." He's talking really fast. "Anyway, it's cool if you don't need any help, it was kind of a dumb idea. Sorry." He takes a quick breath as he turns away.

"Sure." Did I really just say that? My heartbeat is loud in my ears.

He freezes, already several steps away. "Huh?"

"I mean, I'd have to ask my dad, but I think we could use help." Moisture on my palms, across my chest, under my arms. Am I really agreeing to this? I don't even know this guy. But part of me hopes something more is going on here.

"You know where to find me." He smiles, catching my eyes for an extra moment.

"Here it is," I say, holding out the connector across the bench seat of the truck.

He looks up and takes the part between his fingers. Just like mine, his hands are perfectly average. Neither long and thin, nor broad and strong. Unlike mine, however, they're rough with calluses and threaded with lines.

"Looks good, Jackson. How much was it?" Wrinkles around his eyes betray the age that has crept up on him over the last ten years.

I shrug. "Like five bucks, I think. I wasn't really paying attention." Actually I was just distracted.

He runs two fingers across his cleft chin and its covering of stubble. "If you're ever going to run a business or have a good job, you'll need to get better at keeping track of numbers. Accurate record keeping is one of the most important parts of adult life."

"Okay, Dad." I'm careful to add just enough deference into my tone so he doesn't think I'm talking back. "Can we go home now?"

"Sure," he says, starting up the truck.

As he pulls out onto the highway that will take us out of town, I remember the reckless suggestion presented to me only minutes earlier. "So, um, what do you think about getting some help with the roof?"

Dad gives me a look like I should know better. "Like a contractor? I can't really afford to pay for that."

"What about just one person? Like a weekend job for someone my age?"

He shrugs, his voice pensive. "That wouldn't be terrible, I suppose. You have someone in mind?"

When I step into the hardware store for the second time, I've prepared myself enough so that I'm not overwhelmed when Matt's attention lands on me.

He's leaning against the counter beside the cash register, twirling a pen between his fingers. "Hey," he says. He sounds glad to see me, and a feeling of lightness flutters in my stomach.

"I was, uh…" I've never had a problem with public speaking, but this is on an entirely different level. Poking my toe at a dust bunny on the floor, I force my eyes upward to meet his waiting expression. "I was thinking we might be able to use your help on the roof."

He lights up almost before I've gotten the words out. "Seriously? I could totally use the cash. I work here every summer, but they never give me enough hours." When he smiles, his whole face comes alive.

"As long as you're sure that you're up for it. It's a lot of work."

His eagerness not diminishing in the slightest, he nods quickly. "I know. I've roofed before."

"Really?"

"Don't look so surprised," he says with a laugh. "Do I not look like the type?" Judging by his biceps, the physical part of the job won't be an issue. Noticing my gaze, he grins. "That's what I thought."

My face might actually start to burn if it gets any hotter. *Time to bail, Jackson.* Swallowing away my embarrassment, I ask, "Can I leave my number with you?"

Sporting a sly, lopsided smile, he hands me a slip of paper and the pen he's been spinning between his fingers. Hastily scrawling out the number, I push the paper back at him. "When are you free to help out?"

He shrugs, glancing at the paper with my number. "Just let me know a few days ahead and I can make sure my schedule is free."

"Sure," I say, wanting to get out of there as fast as I can. It's getting hard to keep forming coherent sentences with him shooting off that smile of his. Before I go, I remember that Dad told me to find out how much we'd have to pay him before I promised him any work. Better late than never.

"Um, how much do you want an hour?"

Cocking his head to the side, he examines me, as if that has some bearing on how much he'll work for. "Roofing is hard work. Fifteen an hour."

Crap. Dad said no more than twelve. My fingers fidget with the keys in my pocket. "Deal."

"See you later," he says. It sounds more like a promise than the required goodbye.

Giving him a little wave, I step outside. Before I've even gotten in Dad's truck, my phone vibrates with a message from a new number. *Now you have my number too. –Matt*

Chapter Two

Jackson

It's not even eight o'clock yet, but I know today is going to be hot. It's something in the air, maybe the scent, or maybe just the way the morning breeze catches the trailing fingers of the weeping willow trees that encircle our yard. I can't put my finger on it, but you don't spend nearly twenty years out in the country and not start to pick up on these things.

Anyway, about that heat. It's actually a really bad thing, because we're starting on the roof today. When Dad had two pallets of shingles delivered a few days ago, I texted Matt to let him know we'd be starting today.

On the horizon, a column of dust dragged sideways by the wind grabs my attention. That's the one nice thing about dirt roads – it's easy to tell when someone is coming over. The source of the disturbance on the road is an old red pickup truck. Another full minute passes before it coughs its way into the yard, carried on a dusty cloud. Matt hops out and slams the door shut behind him, making the whole truck shake.

I raise an eyebrow. "Nice piece of equipment."

"It gets me around."

Dad picks that moment to come out of the house, saving me from having to think up a witty response. Dad's voice carries easily across the space between us, "So you're here to help us out? Matt, right?"

"Yes, sir." He nods vigorously, reaching out to shake my dad's hand.

"Jeff," Dad states as he accepts the hand offered to him.

"Nice to meet you," Matt replies robustly. I'm surprised. Apparently he can be pretty damn polite when he wants to be.

Dad looks him up and down, seeming pleased with what he sees. And why wouldn't he be? Bundles of shingles are fucking heavy, and Matt has muscle to spare. "You have any roofing experience?"

Matt nods again. "I helped with my uncle's house once. It was steeper than this," he says, shielding his eyes from the sun so he can get a better look at the roof.

"Good, that will make the work go faster. And you're right, this roof isn't that steep, but it's high," Dad warns, gesturing to our two-story farmhouse. "If you fall, you're fired before you hit the ground," he adds with a chuckle.

Dad likes to think he's funny, but he's usually not. Matt has the good sense to laugh though.

Following the two of them up the ladder, I clamber onto the roof after them. My stomach squirms as I get my footing on the curling shingles. It feels like a long time since Dad and I redid the garage roof two summers ago. He'd wanted to do the house at the same time, but he didn't have the money I guess.

"Are you paying attention, Jackson?"

"Huh?" I snap my head in Dad's direction. Matt is standing right beside him. What a suck up.

Dad's eyes narrow at me but he resumes talking. "So today you'll be tearing off. Shingles, tarpaper, roof vents, the old drip edge… everything. I'm hoping you'll have time to take out any leftover nails from the decking once all the old stuff is off, but if not, we'll tackle it tomorrow."

"All clear," Matt says.

"Wait a second, Dad," I interject. "You're not going to be helping us?"

He shrugs. "There are only two shingle shovels, so I'd just get in the way."

That just figures. "Ah… okay." I want to tell him it's a dick move not to help us with the tear off, but I bite my tongue. I don't want to get in a fight with Dad in front of Matt. I barely know the guy, and I don't want to make him uncomfortable. At least that's what I'm telling myself.

Dad doesn't waste any more time before scampering down the

ladder, returning in a minute to hand up a potato pitchfork and the only actual shingle shovel that we own. It's a weird sort of flat and narrow shovel with grooves on the end for catching nails and a pivot on the back to help with leverage. "All right, boys, have at it," Dad says before leaving us alone.

It's early enough the sun is still mostly blocked by the trees, but we don't have more than a few hours or so before it hits us full blast. Matt seems to know it too, because he picks up the pitchfork and raises his eyebrows at me. "Let's get this shit done," he says, shoving the pitchfork tines underneath a row of shingles. As he pries them up, they make the sticky ripping sound of tar separating.

The muscles in his arms are thick, tensing with every movement of the shovel. Continuing in a row, he loosens up an entire section before finally freeing a dozen shingles at once. Giving them a shove with his foot, the piece scrapes across the roof and disappears over the edge. A second later a muffled thud sounds up from the ground. Yeah, it's a ways down.

"You going to make me do this all by myself?" he teases.

"Uh, no, sorry," I say quickly, picking up the shingle shovel.

The work goes surprisingly quickly, or at least it feels that way. After a half hour, we've torn off almost a third of the side we're working on. I think Dad would have been more nervous about this job if the roof were bigger, but our house is skinny and tall, so there just isn't all that much roof.

"Damn," Matt says, leaning against his pitchfork. "Sun's going to be over the trees in a minute."

"It shouldn't be too bad," I say. "We've already gotten a lot done."

Matt turns his gaze on me. "It's going to suck. Trust me." When I shrug, he continues, "I thought you said you'd roofed before. The sun is the enemy, dude."

"It was a few years ago."

"Sure," he says, jabbing the pitchfork under another row of shingles as the first outstretched fingertips of sunlight touch us.

Over the next fifteen minutes, the sun rises above the tops of the trees and begins to broil us. I figured Matt was just being dramatic, but to my frustration, I have to admit he was right. It's not just working in the sun, because any idiot could guess that that's hot and uncomfortable. But the shingles beneath us are *black*, and the heat rolls off them in waves.

"Told you so," Matt says, grinning.

I drop my hand from my forehead, wiping the sweat on my shorts. "Yeah, fine. You were right."

He doesn't seem interested in driving the point home, because he doesn't respond other than to set down the pitchfork and start pulling his shirt off. Except with his arms still in the air, the shirt gets caught, sticking to his back. No doubt courtesy of a layer of perspiration developed in the last few minutes under the sun's searing gaze.

Trying not to laugh as he fights to get free of his own shirt, I step closer to him and loop a finger underneath where the fabric is stuck to his sweaty back. As I lift up, he tugs it off the rest of the way. Now revealed, the contours of his muscles draw my hungry eyes. It's a shame to cover a body like that with clothing. It's not like he's super ripped or anything, he's just… really toned. My eyes wander down his back, to the glistening sweat just above the waistband of his shorts.

"Dude," he says, sounding annoyed.

Is he mad that I helped him get his shirt off? Or because I stared at him a bit too long afterward? I'm afraid to ask, so I pick up the shingle shovel and don't look back. At least not for a few minutes.

After two hours of working under the beating sun, we stop for lunch and rest an hour to avoid going back into the hottest part of the day. Dad made sandwiches for us, but we're too tired to say much.

When we climb back up the ladder to tear off the second half of the roof, we're better prepared. Armed with two Nalgene bottles full of water and gloves to ward off the blisters threatening to erupt on our hands, we dive into the rest of the work.

The flash of Matt's dark hair in the sunlight and the sweat on his skin make it hard to keep my focus on the work. Whenever he digs his pitchfork under another row of shingles, the muscles in his back all tense up together like they're in some kind of competition with each other.

"Why do you keep looking at me like that?" Matt asks after catching me staring.

For the first time today, I'm thankful for the sun beating down. Without it, my embarrassment wouldn't have the mild sunburn to hide under. "I'm not," I reply quickly.

Halting in his work of peeling up old shingles, he leans against his pitchfork and watches me. "Yeah, you were."

Shit. How am I going to talk my way out of this one? Worst-case scenarios stream through my head. Him punching me in the face. Him refusing to help anymore and just leaving. Worse yet – him telling my dad.

His eyes haven't moved from me. If I'm going to salvage this, I have to do it right now. "I, uh... I just am kind of jealous of your, uh, build. Every time I start working out, I never get any results." Fighting to keep my breathing steady, I allow myself a moment to be impressed that I just came up with that on the fly.

"Well, shit," he says, but he doesn't sound mad. A sly smile sneaks onto his face. "I've gotten stares before, but usually it's, um, girls."

"Sorry, I didn't mean to be weird about it." I could kick myself for having just said that. It's not *weird* to check out another guy. It's just not straight. But this isn't a time to stand on principle.

Matt shrugs, picking up his pitchfork. "It's cool. I figure it's just a compliment."

Phew. That was close. Pivoting so I'm aiming at the roof and not Matt, I tear into the next row of shingles. We work in silence until the wind picks up, coaxing us up to the peak of the roof so we can catch the most of the breeze.

"If you're interested," Matt suggests, "I could show you through a workout. It's not hard to gain muscle, you just need to eat properly for your body and do the right lifts."

I glance up from the bland dark gray of the roof. "That'd be great." Assuming that we're still on speaking terms by the time we finish this damn job, I mentally add.

Hours later, we drag ourselves down the ladder. The sun disappeared a while ago, so we couldn't have worked any longer even if we'd wanted to. Every part of my body is sore, including a lot of areas I didn't think could actually hurt. Even my feet feel unsteady on the ground, but somehow, almost inexplicably, we got done with everything Dad hoped we would.

An hour ago, the shingles were all torn off and any last nails had been ripped out, leaving the dirty pine decking boards exposed and smooth. We thought we were done until Dad checked the weather and saw a chance of rain. So we had to go back up and put down tarps and plastic.

I collapse at the kitchen table across from Matt. He sighs, leaning back in his chair. "That was a long day."

I'm so exhausted I don't want to even think about talking, but if

Matt can manage it, I can too. "And we haven't even started putting the new stuff on."

He grimaces. "Don't remind me."

The screen door slams and Dad comes in, looking pleased. "You guys did a good job."

I groan. Matt tries to smile but he just looks like he's in pain. I guess even he doesn't have the energy to be overly polite to my dad right now.

Rubbing a hand across the back of his neck, Dad sits down with us. "If you'd like to sleep over, Matt, you're free to use the guest bedroom. Assuming that you're still up for helping us tomorrow, that is."

"I'll see the job through," he says. "An early start will give us a better chance of finishing tomorrow."

My eyes drift across the table. "That mean you're going to stay over tonight?"

He hesitates, conflict brewing in his features. Finally he shrugs. "Sure, why not?"

A part of me wants to ask if he's interested in watching TV or maybe doing something else, but I'm afraid he'd say no. He's staying over because he doesn't want to drive home and then back tomorrow morning, not because he wants to have a sleepover like a pair of twelve-year olds. A hot swath of embarrassment cuts across my chest, making me glad I didn't suggest anything. If we were actually friends, it would be different. But we aren't. He's just a guy I met last week at the hardware store.

My thoughts stray, thinking back on the day. We talked every now and then on the roof, but mostly we just worked. Which wasn't necessarily a bad thing. You can learn a lot about someone by the way they work. Slow and methodical, or fast and recklessly. Matt was more on the latter end, not that it mattered with tearing the shingles off. Nailing them on is when we need to be careful.

"I'm going to wash up," Matt says as he gets up.

His voice snaps me out of my thoughts. I'm not normally so prone to spacing out, but an exhausted body leads to a wandering mind. "Bathroom is up on the left."

"Yeah, I know."

Oh, right. He came in a few times during the day. Without getting up from my spot at the kitchen table, I watch him retreat up the stairs. He's kind of reserved, but he seems like a nice guy. At the very least, he's a hard worker.

Forcing myself to my feet, I follow him upstairs and wait for him to finish in the bathroom. When he's done, he gives me a half nod before disappearing into the guest bedroom.

I'm too worn out to do anything but brush my teeth and fall into my own bed. I wonder briefly if he needs anything like an extra pillow, but if he feels even half as tired as I am, he'll be asleep in minutes.

Even in the depth of my exhaustion-induced sleep, I'm peripherally aware of the thunder rumbling through the house, accompanied by the soft patter of rain. It's a nice sound, and it doesn't bother me. Not until a yelp from the hallway brings every one of my senses into crystalline focus. "Motherfucker!"

It didn't sound like Dad, so it must be Matt. Throwing off the covers, I move down the hall as fast I dare in the darkness, my fingers trailing on the walls. The moment I reach the doorknob to the guest room, I twist and push, flicking on the light with my other hand.

Matt is sitting up in the bed, the sheet resting across his waist. His shirtless chest is distracting for only a moment, because then I notice the wet circle on the sheet around his crotch.

Any worries about standing in front of him wearing only my briefs are dispelled as I realize what I'm seeing. I give him a look that must contain at least a portion of my bewilderment. "Did you... uh, have an exciting dream?"

He seems confused for a second, his eyes jumping between me, the spot on the bed, and now Dad, who has just appeared behind me. "No... *hell* no. It's the roof, you idiot."

I would be pissed that he just called me that, but I can't prevent an explosion of laughter. Dad is chuckling behind me too, but only until he sees the drips falling from the ceiling and landing on the sheet over Matt's crotch.

"Shit," he growls. "You must have missed covering something up."

My good humor is gone in an instant. I give Dad a sour look. "That means we have to go up on the roof again. In the rain."

As if on cue, a roll of thunder smashes against the house. "In a thunderstorm, you mean," Matt says, scowling as he throws the wet covers off himself. The water must have been dripping on him for a while, because it soaked right through to his briefs. The front of them are wet, making the already tight fabric stick to him.

I look away before he catches me watching him again and bolt to my room, my haste completely unrelated to the water pouring into the house. Closing the bedroom door behind me, I pull on my shorts and t-shirt that I was wearing only a few hours ago. They stink, but I don't care. This is going to suck no matter what I'm wearing. The rain hammers away at the roof while I get dressed, an incessant reminder of the water still leaking into the guest bedroom.

"Come on," Matt calls down the hall. "It's getting worse."

Dad and Matt are already waiting in the entryway with a tarp, a hammer, and a flashlight when I sprint down the stairs and through the kitchen. "I took a bucket from the bathroom to catch the water," I explain.

"I don't care about that." Dad's voice is hard. "It's going to ruin the ceiling if it goes on much longer, which means hurry up," he snaps, kicking my shoes toward me. "If you'd tacked the tarps down right to begin with, this wouldn't have happened." I stare at him, hating that he's talking to me like this in front of Matt. Not that it's unusual, but I don't want him to hear it.

The three of us bundle out of the house into the rain and the dark. My first thought is that I can't even see the top of the ladder. The second is that the wind and rain are *cold*. As I grit my teeth through the beginning of a shiver, Dad clicks on the flashlight and aims it at the ladder. "Be careful."

"We got this," Matt says, taking the hammer from Dad and starting his ascent to the roof. How the hell did we get ourselves into this?

Leaving the tarp with Dad, I follow Matt up the ladder, locking my hands carefully over each dripping rung. *I will not fall*, I repeat to myself. Matt is waiting just beyond the reach of the flashlight when I pull myself up onto the roof. Everything is so wet that it freaks me out to even think about walking around. The wind was bad on the ground, but up here it feels like a hurricane. I can tell Matt is worried too, because his arms are stretched out and braced against the roof for balance.

No longer on the ground, it's easy to see the problem. The area at the top of the ladder where we're crouched should have been covered by a tarp. And it *was* when we went down last night.

"We forgot to secure the bottom," he shouts over the thunder and rain. "The wind grabbed it once the storm started."

He's right. The tarp that covered this section is still held on at the top, but the whole thing has flipped over to the other side of the roof. We'll need to drag it back over to this side and then tack it down at the bottom, making sure we can still get down the ladder. It would be pretty simple if it was day and the decking was dry. But right now it's really hard to see, and the roof is slick.

"I'll get the tarp," I yell back. He nods, still crouched with hammer in hand.

As I climb carefully toward the peak, I spread my fingers out as much as I can to maintain my grip on the slippery boards. In the absence of any actual handholds, I'll take whatever extra friction I can get. It feels like I'm not getting anywhere, but I keep moving higher. Dad's flashlight barely reaches this far, especially with the rain dispersing the beam.

Peering over the peak, I can see the tarp that's supposed to be on my side but instead is currently providing a double layer of useless protection on the other side. The seconds tick past as rain pummels me in the face. I'll have to put myself in a more precarious position in order to pull the tarp back to this side of the roof, but I don't have a choice whether to do this or not. We can't just let rain pour into the house all night. Swallowing past my fear, I rise out of my crouch and grab a hold of the plastic.

Despite losing the assistance from my hands, my feet manage to keep me upright and stable. Exhaling a long breath, I begin to pull the tarp back over. As I drag it toward me, I bundle it up into my arms so I don't have to keep moving backward. Just a few feet left and I'll have the whole wet gob of blue plastic, then I can just back down the roof with it and we'll tack it at the bottom. Easy.

The gust that catches me in the chest isn't much stronger than the others that have been bandying me around. But it's enough. It's enough that I have to pivot my foot to maintain my balance. Without any warning, I'm suddenly sliding down the roof decking. Adrenaline hits my blood in a millisecond, forcing me to experience the coming seconds in slow motion. Arms and legs splayed, I slip downward on all fours. My fingers fight to catch a board, a gap in the decking, hell even a nail… please just let me get a hold on *something*. The inches fly past my face and I'm not slowing down. In the back of my mind, it registers that someone just shouted my name. How far am I from the edge? Halfway there? Oh God, I'm actually going to fall.

A smashing sound reverberates through the roof decking, but I can't tell where it came from – somewhere off to my side maybe. Then my shirt tightens around me, yanking up on my armpits and my neck. I hear the sound of fabric ripping, but it only lasts a second and then everything holds. It's uncomfortable as hell but I'm not moving anymore.

My heartbeats slam my chest, and the rain rushes down. Matt tightens his grip on the back of my shirt. "Got you," he says. From the ground, the flashlight is pinned on us.

If I hadn't almost sailed off the edge a second ago, I might have laughed at how he's splayed out. Half lying on his side, he has one hand stretched out holding onto me and the other wrapped around the hammer with glistening white knuckles. Then it clicks. The sound I heard was Matt driving the hammer's claw side into the decking. It's probably the only reason he didn't go right off the edge with me. Also why he's still holding onto it like his life depends on it.

"You okay?" he asks, his expression still filled with worry. More than I would have expected. Regaining my balance and grip, I tell him he can let go.

If there was anything good about what just happened, it's that the tarp came down with me and has more or less fallen to where it needs to be. Matt waves me down the roof and onto the ladder, pulling the plastic down with him as he follows me.

Pounding several nails directly into the bottom of the tarp, he looks back to my dad on the ground and shrugs. It's sloppy to tack it down that way, but it will hold until morning.

Dad doesn't say anything as we all trudge back in the house, but his face looks like all the blood drained out of it about five minutes ago. My shirt is soaked through, and true to the ripping sound I heard, part of the collar has separated from the rest of the fabric.

"You tore my shirt," I say to Matt. He gives me a wry look, and Dad sighs. I was hoping for a laugh, but I guess they're still too shaken up about what just happened.

"That was too close," Dad says.

I don't know what he expects me to say. I didn't almost-fall on purpose.

When I don't answer him, he lets out another long sigh. "I'm going back to bed," he announces, leaving us alone in the kitchen. A glance at the microwave clock confirms that it's almost one a.m.

"The guest bed is soaked," Matt says through a yawn.

"Shit, I didn't think of that." I bite my lip, unsure what to do with him. "There's… uh, the couch." He makes a face. "Or… we could share my bed if you want." I'm working really hard to make sure my voice doesn't sound hopeful.

"Fine, whatever," he says. "I'm so tired I can hardly think."

Yeah, that just about sums it up.

I don't bother turning on the light in my bedroom because we're already stripping off wet clothes by the time we get there, leaving a trail down the upstairs hallway. I push a pillow in his direction as I take the outside of the bed, making sure to be as far over as possible. The bed is only a full, so it's a bit of a squeeze.

The subdued sound of breathing is the only way I'd know someone else is here with me, because we're not touching anywhere. Now in the silence and the dark, the gravity of what almost happened finally hits me. If it wasn't for Matt…

Ignoring the creeping chill that's only partially from having been out in the cold rain, I whisper, "Thanks. For catching me."

He's quiet so long that I start to wonder if he's already asleep. "You scared the shit out of me," he admits.

I hesitate. "I'm sorry."

He turns onto his back, and his elbow brushes against mine. "You didn't get hurt. That's what matters."

My heart misses a beat, even though I know I shouldn't read into what he's just said. "Weren't you worried that I'd drag you off the roof with me?"

The covers rustle beside me. "Didn't have time to think about it."

I let his words roll around in my head, unsure what to think of them. He definitely risked himself to save me from going over the edge, but even after the limited time I've spent with him, I know it's silly to be getting my hopes up. He's just a nice guy, trying to be understanding of my awkward stares and comments.

His voice touches the darkness once more. "Does your Dad always treat you like that?"

"Not really." *But often enough.* I don't want to tell him that, though, because I don't need him feeling sorry for me or anything. Dad is all I've got.

"That sucks. I'm sorry, man," he says.

After that, we're both quiet – me because I refuse to confirm that he saw through my lie, and Matt because he's probably afraid to push the subject any further. It's better that way, because talking about stuff like that never helps anything.

Despite the thoughts that refuse to settle down, the night eventually drags me toward sleep, just as it did with Matt a while ago.

Matt isn't beside me when I wake up the next morning. Considering our middle of the night escapade, I don't feel all that terrible. After pulling on a ratty pair of shorts and a t-shirt, I meander downstairs to find Dad and Matt at the table drinking coffee.

"Morning, son."

I nod vaguely in his direction and beeline for the coffee pot. When I was younger, Dad didn't really like me drinking it, and I still get all fidgety whenever I do, but this morning I could really use the caffeinated assistance. I'm glad Dad doesn't hassle me about it today, especially because Matt is here.

After a few sips, I'm awake enough to realize how hungry I am. Setting a pair of bowls, a gallon jug of milk, and a box of corn flakes on the table, I join them at the table.

"I borrowed a pair of your shorts," Matt informs me as he shakes the cereal out of the box and into his bowl.

"They fit?"

"Kind of tight, but not horrible," he says between bites.

Once we're finished, we don't waste any time getting up on the roof. Throwing off the tarps and sending showers of water droplets over the edge of the roof, we get to work. We're starting earlier than we did yesterday, so at least we have a few hours without the sun hitting us. Beneath the tarps, we're lucky that the decking is mostly dry, except for a few areas where the plastic didn't cover everything.

Dad comes outside to listen as Matt briefly outlines what we'll be doing and in what order. Apparently Dad is pleased, because he gives us the thumbs up and heads back inside. Most of this is familiar to me, but I'm glad that Matt has taken point and is basically managing the project now. The best part is that I get to spend another day with him and not have Dad hovering over us.

Before we start covering the decking with new material, we move around the edge of the roof, nailing in white metal drip edge. It's supposed to stop water from draining down onto the fascia boards, I think. Unfortunately, it's slow going and takes over an hour before we're done.

Eager to start actually laying down shingles, we rip into the plastic wrapped pallets to get to the rolls of tarpaper and water shield. Carrying one of each up to the roof, we start at the edge closest to the ground and roll out a length of the thicker, gritty water shield. Dad even comes outside to help for a few minutes, holding the bottom from the ladder while Matt and I position it into place. Once we've got it lined up with all the edges and corners, I pull off the plastic covering from underneath, allowing the sticky backside to adhere to the decking.

After a couple rows of water shield, we switch to the tarpaper, which is a lot easier to work with. I hold it in place while Matt tacks it down with the staple hammer. Row after row, until we reach the peak of the roof.

Matt wipes the sweat from his forehead. We're both shirtless again, fully exposed to the beating sun. And to each other. I like working with him and not just because I enjoy the view. He's patient and levelheaded, even when one of us screws up and we have to redo something. But it feels like he's still holding back. The first day I thought it was just because we didn't know each other very well, which is still the case. After last night, though, I thought he might be different. If someone saves your life – or at least saves you from severe injury – does that make you friends? Or is friendship something that can only ever be built with the plodding progression of time?

"What you thinking about?" he asks, surveying me along with the work we've done.

I shrug. "Nothing."

"Doesn't look like nothing."

My gaze sweeps across the swaths of black tarpaper, settling on the path where I slid last night. "I was thinking about that storm," I admit.

"Again? What about it?" Curiosity intertwines itself with his voice.

I give him a long look. For the first time since meeting him, I don't feel awkward about just looking. His jawline is strong and defined, and his bright eyes are staring back at mine. My voice just above a whisper, I tell him what I'm really thinking. "I was just wondering if you saved my life. It's a long drop."

He seems to like what I just said, but his emotion is so well hidden that it's hard to tell. Then he grins. "You would have lived."

"Yeah, probably." But it would have hurt like hell, and I would have broken some bones.

We work for the rest of the morning, getting all the tarpaper down and starting on actually shingling before it's even lunchtime. After getting the air nailer set up, we haul bundle after bundle of shingles up onto the roof. They're god-awful heavy, but Matt doesn't really seem to notice.

As we start nailing them down, I realize he's not only stronger but also just plain better at this than I am. I'm not thrilled about that, but it's true. When I worked on the garage with Dad, that's exactly what it was – helping. And it's the same now. Matt is running the show. I hold the shingles in place, and he nails them down.

The snapping of his fingers brings me back to the moment. "Pay attention, kid," he says playfully, waving the nailer at me. "We don't have all day."

"Yeah, yeah." But he's absolutely right. I really doubt we're going to finish today, not that that would be such a bad thing. I would have to spend more time on this stupid roof, cooking in the sun, but Matt and I would also get to spend another day together.

Not too long after, we climb down to eat. Dad made tacos. Loading up my plate, I sit across from Matt, who's already chowing down. The last day and a half have been hard as hell, but it's kind of cool having him around. In a dorky way, it almost feels like summer camp. And Matt? He's fun to be around, especially now that he's been opening up more. It makes me wish I'd gotten to know him when he still went to Northfield High School, where he apparently also went to school just two years ahead of me.

After lunch we're back on the roof, nailing away. Open the bundle, place the shingle, wait for Matt to nail it down. Wash, rinse, repeat. We're shingling across the roof diagonally, which seems to be the most efficient way. It was Matt's suggestion, and he seemed to know what he was talking about so I didn't worry too much.

The familiar sound of Matt's snapping fingers gets my attention again. He frowns when I look up from where I was staring out at the wispy branches of the weeping willows. "Come on, Jackson. If you keep spacing out, we're never going to finish."

"You think we'll actually get done today?"

"Probably, if we push."

With the end almost in sight, we work straight through dinner without stopping. Matt becomes a taskmaster, snapping at me whenever I get distracted or take too long getting the shingles in position for him. The sun sinks toward the horizon, and the tips of my fingers become so raw from the fiberglass in the shingles that I'm afraid they might start to bleed. And still we work.

I don't know how we do it, but just before it gets too dark to work, we nail in the last cap shingle on the peak. I never thought we'd get done in just two days. I'm so sore I can barely move, but the job is done. From the ground, we finally take a moment to survey our work. It looks good. Dad joins us, walking slowly around the house before giving his approval. "Looks good, guys." He shakes Matt's hand and gives him a check, then leaves us alone once more.

Matt yawns as he stretches his neck from side to side. "I guess I'll head out, then."

"Thanks for your help. I…" I bite my tongue, changing my words. "It was fun."

He laughs. "What do you mean? It sucked. Roofing is horrible."

I look away quickly so he won't see the disappointment in my expression.

After a moment of silence, he adds, his voice softer, "I had a good time too."

I nod, taking a step toward the house. "Drive safe."

"I will," he says. He seems to hesitate, making no movement toward his truck. His eyes lift upward, eventually settling on me. The moment stretches out with a decided reluctance. At last he says, "I go back to college in a few days, but…"

"But?"

He shrugs, looking unsure. "I could show you through a workout if you're still interested. At the very least, I owe you for hooking me up with this job. Your dad paid me like four hundred bucks." He holds up the check.

Ah right, working out. I'd almost forgotten about that, but my heart beats a little quicker at the unexpected offer. "And what do I owe you for saving my life?" I counter, a smile sneaking up on me.

That gets a nod out of him. "So maybe we're even."

After that, both of us are quiet for several seconds, and I'm afraid the earlier awkwardness will force its way back into our conversation.

"You've got my number," he says, catching my eyes for just a second. "Shoot me a text if you want to meet up."

"I might do that," I tell him, trying my hardest to impart at least some pretense of doubt.

Matt gives me a fleeting smile and a two-fingered wave before getting in his truck. Not turning back to the house yet, I watch him back down the driveway and turn onto the dirt road. I wait until his truck is long gone and the dust from its passage has cleared in the evening summer breeze before finally heading inside.

Chapter Three

Jackson

I manage to make it almost a whole day – well, sixteen hours – before breaking down and texting him.

Hey, it's Jackson.

As soon as I've hit send, I throw myself back on my bed. He probably won't respond. He was just being polite yesterday when he offered to hang out. I'm not trying to be pessimistic, but it's really the only explanation. Guys like *that*, they just don't live around here. Especially not hot ones with midnight black hair and wide shoulders and a smile that could get away with murder.

Beside me, my phone buzzes. I'm sitting upright in less than a second.

Lol I know it's you… I saved your number.

He saved my number? Suddenly I'm grinning like a fool. *He saved my number.* We exchange a few messages, concluding that neither of us has been busy. Fingers rapidly tapping back messages as soon as I receive them, I eventually ask, *you still up for the gym?*

His reply comes a moment later. *Sure! This afternoon work?* That exclamation point practically makes me lightheaded. I haven't actually worked out in a real gym before, unless you count the high school weight room, but I know my way around a bench press and everything. Hopefully enough so that I don't embarrass myself.

*   *   *   *

Sun glinting in my eyes, I'm leaning against the brick exterior of Northfield's Snap Fitness when Matt's crappy red truck pulls into the parking lot. I had to search all over for a gym bag, but I eventually found one buried at the bottom of my closet. I don't know if Matt is planning on showering after our workout, or if they even have showers here at all, but I didn't want to be missing anything just in case. Missing, as in, not having a towel. Not missing out on... I push away the thought. I have to be careful, because basketball shorts can be pretty revealing.

"Hey," Matt greets me with a smirk. "You're all ready to go, huh?" He's wearing a tank top and gym shorts like me, but he doesn't have a bag.

"How much is it for just one time?" I ask as I follow him through the glass doors. "I don't have a membership here or anything."

"Don't worry about it." He holds up a plastic fob to the inside door and it clicks open. "This is a twenty-four hour gym, and they don't usually staff it in the afternoon."

It's smaller than I imagined, but the space still contains dozens of weight machines. The far wall is covered in mirrors, and in front of them are racks with free weights. Farther yet from the wall are lifting benches, and beyond those are treadmills and cycles. It feels a bit like cluttered chaos.

"Coming?" Matt calls to me, already at the benches. I'd be embarrassed at him talking across the room to me, but there are only two other people here, both on the treadmills with earbuds in.

Dropping my bag beside him, I ask, "Where do we start?"

His eyes flit over me, appraising. "I suppose I should ask what your goals are specifically. You're slim, so I'm guessing you don't want to lose weight or anything. You're what, like one seventy?"

"Um, one fifty-five," I say, my cheeks growing warm. "Is there a good way to gain muscle all around? Without some crazy complicated routine?"

Thinking for a moment, he points to the bench. "Honestly, if you want to gain weight quickly and keep it simple, powerlifting will get you results pretty fast."

"Powerlifting?" Sounds kind of cool, but I have no idea what it is.

He grins, seeming to enjoy that he's teaching me things. "Bench presses, squats, and deadlifts. It's an Olympic sport class or something, but that doesn't really matter. The important thing is that those are all compound lifts that hit multiple muscle groups. Combine them with eating more, and you'll put on muscle." He pauses, glancing first at me and then around the gym. "Sound good?"

When I nod, he gestures to the bench next to us. "Let's start with this."

Matt starts me at a low weight and then bumps it up for the subsequent sets. As I push through the reps, he gives me tips on form and breathing, but he doesn't make me feel self-conscious. Even when a super ripped guy comes in and starts working out next to us, Matt's attention stays solely on me, so it still feels like it's just the two of us here.

After every set I do, he does the same one, albeit with a lot more weight. After ten minutes, I'm starting to legitimately enjoy myself. I'm four reps into my third bench press set when I feel his eyes on me, moving over my chest and along my arms. More than him just spotting for me in case I can't get the bar off my chest. It's like when I watched him all those times on the roof. Heaving the bar up so my arms are straight, I hold it there, breathing heavily. He's still gazing at me, like he's wanted to do this all along but is only now allowing himself to.

"You're staring," I breathe, daring to fully meet his eyes and not look away.

He almost jumps. "Shit, sorry," he says hastily, flushing as he helps me guide the bar back to the rests. "I just, uh, spaced out. Let's move on to squats."

"Don't you have another set on bench?" I ask.

"I'm going to skip that set today, I think."

The normal squat rack that has the safety wires is already occupied, but Matt is insistent that they should come before deadlifts, so he shows me how to use the unassisted rack. From underneath, he lifts the bar up on his shoulders. It looks a little ungainly, but it works. I watch as he squats down, the muscles in his thighs and butt tightening against his shorts. After his fourth rep, I have to look away.

"You're up next," he says after depositing the bar back on the rack.

Pulling off a few weights, I get under the bar and lift it up just like he did. Except as I adjust my position, my balance is thrown off by all the extra weight on my shoulders and I stumble backwards. In an instant, Matt's hands are on my back, stabilizing me. One between my shoulder blades and the other at the bottom of my t-shirt. He holds them there two seconds, three seconds. I'm definitely not going to fall anymore, but his hands remain. Five seconds, six seconds. Finally the warmth from his touch disappears.

Across the gym, someone coughs. In my peripheral vision, Matt reddens but he doesn't turn around. "Wanted to make sure you weren't going to drop the bar," he says, his voice strained.

"Sure." I think he's lying, because through the rest of the workouts, he's careful to keep his hands and eyes off me. So careful that it becomes obvious he's doing it on purpose when I have to ask him on my deadlift form and he admits he wasn't even watching.

I refuse to let him see that his behavior is bothering me. I don't know if he's testing me, or if he's struggling with his own shit, but regardless, it's not my fault.

When we're done with the three different lifts, he finally looks at me as he speaks. "So that's it, I guess. Maybe we can do this again sometime."

The least he could do is try to sound like he believes what he's saying. Because I sure as hell don't. "Thanks for showing me that stuff."

He waits while I get a drink from the fountain, but he's acting like he's in a rush. You'd think his truck was getting stolen outside. On our way out, I thank him again, but he only nods and says "see you" when we split up at the door. I watch him cross the parking lot to his truck, but he never looks back, not even as he drives away.

Chapter Four

Jackson

My phone didn't make a sound for three days after we worked out together, until this morning when he texted to ask if I wanted to hang out. I was convinced I would never hear from him again, and the look of shock on my face was so transparent that Dad even asked if one of my friends had gotten in an accident. In the end, I had to plead to get the day off from working at Dad's greenhouse business in town, to which he grudgingly agreed.

Beside me, Matt pushes his sunglasses up a little higher on his nose at the same moment that a grasshopper bounds out of the clover, landing on his chest. Grateful for the excuse, my gaze passes over his bare chest as he flicks the bug away. His skin is tan, and the contour of his pecs and abs makes him nice to look at.

Neither of us had any ideas of what to do, but how we ended up sunbathing in a field near my house is anyone's guess. Brilliant sunlight spills over us, lapping at our faces and working to fulfill the promise of being another hot summer day. Eyes half closed, only a slit of blue sky is visible through my lashes. The alfalfa field we're lying in is almost ready for its last harvest of the year, so the flattened vegetation beneath us protects us from the rocky ground.

Our shirts are off and spread out under our backs, filling in where a blanket would have been nice. Who would ever pay for a tanning membership when you could have this? Midwest summers are the best. They're the only reason that anyone even lives here. We pay for it with eight bitter months of winter, but it's worth it.

Matt turns his head, eyes hidden behind his sunglasses. I should have worn a pair too, so it would have been easier to get away with checking him out. I shouldn't be so worried, especially since I caught him doing something similar at the gym.

"It's too bad summer is almost over," he says. "Last year, college dragged on forever."

"Speak for yourself," I say. "I want to finish high school and get out of here."

He's quiet for a moment. "I don't mind it so much here."

"Here, as in Northfield? Or here, as in–" My sentence comes to an abrupt stop as I consider my next words.

"As in?" he prompts.

"Here with me?" I didn't really mean it as a question, but it definitely came out that way. My chest tightens in anticipation of his response. The time we've spent together so far has been fun, and it's not a stretch to think of ourselves as friends, but that voice inside that has wondered since the beginning if it could be more than that... it's still curious as ever.

Matt stares back but doesn't answer my question. No way am I about to let him go that easily. I feel bad forcing this, but only a few days are left before he flies out East for school. Before he goes, I really want to know what this is, or what it could be. The more time we spend together, the more the tension grows. Right now the air between us feels so thick it almost hurts to breathe.

"You're sweating," I say, trying to read the eyes behind those sunglasses.

He swallows, turning to look at me. "It's hot."

Reaching across the space separating us, I trail my index finger over his skin just below the collarbone. His muscles tensing under my touch, he only hesitates a moment before pushing my arm away. "Um, dude?"

"Sorry, just messing around," I say quickly, withdrawing my hand and turning my head so it faces toward the sky.

A breeze whisks through the field, carrying with it the scent of late summer mingled with clover and alfalfa. Everywhere it touches me, coolness replaces the heat, soothing the redness on my chest and arms warning me that I might have a burn tomorrow.

When we were on the roof, even when concentrated wholly on the work, I always felt something. And since the moment we finished, I can't stop thinking about that simmering intensity in him that I can't figure out. I've never done anything with a guy before and I have no idea how that boundary would be crossed, but I'm dying to find out.

As though talking to no one in particular, Matt announces, "I'm straight." His voice cuts between us, sounding a little too high and a little too loud. Sheesh, even he doesn't sound convinced.

I pause, afraid of saying something that might send him running. "Didn't say you weren't."

He seems to relax, at least a bit. After a few minutes of the wind whispering to us, he says, "It's cool if you're… not."

I guess it wasn't technically a question, but he's watching me expectantly. How to answer this one? Can you know you're into guys even if you've never been with one like that? Closing my eyes, I mentally chastise myself for being stupid. Of course I know what I like, and it's stupid to pretend otherwise. If Matt is going to bail on me or hit me or whatever, it might as well be over with sooner rather than later.

Opting for the diplomatic to soften the blow, I simply say, "I like spending time with you."

"I like being around you too," he says innocently.

He better be acting obtuse on purpose, because I'm being really clear. "You don't leave for a few days," I point out.

He smiles. "That's true."

I pause, my fingers on the handle of the refrigerator. I'm not really that hungry. Thankfully my phone saves me from my indecision, choosing that moment to vibrate in my pocket. It's a text from Matt. After he left yesterday, I hadn't gotten a single message that night or all day today. I was worried that it would be another three days before I heard from him, at which point he'd already have flown back East for college. Curiosity winning out, I drag my thumb across the screen to open the message.

Free tonight? Thought we could watch a movie or something.

My focus shifts to the time on the microwave. It's only five thirty-two. Still several hours left in the day.

A movie is fine, but another part of me is dying to know what the "or something" could be. I still don't even know if he's into that, but I would love to find out. At the same time, it kind of scares the crap out of me, but that's not enough to stop me from seeing him again.

Releasing my grip on the refrigerator door, I text him back. *Your place?*

Sure, come over whenever.

So long as I get home before dark, Dad doesn't usually care what I do. Thankfully it's just a bit past the height of summer and "dark" still means hours from now. Walking out to the garage, I hop on my bike – it's an old dirt bike that is technically street legal, if only barely. After turning the key, I jam my foot down on the kick-start and the engine coughs to life, sounding a lot healthier since Dad help me clean all the gunk out of the carburetor last week. I slip on my three-quarters helmet and safety glasses, feeling preemptively self-conscious. It looks dorky, but I don't have a real helmet. I would buy one but they're stupid expensive. At least it beats not having any transportation at all. Backing out, I gun the bike down the driveway.

Matt lives in town in an old two-story house that I've seen before in passing. It's a cool house from the outside, but from the peeling blue paint and the curling shingles, it could use a bit of work. Hopefully his parents can afford to pay someone else to do the roof whenever they decide to have it done.

Dropping the kickstand, I back the bike up to the curb at an angle and jump off. The street is quiet, but I shoot a look up and down the block before pulling off the helmet and locking it to the bike.

I'm here. I wait to see if he'll respond to my text. There aren't any cars in the driveway, but that doesn't necessarily mean his parents aren't lurking inside. I'm glad he doesn't make me wait long.

Yeah I see you, be right down.

Hands stuffed into the front pockets of my shorts, I cross the small yard. There's no space in any of the lots in town. It's like the city made a game of how close they could pack the houses. I can't stand it.

"Hey, Jackson," he says, holding the screen door open for me and showcasing the flowing muscles in his arms. "You brought your bike."

I shrug off the impressed tone in his voice. "Yeah."

"That helmet was pretty stylish too." His grin reaches almost up to his ears.

My face turns red as I step over the threshold, but I ignore his comment. "Are your parents home?" I risk a glance at his eyes, then to his dark hair, styled with some kind of matte-finish product. I don't remember him ever having anything in it before.

"Nah, we have the place to ourselves." Was that a loaded response? I can't tell if he means for me to read into it or not. We're still standing in the entryway. "Um," he says, "want to see my room?"

Yeah, I definitely do. "Sure."

He leads me up the stairs. They're kind of steep, but that's not why I'm steadying myself on the banister. Pushing open a door at the top of stairs that has a black and yellow "Fallout Shelter" sign hung on it, he stands to the side to let me by him, sharing the light scent of his cologne as I pass. His bedroom is small and the ceiling at the outside wall is vaulted for about a foot. The window must be original because sash weight ropes disappear into the walls.

Every inch of the room is covered in posters, the largest of which is spread across the wall above the bed. It's the photo of the Beatles crossing Abbey Road. I think that was the album cover art too, but I'm not sure. Across from Abbey Road, a computer with a giant screen is perched on his desk. I wish I had one like that in my room.

Matt is just sitting on the bed, letting me take my time. "What do you think?"

I shrug, trying to sound nonchalant. "Pretty cool."

"So I uh, invited you over for a movie, so I guess we should watch one." He sounds nervous, almost like he's expecting me to turn him down.

I shrug again. I'm not thrilled about hanging out downstairs, even though his parents aren't home. I make to leave the room, but he hops up and catches my arm. "We can watch it up here if you want." His hand is warm, a hint of moisture across his palm. His eyes lock onto mine for a fraction of second before he lets go.

"Okay," I breathe. Only a swivel chair is at his computer, but if we both sat on the bed, the screen would definitely be big enough. A shiver of anticipation makes the hairs on my arm stand at attention.

Giving the mouse a shake, he opens up the DVD drive. "What do you want to watch?"

I take a seat on his bed, stretching my legs toward the screen. My mouth feels dry, but I still manage to make words. "Anything is fine."

"We're watching Transformers then." Popping in a disk, he joins me on the bed, except he only leaves about half the distance between us that I expected. Not more than a few inches of space remain there. Stretching across me, he grabs a pillow from the head of the bed. Besides his cologne, he smells like the outdoors. Fresh and clean with a vague spiciness, almost like cedar. He stuffs the pillow behind his back.

The movie starts but the volume is quiet. Beside me, Matt's khaki shorts are riding up above his knees. He kicks off his shoes, letting them fall to the floor. His socks are white except for a red band just below the ankle. For some reason, I can't seem to stop my mind from focusing on the most irrelevant details right now.

"What's that from?"

I drag my eyes upward. "Huh?"

He's pointing to the back of my hand. The scar stretches diagonally from the side of my wrist almost to my pinky knuckle. "It was a bucksaw."

He looks up from my hand, a subtle tenderness filtering into his voice. "What happened?"

"I was holding a tree branch last summer while sawing. The wood was green and caught the blade, but I was stupid and kept pushing. The blade jumped and dragged across my hand." I speak the untruth with just enough conviction that it's perfectly believable. Anything to avoid telling him what actually happened with my dad.

Reaching out, he runs a finger slowly over the smooth pale line of healed skin. "Looks like it hurt." His touch feels different than any other touch. It's almost like the day I got the scar, except instead of cutting with pain, he's splitting my hand with the heady rush of anticipation.

On the screen, the giant transforming machine is obliterating a military base. "It bled really bad. I had to run in from the woods to get Dad."

"I wish I'd been there to help." His breath is close, sweet like mint and vanilla, and his hand is just plain resting on mine now. A silent second passes between us. "You like this," he says. It's not a question, and it's not a challenge. It's just… a statement.

My eyes widen. "What do you mean?"

He clears his throat. "You're wearing canvas shorts, Jackson."

I glance down. Okay, it's obvious. I'm not sure I can explain my way out of this one. Luckily, I don't have to. Before I can look back up, he leans over and plants his lips on mine. I freeze at first, but I don't know why.

Whatever the reason for my hesitation, he doesn't stop, and his lips slowly massage mine to life. His eyes are closed. Now mine are too, and I'm kissing him back. Is this really happening? What about him being straight? I'm afraid to ask in case he suddenly remembers and kicks me out.

His hand lifts the edge of my t-shirt and sneaks inside, palm to my stomach. Almost immediately, he pulls away, but his hand stays where it is. "You're shaking," he says, concern in his eyes. "Do you want to stop?"

He's right. Involuntary shivers are sweeping over my skin. "I've never done this before… with a guy."

"Me neither. I'm sorry, we can stop." He begins to withdraw his hand, but I catch him around the wrist. The subtle shaking in my hand doesn't stop, but my grip is firm.

"No," I say. "Keep going."

Sporting a devious smile, he whispers in my ear, "Yes, sir." And just like that he's back, the warmth of his lips and now his tongue on mine. Cautious but steady, his hand works its way up, over my stomach and up to my chest, dragging my shirt up with it. I want to reach out and touch him back, but apprehension holds my hands motionless.

His free hand glides over the back of my head, his fingers weaving through my hair. His mouth slides off to the side, continuing along my jawline. At the same moment, the first of his fingertips touches my left nipple and an instinctive sound comes from deep in my throat.

Matt retreats once more, his brown eyes flashing over me. "You like that, huh?" An impish grin plays across his lips, the same ones that were all over me a moment ago.

"Hell yes." The words scare me the moment they're free. In theory I've figured out what I'm into, but I've never done it before in practice. It might be that or maybe just the tingling in my fingers from hyper-ventilating, but part of me is terrified at what's happening. I don't want him to stop though.

Apparently he doesn't want to either. "Come 'ere, cowboy," he says, his hands moving up along the outside of my t-shirt until they're just under my armpits. Firmly gripping the sides of my ribcage, he deftly rotates me so I'm lying on my back. His knees planted on either side of my waist, he surveys me like a conquistador.

His butt is hovering just above my hips. A thread of panic laces the edges of my voice. "You probably shouldn't, um, sit down or anything."

He's got that same grin, the one that's amused by my nervousness. "Because of that?" He glances at my crotch. "Look, I have one too." He flicks a finger at the tent pole straining against the fabric of his own shorts. Something about the way he's looking at me causes a subtle shift in the battle going on inside me between scared and turned on. Then the humor evaporates from his tone, leaving him with just a smile. "You're cute, Jacks."

Heat rises in my face the moment the syllable steps off his tongue. "Don't call me that," I force out the words, pushing him off me roughly. "I have to go."

"Whoa," he says, his eyes growing wide and raising his hands like I pulled a knife on him. "What's wrong?"

I jump off the bed and adjust myself, aware that he's watching my every move. "Nothing, I just have to go. I'll see you later." Before he can answer, I run out of the room and down the stairs.

The wind blasts my face as I ride out of town. What the hell just happened? My fingers still have that pins and needles feeling, and my heart is racing. I want to be mad at him for pulling that shit on me, but the truth is I loved every minute of it. At least until he called me *Jacks*. I wasn't ready for any of what happened, but that was definitely too much.

It was the first time I'd ever done anything with a guy. And… damn. It was so weird how my body reacted – not my dick, I expected that. The shivering though… it's like deep inside some part of me was seriously afraid of what I was doing. But neither the wrath of God nor that of my father came down. I don't actually know if Dad has a problem with that or not. People seem to like him and he's a sharp guy, but I'm the one who has to live with him. If he does have hang ups about two dudes messing around, I don't want to find out what he'd do.

An instant before the bug makes contact, I see it zooming toward me. It's big and green, like a goddamn grasshopper or something. It nails me right in the cheek before tumbling away in my rearview mirror. It stings, bad, and the little bastard probably even left a welt.

As I ride on, I'm thankful for the coolness of the wind against me, soothing the painful spot on my cheek as well as the turmoil inside.

When I pull the bike into the garage, everything looks the same as when I left, other than the sun being lower in the sky. Inside though, a whole lot has changed.

Ditching the helmet and glasses, I run my hand over the bump on my cheek. It's sore and probably bright red. I'll have to check in the mirror. Sighing, I cross the yard to the house, letting the ratty screen door slam behind me.

Hours later as I curl up under the sheets of my bed, I let the memories of the day sweep me away. *Matt.* His name swells up inside me as I replay every second from when I pulled up at his house to the moment I ran out the front door. He didn't text me or anything afterward. I kind of thought he would, even though I haven't texted him either. What would I have said? *Sorry dude for bailing, I just got a little nervous how hard my dick got when you were kissing me.* Hah, that would be rich. Actually, he'd probably get a kick out of it. The more I get to know him, the more of a good guy he seems to be.

The image of his easy-going grin held in my mind, drowsiness finally wraps me in its arms. Strong, lean, tan arms.

Chapter Five

Jackson

The next morning begins slowly for me. Dad shouldn't still be home, but he's waiting for me at the kitchen table when I get downstairs. "Morning," he says, looking up from his laptop.

I hope I'm not the reason he's home. "I thought you were working today," I say evenly.

"I was just catching up on some inventory planning before I head in," he admits, shutting the computer. "Coffee?"

"Sure." I take a seat across from him while he gets up to pour me a cup. Someone peering into our lives might be confused why he's serving me, but I get it. He's not one of those new age parents that believes in being their kids' best friend or keeping them entertained at all times. Actually he's about as far from that as he can get. But he offered the coffee to me, so he's going to pour it. Dad is old school like that.

He sets a steaming cup in front of me, already mixed with just the right amount of cream the way I like it. We don't have many mornings like these, but after living with someone for so long, you get to know each other. Not just their favorite movie or work schedule, but all the little quirks and pet peeves that make someone who they are. And after knowing all that stuff about Dad? Most of the time he's fine, but he's not someone you want to piss off. Or disobey.

"We're almost out of cream," he says.

"Damn," I groan, refusing to let that lessen the good taste of the coffee. He's not *really* worried about the cream because he drinks his coffee black. It's actually just code for it being my turn to go grocery shopping next. Like a lot of chores, we trade off. Of course when I go, I always make sure to forget a few things. I keep hoping that he'll tell me he can just handle the shopping from now on. Maybe I should feel guilty about that, but teenagers are expected to devise clever ways to shirk responsibilities, right?

Only now do I notice that Dad has been watching me this whole time. "You've hung out with that guy Matt a few times."

"Yep," I say. "He's fun."

He takes another sip of his coffee. "I'm glad you've found a new friend."

I'm not entirely sure, but I think I detect the slightest emphasis on the word *friend.* "Yeah, me too," I say, hoping he'll drop it. One of the things I do really like about Dad is that he doesn't force conversation. He's perfectly content to sit here in silence with me.

I'm not afraid to admit that I'm an introvert. Being around people all the time is exhausting. When I consider it, it's not really a surprise then that my hobbies all involve me being alone. Reading, napping, even swimming… they're all things that are best done alone. Although now that I think about it, curled up with Matt for a nap wouldn't be so bad.

At my stomach's protests, I get up to make myself a bowl of cereal. Dad usually doesn't eat breakfast, so he just keeps sipping his coffee as I putz around the kitchen.

Eventually our mugs are empty and my bowl just has a dribble of milk left in the bottom. "Plans today?" Dad asks.

"Not sure," I say with a noncommittal shrug. I need to at least see Matt before he flies out tomorrow. I'd be happy with a lot more than just seeing him, assuming that he's not too put off about me jetting yesterday. It doesn't make sense to me what happened in his room. He said he was straight and made a point of rebuffing my advances on more than one occasion. I enjoy being with him – a whole lot more, now – but I could really use an explanation.

"You don't have to tell me what you're up to, but…"

"Yeah?" It's a struggle to keep the defiance out of my voice. At seventeen, I'm getting a bit old for him to monitor my summer days, at least when I'm not working for him.

"Straighten up your room a bit? It's a disaster."

I nod. "Sure, if I have time." I would feel bad telling him that the prognosis isn't good, so I quickly clear my spot and run up the stairs to track down my phone.

Before I'm even off my bike, Matt pushes open the screen door of his house, a hand quickly smoothing out his dark hair. Locking up the helmet and tossing the safety glasses over the handlebars, I look up to meet his eager eyes.

"I'm glad you came."

"I said I was going to."

He looks me up and down, as if expecting to find something different from the last time he saw me. "But after you bolted, I wasn't sure."

"I'm here now."

His smile falls as he realizes he might have said too much. Scraping the tip of his shoe against the pavement, he speaks quickly, "So I thought we could walk to this place down the road and get something to eat. You didn't eat lunch yet, did you?"

"Can we hold on just a minute?" I say, feeling guilty for shooting down the enthusiasm in his expression. "What the hell happened to you being straight?"

"You really don't sugarcoat stuff, huh?" Without waiting for me to respond, he says, "All right, here's the thing. I've never really been interested in a guy before. I mean, maybe a bit, but not like *really*. So this is new for me. I was confused at first, and then I was pissed. But I thought, what the hell, why not? I like being with you, so here I am," he finishes out of breath.

"Wow."

"Is that all you're going to say?" He sounds nervous.

I shrug, looking up into those adorable eyes. "Uh, I like spending time with you too?"

"Is that a question?"

"No," I laugh. "I like spending time with you. I think we should do more of that."

"So what do you say to lunch?"

"Sounds perfect."

I follow him across the street, matching his stride once we get to the sidewalk. Somehow he manages to make even a plain white t-shirt and khaki shorts look sexy. With my gaze sliding from his arms up to where his pecs press against his shirt, I don't see the uneven section of sidewalk ahead. My foot catches the edge of the concrete and I stumble. I don't fall, but my face gets hot. I should probably keep my eyes on what's in front of me.

"So where are we going?" I ask.

"Just a little burger place I want to take you to."

Something about the way he says it make me wonder. "As in, take me out?"

A guilty smile awakening at the corners of his mouth, he nods. "I felt bad that things went so, uh… fast last time. It wasn't really fair, because you didn't know what was coming. So I thought this could be like, a real first… date, I guess. Sorry, that sounds dumb," he finishes, the tips of his ears reddening.

"Wait, so you were planning all along on ambushing me in your room?"

"Yeah, sort of." He grins.

Damn him and his disarming good looks. "You're terrible," I say, shoving his shoulder. I've never had a guy take me out before, but I kind of like the idea.

There isn't anyone in the restaurant except for a few old couples scattered at different tables, but Matt directs us to a booth in the back. "Embarrassed to be seen with me?" I tease.

He rolls his eyes. "Not on your life. I just want to have some privacy." He slides onto the plastic bench seat across from me.

It's barely a minute before the waitress comes over. I recognize her as a girl from school who graduated this year, but I don't know her name. Her hair is long and dark and plain, and she's kind of okay looking I guess. For a girl, anyway. "How's your summer going, Matt?" I keep forgetting that he's just two years older than me and probably knows people from my school.

"It was good. I'll have a third pound burger with waffle fries. No cheese on the burger." He says it like it's the end of the conversation with her, which makes me feel warm inside. That, and he's touching my ankle with a shoeless foot. His toe traces a circle around the ball of my ankle. I glance up at him from the menu.

"And what about you?" The girl directs this question to me.

"Huh?"

Her resulting laugh is an irritating noise that sounds like a horse with pneumonia. "What would you like to eat?"

Matt's foot is moving upward past my knee and making it hard to concentrate. "Um, a half pound cheeseburger–" I gulp, swallowing the word I was about to say. Forcing myself to ignore what he's doing now, I give him a look that says *stop it.*

"And?" She taps her pen against the paper.

"Uh, with seasoned fries. Extra fries, too, actually."

"Sure," she says, making a quick note on her waitressy pad before walking away.

Matt is smirking at me, but at least his foot is behaving itself now. "You seemed a little distracted there."

"Ha-ha. I wonder why that was." I sneak a glance under the table. His foot is tucked safely back in his shoe.

When the food comes out, he raises his eyebrows as the waitress deposits a plate with a huge burger and fries along with another plate of fries in front of me. Only when the waitress says, "Enjoy your food, boys," do I remember that Matt said he was paying. Sheepishness bucking to the surface, I venture a guilt-laden look at him. His expression isn't unhappy, but his eyes are wide. "You're really going to eat all that?"

Shaking the red plastic ketchup bottle nozzle-down, I squirt a huge swath into the corner of the plate of fries until the stream sputters to an airy end. I hate that sound, but I love ketchup. "Definitely. I feel like I'm always going hungry."

"If you have enough room inside to put all that away, I believe it."

The rest of our lunch is passed with voracious chewing but otherwise in silence. Afterward, Matt leads us toward a park a few blocks away. It makes me feel weird to admit it, but I like that he paid for me. It made me feel taken care of. No one has ever paid for me like that before except Dad, which obviously doesn't count.

"You didn't actually eat all your fries," Matt points out as a squirrel skips across the sidewalk in front of us.

"That's because you ate the last of them."

"I was afraid you were going to mow through all of them and get sick, and our date would end early." He grins while turning off the sidewalk into the park.

"Whatever, I would have been fine." It's annoying when people try to tell me what to eat or how much. Matt doesn't answer. My irritation rising, I add, "I'm in really fucking good shape, you know."

Hastily shaking his head, Matt brims with deference. "I didn't mean it like that." Then more quietly, he says, "I *know* you're in really good shape." Of course he does, because he's seen me with my shirt off.

Taking a deep breath, I nod and point toward a bench mostly secluded by bushes in the corner of the park. We're alone here, but that doesn't stop me from looking over my shoulder as we sit down. Our knees are touching, but nothing else. A wind picks up, surrounding us with the peaceful rustle of poplar leaves.

"I wish you didn't have to leave so soon," I admit.

"I know. It sucks." His hand is resting on his knee, just inches away from my own. I risk another glance behind us. The park is still empty. Traversing the distance between us, I bring my hand to a rest on top of his. Our eyes meet – his brown, mine blue. His hand rotates and his fingers rise up through mine like the tide, irrepressible and irresistible. His lips parting slightly, he looks at mine and then back upward.

I give his hand a squeeze. "So this is technically our first date, right?"

"That's right," he says, the intensity in his expression diminishing only a little.

The corners of my mouth pull upward. "I thought a gentleman was supposed to wait until the end of the date for the kiss."

His eyes gleam with a mischievous quality. "Who says I'm a gentleman?"

I force back a laugh, pretending to pull away from him. "Well, I only date gentlemen."

"I thought I was your first." He grins, his eyebrows rising together.

"You are, but that doesn't mean you don't have to play by the rules."

"Rules, huh? What happens if I break them?" He nuzzles my neck. His hair tickling my face, I start to pull away again, but the second before we break contact, he pecks me swiftly on the cheek.

"Then there will be consequences," I say, linking my index finger over the collar of his t-shirt and drawing him closer.

His eyelids already drifting down, he follows without restraint. "I can't wait to find out what those are," he breathes, filling the disappearing space between us with his sultry voice. Just like the other day, kissing Matt feels so natural, so *good*. Despite being in a public park, my sense of caution is being eroded by the young man across from me, by his lips and his tongue. They're ganging up on me, combining their strength to drag me to a place where the rest of the world doesn't exist.

When he finally pulls away, placing a hand on my chest to prevent me from following him, I'm forced to open my eyes. His breathing is rough. "Damn, Jackson, you get me going so fast."

I grin, glancing down at myself, then at him. "That's a good thing."

He gives me a half smile. "We seem to keep having this problem."

I'm not sure what makes me do it, but before I can change my mind, I reach out to touch him, moving my hand right over his crotch. His eyes widen in surprise, but he doesn't move to stop me.

For all those times in gym class and all those dreams I've had, I've always wondered what it would feel like to do this. For a moment, everything else is blocked out as my fingers report information gathered through the thin fabric of his shorts. I feel the contour of his firmness extending beyond the base of my palm and his heat beneath my fingers.

Forcing away the burgeoning shame before it can threaten to overwhelm me, I have to remind myself that there's nothing wrong with this.

"You approve?" he asks with the same suggestive grin smeared across his face.

I want him to touch me too. Even though this isn't the place for it, I think something else is stopping him from matching my advance. From the feel of him under my hand and the way his eyes are roving up, down, left, right, all over me, I really doubt it's for lack of interest. So what is it then?

I withdraw my hand. "What's wrong?"

Matt looks past me, as if trying to find the right words before acknowledging my question. "I leave tomorrow."

The emotion rising in my throat catches me off guard. I've known all along that he was leaving, just as well as he did. If anything, it's been on my mind more than his. "I know that," I say quietly. "But who cares?"

"You really want to do long distance?" His tone leaves no doubt that he doesn't.

"No, not really." It's not a lie, but it doesn't mean that I don't want to try.

"I just..." his voice trails. "I just don't think it's a good idea to hold ourselves back like this."

"Huh?" Whatever he's trying to say, I'm not getting it.

He sighs, making a frustrated gesture. "I really like you, Jackson. You're fun and you're smart and God knows you're cute, but–"

"But what?" I snap. I feel like he's breaking up with me, but we're not actually together. I don't even know what it means or feels like to be in a relationship with another guy. How fair is it that I'm getting dumped without ever having enjoyed dating in the first place?

His whole expression seems to slump. "We've only just met. We have known each other for ten days. Ten. Days. You're going to be a senior in high school, and I'm starting my sophomore year in college. And we're going to try to keep this up after I move back across the country?" He takes a deep breath before plunging back in. "That's not fair to either of us. Who's to say that we're not totally wrong for each other? That if we had more time together, we'd figure out after a few weeks that you can't stand my singing voice or you're totally grossed out by my foot hair."

I hate that he's making sense, and that he's making me doubt my newly found feelings for him. Is it even possible to have real feelings for someone after just a week? The dumbest part is that for everything he's said, I can only think of one question. "You have foot hair?"

He laughs, but it's not the playful one full of amusement that I'm used to. Instead it's tainted by a resignation, convincing me that I really am getting broken up with right now. "Yeah," he admits, "I have foot hair."

"Like on the top?" I ask, curiosity overruling my other emotions for the moment.

Rolling his eyes, he answers quickly, "Yes, on top. It goes from my ankle to my big toe. Is that really what you want to talk about right now?"

"No, it's not, but I don't know what else to say."

"I think we should enjoy this for what it is – an amazing week spent together. Even if I disregard the glaring issue that I've never been with a guy before and this feels really fucking weird sometimes... we've only just met. And as much as I like you, I don't want to start a long distance relationship off of *one week*. You get that, right?"

"Yeah," I whisper. "I get it." I don't even disagree with him necessarily, but it just sucks having to get it thrown at me so suddenly. "So what now?"

"We enjoy the time we have left, and then we go our own ways until next summer."

If there was any part of this conversation that suggested even the slightest possibility of a future that includes Matt, this is it. I only wish that I could stop myself from jumping on it with such hopefulness. "Next summer?"

"Sure," he says. "Then we can take the time to get to know each other properly."

Unwilling to stay in the park any longer, we retreat to his house. His parents still aren't home, but getting Matt's clothes off is the furthest thing from my mind. He seems to know it too, because the walk up the stairs to his room is wrapped in a forlorn silence. It's not fair. If only we'd met at the beginning of the summer. Even a few weeks ago would have been enough.

As angry as I am about the whole thing, he's right that a week together isn't enough to start something serious. I might be acting foolish about the whole first crush thing, but I'm not so naïve to think that you can fall in love in ten days. Fall in lust? Absolutely. But that's not love. It can lead to love, but on its own it's nothing.

We curl up on his bed, in the same spot that we made out for the first time. Dropping my head onto his shoulder, I fight to maintain my composure. I'm not going to cry. Closing my eyes, I let his warmth and his scent fill my senses.

With his arm around me, he runs his fingers through my hair. Tracing his thumb along the top of my ear, he leans over and presses his lips to my forehead. "I'm sorry it worked out like this," he whispers. "Next summer, okay?"

Inhaling swiftly to clear the sadness in my sinuses, I repeat firmly, "Next summer."

Chapter Six

Jackson

Nine Months Later

"Where do I start?" I ask Dad, gesturing with my hammer.

"Wherever you want. It all has to come down," he says, meeting my eyes.

Whipping my arm forward, I bury the head of my hammer in the wall. Plaster particles explode outward along with a cloud of dust. When I wrench the hammer out, chunks of plaster and thin wooden lath come along with it.

"Damn, son," he says, sounding impressed.

I shrug, fighting off a grin. "Might as well have some fun with it."

With a grunt, he knocks a hole of his own in the wall. The muscles tensing in his arm, he works the hammer free. I'm surprised he offered to help with this, but I'm glad he did. Otherwise it would have been me alone tearing down the old plaster walls in this room, all fricking day.

Our hammers rip into the wall time after time, until the floor is covered in piles of plaster and broken lath boards. The walls and ceiling in this room were victims of the roof leak when Matt and I re-shingled last summer. So much water came through that the plaster started to crumble in a bunch of places. It wasn't very apparent at first, but after a few weeks it looked like crap. I told Dad we should just putty over it and repaint, but he insisted on doing it "the right way." Sounded like typical bullshit to me, but at least he's not making me do this by myself.

Downstairs the phone rings, and Dad steps out of the room. After the third ring, I hear his distant voice answer it. I keep smashing away.

I'm about to swing again when Dad's voice stops me. "Bad news and good news," he says.

I swivel my head to see him. He has the door cracked open, peering in as though seeing the progress for the first time.

"What?" I ask, the hammer hanging from my fingers.

"It's too bad we didn't start an hour later." His eyes skim over the room. We've ripped down a good portion of the exterior facing wall, right down to the studs. This house is too old to have insulation, so we can see straight through to the substrate beneath the exterior siding.

"Why? I thought you said you wanted all the walls brought down." A wave of frustration builds inside me. If he changes his mind about needing this done, I swear…

"I did," he says, "but something just came up. If I'd known sooner, we wouldn't have started this project. Now we might as well take it all down."

"What are you talking about?" I demand. Lowering my voice to a safer, more deferential tone, I quickly backtrack before Dad can get pissed. "Sorry, I mean, what's going on? Who called?"

Chapter Seven

Ben

"Ben." Mom's voice steals away sleep's comforting embrace. My eyes refuse to open yet, reluctant to give up my dream. Savoring the lingering feeling of absolute comfort and safety for just a few moments longer, I finally give in.

Mom is still standing in the doorway. "Morning," she says, smiling lightly. Despite my disappointment at being wrenched from sleep, I can't help but smile back at her. Mom is beautiful, there's no other word for it. Her long hair is blond like mine, except maybe a shade lighter. It's only possible to tell when we're both in the sun, though.

Crossing the room, she sits on the edge of the bed and lays her hand on the back of my neck. "Morning," I say, my voice scratchy. Her fingers gently massage the muscles of my neck along my spine, moving up and down. No matter how many times she does this, it feels amazing every time.

I know that at work she can be aggressive, and I've heard she's put the fear of God into more than one entry-level analyst – it's how she moved up through her company so fast – but I've never seen that side of her.

I yawn unabashedly, stretching under the covers but making sure to keep in range of her miracle-working fingers.

"I made your favorite," she says, continuing to rub my neck.

"French toast?"

"And bacon." *Yes.* She stands up.

"Don't stop, it feels good." I give her my best puppy dog face.

Mom laughs. "That's all you get, sleepy boy. Now get up, breakfast is ready."

"I'm eighteen," I grumble. "I'm not a boy anymore."

"Sorry. See you in the kitchen, sleepy man-boy."

Stabbing the last square of French toast on my plate, I shove it into my mouth, trying unsuccessfully to keep my jaw defiantly clenched while I chew. I should have known it was too good to be true the moment she mentioned bacon. But this was worse than I ever expected. In fact, it's bullshit through and through.

"I'm sorry, Ben, but you have to go. I wish it didn't work out like this, but it's just the way it is."

She's never left for this long before, not ever. "How can they make you leave for the whole summer? That's stupid."

"I don't like it either, honey." She cups her hand on my cheek.

I push her hand away a little harder than necessary. "Why can't I just stay here? I'm legally an adult."

She braces herself on the kitchen table. "Legally maybe, but I can't leave you here by yourself for that long. Surely you must understand that? You're going to live with Jeff – your dad, I mean – and your brother for the summer."

"And my life here? I have friends and plans and… and this is fucking ridiculous."

Her gaze hardens. "That language is unnecessary, Ben." She turns to empty the dishwasher. "I'm sure Jackson will introduce you to his friends."

I know I'm acting childish, but this whole thing is a goddamn joke. Unfair doesn't even begin to scratch the surface of having the summer before my freshman year at Stanford snatched away from me. "His friends probably suck," I hiss, even though I'm really not sure. The last time I spoke to him was on the phone over a year ago. It was only for a few minutes, and we didn't really dig into details about our personal lives.

"I'm sure you'll figure something out. It's also possible I could get done sooner than they anticipate."

"What is it you're even doing? They've never sent you on a trip for more than a few weeks." I kick the tip of my shoe against the white tile before glancing back to meet her eyes.

She returns a gleaming glass mixing bowl to the cupboard. "They just wanted to get the whole year's travel out of the way in one go. You know, trying to save costs on airfare."

"Except you're having to pay *extra* airfare to send me across the country."

"Yes, well, they've agreed to cover that."

I roll my eyes. "So why don't they just not send you for three months?"

"Can we please not argue, Ben?" She sighs and her shoulders sink an extra little bit. For the first time, I notice the age that finally seems to be catching up to her.

The memory of my conversation with Mom fills me once again, making my stomach roil. It was a week ago, but it still pisses me off to even think about it. I can't believe that this happened.

Someone is staring back at me. Blinking quickly, I glance away. I have a tendency to daydream and stare off into space. Or at people. And with so many people in the airport, it's almost impossible to look anywhere and not be ogling someone.

I'm waiting on one of the benches just outside the main terminal, my duffel bag tucked between my knees. I check my phone, just in case I somehow missed a call in the last thirty seconds. Jeff is late. He was supposed to pick me up at five-thirty, and it's a quarter after six.

An overweight family of five waddles past as I look away down the length of the terminal. Where the hell is he? Is this what it's going to be like living with him and my brother for the rest of the summer? Or do they have some other obnoxious quirk? I haven't actually *seen* either of them in years. Five years? Six? I'm not really sure.

"Hey there, Ben." A hand claps me on the shoulder.

I jump in surprise. "Hi, Jeff." He looks like I remember, except a lot older. His hair is mixed with gray and there are wrinkles around his eyes. He's still thin and tall, though not as tall as I remember.

He frowns for a second, probably because I didn't call him *Dad* but he recovers quickly. "Sorry I'm late. Traffic in the Cities is always a nightmare."

The Cities? I stand and pick up my duffel bag. "Can we go? I'm hungry."

He takes the opportunity to squeeze me into an awkward hug. "It's good to see you, son."

"Yeah, uh, you too, but you're making it hard for me to breathe," I wheeze.

"Sorry." He releases me, and I take a deep breath to refill my lungs. "The truck is this way." He points toward the exit labeled parking ramp.

When we get to his truck, a dark gray F-150, he takes my bag and tosses it into the back. The vehicle looks like a new model, but scuffs and scratches cover the tailgate and the bed. "Your truck is kind of beat up," I say, hopping into the passenger side.

He nods. "She sees a lot of use." The engine rumbles to life, and he shifts into reverse. "Buckle up, son."

Why does he keep calling me that? I get it – technically I'm his offspring. But just because I'm here now doesn't mean he's dear old dad. It wasn't my choice to get thrown back across the country, and if he thinks it's going to change the pitiful excuse we have for a father-son relationship, he's out of his mind.

"Ben?" He's still waiting, foot on the brake. I snap my seatbelt into place.

"How was your flight?" he asks, turning carefully out of the parking ramp.

The bright daylight of the summer evening washes over the truck as we clear the shadow of the concrete parking structure, forcing me to squint until I pull down the sun visor. When I do, a small rectangular mirror on the underside catches my blond hair in its view. "Flight was long," I say. It didn't help that I was pissed off before the flight. And during the flight. And now.

"California is pretty far from here, so I suppose it would be." Scanning his rearview mirror, Jeff merges onto the freeway.

Forcing my gritted teeth to relax, I take a deep breath. "How is Jackson?" I ask. My heart thumps in my chest. I can't believe I'm actually about to see him again. It's been so long. How different will he look?

Jeff taps the button for the cruise control and lets his foot off the gas. "Jackson is doing good. He was going to come along, but he was still out when I left. He'll be home before we are though, don't worry."

"I wasn't," I say.

"You weren't what?"

"Worrying."

"Oh," he says, pausing. "I see."

Thirty minutes of silence pass before we pull off the highway onto a dirt road. I haven't even seen a dirt road in… actually I'm not sure when the last time was. Tall grasses growing alongside the road blow in the wind, and only the occasional tree punctuates the landscape. Otherwise there's only farmland, everywhere. A lot of corn, but other stuff too. Wheat, maybe. The land is too open and empty here, like it might swallow me up whole if it had half a chance.

Up ahead on the left is a white house that stirs faded memories within me. In the yard surrounding it are weeping willow trees, their wiry branches conducting an invisible orchestra in the diminishing light of evening. Beyond the willows is a swath of woods extending back from the yard, providing a stark contrast to the rolling cropland that covers everything else.

"Here we are." He turns into the driveway, bringing the truck to a stop in front of the house at the center of the tree-sheltered yard. It's been years since I was here. So long that I almost don't remember it. Almost. The house is a two-story with red trim and a lot of windows. It's quaint and seems kind of small, at least compared to when I was ten.

I jump as the driver's door slams. Closing my fingers on the door handle, I give it a sharp pull and hop to the ground.

"Go on in. I'll get your bag," Jeff says as he walks around the truck and grabs my duffel bag out of the back, dusting the dirt off it.

I take a breath and my first step toward the front door. He said Jackson would be home. Is he waiting just inside the door? Or in his room?

The screen door is light and opens with a noise that makes me cringe. Jeff catches the door behind me before it can slam shut, following me in. Kicking my shoes off next to the row of boots and shoes in the entryway, I step gingerly into the next room. A couch runs along the far wall directly across from a TV, which is off. Beside the couch is a worn leather recliner, and curled up in it, reading a book, is my brother.

He sets the book down in his lap. Our eyes dig into each other, searching, examining. His hair is blond and a little shorter than mine. Slightly rounded cleft chin, bright blue eyes, and a smattering of light freckles across the top of his cheeks. We stare at each other for a full minute. In the back of my mind, I'm aware that Jeff is just watching us, but that's not where my focus is.

I thought Jackson would look different after the years, but we still appear almost exactly alike. It's like looking in a mirror except there's no glass here. It catches me by surprise, because we haven't seen each other in so long. But looking at him now, it's impossible to miss it. My brother and I share more than a set of parents. We also share a genetic code.

"Hi, Jackson," I say quietly.

He flips down the footrest on the recliner and stands up. "Ben." The word feels empty. Almost as empty as our relationship over the last eight years. "Good to see you."

Tensing my shoulders to force away the shiver dragging its frosty fingers over my skin, I stare at him. I don't know what I'm expecting, because we hardly know each other anymore. I guess I was hoping for more from him than coolness. It seems weird to think of him trying to give me a hug, but I wouldn't have stopped him.

Jeff walks between us and into the next room through a rounded archway. I hear him pull a chair out, so I follow with Jackson bringing up the rear. Jeff is sitting at the kitchen table. "Have a seat," he says.

I sit down as Jackson opens the fridge, reaching for one of several brown bottles in the bottom drawer. He glances at Jeff, who shakes his head. Jackson detours and grabs a coke from the top shelf. "Ben, you want a pop?"

Pop. In case I'd forgotten I was in the Midwest. "I'll have a Mountain Dew."

"We only have coke and root beer."

Who *are* these people? "Coke then."

"Sure thing." He grabs the can and sets it in front of me, taking a seat beside Jeff.

"So how have you been, Ben?" Jeff asks, realizing his phrasing mistake only at the end of his sentence.

I frown. Does he want a serious answer? Because it would go something like, *it's been a clusterfuck ever since Mom announced she was leaving for the summer and I was getting shipped across the country.* "Fine," I say.

Jackson raises an eyebrow. "I'm glad you're still the same old bowl of sunshine."

"Fuck off," I snap, my eyes narrowing.

Jeff cuts in, "Hey, hey. None of that. We're really glad to have you here, Ben, but I have to tell you that we're in the middle of a few things.

I just had two of my employees quit this last week, so I'll need both Jackson's and your help for the next few weeks until I can find someone new."

I have a summer job now, too? "Okay," I say. "And the other stuff?"

"We're also remodeling the guest bedroom. Until we finish up in there, you'll need to share Jackson's room with him." He gives me a sympathetic smile, the kind that parents give to their kids when they're getting hosed.

My eyes shift from Jeff to Jackson, who's taking a sip from his coke. I still haven't opened mine. Pulling back on the tab, I let the crack of carbonation break the silence so I don't have to. "Are you serious?"

"Afraid so. We're going to push in our free time to get it finished, so hopefully you won't have to spend more than a few weeks in Jackson's room."

I take a deep breath, mentally running through the list of what has happened today. Exiled to rural Minnesota for the summer? Check. Drafted into a job? Check. Have to share room with estranged brother? Check. "All right, whatever."

Jeff's expression makes it seem like he's trying to be understanding, but he doesn't respond to me. "Jackson, how about you show Ben the house? I'll bring his bag up to your room in a little bit."

"Come on, Ben," Jackson says, jumping up from his seat and snagging his coke off the table. I don't bother taking mine.

Leading me up the stairs, he points out the bathroom, Jeff's bedroom, and the room I'll have once it's finished. "It kind of looks like hell right now," he says, nudging open the door and gesturing with the can in his hand. "The old plaster and lath got pretty damaged in a roof leak," he explains, making a face that doesn't seem to be directed at me. "So Dad decided we had to take it right down to the studs."

I have no idea what he's just said, but the room is a disaster. I can see the structural boards that form the skeleton of the walls, and the floor is covered in piles of wood chunks and what look like little pieces of concrete. "Huh," I say. "I guess Jeff wasn't kidding about it not being ready to live in."

Jackson stiffens beside me. "Why do you call him that?"

I shrug. "That's his name."

"Yeah, no shit." He turns away and continues down the hall, leaving me in the doorway to the destroyed room. As he walks, the tips of his shoulder blades make alternating impressions in the back of his shirt. Is that what I look like from behind?

I catch up to him as he opens the door to his room. It's about as messy as the guest room with the walls torn out. Clothes cover most of the floor and they're piled on top of the dresser too. Along the wall above the bed, unmade of course, is a huge poster for the latest Star Trek movie. I bite my lip. I actually really like Star Trek, but I'm not about to tell Jackson that.

"A little messy, but it's home," he says. "The bed is just a double, so it's going to be a bit of a squeeze."

My eyes grow wide. "I am *not* sharing a bed with you."

"Why not? It's better than the floor." He says it so coolly, like it's no big deal. Like I'm an idiot for having a problem with the idea. He tosses a pillow out of the way and plops down on the edge of the bed.

I let out a long breath and close my eyes for a moment. If this summer is karma, I have no idea what I did to deserve it. "Why do you care where I sleep?"

"I don't care. Why do you?"

I force myself to breathe evenly and not let him piss me off. "I'd just rather sleep on the floor."

He shrugs. "Whatever makes you happy."

Glancing away, I say, "I didn't ask to come out here, you know."

When I look back, Jackson's gaze is fixed on me. After a moment he says, "Nope, and we didn't invite you either, but here you are."

I'm about to tell him exactly how much I don't want to be here when Jeff knocks on the open door. "Hey guys," he says, setting my duffel bag just inside the room. Scanning the scene before him, he frowns. "Jackson, you were supposed to clean up."

"I did. Kind of."

Both of us give him a look.

"Fine, I'll do some more picking up. Oh and Ben doesn't want to sleep in the bed with me."

Blushing, I look to Jeff. "I just... uh..." I stammer, trying to make it not sound like I just don't want to sleep next to Jackson. Which of course is exactly the reason.

"No problem," Jeff says, saving me from having to lie. "We'll just bring up the air mattress from the camping stuff." Turning to leave, he stops himself with a hand on the doorframe. "Ben, make sure Jackson actually cleans up this time, could you?"

I can't tell if he's joking or not. "Sure." I glance at Jackson. He looks irritated.

Once he leaves, Jackson grabs a laundry basket and starts throwing everything in. I take his spot on the bed from earlier and watch him work in silence. After a few minutes, the place is actually starting to look okay. I consider offering to help, but I don't know what I'd do. I also seriously doubt that he actually has a designated place for any of his stuff.

Jackson is kicking a pair of dirty socks into the tiny space underneath his dresser when he asks, "How is Mom?"

I pause, thinking about how much I miss her already. She saw me off at the airport this morning, but that feels like so long ago. "She's good. Moving up the corporate ladder at her job."

"Does she like it?"

"I think so. She's good at it."

He shoves the overflowing hamper into the closet. "Is that why she had to leave for the summer?"

"A business trip, yeah. They're usually only a week or two, though. Never three months."

"And she didn't trust you to stay home by yourself?"

I bristle at his suggestion. "I would have been just fine. I don't get why she wouldn't let me stay." I hope he doesn't ask anything more about it, because his questions would be the same as my own. She's never left for this long before, and never on such short notice. She told me literally less than a week ago. But I'm an adult. Why the hell did I have to come here?

I shoot a glare at Jackson, but he's not even looking at me, instead busying himself with heaving a pile of papers into the trashcan in the corner. "How about Jeff?" I pause, but decide against correcting myself just for Jackson's sake. "How's he been?"

He gives me an annoyed sidelong look. "Things are good here too. Dad's business does all right."

"What does he do?"

"He runs a greenhouse in town. I thought you knew that."

It sounds vaguely familiar. "Yeah, maybe."

He pushes the comforter out of the way to make room beside me on the bed. "It's not so bad out here, you know."

"It's not where I belong."

Jackson glances at the floor. "I'm going to brush my teeth. Dad will be up with the air mattress in a minute."

"It's only nine."

"We go to bed early, get up early," he says with a shrug as he leaves the room.

I'm not really a morning person, and definitely not when school is out. I'll just add that to the sprawling list of things going wrong this summer. Digging through my duffel, I pull out my bag of toiletries and wander down the hall.

Jackson left the bathroom door open, so I join him at the sink where he's brushing his teeth in front of the mirror. It's funny watching him, because he brushes just like I do – with the toothbrush pinched between his thumb and index finger like a pen and his tongue lolling out to the side. My friends back home always make fun of me for it, which makes sense now, because Jackson looks kind of like a dog with his tongue out like that.

He spits into the sink. "What?"

"You hold your brush like I do." I squirt a line of toothpaste onto the bristles and start to brush.

On his way out, he calls over his shoulder, "You've got it backwards. You brush like me." I want to argue, but my mouth is full of toothpaste.

When I get back to the room, I hook up the pump on the air mattress that Jeff dropped off. The buzzing whirr fills the room as the bed fills. When it finishes, I toss a sheet over it, also compliments of Jeff.

"Here," Jackson says, "You can take one of my pillows." He throws one with a white and brown patterned pillowcase onto the airbed.

"Uh, thanks."

Then right in front of me, he strips off his shirt and cargo shorts. Wanting to avert my eyes but also painfully curious about my brother, I watch him as I undress down to my underwear as well. In contrast to my boxers, he's wearing a ridiculous pair of bright blue striped briefs. For a moment we just stare at one another. It's almost creepy how similar we still look. My muscles are leaner and a bit more defined, but his are a little bigger. If I had to guess, I'd say he has five pounds on me, even though I might be an inch taller. The biggest difference is around his neck. A mini ball-bearing chain is looped around it, and from it hangs a small silver ring in the center of his chest. I wonder where he got that.

The physical differences between us have always been minor. Maybe they've become slightly more pronounced in the passing years, but not nearly so much as the emotional divide that's grown so wide that I'm afraid to look down into it. To see how deep the chasm extends, and to discover what darkness is lurking there.

We're being civil to each other more or less, but what we used to have was so different. It makes our politesse feel forced – an unnatural byproduct of a broken relationship that probably can't be fixed.

Flicking off the light, Jackson crosses the room to his bed as I slide with a shiver into the cool sheets covering the air mattress. The pillow he gave me is a good one, and it smells like him. I know it's stupid to think that, because really we smell the same. I can't explain why it's different, but it is, because I know the scent is his and not my own.

Supposedly some dogs can tell the difference between identical twins. A university somewhere did a study on it, I think. One of those stupid universities that always sent Mom requests to have us put in twin studies. I always used to get so angry when we got one of those letters. I hadn't seen my brother in years, so who the hell were they to assume they could get us together for a study. Eventually I stopped caring. Jackson clearly didn't give a shit that we never saw each other, so why should I?

"Goodnight, Ben," he says, his voice crossing the quietness that hangs still in the air.

I hold my breath, eventually deciding just not to answer him.

A crack of thunder shakes the house, and rain beats against the roof in waves. My heart is thumping fast. My arms tighten around my Jurassic Park pillow, the one Mom bought me for Christmas. My forehead is cold with sweat. I'm so scared. What if I wet the bed? I haven't done that in over two years, but still.

I want to crawl into bed with Mom and Dad, but they're all the way down the hall. Bright light fills our room for a second as the flash of lightning snakes down from the sky. I curl into a ball around my pillow, squeezing my eyes shut. When the thunder comes a moment later, a yelp jumps out of my throat. My eyes are still shut, but tears sneak out of them.

Over the hammering rain, a voice calls out softly from the matching twin bed opposite mine. "Benny, is that you?"

I sniff, clearing my nose. "I'm scared, Jacks."

The hardwood floor creaks, but it's too dark to see anything. At least not until the next flash, and I don't want to be watching when that happens.

Jacks tugs at the covers, and I let him in. Slipping in next to me, he wraps his arms around me. "It's okay, Benny. It's just a storm."

My heart jumps again as the room lights up with the storm's latest attack, but with Jacks here, it's not as bad. My breathing slows as the lightning strikes grow dimmer and the thunder becomes quieter and more delayed.

Eventually Jacks' breathing relaxes too, steady and even, and I know he's fallen asleep. Still tucked in next to him, I fall into a peaceful sleep.

Chapter Eight

Ben

An alarm buzzer cuts through my dream world. My first waking thought is that the air mattress must have a slow leak, because my tailbone is pressed into the floor. It's still dark in the room. How early must it be? I haven't woken up before the sun in a *long* time.

The silhouette of an arm sneaks out from underneath the covers on Jackson's bed, and the alarm is abruptly silenced. A second later, the lamp on his nightstand flares to life, and I toss the sheet over my head with a groan.

"Rise and shine, brother," Jackson says.

"What time is it?" My voice is scratchy.

"Six. Full day ahead of us."

Peeking out from underneath the blanket, I ask, "What are you talking about?"

Pulling on a pair of basketball shorts, he leans over to look in the mirror on his dresser and run a hand through his hair. "We're helping Dad at the greenhouse, remember?"

Oh, right.

"You want to shower first or second?"

"Go ahead," I grumble, taking advantage of another few minutes' rest.

Eventually I hear the bathroom door open just before Jackson yells down the hall, "Done in the shower!"

Forcing myself out of bed and toward the bathroom, I cautiously open the door to a cloud of fog. Jackson is putting some product in his hair, wearing only a towel around his waist.

I stare at his reflection in the mirror until he finally meets my eyes. "Um," I say, "I'm not going to shower with you in here."

He stops, hand midway through his hair. "We don't have enough time for both of us to get ready if we don't share the bathroom. The shower has frosted glass, and don't worry, I won't look or anything while you get in."

I glare at him. This is bullshit. "Fine, whatever." Kicking off my boxers, I step into the shower.

Almost as an afterthought, Jackson says, "It's not like it's anything I don't see whenever I look in the mirror."

Does he think he's being funny? I ignore him. Spinning the shower knob to hot, I let the water pour down, temporarily washing away the knowledge that my summer has been ruined. The steaming water pummeling into my back, I hear the door open and then close. Finally I'm alone. Is that so much to ask while showering?

I've just washed my hair with Jackson's shampoo and I'm about to sample his body wash when I get interrupted by rapid knocking on the door. Through the foggy glass, I see him poke his head into the room. "Why are you still in the shower? We're going to be late. Seriously."

Late for what? Helping Jeff out? I don't give a shit if I'm late for that. "I'm coming. Just get out, okay?"

Jackson sighs. "Sure, but hurry up."

I can hear a conversation happening in the hall while I dry off, but I forgot to bring clean clothes with me, so I wrap the towel around my waist and step out of the bathroom. Jackson and Jeff are at the top of the stairs. Jackson is in shorts while Jeff is wearing jeans with holes forming at the knees, but both of them are sporting silly blue t-shirts that say *Roanoke Gardens* across the front. It's kind of funny to see my last name plastered on a shirt.

"Morning, Ben," Jeff gives me a tight smile. Glancing back to Jackson, he says, "I have to go now if we're going to open on time."

Shrugging in response, Jackson says, "The bike hasn't been running well."

"Shit, I forgot about that." Jeff runs a hand along his jaw. "Take the bike anyway. If it breaks down, just give me a call and we'll sort it out. Otherwise we'll work on it tonight."

Jackson grins. "I can really take the bike? With both of us?"

"No other choice. I'll see you both soon." He gives me a nod and heads down the stairs, his feet pounding over the steps.

"Go on, Ben," Jackson waves me down the hall toward his room. "I set out work clothes on the bed for you."

Just like he said, a pair of ratty cutoff shorts and a blue t-shirt just like theirs are lying on the bed. Dropping the towel, I pull on clean socks and boxers from my bag before changing into what Jackson set out for me.

Jackson is waiting for me downstairs in the kitchen, just popping the last bite of toast into his mouth. "You need breakfast?"

"No."

"Great, that saves us a little time." He flicks his eyes to my feet and then to the entryway. "Do you have shoes that can get dirty?"

"I only brought my Nike's."

"You can borrow a pair of mine then. Size ten?"

I nod but don't say anything. Are we actually going to end up working? Like, honest to God dirt on my hands working? I don't like getting messy.

Tipping back the rest of a glass of milk, Jackson hops up from his seat at the table. I follow him into the entryway where he tosses me a pair of shoes. They're dirty and I'm sure they smell, so I hold my face away while I put them on. Locking the front door on the way out, he leads us to the garage.

"So what's that Jeff said about a bike?"

"Usually Dad and I drive in together, but, well," he gestures off-handedly to me. "We got a little delayed this morning, so we're taking my dirt bike."

"I got ready as fast as I could." Not really.

Shrugging, he says, "It's fine, we might just need to start getting up a little earlier."

I stifle a yawn. "No way."

"We can't be late every day." Jackson yanks up on the garage door and it clatters open along the tracks. The garage is full of crap, and everything is covered in dust, but in the middle is a space cleared out for the dirt bike. It isn't anything like the motorcycles back home. The tires look like fat bicycle tires, and there are massive shock absorbers suspending the front end above the wheel.

"Is it legal to take that thing on the road?"

He pulls on a dorky looking helmet that only covers the top and sides of his head. It doesn't even have a face guard. "Yeah, sort of."

When he picks up a pair of clear plastic safety glasses from the workbench and slides them onto his face, I burst out laughing. "You've got to be kidding."

"You laugh now, but I don't have another helmet or even anything for your eyes," he admits. "So be careful not to look straight into the wind."

"What if we get pulled over?"

Getting on the bike, he kicks his foot down on the starter, and the engine snarls to life like a vicious lawnmower. "We won't. Don and Jimmy don't come out this side of town before noon, guaranteed."

I shake my head at him. "You know your cops by name?"

He cocks his head to the side. "Doesn't everyone?"

I stare back at him.

He sighs. "That was a joke, Ben. Now get on the damn bike, or we're going to get there even later."

I jump on behind him. I'm not sure this thing was meant for two people, but what the hell. Tilting his wrist back, we accelerate down the driveway before taking a right onto the dirt road that leads into town. With nothing but road in front of us, he guns it and the bike surges forward.

Just inside the Northfield city limits, Jackson hangs another right into the parking lot of a small shop. Just like the shirts we're wearing, a sign across the front of the building has the words *Roanoke Gardens*. Having my name on a building tops the t-shirts by far. Especially because it's one with a huge metal-framed greenhouse stretching off the back.

Jackson pulls around and parks next to Jeff's truck. Hopping off, I follow him through the back door into the shop. Every manner of lawn ornaments is stacked along one wall, while another is piled with fertilizer bags and grass seed. The third wall has bins and buckets for dozens of garden implements ranging from hand trowels to leaf rakes.

Popping behind the counter, he picks up a key ring from a hook on the back wall. "Dad probably wants to talk to you about today," he says, passing me on his way to the front door. "He's back in the office."

When my eyes flit around the shop looking for the office, Jackson jerks a thumb in the direction of a closed door next to the cash register. It feels strange to let myself behind the counter as I walk to the door and knock.

Jeff opens the door from the spindly chair he's sitting in, revealing a tiny office. "Hey, Ben. Excited for today?"

I shrug. "Yeah, sure."

"The shirt looks good on you."

No it doesn't, but I can't bring myself to tell him that, because he means well. When he realizes I'm not going to respond, he continues, "A lot of watering needs to be done every morning, so you can help Jackson with that. This afternoon there should be time for some more exciting stuff though, like transplanting." He grins.

I nod. "Is that all?"

He nods, his smile withering just a bit. "Let me know if you have any questions. Otherwise, time to work." He claps me on the shoulder and turns back to his desk covered in papers and spreadsheets.

I shut the door to the office and wait for Jackson to finish counting the cash in the register. "How much you keep in there?"

His mouth is moving silently as he flips through a stack of twenties. Setting it back in the tray and shutting the drawer, he says, "Just five hundred."

"Huh. Interesting." I glance at the door. "Are we like open already?"

"Yeah, but no one usually shows up for another half hour or so. Which gives us time to water. Come on," he says. "Time to get your hands dirty, city boy." I roll my eyes, but he's already walking away.

The greenhouse is huge on the inside, and it smells like fresh earth. Waist-high boards supported by pipes form rows of tables, dominating the center aisle and wrapping around the sides of the plastic-covered structure. Plants cover almost every square inch of the tables, and trays of seedlings are resting on the ground underneath them too. And then there are the hanging plants. There's just so much *green*.

Jackson sets me up with a hose that has a long angled wand on the end to help reach the middle of the tables and the hanging planters. He spins the handle on the spigot and after a few spitting coughs from the hose, water begins to come out in a smooth shower.

I work my way along the first row while Jackson cranks up the plastic on the sides a few feet. As outside air drifts through, the overwhelming smell of earth starts to clear.

"I'm going to head up to the front and make sure Dad doesn't need anything else. You good here?"

I give him a look. "Pretty sure I can handle a garden hose."

"You got it," he says, his tone landing somewhere between encouragement and sarcasm.

It takes over an hour to water everything in the greenhouse, and I'm just finishing when an older woman wearing white pants and a pink blouse enters the far end, poking her way through the plants. I ignore her and keep watering the row of large potted plants along the back wall.

"Excuse me, young man." The woman's voice is right behind me.

My hand jerks and a stream of water flies up to hit the thick plastic. "Jesus," I curse under my breath.

"What was that?" Her tone is friendly, but she's clearly hard of hearing.

I turn to her, flipping the switch on the handle of the wand. The water slows to a trickle. "Nothing, sorry."

"Oh, Jackson," she says, her face splitting into a smile. "How did you get back here so fast? I just saw you up front." Even though her voice definitely belongs to an old woman, it has a youthful quality to it.

I close my eyes and sigh. "I'm not Jackson. I'm his brother, Ben."

Her smile grows even wider. "I didn't know he had a twin brother. It's lovely to meet you, Ben. I'm Cherie Dodd." She holds out a wrinkled hand.

Setting down the hose, I shake her outstretched hand. Her skin is cool, and it's starting to hang off her fingers. "He does. Is there something I can help you with?"

"You know," she says, scooting closer and resting a hand on the middle of my back. "I can't quite remember, but now that I have you… can you point me in the direction of the mulch?"

I bet there are a lot of things she can't remember. "Sorry, I don't know anything about this sh–" I stop myself and rephrase. "About this stuff. I'm just here for a few weeks." *Months.*

"No matter." She waves the topic away with her free hand. With the other she slowly guides me back toward the storefront. "That's so interesting that you and Jackson are twins."

"I guess so."

"I bet you two must be close."

A rope of frustration tightens around my stomach. "No, not really."

"Is that so? That's really too bad. My sister Alma and I were best friends from the time we got out of diapers until she passed away two years ago, incidentally back in diapers before she finally went, bless her soul. Anyway, we were a year apart, so it wasn't like the twinsy connection you and Jackson have."

I grit my teeth. "Sorry to hear about your sister." We're almost back to the store.

"Oh, it's all right. We spent all the best years of our lives together, which of course was college and divorcing our husbands together, so I don't have any regrets." Her attention redirecting to the raised threshold of the store's rear entrance, she winds her leg up like a pitcher to get her foot high enough to step over it. How old *is* this woman?

Following her in, I point across the room at Jackson. "He'll help you." At the moment, my brother is ringing up a young woman's purchase at the register. He smiles as he gives her the change and slips a plastic bag around her plant. What a nice guy, that Jackson.

"Won't you stick around?" Cherie asks. "I understand you're still learning your way around, but I do love to chat, even if you're unable to provide any botanical direction."

"Sorry, I have work to do," I say, dropping my gaze. Her hand falls from my back as I walk away, but the warmth lingers for several moments longer.

The second I'm outside, I kick at the ground and a shower of woodchips explodes into the air. I walk all the way back to Jeff's truck, trying to get a handle on myself. Leaning against the hood, I fight to keep my breathing even. Now that I've finally flown out here to Minnesota, it's impossible to ignore that I have a brother – a twin brother – and I don't even know him. After living half a country apart for nearly a decade, why does it bother me so much now that we've grown apart?

Mom and Jeff's divorce was messy, although I didn't learn that until three years ago on Mom's birthday when she decided to finish a bottle of wine by herself. A divorce that was kept almost entirely from Jackson and me. Our parents tried so hard to insulate us from the consequences of it, and it almost worked, except when it came to the worst one of all – splitting us apart. Even though she didn't explain much, it was enough for me to understand that beneath all of her strength, she was honestly afraid in those last days before she left. Except being here now, I don't know why. Dad isn't some raging drunk or anything.

Anyway, for as hard as they worked to avoid any contact with each other, they never made any attempt to actually keep us from seeing each other. It just sort of happened.

Jackson seems to have changed so much with the passing time.

He even knows how to a ride a motorcycle now. When the hell did he learn to do that?

When I return to the front, Jackson locks eyes with me the moment I step inside the store. "Where did you go?"

"Just took a break for a bit," I mumble.

"Oh. I see you met Cherie. She's a hoot."

I shrug, glancing away. "She seems crazy."

"You should be nice to her, she doesn't have an ounce of meanness in that wrinkled old body."

Sliding my shoe back and forth on the slippery concrete floor, I ask, "So what should I do next?"

"Did you water outside yet?"

"Just the stuff inside the greenhouse."

"Water the little pots outside, and if there's time before lunch, might as well do the potted trees too."

"Whatever you say, boss."

He gives me an impassive look, but I ignore him and walk away.

After lunch, Jackson tells me not to water anymore since it's getting too hot. Instead I'm supposed to be squeezing together the rows of potted tomatoes so we can clear up outdoor space. He doesn't say why, and I don't really care. I just want today to be done.

I'm dragging my third tomato plant to its new home when I see her step out from the end of the greenhouse. Lifting a hand to shield my eyes from the sun, I can't stop myself from staring. Thin and tall with golden brown hair down to her shoulders, she's got on a pair of jean shorts and a blue t-shirt just like mine. She really works here?

When she turns in my direction, I drop my hand and look away, leaving my row of tomatoes half moved as I practically run to the storefront.

Jackson is leaned over the register, counting out the pennies in the take-a-penny, leave-a-penny tray. He glances up when I approach. "Hey Ben, I was just–"

"Yeah I know, you weren't doing anything," I interrupt. "I don't care, but just tell me who that girl is."

"Going after the help, huh?"

"Shut up. What's her name?"

Rolling a penny between his fingers, he gives me a playful look. "Maybe you should just ask her yourself."

"Screw you," I snap, leaving him at the counter staring after me.

* * * *

By the time five o'clock finally arrives, I've never been so ready to head home. It took me half the afternoon to move all the rows of outdoor pots. I saw the girl a few more times but only from a distance. Jeff came out of his office about an hour ago to check on my work before sending me with a shovel to rotate the compost heap at the very back of the property. Blisters formed across both my palms after that particular task, and in addition to my headache, it feels like a desert in my mouth.

I collapse into the chair behind the counter with a bottle of water while Jackson finishes sweeping the floor. I wipe the sweat from my forehead using the side of my hand, even though it's pointless to still be fighting to keep the dirt away. I'm covered in it.

"You did a good job today, Ben," Jeff says, giving my shoulder a squeeze.

I risk a glance at him, a touch of bitterness sneaking into my voice. "How could you even know? You barely left your office."

"I was watching, and you worked really hard. I'm impressed with your work ethic."

"Thanks," I mumble.

"Now if only Jackson worked that hard, we could really get some things done around here." Jeff grins.

Broom still in hand, Jackson raises his arms in a *bring-it* gesture. "I work plenty hard."

"Whatever," I scoff. "You were inside all day."

"I'm not the guy on the bottom anymore," he says. Seeing my expression, he adds, "Kidding. We'll switch off, don't worry."

"All right boys," Jeff clears his throat. "Let's get locked up and get home."

"Sure thing," Jackson says, stowing the broom in the corner and pulling the keys out of his pocket.

Jeff gestures to me. "Ben, let's head out. Jackson can finish up here."

"I thought we were riding back home on the dirt bike?"

"Jackson is, but he's not technically allowed to have passengers on a provisional motorcycle license, so I'd rather you come with me. Besides, as you pointed out, I haven't seen you all day."

As we pull out of the lot, I can just see Jackson in the side mirror locking the last door at the end of the greenhouse.

"So what did you think of your first day?" Jeff asks.

I shrug, then groan as soreness bites into my shoulders. "I wasn't really planning on working this summer. Especially not manual labor."

Jeff nods. "I can understand that. This summer was a bit unexpected for all of us." He waves with two fingers out the window as we pass a black Chevy truck. "But I'm really glad we get you for the summer."

My attention wanders to the greenery flying past. "Free labor, right?"

He sends a disapproving glance my way. "Not what I meant, Ben."

"Sorry."

For a minute, no sound but the hum of the engine fills the cab. "No need to apologize. This is a big change that got thrown at you."

"It's not fair." The moment the words are out of my mouth, I regret them. It makes me sound like a little kid, but it's also the truth.

"No, it's not, but that's just the way things are sometimes." He hesitates, then adds, "I expect you boys to be ready to walk out the door at seven a.m. tomorrow. We're not going to be driving separately every day, am I clear?"

I swallow, running my fingers along the armrest. "Okay." Outside, green fields of wheat and corn sail past just like the minutes. Everything here is so different than back home, and the only comfort is that for every field and every minute that passes, I'm a little bit closer to the fall semester at Stanford.

We've been home about ten minutes when Jackson turns into the driveway and steers the dirt bike into the garage. From the window in his room, I watch him hop off the bike, first setting the safety glasses across the handlebar and then his helmet on a shelf. He strides across the yard, the sun at his back casting his shadow in front of him.

"I'm home," his words carry up the stairs. "Ready to work on the bike, Dad?"

"Sure am," Jeff's distant voice replies.

I sit down on the edge of Jackson's bed. It's strange to listen in on them like this, to hear how they interact. What would it have been like if Jackson had ended up with Mom, and I had lived with Jeff? Would we be the ones having the conversation right now about fixing up the dirt bike? I don't even know how to *ride* one, much less fix the damn thing.

The sound of rapid movement up the stairs precedes Jackson's entrance to the room and his eyes sweeping over me. "Want to help us out with the bike?"

I'm dirty and sore, and there's no way I'm going to willingly play mechanic now too.

"Look," he says. "I know today probably sucked, but it would be more fun if you helped." His voice lowering, he admits, "Just me and Dad all the time can get a little boring."

Despite all the work I've done today, I almost say yes. Then I remember that he was the one who all but cut off the communication between us, and a swell of resentment rises inside me, drowning out any interest in being around him more than I already have been today. What makes him suddenly want to spend time together? Where was that sentiment all the times I called?

"Sorry, Jackson, maybe next time."

Unease permeates his expression, stabbing lines of worry through his forehead like he's just had a bad acupuncture session. I probably could have made more of an effort to sound sincere.

"No worries." He gives me a weak smile, waiting just a moment before retreating down the hall.

I feel like hell, but before I shower and give up on movement for the rest of the night, I need to go for a run. It's the one thing that has always kept me sane. It's my safe place.

Digging through my bag until I find my gym shorts, I change and patter down the stairs in my socks. I forgot my running shoes back in L.A., so I pick out a pair of Jackson's by the door. These stink just like his sneakers I wore today, but they fit pretty well.

Just inside the garage, Jackson and Jeff are crowded around the dirt bike. Jeff is pointing at a part of the engine and saying something to Jackson, who's bent over, hands on his knees and holding a wrench. It's all very blue-collar, and it takes all of my restraint not to roll my eyes.

When I'm just a few feet away, they both look up. Jackson zeroes in on my shoes. "Aren't those mine?"

"No." I give him a deadpan look.

"Liar," he says. "Just because they fit doesn't mean you can wear them."

Jeff's voice cuts me off before I can react, a warning resonating in his words. "Boys…"

"But Dad," Jackson whines, "Ben always breaks shit."

I raise an eyebrow. "I don't break stuff."

Jeff sighs, playing referee. "I think that's a little unfair, considering how long it's been since you've seen each other."

Jackson scowls at me but doesn't respond. With Jeff in the ring, I bite down on my ready remark of how much I really care about his piece-of-shit shoes, instead opting for the diplomatic. "I forgot my running shoes back home," I explain. "I'll be nice to them."

Jackson gives Jeff a long look, then shoos me away with a wave of the wrench. "Just go run, klepto."

"A path follows alongside the road," Jeff says. "So you don't have to run on the gravel if you don't want."

I nod and then I'm off. My shoulders and back are sore, but my legs are eager for the challenge. Quickly falling into my usual rhythm, I cross the road and find the path. Footfalls beating out time like a clock, I let myself take a mental step back from everything that has happened.

It all moved so quickly. It was just a week ago that Mom sat me down to talk about the change in our summer plans. It's almost surreal, being here now. There are no skyscrapers or planes overhead here, no pavement or fountains, and hardly any people. Instead I'm surrounded by a sprawling tapestry of fields and the occasional wooded area, the lines between them stitched by dirt roads and ditches.

A breeze picks up behind me, propelling me forward. The air tastes sweet and fresh, lending an extra lightness to my steps. Like premium high-octane gas, I imagine that the country oxygen is richer, more prevalent.

Practically flying along the road, I stretch my stamina like it wants to be pushed. Not repetitive, agonizing labor, but the thrill of adrenaline-pumping athletics. I love being on a team and I played football all through high school, but something about running really helps me relax.

"Holy shit!" I shout as a rabbit darts out in front of me, zigzagging away when it sees how close I am. It disappears into the brush, but I stop anyway, leaning over to catch my breath. I'm pretty sure my heart rate would have doubled just now if it weren't already near max.

I start back toward the house, going more slowly now that I'm against the wind. The minutes slip away into the sound of my feet striking the ground, until finally I turn back into the driveway.

After my run, a shower, then dinner with Jeff and my brother, I'm exhausted. Staring at the half deflated air mattress, I hear Jackson start brushing his teeth down the hall. I would complain about going to bed this early again if I weren't so tired. Dropping to my knees, I hook the pump up to the air mattress and flip the switch. It sounds like a storm of angry bees, but the bed gradually fills.

On the way to the bathroom, I venture a look into the darkened guest bedroom. I can't imagine how much work it's going to take to get it back to where I can use it, which is frustrating, because after just one night, I'm already dreading sleeping on the air mattress again.

After we brush our teeth and get undressed, Jackson clicks off the bedside light and I climb onto my airbed. "Did Dad talk to you about getting ready on time?" he asks.

"He said we need to be ready exactly at seven."

"You got the easier talk, then. I got an earful."

Maybe that's why Jackson was acting so pissy about his shoes. "Really?"

"Yeah, which is stupid, because it was your fault," he says. "But he took it out on me, because I should have *let you know the expectation*," he imitates Jeff's voice. I can practically hear Jackson's scowl.

"Whatever, so you set the alarm earlier?"

"Fifteen minutes will be fine I think, as long as you shower faster tomorrow morning. Unless you want to shower together, then we don't have to get up any earlier." When I don't respond, he says, "Damn, Ben, learn to take a joke."

I let out a long breath and roll onto my side, the mattress adjusting underneath me. Jackson is such a cocky little shit sometimes.

Chapter Nine

Ben

The next morning, I wake up to Jackson's alarm with a stiff neck and my butt pressed into the floor. I'm starting to hate the air mattress. Yet despite the subpar sleeping arrangements, Jackson and I are washed, dressed, and ready to go by two minutes to seven. The cab on Jeff's truck is pretty big, but it's still a squeeze as the three of us pile in.

I spend the first part of the morning watering again, but before ten o'clock rolls around, Jeff kicks Jackson out of the store and comes to get me. "Ben, ready to learn how to run the till?"

I shrug and follow him back up front. There aren't a lot of customers this morning, but he stays up front with me the whole time, stepping in whenever I need help. He seems to know more than half the people who come through. Must be a popular guy.

After lunch, the same girl from yesterday shows up, working at the opposite end of the greenhouse from me. When it becomes too difficult to keep my eyes away from the tight jean shorts and tank top she's wearing, I walk back to the storefront.

Jeff stops me as I slip behind the counter. "I need you to help out Katie today," he says.

My heart thumps and a thin layer of moisture erupts on my palms. "Is that the, uh, girl who works here? Are you sure? Shouldn't I be–"

"I've got everything covered up here."

"What's she working on?"

He looks at me like I've asked a silly question. "I'm not quite sure, honestly. Go and find out."

Feeling like an idiot and not entirely sure what Jeff is playing at, I walk all the way to the end of the greenhouse. She's bending over, scooping a trowel of dirt into another pot. It's really hard to avoid looking at those shorts right now.

"Hey," I venture.

"Hey, Jackson," she says with a light Midwest accent. Straightening and turning to face me, she freezes. Tilting her head to the side, she gives me an examining look. "Wait a second." She takes a step forward, looking me right in the face. "Holy shit. You're his brother, aren't you? I totally didn't know he had a twin." Crossing her arms, she goes on, speaking more to herself than to me. "That totally makes sense. I could have sworn I saw Jackson everywhere yesterday. It was creeping me out."

"I'm Ben," I say. "And no worries, sometimes I don't even know if I have a twin."

"What do you mean?"

"Never mind. How did you know I wasn't Jackson?"

With a sly grin, she says, "I must be more observant than most people."

I smile back. "I guess so."

"So you here to help me?"

"I was sent, yeah."

"Your dad?" When I nod, she says, "Great. You can help me transplant. I'm working on the peppers right now."

An anxious flutter tickles the inside of my stomach, because I know I'm going to make a fool of myself in front of her. "I've never done this type of stuff before," I admit.

"It's easy," she says, flashing me a flirty look. "Just don't be afraid to get your hands dirty."

An hour later, streaks of dirt cover my arms up to my elbows, and it's even caked under my fingernails. But we've repotted forty pepper plants, and it was actually kind of fun. That might just be because Katie is kind of fun. On the first one we did, she even guided my hands with hers as I moved the plant by the bundle of roots and lightly pressed it into the pot.

"Good job," she says, holding her hand up for a high five. Our hands clap together and a shower of dirt particles falls around us.

It's hot in the sun, but I don't want to report back to Jeff or Jackson for more work yet. "How long have you worked here?" I ask.

"I was here last summer and I loved it. When I asked your dad for a job again this year, he hired me back on right away. And in a week or so, I can start coming in full time."

My eyes shift away to the lot where Jeff's truck is parked. "He's short on help right now, so I'm sure he's happy to give you more hours."

"Is that how you got drafted?"

"Pretty much." I bite my lip, wanting to say more.

After a pause, she adds, "He's a good guy, your dad."

"So I hear. I haven't seen him in years."

Katie nods. "I figured something like that. I'm surprised Jackson never mentioned you."

"I'm not." I absently tap my foot against the base of one of the pepper pots, avoiding her gaze. Something has been bothering me. "How did you know I wasn't him? Especially if you didn't know he even had a twin?"

"Won't let that one go, will you?" she smiles disarmingly.

It's because of that smile that my thoughts actually come out of my mouth. "Did you two date or something?" Of all the things I don't want to share with my brother, a crush on the same girl is pretty high up there.

Hands on her hips, she gives me a defiant look. "I believe it's a little early in our friendship to be asking something like that."

My cheeks smolder. "Sorry."

She sighs, her eyes drifting toward the store, then over to the greenhouse. It's just us out here. "If you must know, we never dated. You could have just asked him that though."

"He's not your type?"

"You're a nosy one, Ben."

I shrug. "Just a question."

"I don't think he's interested in someone like me. I'm not really his type."

It feels like there's more to her statement than what she's said, but I can't guess what it might be. Maybe Jackson doesn't like girls that enjoy working in the dirt. "But if he were interested, would you think he's cute?"

She laughs and shoves my shoulder. "Come on, hot shot. Let's go find out what still needs to get done today."

Apparently it wasn't lost on her that asking if she thinks Jackson is cute was essentially the same as asking if she thinks I am. Grinning, I follow her back to the store.

After work, Jeff and Jackson and I pack into the truck and head home. Just like the day before, I'm covered in dirt and sweat, but I still want to get my run in before showering.

Slivers of guilt prick my skin as I slip on Jackson's shoes once again, but the pair of Nike's I brought with are flat soled. I should buy my own pair of running shoes, so I don't have to keep wearing Jackson's reeking ones, but I don't even know if Northfield has a shoe store, much less where it is.

I've just finished tying the laces when Jeff's voice grabs my attention. "Going out again tonight?" He's in the kitchen, just starting to work on dinner.

Back home, Mom never has time to cook, but it's because her job is so demanding. I'm either home by myself and get take out, or she comes home and we get take out. It probably sounds like Mom and I are counted in one of those statistics on dysfunctional families that never have home-cooked meals around the dinner table, but we're not. Well, we're part of the statistic, but we're not dysfunctional. Mom just doesn't have the time at home like Jeff does.

"Ben?" Jeff prompts.

"Uh, running, yeah. It helps me unwind." I hope he doesn't encourage me to invite Jackson. Running is my own thing.

Setting a tall container of uncooked spaghetti noodles on the counter, he says, "It's good to have something like that. Have fun."

I find my stride faster than yesterday. The soreness in my shoulders is better, but a dull ache in my neck and lower back is making the run uncomfortable. Unlike my sore muscles, which are from the day's work, the new pain is from sleeping on that stupid airbed. Every footfall aggravates the pain, but I need this run, if for no other reason than that being around Jackson can be a real struggle. Not that he's unpleasant, because in general he isn't, but… it's just tough seeing him so much after years of *not*. After all this time, I'm completely lost when it comes to navigating our relationship.

Things have changed a lot between us since we were kids. I understand that, at least in theory. But it's like a bunch of cells in the back of my brain are hardwired to expect a connection with Jackson that just isn't there anymore. The feeling is annoying, like I need to yawn but can't, no matter how hard I strain.

I don't know if I'll ever get used to seeing my brother as nothing more than an unwilling roommate. Maybe it doesn't have to stay that way, but he was the one to break off communication, so he has to be the one to make the first move.

When I get back to the house, Jeff is still working on dinner, so I head upstairs. Jackson is stretched out on his bed, reading a book. I take a seat at his desk stacked with dirty clothes. My heart is still beating fast from the run, and my chest heaves up and down with my breaths.

Jackson's gaze rises from his book and sweeps over me, his blue eyes penetrating but altogether unreachable.

"What are you reading?" I ask. The cover of the old paperback is purple with green text.

"Nothing," he says, flushing. Without any explanation, he shoves the book under his pillow and scoots off the edge of the bed.

"Where are you going?" I call after him.

Pausing in the hallway, he looks at me for only a moment before he speaks. "Going to see if Dad needs help in the kitchen."

My throat tightens as he disappears down the stairs. He's had his life here all along just as I've had mine in California. So why does it hurt so damn much to see him living his without me? Traitorous wetness appears in my eyes.

I wish I could forget about him, as he seems to have done with me years ago. This summer was supposed to be the best of high school. Friends, parties, even a road trip. I had the time and I'd saved the money. Instead I got… this. This bullshit. A full time job in the middle of fucking nowhere, stuck with a brother who can barely be called that.

Gritting my teeth, I curl up on his bed. Tears escape from my eyes, even as I hate them. The bed I'm crying on isn't even my own, and the release from all of this – the beginning of the fall semester at Stanford – feels so far away I can hardly bear it.

Chapter Ten

Jackson

Ben has always been sensitive. I guess it was a lot to expect that to change at all, because nothing else has. He's here, but he didn't have a choice, so even though my brooding brother is now sleeping on the floor in my room every night, it doesn't mean a damn thing. Certainly not that he's sorry for leaving in the first place.

He was quiet all through dinner, probably because he thought I was avoiding him. Which isn't exactly true. Thankfully I have better things to think about than Ben.

I asked Dad if I could take the bike to town and he didn't seem to care, so here I am. Excitement crackles through me, lending a lightness to my steps as I push open the door to the hardware store. My senior year flew by, but whenever study hall was completely silent or I was alone at night in my bed or pushing myself in the school weight room, my mind would wander. And it always seemed to find jet-black hair and broad shoulders.

I never trusted myself to text him or anything, fearing a stilted conversation that would ruin my chances for this summer. Instead I fell back on the hope that he'd be back. Since the beginning of the summer, I've kept an eye out around town, particularly on the hardware store.

It paid off, and even now the reason for my good mood is parked just outside. The first time I saw it was last week. I could have sworn the ailing red truck driving through town was his, but I couldn't tell for sure, not until seeing it up close today.

He's helping a customer when I step through the door, a little bell tinkling above my head. I'm grateful that he doesn't look my way, because it gives me a moment just to watch him. His hair is cut short on the sides but still long enough on top that it has a bit of a sweep, giving him a distinctly collegiate appearance. Otherwise, he looks exactly the same. The muscled curves of his arms and the width of his shoulders haven't changed a bit.

The woman he's been helping thanks him and walks out, giving me an up and down glance on her way to the door. Finally Matt notices me.

"Hey," I say, looking for even the slightest sign that he's excited to see me.

Recognition and surprise jumble up his features, but not in a good way. "Jackson. Wow."

"That wasn't exactly the response I was expecting."

He looks away momentarily. "Sorry, I just…"

"What?" I press, not giving him even an extra second to finish his sentence. Why is he acting like this?

"Sheesh, Jackson. Take it easy, okay?" His voice drops in volume when he continues, making me wonder if other customers are hidden away in the aisles. "I was going to say I just wasn't expecting you. I mean, we haven't talked or texted or anything in almost a year."

If I was going to have to bail out of here, I wanted to do it quickly, so I've been standing by the door. With a shrug, I finally approach the counter. "You should have just said that then."

"Sorry," he says quickly, speaking even more quietly now that we're closer. "Seeing you brought things back. Really quickly. I wasn't quite ready for that."

I smirk, reveling in the pinkness tinting his cheeks. "I didn't forget about last summer," I say, putting extra emphasis on the I.

"I didn't *forget*," he counters, holding his eyes on me. "You bulked up."

The tank top I'm wearing feels instantly tight across my chest, and for the first time since I walked in, I get the feeling he's checking me out. Likewise, I steal the opportunity to let my gaze travel over him once more. My memories of him last summer don't do him justice. I hold my tongue for as long as I can manage, but it's getting hard. Leaning against the counter, I resolve to force the conversation onward.

"Want to grab lunch tomorrow? You can swing by and meet my brother Ben too."

"You have a brother?"

"Yeah…" my voice trails. "We're kind of, um, twins. So don't be alarmed. And please, *please* don't mix us up."

Matt raises an eyebrow. "You seriously have an identical twin? Why didn't you ever mention that?"

"You didn't ask," I reply, defensiveness creeping into my words.

"Sorry, how could I have forgotten that integral part of normal conversation?" he says, his voice ringing with sarcasm. "No really, I ask everyone if they have a twin."

I stare at him, refusing to validate his remarks. "So tomorrow?"

Ben is up front with me, working on untangling several new rakes that have gotten their tines tangled together, when Matt shows up. Ben is in a foul mood today, probably because he's having to work inside. He won't admit it, but for whatever reason, the kid really seems to like being out in the sun and dirt.

First looking pointedly at me, Matt approaches my brother. "You're Ben right?"

Ben looks up with a deer-in-the-headlights expression. "Yeah, who are you?"

"Matt."

"Uh, okay," Ben says, his voice wavering with uncertainty. He nods in my direction. "Jackson is just over there." When Matt looks at me helplessly, I roll my eyes. Ben has always had a talent for pointing out the obvious.

"Sure, thanks," Matt says to him, coming up to the counter where I'm leaning against the till. He holds up a bag. "I got Jimmy John's."

"For me?"

"Three subs," he says, risking another look at Ben who's making an awful racket trying to separate the last two rakes by just shaking the shit out of them. Lowering his voice, Matt asks, "Is he always like this?" The second rake finally dislodges and clatters to the floor.

"Like what? Abrasive, antisocial and with questionable mental capacity?" I ask as Matt suppresses a laugh. "Yeah, pretty much."

Ben glares at us, even though I don't think he could have actually heard what I said.

"Hungry?" Matt asks him.

Just inside a ring of shade cast by a giant oak tree on the adjoining property, the three of us sit down at the frail picnic table beside the parking area.

Across from Matt and me, Ben runs a dirty hand through his hair. Matt is just staring at him. "Something wrong?" Ben asks.

Blushing, Matt says, "It's just so weird how much you guys look alike."

"Yeah, you know, the whole identical thing." Ben gives him a blank look.

"Sorry, I guess you must get that a lot."

"Something like that," Ben replies vaguely.

Matt seems confused by his answer, but I get it. We haven't been around each other in years, so having people comment on our appearance is a novel experience.

Matt tosses the bags onto the table. "Jimmy John's. I wasn't sure what you wanted, Ben, so I hope you like roast beef."

"I don't, but thanks."

Tearing into his own sandwich, Matt shrugs. "Sorry, man." He says it like he's not sorry at all.

Ben shoots him a dirty look, which he pretends to ignore. I frown at them both. Is it so hard to be civil?

"Jesus, Ben," I interject. "Just eat the stupid sandwich."

Now that pissed off face gets directed at me. Sighing, I sink my teeth into the sub.

After we finish, Ben skulks off to the greenhouse, leaving Matt and me alone. "He's kind of pissy," Matt points out.

"He can be," I admit as my stomach tightens. It's one thing to make fun of my brother, but straight up talking bad about him feels wrong. "Try to get along with him, would you?"

Matt tilts his head to the side as if this doesn't make sense to him. "Sure. If that's what you want."

"It is. Especially since you'll be hanging out at my place a lot."

"Oh *really*?" The way he drags out the last word makes it sound like he doesn't agree, but I can't tell if he's kidding or not.

I nod, trying to sound confident. "Starting after work tonight."

Matt looks like he's not sure, and a hurt feeling tugs downward on the inside of my chest. Something in my expression seems to be swaying him, though. "I'll come over. Seven o'clock okay?"

* * * *

I'm helping Dad and Ben with the dishes from dinner when a knock on the front door reminds me that I invited Matt over. Ben's arms are submerged in soapy water while Dad brandishes a dishtowel. The two of them look up from the sink.

"I asked Matt to stop by," I explain, throwing in a "I hope that's okay" for good measure. Dad would never turn someone away, but I should have mentioned it to him before now.

The muscles above their eyebrows pull together – Dad and Ben both. Dad because he's struggling to remember who that is, and Ben because he's being an annoying twerp. Or because he and Matt didn't get along very well earlier. "The guy who helped us roof last summer," I remind Dad.

"Ah, right," he says, brightening. There's another knock on the door, louder this time. "So are you going to let him in?"

Without delaying any longer, I skip out of the kitchen to open the door for him. Matt steps inside carried on a wave of freshness. He smells clean, like soap, and his hair is still wet. "You just get out of the shower or what?" I tease.

"Nah," he says. "Just forgot the window down while going through the car wash."

"Ha-ha. Clearly a lie because your truck is still dirty as ever." I make an exaggerated look past him at the dirty hunk of red metal in the driveway.

"Ouch. I clean it sometimes."

"Annually?"

He scowls dramatically. "Stop ragging on my girl."

Dad's voice calls from the kitchen. "You guys just going to hang out in the entry?" I'm thankful for the disruption so I don't have to think about Matt referring to anything as *his girl*. Gross.

Matt follows me into the kitchen, where Dad shakes his hand and peppers him with questions about college. Yes, he's still an undecided major. No, he doesn't mind being back in Northfield for the summer. And possibly he'd be interested in getting paid to help us put up drywall in the extra bedroom.

"Okay, Dad," I finally interrupt. "Enough with the inquisition. We're going upstairs."

He waves us on, seeming not to notice that Ben never even looked up from the dishes. Matt follows me up to my room, peeking into the torn apart spare bedroom on the way. "Looks like hell in there," he says unnecessarily.

"I know. And until we put it back together, Ben is sleeping on the floor in my room."

He grimaces. "That's unfortunate."

"It's not that bad. He can be a bit testy, but it wasn't his fault that he got shipped out here for the summer. Our mom had to go on a long work trip, and she didn't want him to be alone I guess."

"Hmm," Matt says, throwing himself back on my bed. It shrinks under his weight before bouncing him back up an inch or two.

Joining him on the bed in a less haphazard fashion, I push a pillow up behind me so I can lean against the wall. My eyes wander over him, taking in the tanned forearms and biceps and his tight t-shirt, up to his lips parted just enough to make him irresistible.

"Jackson…" he says, a warning carried in his tone.

"What's wrong?"

"Nothing, but I just think we should…"

My eyebrows furrow. "That we should what?"

"Consider being just friends? I mean, I know we're attracted to each other, but what happens at the end of the summer when we both have to move apart again? I don't want to start something that I know has to be long distance for *years*."

"That's the same reason you gave me at the end of last summer," I say, not bothering to conceal the challenge in my words. "Except last time it actually made sense."

"Look, what I'm saying is that I just don't know if this can be anything more than a summer thing."

"I don't care. If that's all it is, then so what. We'll have an amazing time and then go our own ways." It's out of my mouth before I can really consider what it even means.

Matt's eyes finally make it back to me. "You sure you don't care if it can't be more than that?" In response, I let my knuckles touch his arm. He frowns. "I'm trying to be serious, and you're making it really hard."

"Good." I smirk, hoping he'll catch my double meaning. His expression is conflicted, but his lips are still slightly parted. Abandoning subtlety, I let the words spring off my tongue. "I don't care about what happens next month, or next week, or even tomorrow. I care about now, and right now I want to kiss you. Really fucking bad."

His eyes widen. "Here in your room, with your brother and Dad home?"

"I've waited nine months." I give him a look that rivals all the others I've already sent his direction.

"Don't do that," he says, forcing down a smile.

"Do what?" I ask innocently.

He shakes his head, pretending to be upset. "You know exactly what I mean."

Reaching forward, my fingers close around his t-shirt and pull him toward me. He resists for only a fraction of a second before giving in. His lips are warm and soft, hesitant at first but quickly falling into a rhythm with mine. My tongue edges forward, fighting to break through the last of his barriers.

Yet my eagerness for this contact is offset by his underlying restraint. Like a hidden counterpoint, his reticence is subdued but undoubtedly present.

My hands traveling over his chest and up to his neck, I cup his jaw from each side, letting him feel my strength, to show that it matches his own. His reservation thaws as I continue to kiss him, and finally he relaxes into me, allowing his hands to touch me back.

Hammering footsteps on the stairs separates us to opposite sides of the bed faster than a bolt of lightning could have knocked us apart. I'm just wiping the rogue saliva off my lips when Ben throws open the door and crosses the room to get his basketball shorts. He glances at us but doesn't seem to notice anything odd about our forced casual positions several feet apart on the bed.

"It's nice to knock, you know," Matt says, shooting Ben a nasty look.

Ben whips around, his eyes bulging. "It's my room too, you ass."

"Wow guys, chill out," I snap, panicked. The last thing I want is an ongoing pissing contest between Matt and my brother. If this is the way the rest of the summer is headed, it's going to suck. "Going running?" I ask Ben.

"Yeah," he says simply, giving each of us a last look before stalking out, leaving us alone once more.

"Your brother is a dick," Matt states.

"Give him a break, okay? And you could be a little nicer yourself."

"Sure, whatever." He's quiet for a minute while he gradually prods a pillow with his foot until it falls off the bed. "I'm going to go. See you later this week?"

Disappointment fills me, but I refuse to let him see it. "Oh... okay. See you then."

* * * *

The following days speed by, if for no other reason than that we're all so busy at the greenhouse. Dad keeps saying he's going to hire someone else, but other than Katie, he's not having much luck finding anyone. On the bright side, Ben seems to be getting the hang of everything. If the idea weren't completely crazy, I'd almost say that he likes the work. Every day he insists on being outside, which is fine by me. It's the harder work, and it's dirty. If he likes it though, more power to him.

The longer he stays here though, grumbling at every opportunity about the summer that got stolen from him, the less I feel like anything is going to change between us. It's frustrating and disheartening. Every time I see him, I want to grab him by the shoulders and shake him. He's here, he's finally here, and not a damn thing is different. I don't think he even cares anymore, and I'm too afraid to ask.

Chapter Eleven

Ben

It's becoming harder to get up in the morning. The discomfort from sleeping on the air mattress is actually starting to keep me up at night. No matter if I lie on my back or my stomach, I'm always waking up. And once the bed loses so much air that my butt touches the floor, it's game over. Why did Jeff have to decide to tear apart their guest bedroom this summer? I don't know if I can make it until he gets it fixed up.

By Thursday morning, Jackson has to get me up, because the alarm doesn't cut it. "God Ben, wake up. If we're late, Dad's going to be pissed."

I groan and roll onto my side, transferring the point of contact with the floor from my tailbone to my hip. "Leave me alone."

"Sorry, can't do that. My ass is on the line too," he says, stepping in quick succession on the corner of the air mattress. The resulting shift in the air lifts me up before whacking me back down onto the floor. Repeatedly.

"Ow, ow, ow," I cry out. "Goddamn it, Jackson, stop."

"You going to get up?"

I'm definitely awake now. And angry. "Yes, but for Christ's sake, stop."

He removes his foot from the corner of the mattress. "I'll shower first."

I don't care what he does as long as he gets the hell away. My neck is the worst it's been so far this week, and while my lower back wasn't too bad before, it is now that it's been pummeled by the floor.

While Jackson showers, I dig through his dresser and find a pair of old jeans. I packed several pairs when I left L.A., but they're all good brands and practically new. No way would I ever wear them in the dirt. Jackson, on the other hand, appears to have plenty of ugly clothes. I briefly consider taking a pair of clean underwear from his dresser instead of rifling through my bag, but that's kind of gross, even if they do fit.

A minute after hearing the water stop, I tap on the door and let myself into the steamy room. Jackson is just wrapping the towel around his waist when it slips down a few inches, his backside showing for a second before he can rewrap the towel.

"Can't you change *before* I get in here?" I bark at him. "The last thing I want to see in the morning is your buck naked ass."

"Um, sorry?" He locks eyes with me in the mirror before going on to put stuff in his hair.

Averting my eyes, I drop my boxers and step wordlessly into the shower. The water cascading down feels good, but even its heat can't wash away how tired I am. The one bright point is that I don't have to use Jackson's stupid herbal body wash anymore, since I finally had a chance to buy an array of Axe products.

It's a couple minutes past seven when I trundle across the lawn and jump into the truck, taking a seat beside Jackson. Jeff hasn't even turned out of the driveway when Jackson asks, "What's that smell?" He looks at me and wrinkles his nose.

"Uh, I definitely showered."

He raises an eyebrow and continues to look at me like I just strangled a few kittens. "What did you wash up with? It smells like maple syrup and horse piss."

Jeff's burst of laughter fills the cab. When I glare at him, he gives me an apologetic look and shrugs.

After we pull into the parking lot of Roanoke Gardens, Jackson immediately volunteers to do the watering. He's trying to be nice and let me take the easier job of manning the store, but if I stay inside doing nothing, I'm going to pass out on the counter. And although it makes me cringe to even think this, I'm actually starting to enjoy working here.

The morning passes with me in a daze, but row after row gets watered, more or less. Just before lunch, I notice Jeff watching me from the far end of the greenhouse.

Crossing the space between us, he stops in front of me. "How's it going, Ben?"

I bite down a yawn, straining the muscles in my neck. "Going all right. This is the last section that needs watering," I say, gesturing with the hose wand.

His voice quiets as he studies my face. "So the work is taken care of. But how are you doing?"

Flipping the off lever on the hose, I shrug and lean against one of the tables covered in pots. "I haven't been sleeping very well."

He nods. "I thought maybe that was it. We'll work on the extra bedroom soon, I promise. And I'm still searching for another employee so you don't have to volunteer here all summer. Katie has agreed to start coming in for full days, too."

I appreciate what he's trying to do, but having to spend my days here isn't what's really bothering me. I shouldn't say any more, but with Mom overseas and no friends here, everything is just getting bottled up inside. "It's hard being around Jackson again," I whisper, looking away. I feel like such a kid again when I'm around Jeff. Maybe that's because that was the last time I felt like he was actually my dad.

"It's understandable. You two have been apart for a long time."

"I didn't really notice as we grew apart, but now that I'm here..." I take a deep breath and my lower lip quivers. "I didn't know how much I would miss feeling close to him." I can't believe I'm almost crying in front of Jeff.

"I'm sure he feels the same way, Ben."

I want to put my arms around him, to feel like I really have a dad again after all these years. But I can't bring myself to do it. Shaking my head, I admit to Jeff what I've been thinking all this week. "That's the thing though, I don't think he does." Turning my head away from him, a silent tear slips down my cheek.

"Hey," he whispers, turning my chin with a calloused hand so he's looking me straight in the eye. "It's going to be okay. You two just have to give each other a chance." He smiles tentatively.

I swallow and sniff to clear my sinuses. Holding my voice steady, I can only manage to get a single word out. "Thanks."

Clearing his throat, he says, "Lunch should be arriving in a few minutes. I ordered pizza for us today."

Realizing what I've just shared with him, fear jets through my chest. "You're not going to tell Jackson what I said, are you?"

"Wouldn't dream of it. You can talk to me about anything, Ben, and it will stay just between us."

His expression is sincere, and I believe him. "I need to finish watering the rest of this before lunch," I say, my voice coming out husky.

He nods. "See you in fifteen."

I stare after him as he leaves. For the first time since arriving, a small part of me is glad I got exiled here for the summer. Wiping away the wetness from my cheek, I flip the lever on the end of the hose and continue down the row.

Jackson is counting the till and I'm sweeping the floor as we wrap up for the day. Exhaustion is sending dark splotches across my vision as I work, but I know that once I finish we can head home.

After staring at his phone for a moment, Jackson says, "Hey Ben, if Dad comes out of the office tell him I'll be right back." He's got a stupid grin on his face like he just won a raffle. Before I can respond, he sneaks out the front door.

My curiosity winning out, I walk to the door and peer out through the square panes of glass. Across the parking lot, an aging red truck is idling while Jackson talks to the driver through the open window, his elbows perched on the ledge. It looks kind of like Matt's truck, but I wasn't really paying attention when he came over last week. After a minute, I get bored and finish sweeping.

Taking a seat behind the counter, I wait for Jackson. When he finally comes back in, he's still grinning. "Who was that?" I ask.

"What? Oh, just some customer who had a question." The poorly concealed inflection in his voice tells me that's not true at all.

"Can you just finish up so we can go?"

On the ride home, the warmth of the day and the rhythm of the road make me want to close my eyes. Leaning my head back, I let the memory of my conversation with Jeff in the greenhouse roll through me. Mom has always been there when I need to talk, and I thought I never needed anything more than that. For the first time in years though, I wonder if maybe I was wrong.

Jeff's voice awakens me. "We're home."

Inhaling deeply, I push open my eyelids and raise my head off

Jackson's shoulder. The edge of my mouth feels wet. Wiping a hand across my face, I lift a trail of drool from my cheek. My eyes jump nervously to Jackson's shoulder and the wet spot on his shirt, right where my head just was. God, I actually drooled on him.

"Sorry," I mumble.

He glances to his shoulder. "Thought maybe I felt something."

My face gets hot. "Sorry, that's really disgusting."

"It's fine."

I give him a look. How could that not bother him? "You're serious?"

"You're my brother," he says. "It's fine. Can we head inside though?" He's still wedged in the middle seat.

Jeff catches my eye as we get out of the truck. A warm feeling works its way up my throat, and I have to fight the urge to smile. Maybe there's hope for Jackson and me after all.

My phone vibrates in my pocket as Jeff and Jackson disappear inside the house. It's a blocked number.

"Hello?"

"Hi, Ben." It's Mom.

"About time you called. It's been like a month."

"Barely more than a week, don't be so dramatic," she says. Her voice sounds tired, almost weak.

"Are you okay, Mom?"

A pause comes from the other end. "I'm fine, it's just the travel is really taking it out of me."

"Where are you calling from?"

"Shanghai," she says, her voice tight with stress. "Anyway," she continues, "how is it going with Jackson and Jeff?"

Kicking off my shoes, I pass through the living room where the two of them are already stretched out on the couch and watching TV. "They're good. Just a second, Mom." I give them a little wave with the pinky finger of my phone hand and keep walking. Once I'm out of earshot, I add, "Jeff is keeping me busy working at his garden business while he tries to hire some new people I guess."

"I'm glad to hear you're staying out of trouble at least. And how are things with Jackson?"

"Eh," I say, throwing myself onto his bed. "It's fine. It feels like we have nothing in common anymore. We're really different now."

Mom's sudden laugh comes through the phone so loud that I have to hold it away from my ear. "You were always different, Ben."

"No, we weren't."

"Oh yes, you were. Inseparable? Yes. Loyal to a fault? Definitely. But you were always so different."

"Okay, whatever," I sigh in irritation. "Then we're still different, except that the other stuff you mentioned is gone."

We talk for a few minutes more about what I've learned during the week working for Jeff, but my heart isn't in the conversation anymore. Were Jackson and I always at odds like Mom said? My memories from back then are spotty. A few things I remember as if they happened last week, but for the most part, our first nine years together are a bit foggy.

It's not even eight o'clock when I start yawning. I can't imagine how I'm going to make it through another night on the air mattress. Jackson is reading again on his bed when I take my usual seat at the desk.

He glances up, setting the open book face down on his lap. "You didn't go running tonight, did you?"

Too worn out to care about showing weakness to him, I shake my head and confess, "I wanted to."

"We can go to bed a little early tonight." A moment later, he adds, "If you want."

Although I can't detect even a hint of sarcasm, I wait several moments to be absolutely sure. First his comment in the truck, and now this? Regardless of his motives, his offer isn't going to solve anything. Whether it's seven or ten hours on that stupid mattress, I'm still going to get a shitty night's sleep. "I don't think that will help."

He looks apologetic. "Don't know what to tell you."

A question is crawling around the back of my mind. It was born out of pure necessity a couple days ago, but his reaction to me falling asleep his shoulder is what really set it loose. "I, um… was wondering if the offer to share your bed was still good?"

I hold my breath as his eyes sweep over me. What thoughts are going on behind those brilliant blue eyes? The seconds hover in the air like dandelion seeds, as though waiting for a nonexistent wind to force them onward. If he rejects me now, in this instant, in my moment of vulnerability, I'll never forgive him.

Releasing only a portion of the tense breath I'm holding in, I shift in my chair. The resulting creak demands to be heard in the silence.

My voice is low as I admit, "The airbed is killing me."

Something changes in his expression, as though he's finally seeing me after all this time, and I'm not the person he thought I was. He nods his assent. "If it's what you want, we can share the bed."

Shifting his eyes to the window before bringing them back to mine, he asks, "So do you want to go to bed early tonight after all? You look like you're about to pass out."

"If that's okay."

Slipping a piece of paper into his book, he tosses it onto the desk. "I'll let Dad know, so he doesn't wake us up or anything."

After Jackson leaves the room, the purple and green cover of the book he's been reading beckons me to examine it. *Star Trek: Murders at the Vulcan Academy.* The chuckle in my throat is matched by a bubbly feeling I can't quite place. I never got into the books much, but I love the Star Trek movies. If there's one thing that didn't change in all the years, it's that we're both major dorks.

Before he even gets back upstairs, I'm already under the covers. Jackson's bed is just firm enough that after a minute of lying here, the muscles in my neck and back are starting to relax.

If Jackson is surprised to find me tucked in with the blanket pulled up to my collarbone, he doesn't let it show as he switches off the light and climbs in alongside me. Like he warned me that first night, it's a bit of a tight fit, and our elbows are touching.

Resisting the initial urge to pull away, I force myself to relax. The single point of contact between us doesn't actually bother me, at least not like it would have a couple weeks ago. In a way, it helps a little to solace the part of me that has been so upset about not knowing my twin brother like I should. This forced physical intimacy is no substitute for a real connection, but it's something.

His voice is barely more than a whisper as it glides across the short distance between us. "It feels good to have you back."

"It's not as bad as I thought," I concede.

No sound or movement comes from him, but somehow I know he's smiling. When he speaks, there's no judgment or meanness in his voice. "If you want, Matt and I are going to work out together later this week. You could join us."

My hands tighten into fists under the covers. "That's the annoying guy who came over last week?"

"Yeah." He holds his breath.

It's the first time Jackson has invited me to hang out with him, so I really don't want to turn him down, but that guy Matt has douchebag written all over him. "Maybe, I dunno."

His sigh is the saddest sound I've heard all summer.

"Goodnight, Ben."

"Goodnight, Jackson."

Air rushes past my face as I swoop toward the ground, my legs stretched out in front of me. The dirt rut beneath me is coming closer and closer. I let out a shriek of excitement as I zoom away from the ground and back into the air. The sun overhead shines bright on my face when I reach the highest point and hang motionless in the air for just a moment. That's my favorite part.

My fingers gripping the chains so tight it hurts, I tuck my feet underneath the seat and fly back toward the earth. Jacks doesn't like to swing. He likes to play tag. It doesn't matter which kind of tag. Blob tag where you tag people and link arms with them until everyone is gotten. Or can't-touch-the-ground tag that they play on the equipment. Jacks loves it all. I play with him sometimes, but I really like to swing.

Forward and backward, each time I think I get a little higher. What happens if I get to the top? Is there a highest point on the swings? If I go for the entire recess time, I might find out. My legs pump harder, faster, and I think I rise another inch.

The bell is about to ring. I know because the playground helpers are starting to call in the first and second graders. They're littler and need more time to line up. This year I don't have to line up with them anymore. This year I get to line up with the older kids. I get three minutes more playtime, but it makes sense, because I'm a lot more mature than the little kids.

Last week I saw one of the fifth graders, Nathan Baxter, jump off the swing instead of slowing down first. It looked really cool. I bet Jacks couldn't do that. I told him that he couldn't, but he insisted that he could. He said I was too scared to try it, and he dared me to do it. I can't see him now, but I don't want him to watch when I first try it. I want to practice, then tomorrow I can show him and he'll be so impressed.

The first two times I get scared just like Jacks said. But the third time as I'm swinging toward the ground, I know I'm going to do it. My fingers tingle in anticipation. Jacks will be so surprised when I tell him.

I'm still scared, but I'm going to do it. I let go just a second before I would get to the top point where I float in the air. My bottom sails off the seat, and I go right along with it.

The ground looks really far away. I don't know if Nathan was this high when he jumped. I'm falling so fast, just like when I fly through the air on the swing. Except there isn't a seat beneath me now. Arms outstretched, I hit the ground and scream.

My right arm hurts really bad. It hurts more than I thought anything could hurt. A bloody area surrounds something that shouldn't be there. It's like something is sticking out of my arm. Why does it hurt so much? I start to cry. Where is Jacks?

The bell rings. None of the older kids see me as they run toward the doors. Then I see Jacks. He's looking for me. I can tell by his face. Our eyes meet, and then he's running toward me. I've never seen him run so fast.

Blood drains down my arm, dripping into the dirt to make tiny dark red balls. My brother's racing feet come to a stop in front of me. His face is filled with panic, and he looks more scared than I am. "Oh Benny," he breathes, starting to cry himself. He kneels in front of me, but he must be afraid to touch me, because he's just holding his hands in the air like he wants to scoop me up but can't.

"Jacks, it hurts," I sob.

He takes a deep breath, and the fear in his eyes forms into determination. "Benny, I have to get help," he whimpers.

"Don't leave me," I plead. "It hurts too much."

"Listen Benny, I have to get help. I'll come back as fast as I can, and then I won't leave again. I promise." He squeezes the hand of my good arm, and then he runs.

"Jacks, don't go!" I cry out.

"Huh?" There's movement next to me.

My eyes snap open and stare up into darkness. My chest is tight and my breathing is coming fast.

"Ben?" Jackson's voice is a whisper. "You okay?"

I pause, giving myself a second to catch my breath. "I'm fine."

"You were talking in your sleep. You kind of yelled."

It takes me a moment to remember what I was dreaming about. It was the day in third grade when I broke my arm. "What did I say?"

Silence. Then I hear him turn onto his side. "You said, 'Jackson, don't go.' What were you dreaming about?"

"I don't remember," I lie, rolling to face away from him. Pretending like I'm falling back asleep, I let several minutes pass while faking slow, steady breathing.

His voice is just above a murmur when he finally speaks, but we're so close that I hear every word. "Actually, you called me Jacks."

Apparently he's been ruminating on that instead of sleeping in the minutes since I woke us both up. And I know exactly why. I was the only one to ever call him that, and I haven't used it in years.

It wasn't just a nickname. It meant all of what Jackson was to me. He was my Jacks. He was there for me whenever I needed him, my partner in crime, my best friend, my twin brother. He was everything to me. But none of that's true anymore. He knows it and so do I.

Chapter Twelve

Ben

When we get to work, I head out to the greenhouses to water before Jackson even has a chance to ask if I want to take the till. Watering will let me be alone for a few hours, and that's something I desperately need today.

After having hydrated just a single table of petunias, I flip the switch on the wand to kill the water and kneel next to a tray of funny looking flowers on short stalks.

Brightly colored yellow, red, and orange, their flower structures seem to grow out in two different lobes. Katie showed me last week how to pinch the sides so the top and bottom of the flower open up like a mouth. Snapdragons she called them. I pinch a red one, but it doesn't work. Its yellow neighbor next door does though, letting me see into its gaping maw. At least something will open up to me.

A woman's weary voice calls down the row. "Jackson, is that you?"

I glance up to a somewhat familiar face. It takes me a second to remember her name. "Hi, Cherie. And no, I'm Ben."

A weak smile touches her lips, the wrinkled skin around the corners of her mouth pulling back just a bit. "I was hoping so."

"Why is that?"

She blinks once, and gives a little shrug. "I could use your help picking out something to brighten up the house."

"You should have asked Jackson then, he knows everything here better than I do."

Cherie takes a step closer to stand next to me, slipping her arm around my waist just like last time. "You're right, but he's always so technical. He would ask me all sorts of questions about how much sun it would get and how often I was going to water it and whether it would be inside or outside."

"Jackson is always filled with facts," I agree. "But wouldn't that help you pick out the right thing?"

"No," she says firmly. "It would land me with the plant that best fits the..." She waves a hand arbitrarily as if that will help her find the right word, "...*specifications* of my space, and that's not what I need." She sighs, pulling me slightly toward her. "That's why I need you. You have heart." She glances up with a captivating smile.

I blush, directing my gaze at my feet. An ant is crawling across the top of my shoe. "So what are you looking for?"

"Well, I'm dying." Her voice is so matter-of-fact that it almost hides the sadness.

My eyes widen, a prickling heat spreading in my chest. "You're serious?"

"Yes quite, unfortunately. I want something to brighten up my house."

"Wouldn't something from a flower shop be better? And brighter?"

Removing her arm from my waist, she scoots over to lean against one of the tables. "You know, that was my thought at first, too. Then I considered that a potted plant will last longer, because Lord knows I don't need anything else dying in my house."

Damn, this woman is morbid. I'm not sure if I'm fighting to keep from being freaked out or laughing, but it's a struggle to keep a straight face. "I'm sorry."

"Don't be," she says quietly. "It's all part of life. So, Ben, shall we find the perfect flower?"

Water is still dribbling out the end of the hose wand as we begin to make our way down the first row, her hand tucked around my elbow. I try to point out flowers that would look nice in a pot, but she doesn't want to stop our slow progression down the row to look at anything more closely. Instead, she asks me about how I ended up here for the summer. I tell her, and she asks more questions. About living with Dad, about Mom, about Jackson.

"We used to be really close," I explain. "But then… I don't know. Things changed when we moved apart. Not at first, but after a few years we didn't visit anymore. And then we didn't call anymore. Now we're so different that I'm afraid we'll never get back to the place we used to be."

She's still watching me intently, even though I'm staring at the ground. I know we've circled the entire greenhouse, because at our feet is a puddle from the leaking hose, welling up just like the water in my eyes.

"You really care about him, don't you?" she asks, stopping to give me a hard look.

I drop my gaze. "What makes you say that?"

"You don't get to be eighty-two years old and not pick up on things. Also you look like you're about to bawl all over the place," she says with a smile. "Back in my day, young men were made of sterner stuff, but don't worry, I like you millenials. You've got spunk." She pats me gently on the shoulder.

I wipe at my eyes with the back of my wrist. "You can be kind of blunt."

"I know. I could say that it's out of necessity, as I'm not going to be around for much longer, but that would just be a plain old lie. I say what I think because I like to."

This is the oddest lady I've ever met, but despite everything, I can't help but like her. "We still haven't found you what you came here for," I remind her.

"So we haven't." She sighs, and every one of her years seems to be contained in that breath. "I want you to choose, Ben, pick something that will watch over me and still be around for the funeral."

"Are you sure?"

She nods, and certainty resonates in her tone when she speaks again. "Absolutely. But use your heart, not your mind." Turning away, she calls over her shoulder, "You can bring it up front when you're ready. I'll be chatting with that brother of yours."

As soon as the words are out of her mouth, I know what I'm going to give her. Kneeling on the brick of the walkway, I pick out the black plastic pot containing a trio of snapdragons. The yellow one that opened for me earlier is in the middle beside its stubborn red brother.

Approaching her and Jackson at the counter, I hold up the pot. Squeezing the yellow one's neck, the dragon's jaws open up and stick out a pollen-covered tongue. I give voice to the plant by releasing a playful growl.

Her face breaks into a toothy smile, and she nods. "It's perfect." She squeezes my hand and turns to go, murmuring goodbyes to both Jackson and me.

Chapter Thirteen

Ben

Instead of running along the road, I duck back into the wooded area beyond the yard. The trees extend like a dark wedge between the fields surrounding Jeff's property. Luckily there isn't much undergrowth, and I'm able to maintain a reasonable jog along the little path weaving through the trees. My thoughts drift back to several hours earlier and the conversation with Cherie. The woman is certainly unique.

I haven't gone very far, not more than a quarter mile into the woods when the trail widens into a clearing. The far side is devoid of trees, giving way to expansive wheat fields, but in the middle of the open space is a giant boulder. Not a typical boulder though. Slowing to a walk, I cross the sunlit grassy area to the gray mass. About three feet tall, the top is flat and wide. About as big as Jackson's bed but more rounded, the whole thing is reminiscent of a really thick pancake.

Resting my hand on the smooth, dark gray surface, I let the coolness seep into my skin as my breathing slows. Trailing a finger across the stone, I circle the object until coming up to a wide depression in the ground, roughly the same size as the stone and covered in grass like the rest of the clearing. I wonder if years ago someone heaved this giant rock out of that hole in the ground. Why would anyone do that?

Pulling myself on top of it, I sit in the very middle and cross my legs. It's at a gradual slope, so the top is dry and clean, but still flat enough that I'm comfortable sitting like this. Overhead, the wind rustles through the trees, carrying the lush scent of summer and field crops. Beyond the clearing, countless acres of wheat bow before the breeze in waves, paying homage to the afternoon's graceful breath.

The last few weeks have been such a change. Not just in where I'm living and what I'm doing, but in how I feel about myself. And about my brother. Back in L.A, I never could have imagined that I would actually find gratification in a hard day's work, even when the only things I have to show for it are dirt under my fingernails and a few scrapes.

But even though it's not the way I wanted to spend my summer, and it's no question that living with Jeff and Jackson can be so damn irritating at times, my biggest regret is that I never visited sooner. Summers came and went, year by year, and I never knew what I was missing. If only I could go back in time and talk some sense into myself.

Under my vigil, the sun has dropped steadily toward the horizon, counting the passing time without needing numbers. The wind picks up again, catching the tips of my hair and brushing against my neck. And the wheat, its stalks bend obediently at the command, ceaselessly and tirelessly. The movement is so mesmerizing that I couldn't look away even if I wanted to.

Nothing lasts forever, but if anything could, this summer would be one of those things that persisted on, refusing to relinquish its place in time.

Between running, eating dinner, and watching TV for a while with Jeff and Jackson, it seems like I never have any time in the evenings. It helps that I'm getting decent sleep now, thanks to Jackson sharing his bed, but mostly that just means I'm more awake for the few short hours I have.

Taking my time brushing my teeth, I examine my face in the mirror. A few stray hairs have appeared between my eyebrows. Rinsing out my mouth, I open up Jackson's drawer in the vanity. Toothpaste, floss, hand lotion, deodorant, a tube of acne cream, followed by more boring stuff. How does he not have a tweezers? Reaching all the way to the back of the drawer, I start pulling things forward.

Another deodorant stick, a small mirror, and a half empty bag of cotton balls come out. I reach back again, feeling for small stuff. A clump of objects in hand, I drop them onto the counter. Bingo, a tweezers. Beside them are a bottle of lube and a pair of condoms. Halfway to the tweezers, my hand freezes.

Lube? What does he need that for? We're both uncut, and I assume *that* hasn't changed since we moved apart. Lube might make it more fun, I guess, but it's absolutely not required to have a good time. My gaze jumps to the turquoise plastic squares, a ring inside each indenting against the packaging. Is Jackson having sex, or are these the ones they give out in school "just-in-case"? Hell, maybe Jeff gave them to him.

It's strange to think about my brother in this context. The last time we were close, the biggest issues in our lives were recess plans and what flavor of juice box we got for lunch. Jackson's favorite was berry splash, mine was orange breeze. Or orange wave, I don't remember exactly. I shove the condoms to the back along with the rest of the junk, except for the tweezers.

Jackson is already in bed with the light off when I tiptoe across the room. Sliding under the covers next to him, my elbow brushes his arm.

"Took you long enough," he says.

Jeeze, talk about crabby. "It was like five minutes." I reach up to adjust my pillow, this time bumping his shoulder. "Sorry," I mumble before he has a chance to say anything.

"It was fifteen at least," he hisses back.

I suppose it did take a while to dig through and analyze his toiletries, but I'm not going to validate him complaining about stupid things. "Tough," I say.

"I could kick you back to the floor," he warns, but we both know it's an empty threat. When I don't answer him, he rolls away onto his side.

Chapter Fourteen

Ben

It's been humid all day, and my shirt is sticking to my back as I finish counting the till. Per usual, Jeff has been tucked away in his office most of the day.

Jackson stows the broom in the corner behind the counter. "So I know you said you weren't really interested, but I'm going to meet up with Matt as soon as we finish here. Going to hit the gym quick and then maybe going swimming afterward."

I'm wary about that Matt guy, but getting in the water sounds really good right now, even if I get dragged to the gym first. Reminded of the heat, I wipe a drop of sweat from my forehead.

Biting the corner of his lip, Jackson adds, "I'd like it if you came."

Shutting the spring-loaded drawer, I slip a rubber band around the bundle of cash and checks from the day, leaving only the five hundred in the register. Jackson is still watching me expectantly, a filament of anticipation woven into his expression.

"Yeah, let's go."

His face breaks into a smile. "Great. I'll ask Dad if he'll drop us off instead of taking us home."

Walking out to the parking lot, I hop up on a pallet of landscaping brick while I wait for them to finish. Shielding my eyes from the sun with my hand, I let my vision roam across the store and the greenhouses. If the intake of daily cash is any indication, this place doesn't rake in much money, but it's an accomplishment nonetheless to run a business like this. Jeff has been working hard these last few years it seems, and whether or not it's paying off in a monetary sense, he's built something here that he and Jackson can be proud of.

I'm proud of Mom and her career too. It isn't easy to become a vice president of a Fortune 500 company, but she did it. She has to work a lot, but she always makes time for the two of us. I can't remember a week that she wasn't home for dinner at least twice, and I know that sometimes means she has to go in early and stay later other nights. She makes a lot more money than Jeff I'm sure, but it costs more to live in L.A. than it does here. She also drives an Infiniti compared to Jeff's Ford F-150.

Jackson and Jeff appear outside the store after what feels like almost twenty minutes. Opening the passenger side door, I wait while shimmering hot air escapes from the cab.

"So you boys are hitting the gym tonight, I hear," Jeff says, sounding pleased.

I nod, taking the middle spot so Jackson can have the outside. "I guess so."

Jackson steps up into the cab and squeezes in next to me. Reaching over with the seatbelt, he hits the top of my hand with the metal part. "Sorry," he says hastily, his eyes briefly catching mine. I lean over toward Jeff so he can find the buckle.

"You have dirt on your face," Jackson says, pointing somewhere above my eyebrows.

Usually I'm careful, but I remember wiping the sweat away after counting the till. I brush a hand across my forehead. "Still there?"

"Kind of," he says with a shrug. "But the rest of you is covered in dirt anyway I guess." I rub at my forehead anyway, more vigorously this time.

"Here," Jackson says quietly, licking his thumb and pressing it against my skin just below my hairline. The moisture on his thumb is warm just like the day's heat.

Jeff drops us off at the Snap Fitness in Northfield, and Jackson leads us inside, toting a duffel bag. I assume he has clothes for me, because otherwise why would he have invited me? "I do have guest passes," he says as we pass the empty front desk.

The gym isn't all that big, definitely not like the sprawling weight room at my high school or the Lifetime that I had a membership to for a while. Yet for its size, it's pretty packed. Most of the cardio machines are being used, and a bunch of buff guys are mingling around the free weights without actually working out.

I've been to the gym enough to know my way around, but I've always been self-conscious in front of guys like that. Their macho bravado just oozes out, polluting the air around them far worse than their stinking sweat. If you could wring one of them out like a towel, you'd get at least a quart of testosterone.

"Come on," Jackson says, leading me to a locker room at the back.

Two short rows of lockers and some naked old dude changing are all that's back here. "This place doesn't have showers?" I ask.

"Nah," he says, dropping his bag on the bench between us. "Sometimes I shower at home, but if I just do weight training, usually I don't break enough of a sweat to need one. If I give myself an extra minute or two between sets, I don't sweat much at all actually." He tosses me a pair of basketball shorts and a tank top before pulling off his shirt.

While we change, I give in to a single stray look at him, and it strikes me again how similar we are. His abs have a little bit more definition, which is probably from coming here a lot more often. And there are those sparse freckles at the top of his cheeks, but other than that, I'm staring at myself. A shiver climbs up my spine, despite the lingering heat from the day.

"What?" he asks. "Is there something on me?" He glances down, brushing an invisible something off his chest.

A rising wave of emotion catches me hard in the throat, but I can't swallow it away. I want so badly for us to be close like we used to be. He's part of me, and I'm part of him. No one else in the world can understand me as well as he does. Or I him. We belong together, to be each other's closest confidant and best friend. It seems crazy to think that's even possible, but we had it once. I just don't know if we can ever get it back.

He seems to detect the change in my demeanor. "Is everything okay?" His eyes, the same intense blue as mine, are earnestly searching my face for an answer.

"I'm fine," I strain to keep the gruffness from my voice.

"Hey guys, sorry I'm late," Matt calls over to us. "Just got off work," he explains, dropping his own bag as he begins to change. It's the first time I've seen him without a shirt. He's tan, and definitely the tall and muscular type, so he's not bad to look at.

"Did I miss anything?" he asks.

"I was just giving Ben some tips and tricks."

I roll my eyes at him. "Telling me how not to sweat doesn't count as a tip or a trick."

Matt glances from me to Jackson. "I thought you were Ben."

Jackson gives him an incredulous look. "*Please*, I am way better looking."

"Also, you should be able to see his ego from a mile away and know it's him," I say, raising my eyebrows to Jackson.

The two of them are silent for a moment, surprise on their faces, before they burst out laughing. Matt grins. "Looks like you know Jackson pretty well after all."

"Some things never change."

"So what about those tricks?" Matt grins, eyeing Jackson. "Will you show me some of your tips and tricks too?"

"Um, no."

The two of them exchange a look. Jackson seems irritated. "I'm going to start with cardio," he declares.

"Cool," Matt says. "Ben, want to spot for me on bench?"

Abso-fucking-lutely not. Flying solo with Matt was not part of the deal. I fire a dirty look at Jackson for his treachery. "Sure," I tell Matt.

To my horror, he leads us to a bench in the middle of the pack of drooling gym rats. I don't mind jocks at all. Really. I played on my high school football team for four years, and I loved it. But these guys aren't interested in sports or teams. They just want to prove that their dick is bigger than the next guy's – something that apparently can only be done by comparing the amount they can lift.

Matt loads up the bar with two forty-five pound plates on each side. Holy shit, this guy can lift. The guys around us seem to perk up too, especially when Matt powers through a set of ten, only struggling on the last two reps. On the last one, I help him get the bar all the way up, but I'm not convinced that I was contributing that much.

"Your turn," Matt says with a smile that borders on sardonic.

Approaching the bar, I pull a plate off each side. Matt raises an eyebrow at me. Cheeks reddening, I lie down on the bench. I should have grabbed different weights to drop another ten or twenty pounds, but after the look he just gave me, I'm already embarrassed. At my best, I could only ever bench this amount, but that was at the height of the football season last year. I haven't lifted much since then.

Doing my best to ignore the guys standing just a few feet from us and laughing about some stupid bullshit, I lift the bar off the rests. Fuck this is heavy. I get it down to my chest, then push, driving my shoulder blades into the padded bench. The bar moves up an inch. Then another. But it's too much weight, and I'm just pushing myself toward muscle failure.

Matt is watching all of this, but he's just smiling. Smiling like a douchey asshole. "Help," I manage through gritted teeth.

"Seriously?" He waits for a second, but I don't know what for. It's obvious that I'm not going to get this thing more than a couple inches off my chest. Finally he reaches down and helps me set it back on the rests.

My face burns. "Can we drop another twenty pounds?"

"If you think that will help," he smirks. Behind him, one of the guys closest to us laughs, but I can't tell if it's at my expense or not.

Matt watches while I exchange the forty-five pound plates for a twenty-five and a ten. I hope to God that's enough.

Thankfully, it is, and I push my way through eight reps. He doesn't make any more comments as we alternate to each finish our three sets, but my blood teems with a seething rage that refuses to cool.

"Jackson is a lot stronger than you," he says as I sit up from my last set. Who the hell does this guy think he is? I came along because I wanted to spend time with Jackson, not because I wanted some asshole to critique my lifts.

He seems to notice I'm getting pissed, because he raises an eyebrow at me. That's it, I'm done with this. "Hey, where are you going?" he calls after me.

Turning, I give him the coldest glare I can manage. "Tell Jackson I'll be waiting outside."

By the time the two of them emerge from the glass doors, I've been leaning against the outside of the building for over a half hour. My anger with Matt has abated somewhat, leaving me with a pervasive disdain for the guy. What does Jackson even see in such a shitty friend?

"You need a ride home?" Matt asks as he passes me.

"I guess," I say, annoyed for having waited so long.

Like its owner, the truck's charm is a bit lacking once you get close. The paint is cherry red, but rust is creeping out from under the fenders. I tug the door open for Jackson, because I refuse to sit right next to Matt.

A funny smell permeates the cab. Vaguely like old engine oil mixed with rancid dreadlocked cat fur. I make a face at my own analogy.

"What is it?" Matt asks as he reaches a hand under the dashboard.

"Nothing," I reply quickly. Concentration bounces around his expression as he fumbles down near the pedals. "What are you doing?"

Out of nowhere, a metronomic clicking noise begins emanating from the instrument cluster. Except not like a metronome at all, because the clicking is completely irregular. Click, click. Pause. Click. Pause. Click, click, click. He grins as he sits back up in his seat. "Hooking up the turn signals."

I glance at Jackson, then back to Matt, waiting for him to laugh. But he doesn't. Click, click. Instead he turns the key into the ignition. The engine awakens with a tyrannosaurus roar.

"Jesus," I say. Jackson shifts beside me, his bare arm grazing against mine. Click, click, click.

Matt pats the dash. "She's a good old girl."

Click. "What *is* that noise?" Jackson demands.

"I told you, the turn signals. The relay or whatever is busted. The signals work fine, but the thing that makes the noise when the signals are on is totally broken. But if I let it do that when the engine is off, the battery goes dead, so I just disconnect the whole thing when I'm not driving."

"It's annoying," I say, barely able to hold back a flood of other comments.

Matt shrugs and presses on the gas. The engine grumbles but it takes a full three seconds before we actually start to move. "I'm going to take you guys home," he says. I guess swimming isn't going to happen after all, which is fine with me. I don't want to spend any more time with Matt than I already have.

The twilight of evening settles over the endless rolling fields of green as we travel. It's a wonder his truck can actually get to highway speeds, but it does, and soon wind is rushing through the open windows. I look over to see how fast that actually is, but the speedometer is stubbornly stuck at zero.

"Your speedometer is broken too?" Jackson asks, apparently noticing at the same time.

Grinning again, Matt nods. At least the noise of the wind and the engine almost drown out the clicking of the turn signal relay or whatever.

106

When Matt finally pulls into our yard, it's with more than a little amazement that I jump out of the truck and find myself on solid ground. Jackson hasn't moved from the center seat. He can do what he wants, but I'm going to bed.

"Later, Ben," Matt calls after me. I flip a hand in the air to show that I heard him but I don't turn around.

Chapter Fifteen

Ben

The next day, Katie comes in before lunch for the first time since I started working for Jeff. She finds me in the greenhouse talking with a lady and her daughter.

"So these all require full sun?" the woman asks me, gesturing to the rows of pots on the far side.

The ever-present hose dangles from my hand, a steady drip of water draining from the end. I think the shut-off valve on the wand is failing. "Correct, except for those waxy looking ones with red and white flowers," I point to a tray about ten feet away.

"What flower is that?" she asks. Her daughter stoops to examine a woodchip.

Katie catches my eye from across the center tables, a subtle smile playing out on her lips. "Um," I say, "they're begonias." Katie gives a little nod, and I know I got it right. I'm glad that she's here to see this, to know that the hours she's spent teaching me about all things garden related were worth it.

"Thanks," the woman says, taking her daughter's hand and continuing down the row.

Katie cuts through a narrow space between the tables. "Good thing she had Mr. Expert over here to help."

I shrug it off. "I thought you didn't start coming in this early until tomorrow?"

She elbows me in the ribs. "You're not happy to see me or what?" Before I can respond, she shrugs and says, "I was bored. I thought I'd swing by and help you be less hopeless when it came to plants." She walks her fingers along the edge of the table, then raises her eyes to mine, forcing me to look away from the tight cutoff shorts she's wearing again.

"Turns out you already have everything covered, so no need for me."

"Don't go." The words are out before I can stop them.

She gives me a coy smile. "Actually, I am going to go, and so are you. I want to take you somewhere."

I like the sound of this. "So uh, what did you have in mind?" I could suggest a few things.

"Don't get any ideas, big guy. I'm talking about ice cream."

"What? That's totally what I was thinking." I raise my eyebrows in mock indignation.

Water is still dribbling from the end of the hose as I glance at the ground, my hand sneaking up to rub my neck. "But I can't just go. I have to finish watering, and you know, I'm on the clock... I think."

"Do you actually get paid?" When I don't answer, she adds, "That's what I thought. Now let's get out of here, hot shot."

"What about Jeff and Jackson?"

"They'll be fine. How do you think they managed before you got here?"

"Good point. Let's get out of here then, but I don't want to be gone too long."

It feels like I must be breaking some kind of rule as I slink away with Katie, but Jeff has never mentioned anything about getting paid, so it's not like I'm stealing company time or anything.

Katie seems to know where we're going as she leads me through a swanky residential part of Northfield. Overhead, the sky is almost cloudless as we move down the sidewalk. Around us, the houses grow bigger, surrounded by perfectly manicured lawns and built-in sprinkler systems sending arcing waves of water over lush green grass.

I've never been interested in this kind of living. It feels too fake. Every object in theses houses will be in its correct place, and not a single blade of grass will be bent in the yard, but the people are just as screwed up and human as the rest of us. They just hide it a little better.

Not that I have anything against money. Mom does pretty damn well for us, but we don't have a cookie-cutter house like these. Instead we live in a condo with a great view and amazing art on the walls.

"What are you thinking about?" Katie ventures.

I step around a wet area where an overzealous sprinkler is spraying onto the sidewalk. "Nothing." I pause, then say, "Home, actually."

"Is it like this?" She gestures vaguely to the houses around us.

"Not at all." I chuckle, gazing down the street. The tasteless houses stretch on for blocks. "Where are we? Aren't we supposed to be getting ice cream?"

"That's just what I used to get you out here." She says, sticking her pink tongue out at me.

I'd love to investigate that more closely. "Oh really," I grin. "So now that I've uncovered the deception, what was your actual plan? Kidnap me and then interrogate me about L.A.?"

Her eyes aimed ahead, she gives me a wry look. "Something like that."

It hits me again how beautiful she is. Her hand swings at her side, carefree. I want to take it in mine, just slip my fingers through hers. "But really, why are we out here?"

"I wanted to get to know you a little better, and it was important to avoid the work friend trap."

"What do you mean?"

"You know," she says, kicking at a rock on the otherwise spotless concrete. "If you wait too long to hang out with someone outside of work, it will never happen. You become work friends."

Warmth spreads in my chest, emanating from the pattering in the center. "Except I'm still on the clock, so this doesn't count."

Rolling her eyes, she pushes my shoulder. "That's such crap."

I scan the store and greenhouse as we approach, hoping Jeff didn't notice that we were gone so long. Through the open front doors, I can see him leaning over the counter reading a book. It's usually quiet around noon.

As it turned out, Katie took us to an ice cream place after all. Waffle cone in one hand and purse in the other, she starts to veer away from me.

"You coming?" I ask, already halfway to the front door.

She waves me on, "I'll catch up with you after lunch. I need to grab something from the gas station."

Taking a lick of my ice cream, I watch her walk away across the street. Spending time with her is just so awesome. I also got her cell number. It was kind of sexy to be kidnapped by her this morning, but it would be nice to do a little planning of my own. I won't text her for a few days though, so it doesn't look like I'm overeager.

"Hey, Ben," Jeff says, looking up from his book. "You brought me ice cream."

I hold the cone out to him, and he takes a bite from the top. From a bacterial perspective, I guess that's better than licking, but teeth marks in ice cream just look gross. I quickly smooth over the top with my tongue.

"Thanks, that hit the spot." Then he smirks. "So how was your morning?"

I give him a sidelong glance, but I'm glad he doesn't seem to mind that I disappeared for quite a while. "It was fine. Katie is nice." The last thing I want is for this conversation to continue. "Anyway, where's Jackson?"

"Back parking lot. Have him come up here, would you?"

"Sure," I say, moving toward the door leading out the back. I never thought I'd start to enjoy working here with Jeff and Jackson, but it's starting to feel almost natural. I still don't know a ton about the plants – other than most of their names now – but there's something to having a solid daily routine. Get up, shower, eat with Jackson, water plants until noon, do odd jobs with Katie until closing time, dinner with Jeff and Jackson, go for a run, go to sleep. Whatever I do with Katie is usually my favorite part of the day.

I wonder if Jackson has the same feeling about working that I do. He's been doing it a lot longer, so he might get bored of it more easily. He also doesn't have someone like Katie he gets to work with every afternoon.

My fingers wrapped around the handle of the back door, I peer through the glass. Matt's truck is parked next to Jeff's. I figure he must have come for lunch, and I'm about to open the door when a hint of movement catches my eye. In the back corner of the parking lot are Matt and Jackson, laughing together. Something about the interaction between the two of them rubs me the wrong way. Their movements and words seem to come so easily.

I'm hit by a sudden jealousy at watching this private moment. Breath catching in my throat, my fingers tighten around the metal handle. Closing my eyes, I swallow, take a deep breath, and turn around. Slowly walking back up to the front, I take a seat on a spare stool. My vision gradually blurs as my gaze cuts into the wall with the rakes and shovels.

A sinking feeling fills my chest when I realize what bothers me the most about all this. Jackson just doesn't want me to be a part of his life here, and he doesn't enjoy spending time with me, at least not the way he does with other people. Christ, he's my brother, and even though I've been living with him for a few weeks now, I still don't know hardly anything about him. I clench my teeth, forcing a swallow past the rock in my throat.

"Ben, is something wrong?" Jeff asks.

"I need to go," I say through a dry mouth, walking past him.

Hesitation echoes in his voice when he speaks. "What's going on?"

His words sound distant, as though a glass wall divides us. I wave a weak hand in his direction as my shoe catches on the threshold. "I just... I have to go."

Up ahead, Katie is just coming back from the gas station. "Where are you going?" she asks, trying to catch my eye.

Tightness in my chest reminds me I haven't been breathing. Releasing the pent up air, I drag a shallow breath of hot humidity into my lungs. Her stare barely registers as I take plodding steps past her. Behind me, her voice calls out, lined with fragility. "Aren't you going to answer me?"

My feet carry me forward past streets and houses and down more streets until finally depositing me at the edge of a stream cutting its way through a park. Dropping myself to the ground, I cross my legs and wrap my arms around my chest. Beside me, the stream gurgles along, catching the occasional shred of sunlight that slips through the trees overhead.

Jackson. The name that long ago used to have a calming effect now leaves me insecure. *Jackson.* A chilly current sweeps through my chest, cupping my heart in its undertow. What we had when we were little, it was special, but we didn't understand it back then. We didn't know how precious it was. At least I didn't.

It didn't bother me being away for so long, because I always believed we could get it back – the closeness – when we saw each other again. Except the years flew by and we didn't see each other like I thought. Vacations, sports, friends, it was all bullshit. None of it mattered at all, but I let those things be the priority, let them take precedence over my brother. All along I was destroying something I could never get back. My eyes drift across the rippling water, and one after another, tears slide down my cheeks.

It's almost five o'clock when I finally drag myself back to the store. The sun isn't high in the sky anymore, but it still feels hot on my neck and my mouth is dry. Jackson stops the second he sees me, a thirty-pound bag of grass seed slung over his shoulder. It's nothing compared to the weight I'm carrying.

His squinting eyes look me up and down, like he's not sure if I'm real or not. The bag shifts slightly as he sighs. "Dad wants to talk to you."

I nod, and he doesn't say anything else.

The white door to Jeff's office is closed, and my hand is heavy as I lift it to knock.

"Come in." His voice isn't raised or even upset. Is that a good or a bad thing? As I open the door, he glances up from a ledger, his eyes scrutinizing me from under a pair of reading glasses. "Have a seat." He gestures to the empty chair across from him.

Pulling the door shut behind me, I sit down. The air is stuffy and the chair is hard. His gaze is fixed on me, but I look away.

"I've been impressed with you, Ben. You've been a hard worker and a good sport about things suddenly changing on you this summer. I think I've given you a fair bit of freedom as well." His tone is sincere. He wants to understand, but how can I even begin to explain? The more I get to know my brother, the more I realize I don't know him at all anymore. How can I communicate how much that's killing me inside? He would never understand, no matter how hard he wants to. He never had Jacks. I did.

I've never been able to hide emotion, and I'm not able to now. The storm plays out across my features like performers on a theater stage, but that doesn't mean he knows *what* I'm thinking.

When I'm silent, he lets out a long breath. "Mind telling me what happened today?"

My mouth opens just a bit before closing again. If I can't speak the truth, there's only one alternative. "I was upset about… Katie. We sort of got in a, uh, fight."

Jeff rubs his jaw. "Anything I should know about?"

"No, it was just dumb stuff. I needed time to cool off, so I left." My breath comes more easily as I spin my lies with increasing conviction. "I'm sorry, it won't happen again."

He gives me a serious look, his tone adopting a hardness he hasn't used with me before. "Make sure it doesn't. If you need to take a break, or if you need to cool off, that's fine. But you check in with me first, got it?"

I stand up, matching his expression. "Understood."

"Good, now let's get going."

As soon as we're home and out of the truck, I sprint up to the house and change into basketball shorts. Jackson and Jeff are just getting water from the fridge when I race back down the stairs and slip on Jackson's running shoes. He locks eyes with me for a fraction of a second before I'm out the door. They're the same blue eyes as this morning except not the same at all. God I really need to run. I need to run until my heart bursts or breaks, it doesn't matter which. Either way it's not coming back whole.

Today I head west. Crops on both sides of the road fill my vision as my feet beat the ground into submission, forcing it back under my advance. Endless rows of corn stretch to the south, while wheat dominates everything to the north.

If only he would let me in, maybe we could find something close to what we had. I have things I'd like to share with him too, if he were willing to listen. Stuff about living with Mom and about getting to know Katie. Stuff like how a gaping crater inside is threatening to engulf me. Maybe it's irrational, maybe it's bizarre, but I need him.

After what feels like forever, I turn toward home with a growing headache threatening to split my head apart and my chest so tight I can barely breathe. For the hundredth time, I regret not drinking any water before I left. I shouldn't run this hard when I'm dehydrated, but I don't care. Barely more than the balls of my feet touch the ground. If I push myself hard enough, the physical pain will cover the other, deeper pain. It will be a welcome relief if I can get there. So I keep pushing.

Finally crossing the road into our driveway, a sickening roil grips my stomach, and I know I've overdone it. I slow my pace to a walk, but it's too late. Gritting my teeth through the razor-edged headache, I try to burp but I can't get anything out. I'm ten feet from the front door when I double over in the grass and start dry heaving. This is the closest I've been to throwing up in a long time.

The caustic taste of acid fills my nose and mouth, but nothing actually comes up. Once it's over, I take a few minutes to just let myself breathe. Spitting a few last times into the grass, I push myself to my feet and head inside.

Jeff and Jackson are on the couch watching TV. I turn my face away as I pass the living room so they won't see how flushed it is. Pouring myself a glass of water, I rinse my mouth out first and spit the bile into the sink. Topping off the glass, I drink it all. From the cabinet above the sink, I take three ibuprofen and down them with a second glass.

Half dragging myself up the stairs by the banister, I stumble over a pile of dirty clothes as I enter Jackson's room. My head pounding and my throat still raw, I pull the shades down and drop into his bed. It's not exactly what I wished for, but straight unconsciousness will suffice.

Hours later, I awake as Jackson climbs quietly into bed beside me. Everything is dark, but my headache is gone. Neither of us says anything, and in a minute I've fallen back to sleep.

When I awake for a second time, the room is still smothered in darkness and silence. My legs are stiff and my throat feels like an animal clawed its way out sometime during the night, but at least I'm well rested. A few inches to my left, Jackson's steady breathing counts time to the passing seconds. With only the top sheet covering him, I reach out across the space between us and lay my hand on his stomach. Under my palm, it rises and falls in cadence with his breaths.

He rolls his head to the side, but I know he isn't awake because my hand on his belly still moves evenly up and down. This moment feels stolen, like it will never really belong to me. Because as much as I'm craving connection with Jackson, it has to be freely given, not taken. I withdraw my hand.

Chapter Sixteen

Jackson

Another week has passed, and we're still working at Dad's greenhouse. The days move quickly, and the evenings even faster. It's taken a little time to get used to Ben being beside me every night, but I don't really mind anymore. In a way it's kind of cool, even if our frequently whispered conversations before we fall asleep are stilted and awkward at times.

Tonight Ben doesn't say anything for almost fifteen minutes, but I know he's awake. It's something about his breathing, but I'm not sure exactly what. At last he says, "So do you have a girlfriend?"

I shift under the sheet, wanting to take back my earlier thoughts. He's never dropped something like this on me, and I really don't want to get into it with him. "No girlfriend. You?"

"No," he says, answering quickly, "but I'm kind of hoping to get to know Katie better." He pauses for a second before continuing. "She's got the best smile… and laugh. And don't even get me started on those shorts. She always wears the sexiest shorts."

"Um…" I guess I should be proud of him for going after someone here and trying to make the best of this summer. Still though… it's Ben, and I don't want to think about him that way.

He rolls onto his stomach. Jesus, I hope he's not doing that because he's getting hard. So gross. I scoot away from him a little bit. "You like her a lot, huh?"

"So what if I do?" He's silent for a moment, then asks. "You and her didn't have like a thing, did you?"

I actually laugh this time. "Uh, no."

"What's so damn funny?"

"Nothing," I say quickly, holding my breath. I *really* don't want to get into this right now.

Ben is quiet for a bit, long enough that I think he's given up, when he restarts the conversation. "You'd tell me, right?"

"Huh? I was almost asleep."

"Sorry," he says quickly. "But now that you're awake again…"

"Yes?" I grumble.

"You'd tell me if you were interested in someone, right? I know that–" He stops midsentence, like he's afraid of what he might say. He tries again. "I know that things aren't like they used to be, but we're still brothers. We're supposed to share stuff like that."

How can I possibly answer him? *Oh yeah, Ben. Actually I do have something of a love interest. He's six foot one, a hundred and eighty pounds, and his dick really puts to shame those push-pops we used to like as kids.* Yeah, not going to happen. Not that I've actually *seen* Matt like that yet, but I had my hand on it, so that counts. "Sure, I'd tell you."

"I thought so," he says. "I was just checking." From his voice, I can tell he's smiling. I don't like lying to him, but what choice do I have?

Dad delivers the good news that business has slowed down enough for the summer that he can manage with just him and Katie, who's now working full days. The caveat, of which he somehow managed to inform us no less than seven times in that one conversation, was that he still might need our help sometimes.

He's also decided that it's time to fix up the guest bedroom so Ben doesn't have to keep rooming with me. It's funny that a few weeks ago I would have done anything not to have him in my room, and now I'm going to be sad to see him go. Despite his rocky time here, there have been brief moments where it feels like everything was like it used to be between us. For the first time in years, it was just him and me, together.

I don't quite understand the intense need to be close to him. It was easier to ignore when we lived apart, but now that we're in the same house, it's an emptiness inside that demands to be filled. What makes me feel like this? My mind supplies a rogue explanation, but I know it's not *that*, there's no question about that. I'm no more attracted to Ben than I am to a houseplant. It's something else, something deeper.

The following morning, Dad gets a friend of his to manage the greenhouse so he can work on Ben's room for the day. When Dad asks which one of us wants to go to Menard's with him to get the drywall sheets, I gladly let Ben go ahead. I've been to that store way too many times over the years. Each trip drags on until we've been there for hours and I'm hauling around a cart or lumber trolley filled with so much stuff it borders on being unsafe. So yeah, Ben, go right ahead.

After they leave, I text Matt to let him know he doesn't need to come over to help until after lunch. Dad said they'd be back by eleven, but it always takes longer. Dropping my phone onto the bedside table, I strip off my jeans and t-shirt and lie down to get a bit more sleep. As much as I don't want to admit it, I haven't been sleeping any worse since Ben started sharing the bed. I don't know how that's possible, since it's a double and we're not scrawny guys. We've got shoulders.

Once on a field trip in middle school, I had to share a bed with another guy, and I slept like shit. Every time he moved I woke up. It was miserable.

But with Ben? I'm out cold, every night. Except for that time he said my name in his sleep. *Jacks.* Fuck if I wasn't wide-awake from the moment that syllable passed his lips. For a split second it made me feel amazing, and then I remembered. I remembered he never calls me that anymore and probably never will again. I bite down, suppressing the emotion smoldering in my throat before it can really take hold. Forcing my eyes closed, I make myself take steady breaths until I no longer have to force it. Rest is a welcome relief when it finally comes.

"Hey," a whispered voice coaxes me from sleep. *Ben? No, that's not right.* Sleep clouds my brain, so it takes some effort to open my eyes. Matt is sitting at my desk, just a few feet away.

"What are you doing here?" I glance around, trying to make sense of everything. "Did I oversleep?" The shades on my window are drawn, leaving the room cloaked in murky shadows.

"It's only nine thirty," he says a little louder than his earlier whisper. "You said your dad and brother weren't coming back for a while, so I thought I'd come over."

I sit up in bed, acutely conscious of his eyes as they skim over my shirtless chest. Even in the semi-darkness, I can see him turning red. "Huh?"

"I, uh, thought you meant for me to come over before they got back."

I give him an incredulous look. "Um, no, I didn't mean that. How could you have gotten that from my text?"

"All right, I know you didn't say that," he admits. "But I wanted to see you. Without your family around for once."

Hearing Matt refer to Dad and Ben as my family feels off for some reason, if only because it's just been Dad and me for so long. I sigh. "I don't feel comfortable, uh, fooling around here. Ben has been asking questions, and I don't want him getting ideas."

"Who gives a shit?" Matt breathes, fire instantly kindling in his expression. "I'm pretty horny, and I bet you are too. It doesn't matter if your brother is here for the summer."

"It does." My words hover in the air, a challenge.

"Fine. I'll go then."

Am I really going to let him leave? It's been impossible to get him out of my head lately, but the thought of Ben finding out about us scares the shit out of me. The sounds of his footsteps on the stairs echo back to me as melancholy notes.

Without caring about the yellow and orange striped boxer briefs I'm wearing, I toss the covers off and bolt down the hallway. If he leaves, he's not going to come back. I don't know how I know, but I do.

Bare feet slapping the smooth oak stairs, I burst into the kitchen and run through the living room, catching his arm just as he reaches the front door. "Don't go," I say, my breath heavy. His skin feels hot beneath my fingers.

He glances downward, no doubt taking in the fact that I'm not wearing anything but a pair of skintight underwear. "Don't go," I repeat. His eyes snap up to mine before being drawn back down just a little.

"I don't want to play games. You said you were okay with just having fun this summer, but that's pretty hard to do if you're being a paranoid closet case. I don't care, because that's your deal, but there's no one even *here* today." He pulls out of my grip.

I bite my lip. "I'm sorry. It's just kind of confusing with Ben here."

He sighs. "I'll be back in a few hours to help you guys with the room."

"Really?"

"I said I'd help, and I kind of need the money." Then he turns and disappears out the door. Behind him, the screen door slams with a screech. I hate that sound.

Climbing the stairs back to my room, I throw myself onto the bed and pull a pillow into my arms, unable to shake the feeling that I'm messing something up right now. And for what? Because Ben might be upset if he found out?

The rest of the day passes in a blur. Matt shows up at one o'clock just as we finish lunch, and he works with us the whole day, just like he said.

Dad took time at the beginning to show both Matt and Ben how to hang drywall properly, but he kept saying things that made it seem like he was impatient. Once they each mastered scoring and snapping apart the pieces, positioning them properly on the studs, and finally drilling the screws to the right depth, the work started to go a lot faster. I would have preferred not to team up with Matt, but Dad told us to work together. Probably thought he was doing us a favor.

After the walls went up, we mudded between the joints, keeping the work clean enough that we won't have to sand it much afterward. We'll still have to paint before Ben moves in here, but at this point I think Dad is in more of a rush to get Ben out of my room than either of us are.

Without anything else to do, Matt and I just watch as Ben and Dad clean up. We aren't talking, but that's not really a surprise since we haven't said much all day. We didn't talk while we were working either, at least not any more than we absolutely had to. I know it would have taken a lot longer if it had just been Dad and Ben and me, but I wish Matt hadn't come back to help.

"I think I'm going to head home," Matt announces, shooting a look at me.

Dad sets down the drill and pulls out his wallet, handing Matt several twenties. "Thanks for the help, Matt. Was good to see you again."

"No problem. Glad to help out."

My eyes catch Dad's, and then I say, "I'll show him out."

An hour later, the sun is already casting evening shadows from the deck railing as Dad tosses three steaks onto the grill. Beyond the deck, the willow branches hang down, completely still.

"You and Matt didn't talk much today," he says.

The edge in his voice makes the hairs on the back of my neck lift into the air. "Not really," I say cautiously, glad that Ben is still inside the house.

"Did you guys get into some pissy fight?"

His words make my chest constrict, forcing the air out of my lungs. I don't know what he's getting at, and I don't want to find out. "No," I state. "We just didn't talk much."

"Hmm," he says as Ben steps onto the porch and sits down on one of the deck chairs.

I refuse to look at either of them.

"You picked up pretty quick on the drywall work," Dad says to Ben. "Have you ever done any type of construction before?"

Ben flushes and shakes his head, his hair brushing against the back of the chair he's reclining on. He must like getting a compliment from Dad. "In a weird way," he says, "it was kind of fun learning to put walls up."

Really? I'm surprised that he enjoyed himself, but there's more to the thoughtful expression he's wearing, although I can't quite figure out what it is.

"You and Jackson do a lot of this stuff?" he asks.

"Not often, but sometimes." Dad closes the lid on the gas grill. "Be right back," he says, stepping through the screen door.

When he returns he has three dark brown bottles. He hands one to Ben and another to me. "You've earned it," he says.

Prying the cap off mine with the opener on my keychain, I take a long swig.

Ben rotates the bottle in front of him, eyeing the label with green writing and a picture of a cow jumping over something I've never been able to identify. *New Glarus Spotted Cow.*

"You're serious?" he asks, raising his eyes to Dad.

"Yep," he says, taking a drink.

I watch Ben out of the corner of my eye as his fingers close around the neck of the bottle. Like mine, it's cold and covered in a layer of condensation. I hand him my keychain. He opens the bottle and takes a drink, seeming to savor it. "Thanks, um, Dad," he says.

My eyes jump to Dad and the smile awakening on his face. Ben hasn't called him that even once since arriving here.

"No problem, son."

"Today was actually kind of fun. Dad has been pretty cool lately," Ben says from beside me. The lights have been off for a while, but he clearly hasn't fallen asleep yet.

I roll over to face him. "You're just saying that because he gave you a beer, but Dad isn't all sunshine and rainbows."

"It's not that. I just… I mean, it feels good to get to know him again."

If I'd known Ben was so easily bought, I would have set a cold one in front of him the moment he first stepped through the door at the beginning of the summer. I know I should be more gracious that Ben is finally warming up to being here, but I can't stop myself. "If you hadn't left in the first place, you wouldn't be needing to get to know either of us again."

"I didn't exactly have a choice," he snaps. Jagged silence cuts between us and tension pours into the air. If I'm perfectly honest with myself, I'm not really mad that Ben is starting to rebuild his relationship with Dad. I'm mad that Dad treats him better than me.

It feels like Ben is trying to work up the courage to say something more, so I wait, but the only answer I get is soft breathing.

Chapter Seventeen

Jackson

The door to our bedroom is shut, but it still makes me feel a little uneasy doing this without a lock on the door, even though Ben made it clear that he was going for a long run today. With just Dad and me, I never really worried, because he never came knocking. But Ben? He's actually living in this room with me – at least until his room gets painted – so there's a better chance of... I push the thought out of my mind. There are other things I want to think about.

Leaning back on my bed, I reach underneath the mattress and pull out a magazine. It's definitely not the most original spot to hide a porn magazine, but it hasn't been discovered yet, so there's that. Flipping through the pages, I adjust the position of my restless hips. I don't need some smutty magazine to get off, but the thing with Matt... it's my first time with a guy, and I want to make sure that it's not just him. I feel stupid for thinking that could even be a possibility, because it's obvious that I'm into guys. But I've never had a gay experience before, at least not before Matt. I've barely even seen other guys in the locker room. Quick glances, but nothing more. It was high school after all, so I had to be careful.

So about the magazine... I guess I wanted to see how my body reacts to this kind of thing. Do guys in pictures do the same thing for me that being around Matt does? I flip to the next page, my eyes devouring the photos. Wow. I didn't even know guys did this stuff with each other. And *to* each other. I also can't erase the giddy smile from my face.

Easing open the zipper on my jeans, I work them downward toward my knees. Wrapping a hand around my dick, I start to give myself some attention. When I was younger, I tried to jerk off to straight porn a few times but it was nothing like this. The boobs were always such a turn off.

My hand continues eagerly, sending sunny waves through me. This is so much different than the straight stuff, which always made it such a struggle to finish. In contrast, this is… this is fucking fantastic. If I'm not careful, I'm going to get off in the next minute or so.

The voice is so unexpected that it takes me a moment to even stop what I'm doing. "Hey Jackson, do you–" Ben stops dead, his hand on the doorknob and looking like the scene has slapped him in the face. He's riveted in place, his eyes flicking downward for only a fraction of a second before settling on the magazine.

Like my hand on my dick, his face is frozen, covered with an expression you'd expect from someone watching a plane crash.

With the blankets and sheet in a pile on the floor, I throw the magazine over my crotch to cover myself and lash out with my newly found voice. "Jesus, fuck, Ben, get out!"

Slamming the door behind him, his steps thunder in the hallway and down the stairs. No fucking way. Just absolutely not.

Chapter Eighteen

Jackson

I could sprint to town and back, and my chest wouldn't be this tight. And my nose wouldn't burn like it does now. As if that weren't enough, a sadistic heat fans out across my stomach, rising up to my face. "Fuck!" I shout again, throwing the magazine as hard as I can. It slaps the wall next to the window and thuds to the floor, pages splayed. "Fuck!" My breaths are coming fast. Goddamn it, why did he come back so soon? I would have jerked off in the fucking shower if he hadn't made it clear he was going for a long run. It's been weeks since I've beat off to anything but the smell of shampoo and the drone of running water. I wanted a break, so I waited until Ben was going to clear out for a while.

My erection has long since collapsed onto my stomach, so I barely have to adjust when I pull my underwear and pants back up. What the hell am I going to do now? A spasm of fear strikes me in the chest. *What if he tells Dad?*

I tug a clean shirt over my head. I'm going to have to talk to him. This isn't a conversation I wanted to have today, but it's as good a time for it as any, I guess. Taking a deep breath, I venture a look in the mirror. I'm still in one piece – that's something to be thankful for at least. Not that Ben would ever have taken a pot shot at me for getting off to gay porn, but I've never actually *told* anyone before, Matt excluded. I wasn't really sure what would happen to me when the first person found out. Somehow I thought a piece of me might crack under the pressure, but hey, I'm still here. Not to say that Ben busting in on me counted as *telling* him, but he sure as shit knew what was going on.

Ben isn't in the hallway when I leave my room. Tiptoeing down the stairs, I scan the kitchen and living room, but it's just Dad watching TV. "Have you seen Ben?"

Dad mutes the show. "He ran out the door just a minute ago. Did you guys have an argument? I heard shouting."

"No argument. I just stubbed my toe." I meet his gaze so he doesn't think I'm lying. "I'm going for a walk, I'll see you later."

Dad nods and the noise from the TV resumes as I kneel to put on my shoes. "That fucker keeps stealing my running shoes," I mutter and slip on his white and green Nikes. See what he thinks about that.

It takes a good ten minutes to find him, but eventually I do. He's sitting in the grass, leaning up against the back of the garage with his arms propped up on his knees. That's Ben all right, never sure how to handle things. He wrestles with a problem in his own little world until he realizes he can't solve it by himself. That's when he looks to me. At least that's how it used to work.

"Hey," I say. He glances up, holding my eyes in his own – within them are clouds of emotion so thick that I can't even begin to decipher what's going on inside him. I sit down, leaving some space between us. He was bound to find out sooner or later, so why am I so afraid?

The wind picks up, forcing the grass in our lawn to bend under the onslaught. My position mirrors Ben's, except my arms are crossed. I wait for him to speak. Ben needs his time.

Still staring off into the woods at the edge of the yard, he puts together his words one at a time. "You like… guys?"

The answer is heavy in my throat. "Yeah."

A long sigh takes place next to me. You'd think someone had died. "Why didn't you tell me? Why did I have to find you whacking it to gay porn? You know how shitty it makes me feel to find out like that?"

He doesn't have any right to be mad at *me* about this, especially considering the way he left eight years ago. "Don't you dare get self-righteous with me. I didn't tell you because we haven't been close in *years*."

Ben shakes his head, biting his lip. "Are you and Matt hooking up or something?"

I look away, releasing an anxious breath.

"Jesus, Jackson. With Matt? Seriously?"

His accusing eyes bore into the side of my face, cutting scorching streaks across my cheek as I turn to him and shrug.

"*Seriously*, Jackson?"

"I know you don't really like him," I concede.

"He's a first class douchebag," he scoffs. "I cannot believe you not only never told me, but that you're messing around with such a–"

"Shut up!" I shout, my rage burning. "It's so typical of you to make this all about yourself."

Ben flicks his eyes up to mine but remains quiet. He's processing. Maybe it's more about him than I think? "And besides," I venture, "I figured you had a similar experience."

His voice is taut with suspicion. "What do you mean, 'similar experience'?"

Shrugging, I answer him honestly. "Same genes, little brother. I always guessed you might be the same way. Are you?"

"I'm not fucking gay," he snaps.

Staring off into the wheat fields that stretch away from our property, I fight to bury the searing heat in the back of my throat. Of all the people in the world, Ben was the one supposed to take it the best. Even the years apart couldn't change *everything* between us. At least that's what I thought.

"So what is Matt to you, really? You guys just get frisky whenever you need to get your rocks off, or are you actually a thing?" he asks, his voice probing.

"None of your goddamn business, that's what." From the corner of my eye I see him flinch at the harshness in my words. I release a grunt of frustration. "Look, you can think what you want, but–" My voice catches in my throat. "Just don't tell anyone, especially not Dad, okay?"

"Whatever." The muscles in his face are working overtime, as if that will help him figure this all out.

I can tell from his tone that he's really upset, almost about to shut down completely. He has already passed the point of no return, closing himself off to everything. He won't talk about this with me anymore, at least not right now. Standing up, he walks away from me. I know better than to follow. He wants me to, but until he sorts out his emotions, he's like a cornered animal. If I force the conversation, we'll just end up laying into each other and saying things we regret, so the conversation has to be over.

I wish it weren't, though. I wish he would tell me that it's cool whether I like dudes or old ladies or golden retrievers. But he didn't, and he won't. Ben always seems to need me for everything, but he can't step outside of his own head for two seconds when I really need him for something. When he showed up here this summer, I was hopeful that maybe we could start over again. It didn't matter that he didn't choose to come here.

But he's clearly content to be miserable. He probably doesn't even care how much we've grown apart. Well, fuck him. I don't need anyone. My fingers wrap around a clump of grass like a boa constrictor, squeezing the life out of it. I need to get out of here. I pull out my phone and text Matt.

Hey what are you up to?

Nothing, you?

Same old, fighting with Ben.

Sorry man.

My fingers hover over the screen, hesitant. Oh, what the hell. I tap out the message. *Can I come over?*

I toss the phone into the grass beside me and let my head fall back against the garage, remembering my last real conversation with him. It was clear that he was still willing to keep doing what we're doing, whatever that is, as long as I figure my shit out. I can't believe Ben had the balls to ask if anything was going on between us, but now that he knows, there's no point in hiding it any longer.

My phone buzzes with Matt's reply. *Sure.*

The ride over to his place feels like it takes an hour, even though it's only a few miles. When I arrive to find the driveway empty, I feel a pang of guilt at the excited flutter in my chest. I shouldn't be looking forward to this as much as I am, but I can't help it. Ben interrupted me trying to release my pent-up energy earlier, and if anything it's even worse now than before.

I'm barely in the door when his hands slide around my biceps, pushing me up against the wall and locking down my lips with his. Damn he tastes good. His lips are soft, surrounded by just a shadow of roughness. Just like last time, I can't get enough, so when his tongue nips into my mouth, I eagerly push back with my own. His hands rise to my neck, his thumbs pressing against my jaw as his mouth goes after mine.

My shorts feel tight against me when he finally pulls away. "I've been waiting to do that." He says it like it's been years. "Took you long enough to finally text."

"Me too," I breathe. "Been waiting, that is." Letting my hands grip his waist, I add, "Let's go upstairs."

"You sure you're not going to bolt out of here or anything?" His eyes flash darkly.

Forcing away my hesitation, I nod. That must be good enough for him, because he pulls away from my grip and gestures for me to go first.

"I like your shoes," he says with a pointed look at my feet.

I remember I'm still wearing Ben's white and green Nike's. "Thanks," I say, brushing the thought of Ben out of my mind.

Self-consciously covering the bulging section in the front of my shorts, I lead the way upstairs as every square inch of my skin burns with desire.

I've barely shoved the covers on his bed out of the way when Matt is on me again, more voracious this time. Maneuvering me so I'm lying on my back, he picks up where we left off at the door, melting into me with his mouth, with his hands, with a steady rhythm in his hips. Damn it if my hands aren't all over him too, pulling up his shirt as he takes off mine.

The warning voice inside that held me in check when we were here a year ago is quieter now. Still present, but more subdued and easier to ignore. I want this. I *really* want this.

Matt lowers himself from outstretched arms down to his elbows, shrinking the space between us until our chests touch. His stomach is soft against mine, and his dick is hard through his shorts, nestling alongside mine likewise concealed – for the moment at least.

I groan as he traces a line downward with his tongue, pausing at my left nipple and zigzagging across to the other before continuing lower. His breath on my stomach causes me to suck in, but I relax into it after a moment. Matt's hands wander along the sides of my chest, gently kneading the muscles that wrap around into my back. I squirm as his tongue darts into my navel, leaving a trail of moisture that brings with it a touch of coolness as he exhales.

By the time he reaches the waistband of my briefs, I can hardly stand it anymore. I'm convinced I'm going to tear the fabric of my underwear if he keeps going like this. Sneaking a finger under the elastic, he tugs them down, freeing me in a way that should make me self-conscious as hell. But it doesn't.

"Damn," he says, just looking at me. "It's hot that you're uncut. And kind of big."

I might be feeling some warmth at the compliment, but I can't feel a damn thing over the heat gripping me from my core. "Thanks," I murmur, not wanting to distract him. Is he really going to do this? Do I really *want* this? The pesky voice inside says no. But every other part of me is saying something else.

His tongue continues, breaking like waves against my skin as he moves to the side, bypassing the place where I really want him to go. The light stubble on his cheeks rasps against the side of my dick, sending even more powerful ripples of desire through me.

"You're teasing me," I say, trying to keep my voice light.

Matt's gaze rises to my face. "Are you sure that's what you want?"

"Yeah," I growl. "*Hell* yeah."

His eyes soft and fixed on mine, I feel his hot breath a half-second before he takes me in his mouth. "Damn," I whisper as he looks up. Those eyes, all for me. Tipping my hips up to let him take me deeper, I groan, each of my hands squeezing a fistful of the sheet.

His head bobs up and down as his hands work in tandem with his mouth. "Fuck, that feels so good." He doesn't respond, but his mouth is full, so I don't hold it against him.

My breathing comes in clipped bursts as he continues. Releasing my grip on the sheets to run my fingers through his hair, I have to make a conscious effort to prevent all my muscles from tensing. I don't want to hold back.

"Oh God," I breathe. His eyes are on me again, and in them I can see his awareness of what's about to happen, but he doesn't stop. Closing my eyes, I tighten my grip in his hair. It seems like an eternity between the moment I lose control and when I actually come. He slows as I do, and I can see him swallow several times. Watching him do it gives me a pleasant satisfaction, but I'm not sure why.

When he finally looks up, I feel an urge to turn away, exposed as I am. But I know he gave me the chance to stop it before it went this far. The truth is, I didn't want it to stop, and I don't regret it now.

We just look at each other, taking in the abrupt change in our relationship. We're definitely not just buddies anymore. I'm pretty sure that happened the moment he took me in his mouth.

Watching him stare at me with that earnest look in his eyes makes me flush. "Why are you smiling like that?" I ask.

He drops his voice, but it's not enough to keep from understanding him. "I like the way you taste."

Embarrassment burns in my face at his confession. What he just said could easily top the list of things I never thought I'd hear from another guy. He's still watching me, and after a moment I realize that he still hasn't gotten off. Sure enough, he's hard against the fabric of his shorts.

Resolving to fix that problem, I lean forward just as the sound of a door shutting downstairs makes us both freeze. The bottom drops out from under my stomach as my eyes grow wide.

"*Shit!*" Matt hisses. "They weren't supposed to be home for at least another hour."

The clink of keys being dropped on a table is followed by the creaking of someone coming up the stairs. I stare at him unmoving, gripped by panic. This can't be happening. Matt has already landed on the floor, scrambling to pick up our shirts. "Don't just sit there. Put your clothes back on!" We both still have our shorts on, albeit unzipped in the case of mine. Tugging my shirt over my head, I hastily rearrange myself and zip up.

By the time Matt's mom stops by the room, we're both fully clothed and in the middle of a TV show on Netflix. God knows how it loaded in time. I have no idea what we're even watching, but my attention is locked on the screen like it's a preview of the apocalypse.

"Hi, Jackson," she says. I've seen her a time or two this summer, but for the most part Matt has managed to minimize our contact. I'm not sure if that's intentional or not, but it doesn't bother me.

"Hey," I manage, certain that my voice betrays what we were just doing. If not that, then the mess of blankets we're sitting on that make it look like a tornado ripped through here. Even Matt's hair is a disaster. We chat for a little bit, and finally she leaves without hassling us further.

"So," he says, weaving his fingers through mine. "What happened between you and Ben?"

The sound of a humming garbage disposal carries up from downstairs. It makes me feel like even when we're alone, we're not. "Ben got pissed at me," I admit.

I feel his eyes on me, but I don't turn toward him. "I gathered that, but what actually happened?"

Hoping to dodge the question, I muse, "We used to be so close, but we just aren't anymore." I sigh, glad for the chance to talk to someone about this.

Matt adjusts his fingers still linked with mine, the moisture from his skin making his hand feel hot. "You still haven't said why he's mad."

"It's probably a few things. I think he's upset that we've changed," I say, pausing. Pulling a full breath into my lungs, I spit out the words before I change my mind. "And he's mad because I'm into guys."

Letting out a low whistle, Matt squeezes my hand. "I'm sorry, man." A moment passes, stillness overwhelming the air between us. "I thought you weren't going to tell him."

"I *didn't* tell him."

"Um… how did he find out, then?" When I don't respond, his voice becomes more insistent. "How did he find out?"

Matt sounds worried. But about what? Does he think Ben caught me with some other guy? "Are you jealous?" I ask, disbelief flitting through my words.

Matt pulls his hand away. "Don't screw with me, Jackson."

"Whoa, it was nothing like… whatever it is you're thinking."

"What was it, then?"

I bite my lip. "I'd rather not say."

Crossing his arms, he shifts over a little bit. Jesus, he can be touchy. He and Ben should start a club. I run my hand lightly along his leg, but he pulls away. "For fuck's sake, Matt, he walked in on me jerking off, all right?"

His expression softens, but only a little. "Everyone jerks off, it doesn't make you gay."

"It does if gay porn is involved."

His laugh obliterates the uneasiness between us. "That's so awesome."

"No, it sucked," I say, glaring at him. "He just stared at me like he couldn't figure out up from down."

"Clearly it was up." Matt snickers.

"That's not funny."

He smiles like he disagrees, but he has enough sense not to say so.

"Um," I say, "I'm going to head home now."

"Sure." Matt doesn't sound irritated, even though he's probably horny as hell. In a way I'm kind of glad his mom showed up, because it prevented me from having to decide if I was going to reciprocate. The idea of doing that really turns me on, but it's also the scariest thing I can imagine. Receiving is one thing, but taking the active role is different. Way different.

I wave to Matt's mom on the way out, convinced that my guilty expression will give me away, but she just smiles and says goodbye.

As I ride homeward, I allow myself to think what I was holding back in his room. Him acting all suspicious or jealous or whatever, it made me feel like he really cared. In the moment, it was annoying and a little unsettling, but I like that he feels possessive about me.

If I thought *he* was seeing some other guy, I would probably deck them both. I might not hit Matt as hard as the other guy though. It would be a shame to damage such a nice face.

Finally passing the city limits, I twist down with my right wrist, and the bike buzzes forward. The sun catches me in the eyes as I take a long curve in the road. With a few hours left in the day, I should really try to patch things up between Ben and me. He is my brother after all. My thoughts wander to our fight earlier. Two hours ago seems so far away, almost like it happened to someone else. As much as I don't want to think about what he said, it's the things he didn't say that actually hurt.

Dad's truck is gone when I get home, which means that I can talk to Ben without interruption. Dragging myself up the stairs, I push open my door and drop face down onto the bed. Ben's probably out running or something. My eyes closing, I let the moments from the day replay in my head. My body reacting so strongly to that magazine, Ben bursting in on me, and Matt. Just… Matt. I don't even know where to start with that.

Propping myself up on my elbows, I realize that something is off. All of Ben's shit is gone. His bag, his clothes, even the pillow I tossed him that first night isn't here. Trepidation creeps down my spine. I hope he didn't do anything stupid. Dad's truck was gone. Did Ben tell him what he saw? Did Dad agree he didn't have to live here with a homo and then took him to the airport? I hope I'm just being paranoid.

Chest thudding, I dash out of my room but catch myself at the top of the stairs. The door to the spare bedroom is shut, but earlier today it was ajar. I try the handle. It's locked, but I hear movement behind the door.

Rapping a knuckle on the wood, I call softly, "Ben?"

The sound of cheap metal clinking precedes the door opening.

He's trying to block the door with his body, but I can see all his stuff shoved into the corner. The walls aren't even painted yet, and dust still covers the floor. "What do you want?" he asks.

"What are you doing?"

"I'm not going to sleep in a bed where you're jerking off all the time," he spits. "That's fucking gross."

Pressure builds in the back of my throat, and I drop my eyes. "That's the stupidest thing I've ever heard. You should just say what you mean. You won't sleep in my room anymore because I..." The words get caught on something on their way out, but I force them free. "Because I like guys," I finish quietly.

"I meant what I said," he counters. "This is what you wanted anyway, to have your own room. And your own life."

The hurt building inside from hearing his lies and his attempt to cover them morphs into anger. So many times I've held back with him and said what he wanted to hear instead of what I really thought. But not now. "You know what, Ben? When you first got here, I thought you were the same as when we were kids, but I was wrong. You're definitely still a coward, but you're an asshole now too." I hope he can hear every bit of my churning rage.

He flinches like I've just hit him. In return, his tone is pure ice when he speaks. "Go fuck yourself, Jackson. I know you're good at that. Just remember to lock the door next time and save me having to see it."

"Fuck you!" I scream, my face red with fury. I want to slam the door in his face, but I'm on the wrong side for that. Instead I shift weight to my back foot, readying myself to lunge at him. Apparently he anticipates that, because his flat palm slams into my chest, driving me back. A moment later the door flies closed with the force of an avalanche, the shrieking protest of the breaking trim boards almost being swallowed up by the bang of the door.

"Argh!" I shout my rage, kicking the wall as hard as I can. My foot goes through, and the impact knocks a picture frame off the wall. It falls and the glass shatters when it hits the floor. Chest heaving, I stare at the pile of broken glass. It's a photo from years ago of the four of us. Mom, Dad, Ben, and me.

Dislodging my foot from the wall, I make it down the stairs and through the front door before I double over and collapse on the front lawn. Tears slide down my face. Arms clutched around my stomach, I rock back and forth on my side.

It shouldn't be a surprise. It was his fault we split up in the first place, all those years ago. I was stupid to think he'd have changed, or that he'd want to fix things. To think he would want to be the brother I desperately need. Pushing down the pressure building in my throat, I force myself to breathe normally.

The weight of the world. I always thought that was a stupid expression. I think it's based on the Greek god Atlas. Or was he a Titan? My knowledge of fictional entities doesn't extend much beyond Star Trek. Regardless, the world feels pretty goddamn heavy right now.

I don't know how long I've been staring at my feet, but only now do I notice my shoe. Ben's shoe, actually. The trip through the wall tore up a section of leather from the side, the stitches now hanging loosely from a two-inch wide strip. A hoarse laugh erupts from me in stilted bursts. Ben is going to be so mad. It gets easier to laugh as I continue, imagining his face and him throwing a fit. I'm laughing so hard now that I've actually started to cry again.

Finally sitting up, I wipe the moisture from my face and the plaster dust from my shoe. Ben's shoe, whatever. Taking a deep breath, I start toward the woods. Walking through the trees blunts what's left of my anger, and by the time I reach the giant stone at the very back corner of our property, it's possible to think clearly again. Lying back on the flat gray surface, I rest my head on the palms of my hands. All the years that Ben wasn't here, I would come here to sort through stuff without him. Ironically, he's now the problem I'm trying to figure out.

I wish I could make myself not care about what Ben thinks. I shouldn't have said what I did earlier, but I don't think it was untrue either. Ben *is* being an asshole, and he can be pretty spineless at times, but damn it he's my brother. At the last thought, longing flares in my chest.

Picking up a fallen stick from the stone's surface, I turn it over in my hand. When did he turn from mild-mannered Benny into angsty, spiteful Ben? What I said was mean, but at least it was founded on what's actually going on between us. He was just trying to be hurtful. And it was. I toss the stick into the weeds and get up to head to the house. Today I'm going to take the long way back.

Dad's truck is in the driveway when I traipse back into the yard through the darkness. Taking a deep breath, I let myself through the screen door. It slams behind me, sounding louder than normal. Dad is sitting at the kitchen table sipping a beer, and his eyes rise slowly from the table to my face. Yeah, he knows about the trim and the wall. His gaze dissects my expression with the ease that only a parent of almost two decades can achieve. Even if he didn't already know that something had gone down between Ben and me, he would have read it off my face just now. I'm not as painfully obvious as Ben, but Dad can still figure me out.

"Follow me, son." He waits until I nod before standing and ascending the stairs. I venture a glance at his beer left half full on the table. Downing the rest would make the next few minutes go a little smoother. If only I could ever get away with something like that. "Jackson," Dad calls down the stairs. His tone doesn't leave any room for interpretation. *Get up here, now.*

He's standing at the top of the stairs in a spot where he can survey the damage on both the door and the wall. Light spills into the hall from the spare bedroom where Ben is silhouetted in the doorframe.

Dad runs a hand across his forehead, massaging the skin above his eyebrows. Not quite as harsh as when he summoned me up the stairs, he says, "Either of you want to tell me what the hell happened here?"

A second passes. "He did it," our voices overlap each other, the nearly identical pitch making us sound like those musicians who record their own voice on multiple tracks of a single song. Ben and I meet eyes. Why is he glaring? He busted the trim on the door, no question about that. I know I'm the one who kicked the hole in the wall, but he was trying to piss me off the fastest way he could, so is it really my fault if I took out my Ben-induced rage on the wall?

"Fine," Dad says with a sigh that sounds more pissed off than resigned. "If you won't tell me, then you boys will just have to sort this out on your own." Jabbing a finger at the damage, he says, "This needs to be fixed up by this weekend. Jackson, you know how to do the work. I don't care who does what, but it gets done and it looks like new." He surveys the two of us like we're juvenile delinquents. "Understood?"

"Yeah," I mumble. Ben nods.

"Good," Dad says. His voice losing some of its gravity, he continues, "I'm always available to talk, and that goes for both of you." He looks at me and then at Ben. "But if you're going to keep things between yourselves, take it outside the next time you work out your issues, and for God's sake, please don't break any bones."

Something strikes me about what he's saying. I lift my eyes to Ben. Does he remember too? Dad told us this before, years ago. His message has changed slightly though – last time he forbade us from even drawing blood, but we were a lot younger then.

"Understood?" he asks, his voice sharp. He's serious and he wants us to know it.

"Yes," I say.

"Clear," Ben says.

Dad gives us a last look before retreating down the stairs. Ben seems like he wants to say something, but then he just turns back into the spare room, closing the door quietly behind him.

Chapter Nineteen

Jackson

For the first time in a while, I can stretch my arms and legs out to the edges of the mattress. The sheets are cool against my skin, but it's not the same refreshing welcome that they always used to bring. It bugged me that first night we both slept here, but after that I realized I actually liked the warmth escaping from Ben sleeping next to me. Because I knew he was there. Without stimuli from light or sound – even completely unconscious – it let me sense his presence all through the night. I doubt he felt the same way, but as much as he pisses me off, it felt good to have him close.

I'm still mad at him, though it's hard to decide what I'm most upset about. It irks me all the more that he's the reason it's taking so long to fall asleep tonight. What gives him the right to swing into my life after all this time and start tossing shit around? I roll onto my back and shove a pillow under my knees. I think it's better for the spine or something.

The next morning, the fog in the bathroom is already fading by the time I roll out of bed to take my shower. Ben has already been in here. The realization slowly hits my groggy brain that he probably got up early to do that. I take a moment to allow the exasperation to roll through me, filling every cell inside me from my toes to the tips of my disheveled hair. He's taking this way too far. I'm still Jackson. Plain old Jackson. Why doesn't he see that?

Stepping into the shower, I force the handle hard over to hot. With one hand on the glass, I let my head hang. Water filters through my hair, dragging it down into watery strands. Like the branches of the weeping willows outside, the curtain of my hair hangs around me, a barrier to the world outside.

The water borders on searing, and everywhere it lands, my skin turns bright red. Blood rises to the surface, and the veins become fiercely defined on my arms. Let the water scorch, let it scald. Let it take away all the bad things, please, just burn them from my flesh. Take it all away until nothing is left.

The next few days are quiet. Ben does his own thing, and I do mine. Now that we're not slaving away for Dad anymore, we have a lot more time, which just gives me more hours to think about everything that I want to ignore. Dad seems to recognize that things are messed up between us, but he doesn't say anything about it. It's no surprise that he figured it out, because the tension between Ben and me is so thick you could cut it up and serve it as some kind of cake. Calorie free but certain to cause indigestion.

I'm reading on my bed when my phone vibrates in my pocket. It's a text from Matt.

Hey I was thinking of stopping by for a few hours today… your dad is working, right?

Moisture breaks out on my palm. I glance out the window. *Um I don't think that's a good idea.*

Did I do something wrong?

No. I'd just rather hang out this weekend.

Ok, you'll text me?

Yeah.

I'm not putting him off. Really. I just don't want Ben getting any more ideas.

Chapter Twenty

Jackson

A knocking on my door wakes me up Saturday morning. I roll over, blinking the sleep out of my eyes. More knocking. Christ. "What?" The word comes out hoarse and barely loud enough to carry through the door.

"Are you decent?"

"Come in." The door opens slowly. Really slowly. "A little paranoid, don't you think?"

Ben is wearing a stained white t-shirt and a ratty pair of cutoff shorts that look suspiciously like the ones I haven't seen in a few weeks. "Do you blame me?"

Dropping my head onto the pillow, I roll my eyes at the ceiling but ignore his question. "You look pretty flashy. You have a date?"

"Screw you. I'm wearing this so I don't mess up my good clothes while we fix the hole *you* kicked in the wall."

"Oh yeah, that." I wrap the covers around me a little tighter. The air is cool this morning.

He glares. "Yeah, *that*. Now get up."

"I need to shower." I stretch my arms out of the blankets and over my head.

His eyes jump first to the window before hitting me with their intensity. "You don't need to shower. I want to get this done."

I curl back into the blankets. "Damn it, Ben, then do it yourself."

He crosses his arms. "I don't know how to fix drywall, you do. And it's your own stupid fault, anyway."

I roll over, facing away from him. When he doesn't say anything, I think he might actually let me sleep longer, but the next second, the blankets are flying off me. "What the hell, Ben!"

He smiles remorselessly, tossing the ball of sheets and my comforter into the far corner of the room. "Now get up, you lazy bum." He throws the pair of shorts at me that I wore yesterday.

I kick him out of my room so I can get changed, but before long he comes knocking again. Might as well get the stupid project done sooner rather than later.

"So how do we patch this thing?" he asks, squatting beside me in front of the busted wall.

"We have to cut back to the studs. Here, and here." I draw imaginary lines with my finger on the wall. Feeling around the edges of the hole, I start ripping out chunks of drywall until the gap is big enough for me to see where the studs are.

"You have the knife?" I ask. He grunts and digs in the toolbox behind him, handing me the bright green utility knife a moment later. Leveling the long metal drywall square against the floor, I line it up with the center of the stud as best as I can. "All right, now hold the square."

His hands reach across mine to press the metal T-square against the wall. Starting at the floor, I drag the knife blade up the wall, flush against the square. "Careful of your fingers," I breathe, maintaining pressure on the blade. I feel his eyes on me for a long second before his grip on the square moves away from the knife's progress.

We repeat the same procedure for the opposite side and finally the top of the hole. Delivering a swift strike with the side of my fist, the pieces snap off, leaving a relatively square hole, cut so the studs are partly exposed. I glance at Ben and nod. "That'll work."

His fingers are turning white from holding the new piece tight against the studs while I drill in the screws. After we tighten it down, a bit of a gap remains around the top, but it's nothing that can't be fixed with a bit of mud and sanding.

"Good work," I tell Ben.

He holds his breath for a moment. "Yeah, you too."

Setting the drill on the floor between us, I lean back against the opposite wall. "Why are you in such a rush today anyway?"

"Um," he hesitates. "I'm actually going to hang out with Katie tonight."

I raise an eyebrow. "This isn't going to take that long." As an afterthought, I add, "I didn't know you guys had become friends."

He averts his gaze, absently spinning the utility knife in a circle on the floor with his outstretched finger. "This is the first time we're hanging out. Outside of work, that is."

"Cool."

He opens his mouth a fraction of an inch, like he wants to ask something. After a pause, he says, "How about you, any plans to spend time with… anyone?"

He was going to ask if I'm seeing Matt today. "Uh no, not yet." Behind him, the sun is partway up the sky, visible through the hallway window.

"Maybe Matt is free," he suggests. "I haven't seen him around here in a while."

I grit my teeth. "Maybe you could mind your own fucking business." I regret the words as soon as they're out. I didn't mean to freak out on him, but he's made it clear that he doesn't approve of me, so why does he even bring it up?

Ben bites his lower lip, his expression tinged with resignation. "I'm going to go," he says.

"You're just going to leave me to finish all this?" I snap, tossing the T-square onto the floor so it clatters against the hardwood.

"You made your point. I don't think you really want me here anyway," he says softly, flashing me a last look before disappearing into his room. Waiting until the door is safely closed, I pull out my phone. No new messages. About time to create one of my own, I think. *You free today?*

I haven't even got the phone back in my pocket before the screen lights up.

Hey you, sure am! When do you want to meet up?

In like an hour? What do you want to do?

Parents are home all day, but we can find something to do. Meet at my house?

I feel like a dork, but I can't help but smile while I tap out my reply. *See you then.* I still need to finish mudding and sanding this, so maybe two hours is more realistic. If I make Ben paint it later tonight, it will save me some time.

Chapter Twenty-one

Jackson

After spending the afternoon at Matt's house, engaged in G-rated activities because of his parents downstairs, I'm ready for a quiet evening. Walking up the stairs to my room feels like it takes longer than normal. Maybe it's because I'm not sure what I'm going to find at the top. A trio of empty rooms, and nothing to pass the time but hours on my bed reading?

A thin stream of light is dripping out from underneath the door to Ben's room. Ear to the door, I hold my breath and listen. He's on the phone, but I have to strain to hear his words. Is he talking to our mom? I haven't spoken with her in a long time. She used to call a lot, way more than Ben did, but about five years ago, that changed.

She tried to get back custody of me from Dad. At first, the idea was tempting – a chance to live with Ben again – even if it meant leaving my life here behind. Except when Dad found out, he sat me down and told me about the divorce. About how he wanted to keep working on the marriage, but Mom refused to even go to counseling. He said he begged her to at least stay in the area, but she moved away to California anyway, taking Ben with her. *Ben*. Her first choice.

If she hadn't wanted me when she left, why did she want me then?

The next time she called, I refused to talk to her. And the next time, and the time after that. Eventually she stopped calling, and she dropped the pursuit of custody.

Behind the door, their conversation continues. Unable to distinguish the individual words, I listen instead to the sound of my brother's voice as they talk. Mostly it's soft, deferential, but at times adamant. I've made a point to not need anything from either of them over the years. They left me, not the other way around. But overhearing their conversation makes me wonder what it would be like to have a relationship with my mom again.

Finally Ben's voice says a muffled goodbye. After he hangs up, I hear movement inside the room, but it's hushed. What's he doing? Brandishing the knuckle of my index finger, I tap a few times on the door.

The noises are abruptly silenced. "What?"

"Can I come in?"

"If you want."

Turning the handle just until the latch disengages, I apply precisely enough pressure for the door to swing ajar. Not even a light breeze wafting it open could be subtler. In the center of the room is the bed that used to be in this room before we started redoing it. The air, heavy with the scent of wet latex paint, drags my attention away from Ben's sleeping accommodations. The dull gray of the drywall is now a soft blue, at least on the wall across from me – the others are still unpainted. Ben just watches me. Paint roller in hand, he dips it into the tray on the floor and turns away from me, wheeling it up the wall.

"When did you move the bed in here?"

"Dad helped me move it up from the basement a few days ago." From his voice I can tell he doesn't want to be talking to me.

"Oh." Taking tentative steps into the room, I sit on the corner of his bed and slip my hands under my thighs.

His roller is running low on paint, but he keeps pushing it up and down the wall. "Did you want something?"

I flinch. "I…uh…thought we could talk."

Finally turning away from the wall, he locks eyes with me. "What do you want to talk about?" He doesn't make any move toward the paint tray.

His dense stare is hard to withstand, but I don't let myself look away. "I thought we could talk about the… um, gay thing."

"What about it?" His tone is like cold steel, cutting and chilling all at once.

"Why does it bother you so much? I'm still me. Nothing has

144

changed." I should give him a chance to respond, but I deserve to get this out. "What does it matter if I'd rather be with a girl or a guy? I'm still your brother. Jesus, Ben, I can't believe *this* is what you can't take. After years of being separated, you'd think you'd be happy being back together again, but you won't even brush your teeth next to me anymore." Wetness is slowly gathering in my eyes as I speak, but I've said what I need to say. Almost. My voice is quiet. "Why are you doing this?"

He's always been so easy to read, but right now I'm not sure what I'm seeing. His expression is conflicted, but with what? When he speaks, his words come slowly, but they're determined and purposeful. "You clearly don't know the first thing about what I can or can't take. Why don't you get it?"

"Help me understand. Help me get it." I stand up and grab a regular paintbrush off the floor. "Here, I'll help you paint. Just you and me." Raising my eyebrows a quarter of an inch, I smile tentatively.

There's that torn look again, but it's clearer to see what he's feeling now. It's pain. "I don't want your help."

Dipping my brush into the tray, I say, "Well, I'm going to help anyway." Aiming the brush for the corner where his roller can't reach, I start up the wall.

A clunk beside me seizes my attention. He's dropped the roller onto the tray. "You want to paint so damn bad," he says, "then you can do it yourself." Without another word, he walks out, leaving me alone with the paint. I stare after him – at the door really – until long after the sounds of him tromping down the stairs have faded into the old bones of the house.

The faintest sound of a drip murmurs up from the floor. I glance down. A single round dot of blue paint has fallen from the brush in my hand. Forcing out the stagnant air in my chest, I crouch and sweep up the drop with the side of my thumb.

Why is it so hard for us to figure this out? I know Ben well enough to understand that he's having a tough time now too, but I can't do *everything*. He has to take some responsibility in this. And him being such a colossal dick about the sexuality thing isn't something I can ignore.

The blue on my thumb is still wet. Wiping it in a long streak on an unpainted part of the wall, I glance down at the tray and dip my brush into the viscous blue. Taking the brush to the wall, I let it glide in light strokes as I scrawl a line of cursive. I've always had great penmanship – much better than Ben's. Stepping back, I examine my work with satisfaction. I think it gets the point across. *Fuck you, Ben, go home.*

Forcing my eyes away, I scan the rest of the room. It would be a mess, but there isn't enough stuff here to qualify. His travel bag and a bunch of dirty clothes are piled at the foot of the bed, which itself looks like a herd of bulls tore through it. It's a full bed just like mine. I must have been off with Matt when he and Dad moved it back in here.

Squatting in front of his bag, I unzip it and peek inside. I dig through more clothes that – from the smell of them at least – are dirty as well. A can of Axe body spray clunks against my wrist as I push a nest of socks out of the way. How did I ever think Ben was anything but hopelessly straight?

My breath stops in my throat when I catch sight of the next thing. It's the picture from the hallway, the one that fell and broke when I kicked the hole in the wall. The four of us are there, all smiling. It's in a new frame though. It has to be, because I remember the glass shattering on the original.

The frame slipping from my slackened fingers, I zip the bag back up so fast that the zipper jams and I have to back it up and try again. I shouldn't have looked, but now that I have, I can't un-see that picture or what it means. I can't imagine how hard it was to give up his summer to come live with Dad and me. Like, *really* hard.

Even that nagging voice inside me, whispering that it was Ben's fault anyway, his choice to leave, can't shake the conviction that this has been one tough summer for my brother. My eyes flit around the room. It's just so… empty. The only thing of note is the message I've scrawled on the wall for him. Guilt hits me in the gut so hard I almost double over. I can't let him see it.

Dried smears of blue cover my hands and arms when I finally finish. I didn't stop with covering the anathema I'd inscribed onto the wall, but instead continued until the whole room was painted. Slipping the brush, roller, and tray into a plastic bag so I don't have to clean them tonight, I scan the room one last time before stepping into the hallway.

Not bothering to wash the paint off, I collapse into my bed and switch off the light. Eyes adjusting to the moonlight navigating past the trees to splash through the window, I curl up on my side and wrap my arms around a ball of blankets. They smell like me, but there's an unidentifiable hint of something else that makes me know part of Ben is still in them as well, from all those nights he slept here with me. I inhale again, deeper this time, savoring the tiniest portion of the scent that is uniquely Ben.

Benny's fluffy tuft of blond hair catches the sun, making it look almost white. He's next to me at the kitchen counter. We're sitting on the tall chairs, eating popsicles. Mom is drying dishes. Dad is mowing the lawn in the backyard. I know because I can hear the loud noise through the open window. Sometimes the sound gets quieter but then it always gets louder again.

When Benny turns to me and smiles, I point at his face with my popsicle and laugh. "Your lips are all blue, Benny."

"Are not," he says and makes a pouty face. "Don't make fun of me."

I can't stop laughing, so I try to cover my mouth instead. "Are too."

His eyes are wide. "Are my lips blue, Mom? Jacks says they're blue."

Mom stands up straight and crosses her arms. The sound of her laugh fills the whole room, making it feel warm. Not warm like it is outside, but warm like everything feels safe and happy. "They are a little blue, honey."

He sets his popsicle on the counter and lowers himself onto the floor. His shorts pull up as his bottom slides off the stool.

"Benny, where are you going?"

He glares at me. "None of your business." His voice is whiny.

Popsicle in hand, I follow him out of the kitchen and to the bathroom. He leans over the counter and turns on the water, trying to wash the blue off his face. Benny is so funny about being dirty or messy. I don't know why he doesn't like it. Maybe it would help if he were messy more often. Then he wouldn't be so scared of it. I grin.

He's so busy cleaning his face that he doesn't notice me behind him. As fast as I can, I pull the collar of his shirt out to make a gap around his neck, and I shove my dripping popsicle down his back. I watch with glee what happens next. He arches his back and screams. He twists, his hand reaching around in his shirt. He can't get a hold of it. A wet spot forms in the middle of his back where the frozen treat is stuck. He does a silly little dance in a circle, wailing the whole time. I laugh and laugh until I can hardly breathe.

A second later, a melted red blob falls out of his shirt onto the floor. Benny's eyes fill with a mixture of tears and fury. "I hate you,

Jacks!" he screams through his sobs.

Then I run. I'm already out of breath from laughing so much, but I'm not worried. I'm quicker than Benny. Especially when he's upset.

Mom tries to catch me when I sprint past her in the hallway, but I duck and her fingers miss me. Now Benny is right behind me. I could stay away from him if we were outdoors, but there are too many obstacles in here. He chases me around the living room. Next to the couch he catches me by the hair and tackles me.

"I hate you, Jacks!" he shrieks again. I try to roll away but he won't let go, so we move together. We roll right into an end table. I'm on my back, and Benny is on top. Above him, the lamp rocks from side to side. It's going to fall. It's going to fall on Benny. He's going to get hurt. *My Benny.*

The lamp tips off the edge of the table, and I throw him off me as hard as I can. A second later, it hits me and the bulb bursts in a flash of light.

I wake up pulling a deep breath into my lungs. Cycling through the rest of the memory, I put together how it ended that day. After the lamp broke, Mom quickly checked to make sure we were both okay before running to get Dad. That's when he gave us the talk about sorting things out, as long as there was no blood. In retrospect, I think we were a little young for that particular message.

Dad asked me afterward why I'd done it, especially considering that I knew perfectly well how fast Benny got upset about things. I didn't have an answer at the time, but now I think I did it *because* he got upset so easily. It was a little game that I would always win. How fast can I make Benny cry? It makes me feel shitty thinking about it, but there's nothing I can do about it now. What bothers me the most is that I can't shake the feeling that I'm still hurting him. It's not like it doesn't go both ways, though. He has said some pretty hurtful shit, and what he hasn't said is worse.

I stretch my arm across the open space next to me, to where Ben slept while we shared this space. It's empty here without him. Drawing in another deep breath, I roll over to his side of the bed. Wrapping the covers around myself like a cocoon, I clench my teeth to stifle the ache inside.

Chapter Twenty-two

Ben

The house is steeped in darkness when I get home, so I'm careful making my way up the stairs. Stopping first at the bathroom, I brush my teeth and take a piss before tiptoeing across the creaking hardwood to my room. Brushing my hand up the wall, I trip the switch about halfway up and the space is bathed in light.

The blue color I picked out for the room glistens from every wall. Running my eyes along the seams between the walls and the ceiling and around the windows, I realize how meticulous the work was.

Why the hell did he paint my whole room? Is it really cold, aloof Jackson that did this? Part of him is clearly reaching out for connection, but if he's going to ignore or insult me the majority of my time here, then I don't want whatever he's selling.

I'm not sure if it's because he painted my room – doing a damn good job of it at that – or just because it's sucked so much hardly spending even ten minutes with him in the last few weeks, but it strikes me how much I miss him right now.

Turning the light back off, I strip down to my boxers and climb into bed. Ignoring the memories of Jackson, I focus on the last few hours. Katie lives on a few acres outside of town, just like Dad and Jackson. Between the sun plodding across the sky and the light breeze, the evening felt perfect. Then she suggested we go for a walk, and I realized how much better it could get. The stalks of the wild grasses bending into the wind alongside the path, she took me all the way out to the edge of their property. Unlike everywhere else growing corn or wheat or something else equally boring, they just let the wild grasses grow on their land.

I kept expecting something to happen. I guess in a way it did. We just… talked. She told me about growing up in rural Minnesota and about her first boyfriend. Her fingers sliding lazily along a blade of grass, she told me about her love for all things that grow. Then she asked about me, and whatever she asked, I answered. My life in L.A. with Mom came out first, but quickly I found myself telling her about living with Dad and Jackson. Getting to know the Dad I'd forgotten about, and the brother who'd forgotten about me. Unreachable Jackson, my other half, living a life I know almost nothing about.

It didn't feel right to share what I'd most recently learned about Jackson, but I did share the way he made me feel. Somewhere between explaining my feelings of rejection and the building anger becoming ever harder to ignore, I felt her hand slip into mine.

Darkness around me once more, I bite down on my cheek, working through the emotions that the memory conjures up within me. Katie is beautiful, smart, and she's into me. It's not that I'm not interested, because I definitely am. Or was, I guess. I don't know. When she touched me, I got the sudden feeling that I wasn't paying attention to the right things. To the thing that really mattered. Like I was mowing the lawn while the house burned down behind me.

My unease grows as I remember what happened next. Those moments of hesitation, my eyes reluctantly rising to hers. The look in my face that she must have interpreted as nervousness. For a few seconds, she tried to take me to somewhere else. Somewhere far away from everything dragging me down. She tasted like lavender and the ocean, but it was wrong. All wrong. I shouldn't have been there at all. I should have been here, accepting my brother's help to paint my room.

Chapter Twenty-three

Ben

My knees digging into the moist dirt, my hands are wrapped around the supports of one of the tables in the greenhouse. The whole goddamn thing collapsed while I was watering this morning. It took me a half hour to get all the plants off it before I could even try to start fixing the table itself. Now I'm trying to reattach the supports from underneath, but it's messy work.

Dad wasn't lying when he said I wouldn't have to work for him all summer, but after so many days stuck at home with only Jackson and the daily strain between us, I asked Dad if I could start coming to work with him. He was more than happy to oblige, and I'm even getting paid now, so that's a plus. If I'm completely honest with myself, deciding to continue working for Dad isn't all about Jackson. I actually like getting into the dirt and feeling like I'm taking care of something alive. Being able to fill my days this way and get some money on the side are merely perks.

I've just shoved the steel pole into the slot and tightened the lock nut when a familiar voice calls out from behind me. "Hard at work, it looks like." Her usual warmth is lacking, and her voice sounds tired.

Glancing back at her, I give a nod. "Morning, Cherie," I say, just starting to wipe my hands on my pants when she pulls me into a hug that I have no say in. Arms pressed to my sides, she squeezes me tightly. She's apparently unconcerned with how dirty I am, even though she's wearing white pants and a peach blouse.

Finally she lets go. "It's good to see you, Ben."

My eyes pause at the new smudges of dirt on her top. "How are the snapdragons doing?"

Smiling, the wrinkles in her cheeks move aside to make room for her dimples. "They're wonderful."

"And how are *you* doing?"

"I'm still alive and on my feet," she says. "So it could be worse. My doctor is amazed I'm still able to move around, but I think he wrote me off ages ago, so I don't pay much attention to what surprises him anymore."

I can't believe she's sharing this with me. I hold my breath to ward away my own emotions and reach out to give her shoulder a squeeze. My hand leaves more dirt on her. "I'm so sorry, Cherie. Is there anything I can do?"

Waving her hand dismissively, she says, "Not really–" She stops, seeming to reconsider. "You know, my raspberries are quite overrun. Would you like to stop by later today to help?"

I can feel my stomach tighten and my face grow warm. "Like, over to your house?" My second thought is surprise that she can still do garden work. Conversely, maybe she *can't* and that's why she wants help.

Cherie is watching me intently. "I bake the best cookies, so you won't go hungry." Her expression makes it really hard to say no – everything from the wrinkles lining her face to the shimmering eyes that defy her age. "I could really use the help."

"Um, sure." I think it's pointless to be weeding a garden if you're weeks or months from death, but if that's what Cherie wants, she's going to have the best damn raspberry patch in town.

Her mouth breaks into a wide smile. "How about this afternoon?"

"I'll have to run it past Dad, but I think it'll be fine. Two o'clock?"

"Perfect." She smiles one last time before doddering unstably toward the front. I follow her at a distance to make sure she makes it. I agree with that doctor of hers – it's a wonder she's still mobile.

"Hey you," Katie's silky sweet voice calls across the parking lot. I'm grinning before I've even turned around.

"You're late."

Shrinking the distance between us, she stops a few feet from me with raised eyebrows. "You are a rude boy."

"Nope, not that," I say with a smile. I've backed off ever since that first and only night we kissed, but sometimes it's hard not to flirt.

Rolling her eyes, she turns back toward the greenhouse. "You're such a guy, Ben."

"What's that supposed to mean?" I follow her, suspicious that my voice sounds whiny.

"You know what I mean. So what's on the agenda for today?"

"Well..." I say, getting a dirty look thrown my way. "Okay, okay." I finally ditch my grin. "I think we should check all the tables in the greenhouse to make sure they won't collapse."

She stops, tilting her head to the side. "You're serious?"

"Completely. One went down earlier while I was watering. I figure we should make sure the rest aren't at risk."

Snickering, she resumes walking. "So that's why you're covered in dirt?"

An hour later and we've checked the supports on almost all the tables – indeed finding a few that needed tightening – when Katie asks, "So are you going to Austin's Fourth party this Friday?"

"Fourth party?"

"You know, the Fourth of July."

"Oh, right." That's two days from now. It's been exactly six weeks since I got on the plane that brought me from L.A. Only six weeks? Already six weeks? I'm not sure which is more accurate.

"So you *are* going?"

"Um," I say, pulling my gaze away from the far end of the greenhouse, "I didn't know there was anything happening."

Her eyes narrow. "Jackson didn't tell you?"

"No. Does that surprise you?"

"I guess not."

"Do you think maybe Jackson just doesn't know about this thing on Friday?" I watch Katie to see how she answers, to see how sure she is.

Her expression is sympathetic. "He definitely knows. Pretty much everyone from our graduating class is going."

It's weird to think that besides her and Matt, I haven't met anyone else from their school. It's not like Jackson invites me along whenever he disappears.

"Forget about him. You can't keep letting him get to you," Katie says, resting her hand lightly on the back of my neck. "You can come with me." Our eyes meet, and the pressure on my neck disappears the same moment. "So how about we start teaching you the scientific names of everything," she changes the subject with a grin.

"Yeah, right. It's hard enough to remember all this crap as it is." I sweep my arm toward the numerous rows of pots. She doesn't answer though, and it's by unspoken agreement that we don't talk anymore as we finish tightening the rest of the tables.

Kicking at a rock lying on the sidewalk, I watch it bounce along before it skids off into the grassy boulevard. I sigh, checking the street signs to make sure I haven't gone too far. Cherie is cool, but how I got roped into this is a mystery to me. Does she normally invite young neighborhood guys over for some manual labor and cookies? Twenty minutes ago I gleefully strode into Dad's office, reminding him that he'd have to let me take his truck. Turns out she only lives like ten blocks away.

Coming to a stop on the sidewalk in front of the house number Dad gave me, I take in the view. The house is a small rambler painted pale green. In the front, the lawn is full of flowerbeds, exquisitely tended into flowing washes of color. Reds, violets, yellows, floating in a sea of green. From the beds in front of the house, vines creep up trellises toward a gently sloping roof.

At night this place probably looks like a Thomas Kinkade painting. If it were anyone else's house I would call bullshit, but I can see Cherie actually enjoying creating this. Just like the warmth in her personality, this garden feels authentic, not staged or contrived.

Taking a deep breath, I knock on the door.

However I managed to exchange working in the dirt at Dad's greenhouse for working in the dirt at Cherie's, I'm not really sure. But it's not all that bad, especially because I've more or less given up pretending that I don't enjoy this kind of work. I never would have imagined it, but it's fun to get into the dirt.

Kneeling at the edge of a row of raspberries, I pluck out weed after weed and toss them into the bucket. The first hour was fine, but the sun is starting to get to me. I'm becoming suspicious whether raspberries need weeding at all, because they seem tougher than anything else out here. Although if I consider the rest of her manicured lawn and garden, maybe it makes sense that she wants to abolish every last weed from her yard.

All the while, Cherie has been sitting beside me in a folding chair, but she hasn't really been doing anything besides talking about her late ex-husband. She's also safe from the sun, comfortably basking in the shade provided by an expansive sun hat. What is it with old ladies and wearing white?

As I dispose of a particularly aggressive dandelion for whose taproot I needed the trowel, she catches my hand lightly around the wrist.

"You bite your fingernails," she says.

"I'm trying to stop."

"Hm." She lets go of my hand. "So why don't you?"

I shrug, sitting back on my heels. "I do it whenever I'm nervous. Or hungry. Or bored. So, all the time I guess."

She gives me a long look, like an art dealer would assess a painting that might be a forgery. "If you want something, you can't just wait for it to happen. Life will go on without you."

Is she still talking about my fingernails? I can't really tell. "Um, all right."

She smiles, and I get the feeling she knows a lot more about what's happening around her than she lets on. "Enough staring," she says. "There are more weeds to pull."

I turn back to the raspberries.

Eventually she decides I've worked long enough and ushers me back inside to wash my hands and have a "little snack" with her. Sitting at the kitchen table with a glass of lemonade and a plate of homemade cookies in front of me, I wait for her to take a seat, which is apparently quite the process. She has to brace herself on the table and line up the chair just right before attempting a landing.

I take a polite sip of lemonade. It's too sweet and too sour at the same time. How that's even possible, I'm not sure. Maybe it's a Minnesota thing.

"How is Jackson?" she asks, crossing her legs at the knees.

With no idea where to start, I just sigh, staring at the plate of cookies and horrible lemonade on the table.

"That good, huh?"

"Pretty much. I feel like I don't even know him anymore. Even the most basic parts of him seem to be nothing like I remember." I mull over how far I really want to dig into this with Cherie. She's old, so she might not be able to handle it. "I always believed that Jackson and I were on the same page, but we're just… not."

"What do you mean?"

My voice rises in pitch as I speak, finally getting the opportunity to let out this frustration. "Take this girl at work that I like. I tried to ask Jackson if he was into anyone, only to find out…" I bite my lip, afraid I've said too much.

"Only to find out," Cherie echoes me, raising her eyebrows. "That he went in a different direction."

"Wait, you… know about that?"

Taking a drink of lemonade, she looks at me with blatant understanding. "I always guessed, but what kind of person would I be if I asked whether he liked boys or not? Besides, old ladies like me are supposed to pretend that boys never have sex with other boys."

I drop my eyes, as if that will conceal my blushing. "Everyone seems to see into him so easily. Not that he's gay necessarily, but just understanding him in general. You, Dad, the girl Katie from work, hell even that asshole Matt – no one has a problem. Why am I the only one who can't figure him out?"

"Because you love him the most." Her words come quickly, but I wouldn't have been ready for them if I'd had an hour to prepare.

As I look dumbly at her, she takes another sip of her lemonade in defiance of its repulsive taste. I let her words roll around in my head. "Even if that's true, Jackson definitely doesn't think so."

Cherie's weathered features stare me down. "So why haven't you told him?"

Later that night I ask Dad if I can go out on Friday. He mutes the TV and looks at me until my fingers start to fidget with the cell phone in my pocket. "I don't suppose I can tell you no, but I know what goes on at these parties. Drinking, probably some drugs too."

Should I admit that he's right or just feign innocence? Luckily, he continues talking and saves me from my indecision.

"Being young is about making mistakes, but I just want you to keep a good head on your shoulders. Don't do something that makes you uncomfortable, regardless of what everyone else is doing, and if you need a ride home, feel free to call, no matter how late."

I look up at him, stuffing both hands into my back pockets. "You really wouldn't be mad?"

His tone cools a bit as he says, "I didn't say I wouldn't be mad, but

I can promise you I would be a lot less mad if you called than if you ended up in the ditch or in a police car or the hospital. The key is to not get into trouble in the first place, though."

"Fair enough," I say.

"And that's on Friday, you said?"

"Yeah."

"You and Jackson going together?"

"I don't know."

Dad looks puzzled. "You don't know if you're going together, or you don't know if he's going?"

Swallowing hard, I avert my eyes. "We don't really talk a whole lot these days."

He sighs but doesn't say a word until I look up. "You boys will get through this, I know it."

"Okay, sure." I can't bring myself to tell him I think he's wrong.

Chapter Twenty-four

Ben

Music pounds through the house as I follow in Katie's wake through the crowd. No one looks older than eighteen, and quite a few look a lot younger. I'm surprised that this place hasn't gotten busted already. We'd never get away with a party this loud and blatantly underage back home. But we're also miles out in the country, so maybe it makes sense.

Slipping her fingers into mine, Katie pulls me through a particularly dense clump of guys surrounding the keg. The two guys manning the silver drum run suspicious eyes over me before focusing on Katie. I don't detect any recognition in their expressions, but there's definitely something else there.

The guy with his hand on the tap speaks first. "Hey Baby, what can I get you?"

She flashes him a smile, "A couple beers."

"Sure you don't need just one?" He flicks an irritated look back at me. Shoo fly shoo, it says.

"Definitely two."

Red Solo cups in hand, she guides us back through the mass of bodies to the sliding glass door off the kitchen. Humidity hits us like a wave as we step out onto the deck. Quickly shutting the door behind me, I follow her to the railing overlooking the lake behind the house. It's a bit quieter out here but not much. Apart from two skinny girls sharing a drink on the other side of the deck, we're alone out here. No one else wants to leave the air conditioning inside, and considering how sticky it is out here, I don't blame them.

"It's still early," Katie explains. "Once the fireworks start it's really going to get hopping in here."

"Hopping, huh?" I smirk.

"Careful, punk," she shoots back. "You're a long way from home." I'd be worried that she's actually upset, but I've long since gotten used to her snappy retorts.

When the head on my beer has settled enough that I can drink without fear of getting a foam mustache, I take my first sip. It's cold and refreshing, but it's not as good as the Spotted Cow beer that Dad gave me. Unbidden, Dad's warning on staying out of trouble springs to mind. It's silly, because I'm sure he doesn't care if I have a few beers. At the same time though, I don't want to risk disappointing him. Did Jackson get the same talk as me?

"What are you thinking about?"

"Huh?" I pull myself out of my thoughts. "When do the fireworks start?"

She gives me an incredulous look. "You were thinking about the fireworks?"

"Yeah." I sigh and lean back against the railing, resting on my elbows. The edge of the top rail digs into my lower back, but I don't want to look dumb by changing positions so soon.

"They'll start shortly, I think."

The light from the kitchen spills out onto the deck, silhouetting her face against the darkness. She's beautiful like always. "Thanks for inviting me tonight," I say.

Katie takes a sip of her beer. "I still think it's stupid that Jackson didn't ask you himself."

I look away, the moment broken. It strikes me how much of a real pain in the ass Jackson is. Not only can I not get close to him, somehow I can't get away from him either, not even when I'm trying to have a private minute with Katie.

"Sorry," she says. "I didn't mean to bring him up again."

"How did you know it bothered me?"

"You've got a Jackson look."

I laugh and take a longer swig this time, wanting to speed up the carefree feeling spreading through me. "Oh, do I? You do know we're identical, right?" I tease.

She rolls her eyes and elbows me in the ribs. "I mean, you have a look when you're *thinking* about Jackson. I know that you look like each other, you dork."

"You're sexy when you're trying to insult me." I grin playfully, reveling in the fact that the drink in my hand is already curbing my inhibitions.

Katie is shaking her head when the first firework explodes over the far end of the lake, green and orange flaring into life high in the sky. After just seconds, the glass door to the kitchen flies open and the deck begins to fill as more fireworks go off. In a few minutes, the deck is packed, and Katie and I have been squished into the corner. I take the opportunity to let my arm slide around her waist. She tenses, but only for a moment.

The display continues, painting the celestial canvas of southern Minnesota with vivid pigment, all reflected up from the lake as wavering ghost images of the originals. The display isn't anything like the showy extravagance of the one I see in L.A. every year, but it's still pretty cool, especially since it's over a lake. Without the light of a sprawling city washing out the sky, the colors are certainly more intense. Quality over quantity, I suppose.

I finish my beer before the finale, so when the explosions reach their climax, I have a free hand to pull Katie toward me. "Happy Fourth of July," I whisper, pulling her in. Bursts of color bathe the sky as I kiss her for the first time since the night I left Jackson to paint my room.

When I pull away, she says, "That's not fair."

The crowd around us thins as people migrate back inside the house. "What's not fair?"

"Fireworks aren't fair." She sticks her tongue out at me.

A breeze picks up, giving us some relief from the heat as I shake my head. "No way, they're totally fair. You want another drink?"

"Yes, sir." She salutes me. Apparently I'm not the only one who isn't used to drinking very much.

This time, I'm the one leading the way as we cut back through the kitchen to get to the keg. At the edge of my vision, I glimpse Jackson near the dining room table taking a shot with two other guys. Matt is one of them. I continue toward the keg, wondering when they arrived. Fighting back the flood of frustration, I try to push him out of my mind. I'm having a good time, why bother changing that?

Katie and I get our second round of beers and return to the deck.

It's not as deserted as when we first came out here, but definitely not as busy as during the fireworks. I down half the beer in the first drink, making my Adam's apple bob up and down repeatedly before lowering my cup. In front of us, the lake stretches out like a mirror, harboring a pinpoint of light for every one of the myriad stars spread across the night sky. A moment later, a flash of distant lightning snakes across the blackness just above the horizon, illuminating distant clouds. Maybe the humidity will break tonight after all.

"You saw him, didn't you?"

I wait a full minute before responding. "Yeah."

"You want to go inside?" There's another half to her question, but she doesn't need to say it.

"No. And yes."

She lets out a breath so long I can practically feel her shoulders drooping. "Then you should go."

"I'll be back, I promise," I say as I turn to her, hoping to find something other than disappointment in her face.

"Sure," she says, turning her back to me as she leans against the railing.

Leaving her, I head back inside to find Jackson still standing with Matt and the other guy I don't know. The music thuds, forcing everyone to yell to be heard.

"Hey," I say, joining them.

"Holy shit," the guy next to Matt exclaims, "I didn't know you had a twin, Jackson." He's built, especially in his shoulders, and he's a little taller than Jackson and me.

Across from me, my brother's eyes narrow just a bit. "Surprise, surprise," he says. Matt looks amused.

"That's so crazy," the guy says. "I'm Justin, by the way."

I shake his hand. "Ben. Nice to meet you."

Over the next ten minutes, Jackson does his best to ignore me, but Justin continues to include me in their conversation. Even Matt directs the occasional comment my way, although they're more like snarky quips. I really do hate that guy.

I'm not sure where I'm hoping this will go, especially since the topics begin to center more and more on students in their graduating class that I've never met.

"Oh God," Justin interjects, struck by some sudden recollection. "Did you hear about Stephen Waymire? I always knew that kid was a fag, but I guess he finally admitted it after we graduated."

Matt and Jackson both laugh, but a nervous note skates through it. I lock eyes with Jackson, sensing the unease there. He doesn't look away, and a brief moment of silent communication passes between us.

I feel Matt watching me while Justin goes on about how disgusting he finds fags, oblivious of everything else. Dropping my gaze, I take a quick drink from my Solo cup. I can't imagine how this is making Jackson feel, having to laugh along. My stomach twists as I realize that he probably still thinks I have a problem with his sexuality too.

I look back up at Jackson. He's staring off into space, but anxiety permeates his features. A bitter taste diffuses across the back of my tongue. This has to end. "Jackson," I say, interrupting Justin. My brother's attention snaps onto me. "Can I talk to you for a minute?"

His glare makes me wince, but he lets me take him away from his friends, my hand on his shoulder guiding him toward the door. Once we're outside, he keeps walking away from me.

"Hold up," I say, catching his arm. His bicep tenses beneath my hand. "What do you want?" Jackson demands, yanking his arm away when I don't let go. The muffled bass from the party thumps like an erratic heartbeat.

With everyone either outside or out back, we're completely alone. I open my mouth to tell him to stop being such an asshole, but then I close it and rethink my strategy. I can't afford to let him keep slipping away, and I can't waste any more time. "I'm sick of us fighting. I miss what we used to have."

He hesitates like he wasn't expecting that from me. My eyes dart to his t-shirt and the damp area under his right arm before his voice pulls my attention back. "Then what the hell is going on? Why are you acting like this?" He still sounds pissed off, but I can hear curiosity there too.

"Why am *I* acting like this? Why are you? Fuck, Jackson, we used to be best friends and way more beyond that. You–" My voice catches. More quietly, I press through my hesitation. "You used to… you know, watch out for me. And now? It's like you couldn't care less about anyone but yourself. You just don't give a shit anymore, Jackson, and I have no idea why. You've tried your damndest to keep me out of your life here, and it's working." My chest is tight with emotion, but I need him to hear all of this. "You want to know why I'm pissed all the time, why I moved out of your room, why it hurts to even look at you anymore? It's because you're not the brother I remember. The one who held me through thunderstorms and stuck his neck out for me all those times. Where did he go?" Inside my head, the question I really want to ask confesses itself silently to the night air. *Where did Jacks go?*

Across from me, Jackson shifts his weight from one foot to the other. The porch light behind him makes it hard to see his face clearly, but when he inhales it sounds like his sinuses are wet. Was he trying not to cry?

His voice is clear of emotion when he speaks. "Sorry to tell you, Ben, but he's gone. I'm still your brother, always have been, but things are different now. You might as well forget about the way it used to be between us, because that's in the past."

A rustling in the trees precedes the wind picking up. It's cool and tastes like rain. "I don't believe that. It doesn't have to be that way."

"Maybe, but that's the way it *is*. I'm sorry if you think I've been pushing you away. I'll try to include you more, okay?"

I sigh, feeling like this didn't go at all how I wanted. "Yeah okay, Jackson, thanks."

He frowns, exhaling a breath teeming with frustration. "I'm trying here, all right?"

Except it's not true, because he's still holding back. We might have drifted over the years, but I know myself well enough to recognize the expression he's wearing now. His eyes – sullen on the surface – hold deeper emotion than what I can see. Is he hung up on me discovering he was gay? I was upset at finding out the way I did, but the actual fact of him being into guys doesn't really bother me. He's my twin, and I want him to be happy. If a guy is going to do that for him, I'm all for it.

But does he know that? We never really discussed it, but I figured he wanted it that way, that he wasn't comfortable talking to me about it. Which hurts just like everything else.

"Are you still upset I found out you're gay?"

Jackson's gaze digs into me before another voice slices through the air. "What the fuck?" A guy walks out from the dark side of the house, zipping up his fly. "Long line for the bathroom, so I came out to take a piss, but I guess I got more than I planned on." The guy has wide shoulders and a stupid jock look to him. "I always thought something was off about you, Jackson. Also funny, I didn't know you had a brother. A twin even, looks like. He queer too? I wonder how many other fags in our school were just waiting for graduation to finally come out."

I bristle, anger mixing with alarm. Was he listening the whole time? Not that it matters anyway – I know the damage is already done.

"Go to hell, Tyler." Jackson's words are laced with barely concealed undertones of fear. My face prickles with anxiety.

Tyler chuckles mirthlessly. "Oh I won't, but you probably will." Turning back toward the house, he calls over his shoulder as he swaggers away. "See you boys around."

The moment he's back in the house, Jackson doubles over with his hands on his knees, taking sharp breaths. Squatting next to him, I reach out a hand and rest it on his shoulder. Without warning, his hand whips up with the speed of a striking viper and knocks my arm away. "Fuck you," he says through his teeth.

"Jackson," I plead, regret staining my words.

"Fuck you!" he shouts, jumping to his feet. "This is why I didn't want you to come here, and why I never wanted to let you into my life. I knew it would mess up everything."

I take a step toward him, but he backs away from me, shaking his head. "Just leave me alone." His voice breaks as he runs away across the lawn and into the trees, the sound of his footsteps over twigs and dead leaves quickly fading.

In case the wind and the coolness in the air weren't warning enough, a roll of not-so-distant thunder grumbles around me. Frustration thrums in my chest, accompanying the indecision of whether to follow him or not. Would it help or just make things worse?

Another question leaps into my mind. Is that guy Tyler going to out Jackson to everyone here? Something like that would barely be news back home, but middle-of-nowhere Minnesota is a different story. It's also not lost on me that since I look just like Jackson, it might not be a good idea for me to stick around here much longer either.

Digging my phone out of my pocket, I call Katie as I cross the driveway and come to a stop at the line of trees through which Jackson disappeared.

"Where did you go?" she demands, her voice mingling with the music.

"Sorry, I sort of got caught up in something with Jackson."

"Matt is here with me. Where did you guys go?"

"Um, outside. Can you come out here?"

A barely audible groan of exasperation comes through the phone. "Fine, we'll be right there." The echoed music from the other end disappears as she hangs up.

I didn't mean for them both to come, but maybe it's for the best. I only have to wait a minute before the front door opens. "What the hell, Ben," Matt growls as he gets closer. "You guys just disappeared on us."

"And you left me alone on the balcony for even longer," Katie adds with an irritated stare.

Part of me knows I should be concerned that the only friends I know here – if they can even be called that – are both pissed at me, but just one person is on my mind right now. "We should go home," I say.

A shadow of fear flickers over Matt's face. "What happened?"

"We were talking stuff out, and some guy pissing in the bushes heard at least part of it."

Matt pales. "Oh shit."

"What's going on here?" Katie examines the two of us.

"Nothing," Matt and I say in unison.

All around us, the light patter of isolated raindrops whispers a warning, reiterated only a moment later as lightning streaks through the sky, illuminating the puffy gray masses of clouds overhead. Jerking my head toward the woods, I say, "You should go after him. He's got a few minutes on you, but Jackson doesn't like to run so he probably didn't get far." Matt waits a moment longer before he nods and sprints off into the woods.

Katie crosses her arms. "You want to do some explaining?"

About a hundred feet away, the front door of the house opens and a few guys step out. One of them points at us, and I think it's that guy Tyler. "Yeah, but let's just get out of here, okay?"

Following my gaze, she watches them for a moment. They're not coming toward us, but they're not going back inside either. "Okay," she says. "Come on."

My breathing doesn't come easily again until we pull off the dirt road onto the highway as rain batters against the windshield. Luckily we didn't park in the driveway, so we didn't have any issues leaving. In the driver's seat, Katie adjusts her hands on the steering wheel. "You want to tell me what that was all about?"

I bite my lip, unsure how much I should say. Tyler probably told everyone at that party, so there's no reason not to open up to Katie. I'd rather her hear from me than someone else. "Jackson is…"

"Gay?" she finishes for me.

"You knew?"

She shrugs, slowing down as we take a sloping corner in the road. "I always kind of figured, but I didn't know for sure. So he's getting outed tonight, huh?"

The way she says it hits me hard in the chest, sympathy for him welling up inside me. It's shitty that it had to happen this way, through no choice of his own. It's not fair that he grew up here where it's despised while I grew up thousands of miles away where no one cares. "I assume so," I say, my voice heavy.

As we drive, the passing minutes are defined only by the sound of pouring rain, until finally she says, "You really love him, don't you?"

"Why does everyone keep saying that?" I turn to her, trying to figure out what she means, and why she sounds surprised. "And of course I do. He's my brother."

"Right, right, but it's like…"

"Like what?" I prompt.

"Like it's more than that."

"Um…"

She laughs, waving her hand dismissively. "I totally didn't mean it like that. I meant, most siblings just tolerate each other. Sometimes, they not only tolerate but actually like each other. Yeah, there's family love too, the kind that you know is there somewhere but you never actually feel it unless the person is dying, but that's not what I mean either."

"So what *are* you saying?"

"The way you always think about him, like just now how you're so concerned. I don't know, it's like you really… adore him. I've just never known anyone to feel that way about a brother or sister."

"I'd do anything for him." It's the truth, and I know that without having to think about it.

"Jackson doesn't seem to feel the same way," she points out. The wipers squawk across the windshield as the rain lets up momentarily.

My expression hardens, but she's right. "He's just forgotten. I wish he'd hurry up about remembering, but he's just so goddamn stubborn." I still want him to be my protective Jacks, the one who watches out for me, but what if that's not what he wants? What if it's not what he needs? If anything, tonight I was looking out for *him*.

When Katie pulls up in front of Dad's house, I can feel her eyes on me, but I can't bring myself to look. Whatever she wants from me right now, I'm not in a position to give it. "Thanks for inviting me," I say, still staring out the window past the water running down the glass. "And for driving."

"Sure." She says it with just enough coolness that I know she's mad. If she were any other girl, I'd have to wait, but Katie doesn't hesitate. "I get that you're dealing with a lot right now, but you can't always push me away in favor of your brother." She bites her lip. "I mean, you can, but I'm not going to stick around while you figure your shit out. He's really important to you, and I understand that. But you have to at least act like you want to spend time with me. Even when we're together, you're always thinking about him."

"Okay..." I say quietly.

"Is that all you're going to say?"

"I don't know if I can give you more than that right now." It's not what she wants to hear, but anything else would be a lie. "See you on Monday?" I ask, stepping into the rain.

When she doesn't respond, I shut the door and walk toward the house. Not caring that I'm getting soaked, I watch her drive away. I don't like that I left Jackson in the woods, but there wasn't much of a choice. I try to convince myself that I did the right thing, sending Matt after him. Whatever is going on between them, Matt has a better chance of getting through to him right now than I do. I hate that it's true, but there isn't anything I can do about it.

Inside the house, every light is off except for a solitary bulb above the kitchen sink. Dad must have already gone to bed. Tiptoeing up the stairs, I make a stop by the bathroom to relieve myself before taking a long drink of water from the glass beside the sink. Hands planted on the vanity, I stare into the mirror, wondering at the miracle that there is another person out there who looks almost exactly like me. Except for the freckles smattered on the tops of his cheeks, and a few other tiny things. An inch or two, maybe five pounds, but that's all that separates us. Physically, at least.

A gnawing feeling at the bottom of my stomach drags my attention away from the mirror. My stomach isn't upset from drinking, though. It's because I left Jackson out there in a thunderstorm. I briefly consider calling him to make sure he's all right, but he would never answer, not right now. Concern mingles with regret for having left him, so instead of returning to my room, I go toward his.

I haven't been in here for more than a minute or two since the night I moved all my stuff out, but under the light of his bedside lamp, nothing seems to have changed. On the floor beside my feet is a pair of his colorful boxer briefs, half turned inside out. These ones are gray and pink leopard print. My chest and throat grow tight as I stare at the pair of briefs.

I won't be able to sleep if I'm worrying if he's okay, wherever he is. And if I'm going to stay up waiting, why not do it here? Ditching my jeans and shirt, I lie down on the messy bed, tossing one of Jackson's dirty t-shirts to the floor as I curl up into the blankets. His scent surrounds me, affording me a morsel of comfort where I would otherwise have none.

Acting on an impulse, my fingers reach to turn off the lamp on the nightstand. Blackness immediately descends into every corner, but as my eyes adjust, the weak light distilled through the storm clouds coaxes definition and depth back into my surroundings. Warm and cocooned in Jackson's safe place, I wait. Eventually the apprehension in my chest fades, but still I wait. Time plods onward, although I'm unsure if it's moving of its own accord or is pushed forward only by my steady breathing.

Chapter Twenty-five

Jackson

I don't know how long it's been since I ran. Away from Ben and the party and that asshole Tyler and the incessant beat of the shitty music. Since the first raindrops began to fall.

I'm leaning against a tree, which provides some shelter at least, but my t-shirt was completely soaked after the first few minutes. Alone in the cold and wet darkness, my mind wanders back to an even colder time eight years ago.

It's cold outside, and snowy too. That's why I'm waiting inside. Mom and Dad are loading up the car. They have so many suitcases. Some are blue and some are black. The little one that Mom is carrying is the same one that Benny and I shared when they took us camping two years ago.

Benny is outside helping, all bundled up in his snow pants and coat. He looks like a big, puffy gummy bear. A gummy bear carrying a box. When he turns back to the house, I can see his face framed by a furry hat, the kind that hangs down on the sides with little pompoms at the end of the strings. He waves to me. I raise my hand and move it from side to side.

Mom and Dad sat us down a week ago, and they told us that we were going to be moving apart. They said we would still see each other, but I don't understand why Mom and Benny need to leave. The house is big enough for all of us. Benny and I share a room, but we've never complained. Not a single time. We fight sometimes, but that's not because we don't like sharing the room.

All three of them come inside, stomping their feet like they want the floor to collapse. Pulling down his hood, Benny comes over to me. "I guess we're leaving soon," he says. I stare into his eyes. They're blue just like mine. I don't want him to go. I don't want Mom to go either, but it's losing Benny that really scares me. I won't actually lose him though, right?

They'll come back. They have to. It'll be like when Mom went on a work trip for a month. It was a really long time, but she came back, and then it was just a memory that she was gone for so long. Everything went back to normal. That's what will happen this time, too. Benny and Mom will leave, but they will come back. I might be a little lonely, but I can take care of myself. I'm a big boy. Mom is always telling me that, so it must be true.

Mom and Dad are talking, but they don't hug or kiss when Mom zips up her coat and stands next to the door. They're watching us.

"Jacks," Benny says quietly. He's still wearing all his winter clothes.

I want to tell him not to go. Why does he want to go? I'm staying here, Dad is staying here, why can't he stay too? But I don't tell him to stay. "What?" I say.

I don't understand his searching gaze, even though Benny is always so easy to read. Reaching into his pocket, he pulls out a small plastic globe that fits in the palm of his hand. It's from those vending machines that spit out random prizes. The one in his hand is bigger than normal though. It's one from the expensive machine at the grocery store. I know because we always talk about buying one, just to see how good the prize inside is.

"I got this for you," he says, handing me the globe. The object is hidden by plastic wrap.

Mom calls from the door, "It's time to go, Ben."

"Goodbye, Benny," I say.

"Goodbye, Jacks," he whispers, his bottom lip quivering. Why does he say it like that? We're going to see each other again soon. Mom and Dad promised. Benny pulls me into a hug, his puffy coat deflating as he squeezes me. A couple seconds pass before I hug him back. What if this really is goodbye? It can't be. We're brothers, and nothing will ever separate us, not really.

Mom gives me a hug, and Dad gives Benny a hug. Dad and I watch as they push through the door and into the cold and snow. Mom gets into the car, and the lights turn on. Benny stops halfway to the car and looks back at me. We hold each other's eyes for as long as we dare. I want to scream for him not to go, just demand that everyone stop this. I could run outside right now and stand in front of the car. But I don't, and Benny turns away and gets in the backseat.

Dad puts his hand on my shoulder. The car pulls away, and I pull away from Dad. I run upstairs as fast as I can, heading straight for the window. From my spot beside our bunk bed, I watch the car drive into the distance. Tears slip down my face, but I don't move, not until long afterward.

Sitting down on the bed, I pry open the bauble. A plastic baggie falls out. Inside is a shiny silver ring. It's not like the cheap ones from the twenty-five cent machines. No, this one is from the dollar machine. It's heavy and solid. It's a lot smaller than Dad's ring that he doesn't wear anymore, but it's still too big for any of my fingers. I hold it in my palm, feeling its weight. It's not just a ring. It's a promise. A promise from Benny, that we'll always be brothers. A promise that he'll come back to me.

The scent of earth heavy in the air, I bear down into a shiver and push my shoulders back, feeling the rough bark along my spine. The heavy drum of rain hitting the leaves would almost be calming if it weren't for the thunder and flashes of lightning.

"Hey." The voice in the darkness sounds relieved.

I look toward the sound, just a few feet away. "How did you find me?"

Matt sits with his back likewise to the trunk, his shoulder pressing against mine. "It wasn't easy," he says with a sigh. Despite the storm and the dark, he's so close that I can make out his features.

"Ben sent you after me," I say. I'm not sure if I would have preferred Ben to come himself or not. I might have just run away from him again.

"He did. If you'd gone any farther I would never have found you."

The bark digs into my shirt as I shrug. "Maybe I should have."

"You want me to go?" His tone is a challenge, but I ignore it.

A fat rain drop hits the center of my forehead, the slippery liquid gliding down my nose to form another droplet at the end. I wipe it away with the back of my wrist. More quietly this time, Matt asks, "What happened?"

"Ben's usual idiocy, nothing new. He outed me in front of this guy I graduated with, Tyler."

In the shoulder and arm touching mine, I feel him tense up. "On purpose?"

"No, but that doesn't make it any better."

"Care to elaborate?" he asks as rain continues to pound down around us.

"Because he hasn't done a damn thing to show me otherwise," I snap. Crossing my arms to preserve body heat, I'm peripherally aware of my eyebrows pulling together.

When he speaks again, Matt's voice is pensive. "I'll be honest, I think your brother is kind of a bitch, but he cares a lot about you. Like, a *lot*."

"What do you know about that?" The venom in my words surprises me. I like Matt, but he's getting close to crossing a line.

"The way he acts around you, it's obvious."

"He's the one who doesn't want things to get better between us."

"Then why do you push him away?"

I force the words out. "I'm. Not."

"I think you should–"

"Back the fuck off," I interrupt. "He's *my* brother."

Matt doesn't speak again. Not as the rain lightens up, and not when the thunder becomes so distant I'm not sure I'm even hearing it anymore.

"Let's get out of here," he says at last, standing up. "I parked down the road from the house, so we can leave without having to deal with anyone there."

Lethargy tugs at my limbs as I follow him away from the tree. Every part of me from my hair to my shoes is sopping wet.

When we get to Matt's truck, he drives us a few miles before pulling to the side of whatever dirt road it is that we're on. He's looking at me, and I'm looking at him. We're both wet, and he's probably just as cold as I am. But where his expression contains optimism, mine holds none. If only I could blame everything on Ben, make it his fault for what happened tonight, it would make everything easier to understand. I could quantify it then, at least. Ben did something, and now I hurt.

Except that wouldn't be true. It doesn't really matter what a bunch of dumb pricks at my school think about me. The real reason I hurt is because of regret and resentment, and those are buried a lot deeper than what happened tonight.

"Jackson?" Matt is still watching me, even though my own eyes have long since faded into fuzziness.

"What?"

"Come over here." He unbuckles his seatbelt and pats the area of the bench seat between us.

Seriously? What's he going to do, give me a hug? I stare at him.

"I could drag you across the seat," he threatens playfully.

I'd like to see him try, even though he does have a good twenty pounds on me. After a moment, I do as he says and scoot over.

"All right," I say, sitting next to him. "Now are you going to tell me what the hell we're doing out here in the middle of nowhere?"

His answer is a bottle of vodka, retrieved from under the seat. "I think we got shafted out of a number of drinks tonight that were right-fully ours," he says with a grin.

"Shafted, huh?" I raise an eyebrow at him.

He shrugs as he takes a drink from the bottle, making a face when he swallows.

"Well?"

Shaking his head, he coughs. "It burns."

Good enough for me. I take the bottle from him before he can put the cap back on. Tipping it back, I let the clear liquid flow over my tongue and down my throat, searing all the way. Biting down to stifle a cough, I hand him the bottle.

Giving in to the renewed buzz stretching its fingers through me, I steal the moment to look at Matt. At his strong jawline and the covering of stubble that I'd love to run my lips over. And the hair so glossy black that it passes in and out of focus against the dark backdrop of the night. "What's it like?" I ask.

"What's what like?"

"Being so gorgeous all the time." As soon as I've said it, I realize how stupid I sound.

He laughs. "I think you've probably had enough there, bucko." I roll my eyes, even though I doubt he can see it in the dark.

Despite his assertion that I should be cut off, we pass the vodka back and forth several times before Matt caps the bottle and stows it back under the seat with considerably less left inside.

"So what now?" I ask, my mouth reluctant to move properly.

His answer is his arms encircling me. Wet fabric presses together as he draws me to him. It catches me by surprise, because we've never had this sort of intimate contact. Before now, it's always been... well, sexual. This is different.

Shifting in my seat, I sink into his embrace. "I can't believe what happened tonight," I eventually say, the beginnings of tears forming under my eyes and infiltrating my voice.

"Everything is going to be okay," Matt whispers. "You're going to be okay." The distinction isn't lost on me that he said *you're* and not *we're*, as if I'm all on my own and he just happens to be along for the ride. At least the alcohol blunts the impact of his unintentional admission.

Dropping my face into his shirt, I let go of what I'm holding in, my fingers curling to dig into his back. At the beginning of this summer, I never imagined opening up to anyone like this. The only person I was ever this close to was Benny. The name is a like another shot of vodka in my thoughts. *Ben*, not Benny.

But it's not him who's here with me. It's my boyfriend. In that instant I realize how lucky I am to have Matt. What kills me is that an insistent nagging inside wishes that the shoulder I'm crying on was Ben's.

Chapter Twenty-six

Ben

Hours have passed when I hear a creak in the hallway and the soft protest of the door's hinges. As Jackson's darkened shape moves toward the bed, I roll over. He jumps backward, exploding with a whispered exclamation. "Holy mother of hell!" His breath reeks like booze. He must have had more after I left him. But where? With Matt?

"Sorry," I mumble. "I just wanted to know that you were home safe. I didn't mean to scare you."

"Well, you did." He moves back toward me. "Scoot over if you're gonna stay," he says, his words running together.

"You're not kicking me out?" I ask, untangling myself from the blankets and making room for him. His only answer is the rustle of fabric and denim as he strips down to his underwear before climbing into bed beside me. Now that he's under the covers, I can smell the alcohol even stronger.

"How did you get home?"

"Matt," he says.

"What were you guys doing?"

"Had a few drinks in his truck."

I'm wide-awake now. "Of what exactly? You smell like a distillery."

He tries to laugh but interrupts himself with a burp. "I dunno… vodka I think."

Tension flares in my chest. "He drove you home after that?"

"Yeah. We didn't fool around or anything, so don't act so grossed out. Jesus, Ben..." his voice trails.

"I don't care about that, dumb ass. He drove you home drunk?"

Jackson doesn't answer me at first. When he speaks, his words are barely more than a whisper. "Why are you always mad at me?"

"I'm not mad at you," I say, keeping my own voice soft. It's easy to do, because what I'm saying is true. The one I'm mad at is *Matt*. If Jackson's level of intoxication is any indication, Matt should definitely not have been driving at all, much less endangering my brother while doing it. But if I go off about that, Jackson will just freak out on me.

Instead, I apologize. "I'm sorry, for what happened tonight."

First a pause, then he sighs but still doesn't respond.

"What's going to happen now?" I ask.

His voice is heavy in the darkness. "I don't know."

"At least you're graduated and about to get out of this town."

"Yeah."

I'm tired, but I don't want tonight to end with those words. My teeth nibble on my lip. "I was worried about you," I admit.

He shifts beneath the covers, then pushes himself up to a sitting position and turns on the bedside lamp. Squinting in the sudden illumination, I sit up so I'm leaning against the headboard beside him. What does he want?

As if in response to my unspoken question, he reaches over and runs a hand through my hair just like he always does with his own. It happens so abruptly and unexpectedly that when the moment is over, I think I may have just imagined it.

Jackson looks at me, and I look back. His face has a crooked grin that I recognize as alcohol induced. Seeing him like this makes me want to grab a hold of him and never let him go.

It's possible that I'm channeling the same chord of spontaneity and lack of restraint that he just acted on, or maybe I'm just doing what I want to. Stretching out my hand toward his face, I let the tips of my middle and index fingers lightly touch his cheek. He doesn't flinch or pull away, instead letting his bright eyes – somewhat dimmed by the alcohol but nevertheless brilliant blue – continue to hold me captive.

He lets me simply touch him as I run my fingers across the freckles at the tops of his cheeks. I love them, and I have no idea why. Jackson and I had something special once, and at its heart was our sameness. So it doesn't make sense that the thing I appreciate most about him is one of our few differences.

Maybe it's because physically, it's the only thing that I can love about him that is him and only him. If I admire his biceps or his hair or his eyes, I'm inadvertently complimenting myself at the same time. But those light brown spots just below his eyes, those are Jackson's alone.

Dropping my hand, I try to interpret his expression. Part of it is wistful, but its composition includes a darker aspect, too. He clicks off the light and slides down until his head rests on the pillow.

Now that Jackson is home, the exhaustion from the day finally settles over me, dragging my eyes closed. With the steady breathing of my brother beside me, I quickly slip toward a peaceful sleep. My last thought before disappearing into unconsciousness is how at home I feel.

Chapter Twenty-seven

Ben

A swift rapping noise drags me awake. The door opens at the same time my eyes do. "Jackson, where the hell is–" Dad stops midsentence. "Oh, Ben, you're right here."

"I, um," my brain struggles to find a plausible explanation why I'm wedged in bed next to Jackson when my room is just ten feet down the hall.

Dad holds up a hand, shaking his head. "I don't want to know." I expect him to laugh away the bitter note in his voice, but instead he turns and walks out of the room. The only sound louder than my thumping heart is that of Jackson's beside me.

My eyes scroll to meet his. He looks scared. "He's not really upset is he?"

Jackson tugs the blanket up a few inches so only his neck is exposed. "I don't know, but you should probably go."

A half hour later I head to the bathroom to take a piss. Jackson is taking a shower, but with frosted glass on the enclosure, co-usage of the bathroom is nothing new to us. When I try the handle, the door is locked. Sighing, I turn away with no choice but to hold it and wait.

Hair wet but fully dressed, Jackson shows up at my door a while later. "I'm going over to a friend's today, but I'll see you tonight," he says. I know better than to ask who he's visiting, since it's probably Matt, but it's still nice for him to tell me that he's going somewhere.

He's never done that before, so maybe the conversation last night actually connected with something inside him, despite its ending.

"Thanks for letting me know. Have a good time with… your friend." I try not to look annoyed that he won't admit to who he's seeing, and I do a pretty good job at it.

"Sure," he says, lingering only a moment before leaving me alone.

With Jackson gone, I try to pass the time by organizing my stuff, but there isn't enough of it to really organize, so I settle for stacking my clothes into a neat pile in the corner. The activity makes it obvious that I'm acutely lacking in the furniture department.

Long after the sounds of Jackson's feet on the stairs have faded into silence, Dad comes to my door. "Ben," he says, his earlier ill temper gone. "I'm going to visit Cherie and see if I can help out with anything over there. You'll be fine here while I'm gone?"

"I'm eighteen, Dad. Of course, I'll be fine."

"Right. See you this afternoon then."

I listen as he moves down the stairs. When the screen door slams closed, I toss myself back onto my bed. It's one of the few times I've been home alone without either of them. A familiar impulse slinks through me, tapping the back of my throat, the tips of my fingers, and my midsection all at once. I might as well take advantage of them being gone.

Lying on my back and propped up against a pillow, I take my time, stripping off my shirt first. I run a hand across my chest and another lightly over my stomach, tucking my thumb into the waistband of my shorts. I push everything out of my mind. There is no Jackson or Dad or Matt or working at the greenhouse or being sent away for the summer. Even Katie is banished along with the rest of it. This is about me, about finding my center, a release, and bringing back balance where I'm losing my grip.

When I pull my shorts down, I'm already hard. Closing my eyes, I wrap my fingers around myself. With the movement up and down, I let the waves of relaxation and pleasure build and roll into me, swelling like a secret tide. Not wanting to rush, I drop my hand and take deep breaths until my arousal just begins to fade. Starting once more, I find myself quickly back at the brink and have to pause again.

Holding my breath steady, I resist the urge for as long as I can. For a third and last time, my hand begins to glide up and down. Slowly at first but moving faster as I ride the feeling escalating inside me.

Forcing out my breath, I tug down a final stroke, holding my hand at the base. Quivering with uninhibited enjoyment, my stomach tenses, pulling me forward as I come on my chest. "Holy shit," I breathe.

Not bothering with my clothes, I saunter to the bathroom and clean myself at the sink. I never used to be this comfortable being naked, and I'm not sure when that changed. Maybe it's because of Jackson and how he's always so confident. We have the same body more or less, so if he can wear it proudly, then I can too.

Leaving the bathroom, I glance into Jackson's room. Through the window, movement outside catches my eye. Doubling back, I cross his room at a crouch. It's Dad, walking across the yard from the woods toward his truck. I guess I should have made sure he'd actually left before I...

Stealing back to my room in case he comes inside, I dress quickly, but the sound of his truck starting shows there was no need. This time I listen carefully until the noise of Dad's truck retreats completely before concluding that I'm alone. Pulling out my phone, I send Katie a text. *Hey, sorry about last night, I was upset about Jackson and not thinking clearly. What are you up to today?* I stare at my phone for a full two minutes before setting it on the nightstand beside my bed.

One physical need has been satisfied, but another is calling me now. It beckons me toward fields and dirt roads. I need to run, more than anything right now.

I'm watching TV on the couch when the front door opens. I expect Dad to come in, but instead it's Jackson. "Hey," he says.

Sprawled out with my legs stretched across the cushions, I mute the show about out-of-control teenagers. "How's Matt?"

"Fine," he says. A moment later his eyebrows scrunch. "I mean, I wasn't..."

I roll my eyes but aim a sincere look at him afterward. "Jackson, it's cool. Don't be embarrassed. I don't care what you do with him, as long as he's not driving you around drunk."

"That was a one time thing." He stays standing for a few seconds, finally gesturing toward my feet. Bending my legs at the knees, I make room for him and unmute the TV. We watch without talking as the show's host tries to mediate between the screaming, frazzled mother and her equally bratty child. Jackson laughs when the kid kicks his mom in the shin and she falls back into her chair.

I'm not quite as impressed with this show as Jackson is. "How did Dad end up running a greenhouse?"

Quieting himself, Jackson explains, "He always wanted to, I guess. A few years ago, he just went for it."

"He's really into the plants, huh? I thought it was just a failing business he happened to fall into."

"Nope, he runs a garden store because he likes that shit." Jackson stares at me for several long seconds. "You know that he has a master's degree in botany, right?"

My eyebrows rise. "You're serious?"

"Absolutely."

It's weird that I had no idea Dad has a graduate degree. It takes a minute for me to process. "If he loves it so much, wouldn't you think he'd try a little harder to make it profitable?"

Jackson looks back to the TV with a shrug. "Heck if I know."

Reluctantly I let go of my curiosity and enjoy the Saturday afternoon for all that it is – namely, hours spent with my twin brother. We laugh and make fun of the people on the show, and time is a concept both of us forget about.

After coming back from the kitchen with a glass of water, he even begins to talk about Matt. He only shares little things and definitely no specific details, but it's enough to imply that they're together, in some way at least.

"You really don't like him, do you?" Jackson asks me.

Before answering, I take a drink from his glass, but he doesn't seem to care. "He's all right."

A dejected gleam forms in his eyes. "I figured as much. He's not a bad guy. I wish you two got along."

After that, Jackson stays quiet for a long while, letting the TV do the talking for us until Dad's truck rolls into the driveway.

Something about the way the front door opens, or maybe just a subtle shift in my brother's bearing, but the foreboding feeling coursing through me is unmistakable. The door shuts harder than necessary, like it was meant to be slammed but Dad just didn't have the strength to do it.

The expression in his face is impossible to decipher as his eyes jump between us. Ultimately his gaze lands on Jackson. "Turn off the TV." A hot current of fear tightens like a constrictor around my chest as I press the power button on the remote.

Muscles twitch at the base of Dad's jaw. "After I left Cherie's, I stopped by the hardware store."

Jackson tenses beside me, but I don't understand why for another few seconds. Dad continues, his words plodding toward an unspoken conclusion. "I talked to Tyler's father, and he shared something upsetting." My mind races back to the night before. *Tyler*, the jerk pissing outside who caught us talking. Jackson sits up straighter, which must be difficult because the couch is so lumpy.

"Is it true?" The syllables echo in the room like thunder tumbling across farmland.

Jackson's voice is subdued. "Is what true?"

I shift to a sitting position. It's not right what's happening. Confident, indomitable Jackson, reduced to the timid boy beside me.

Dad's voice crackles with anger. "Don't screw with me, Jackson. I was humiliated today, and I'm pretty sure you know exactly what I'm talking about."

As much as this accusation bothers me, it's nothing compared to the emotions on Jackson's face. He looks like he's about to cry, and he won't meet the eyes of his interrogator. He nods.

Dad runs a hand through his hair, turning away from us as he releases a breath so deep I expect his chest to collapse into the vacuum created inside. He brings his hardened gaze to bear on us again. "Why?"

"What do you mean?" asks Jackson huskily. "It's not like I did this to piss you off or something." A tear slides down his cheek.

Dad drops into the chair across from us, looking like he's had the wind knocked out of him. "How long has this been going on?"

Jackson shrugs, unwilling to look up. "Always, I guess."

I'm staring at Dad, who's staring at Jackson, who in turn is staring at the floor. "Ben turned out normal, so I don't understand what happened." Dad hesitates, finding his words. "I want you to see a therapist."

I've enjoyed getting to know Dad again this summer, but if he thinks I'm going to watch him tear down my brother like this, he's got another thing coming. Before Jackson can respond, I break my self-imposed silence, staring Dad down. "There's nothing wrong with him. He doesn't need to get *fixed*."

Dad looks between Jackson and me, shaking his head with a mix of resignation and frustration. Almost a minute passes before he speaks. "Fine. You're both adults now, you can live your lives how you want."

Directing his attention back to me, he adds, "But that doesn't mean I agree with any of this, and I sure as hell don't want to ever see you boys sleeping in the same bed again. Ever." I can't tell if that's a threat or not, but it sure sounds like one.

With a last look at me, he walks out of the room, slamming the front door for real this time. Jackson gets up too, moving silently toward the stairs. As I watch his retreating form disappear up the steps, the nearly incapacitating apprehension I felt during the conversation gives way to outrage at how Dad is handling this. My brother deserves better than that. The man might be my father, but my loyalty will never lie anywhere else but with Jackson.

"Jackson," I call after him, but he doesn't respond. Sprinting up the stairs, I catch him at the entrance to his room. "Jackson," I repeat.

He stops and turns. "Don't," he says. "Just… don't." His eyes sink toward the floor as he closes the door. The click of the latch snaps into place with a certain finality.

Pushing my way out the front door, I run from the house. I want to leave it all behind. I want to go somewhere that I can forget it all. And that somewhere is a huge flat object that marks the tip of the property. Laying myself onto the cool stone, I stare up into the sky. The days of stifling humidity have abated, leaving sunny afternoons and cool breezes that remind me of home. Why can't I help Jackson through this? I want to be there for him however I can, but he doesn't seem to want that at all.

Staring up through the gap in the trees above me, I watch the clouds drifting past, wishing I could jump aboard and just sail away with them, to let them take me somewhere life is simpler. But only if I could bring Jackson with.

Chapter Twenty-eight

Ben

For me, the next few days pass as if almost nothing happened. Jackson keeps to himself for the most part, and after a few failed attempts to drag him into conversation, I give up and grant him the distance he wants. When I'm working at the greenhouse, Dad is likewise aloof and barely leaves his office during the workday. Not that it's a huge change from before, but he appears even less than he used to, leaving me and Katie to keep everything running smoothly.

Katie seems to have forgiven me for the night of the Fourth, but it's not the same between us anymore either. She's not flirty like she used to be, and if we end up working near each other, it's purely by coincidence. I know I should apologize again and tell her that she's important to me, but I can't bring myself to worry about anything besides my brother right now. Maybe she knows it, and that's why she's keeping her distance from me too. It's probably for the best. I can't give both her and Jackson the time they each deserve, at least not right now, and it's no contest who comes first.

A soft knock on the door precedes Jackson's nose poking inside my room. I glance up from my phone. "What's up?"

"Can I come in?" he asks, stepping inside and taking a seat on the bed. "Don't freak out, but I invited Matt over."

Working to control my annoyance at realizing he's coming over, I do a pretty good job of keeping my voice level. "Okay..."

"I, uh, thought we could do something together. I hate that you guys don't get along."

I sigh, briefly closing my eyes while I massage my forehead. "That guy is trouble."

"I know you think that," he says with a touch of exasperation. "But if you guys spent time together and actually tried, you'd see that he's not such a bad guy." He takes a deep breath, adding for effect, "I really like him."

"I get that, but that doesn't mean he's not an asshole."

"Please?" Jackson is practically pleading now. I suppose it makes sense that this is important to him, but how am I supposed to ignore my deep and abiding dislike for Matt? He's obnoxious, and Jackson deserves better.

I make a face, but then concede. "Fine. What did you have in mind?" The only reason I'm agreeing to this is because Jackson has had a rotten week and he's been shut in his room so much that I'm desperate to actually spend time with him.

Jackson's smile stretches as wide as the wheat fields outside. "I got a hold of some weed."

My eyebrows lift upward. "Really?" I was never that into smoking pot, but I've always been curious to smoke with Jackson, to see how he reacts.

"Yeah! I knew you'd be interested," he grins, genuinely excited.

"Why not just us, though? Or if you really want to smoke with someone else, can't you find someone other than Matt? Like a random homeless person or something?"

"That's not funny."

I shrug, my face impassive. "I wasn't really kidding."

"You said you'd try," he insists.

"No, I said I'd hang out with you guys. I didn't say I'd try to be nice."

A knock prevents Jackson from responding. "Hey guys," Matt says, pushing the door the rest of the way open. "You got the stuff?"

After some back and forth, we decide to smoke on the boulder at the edge of the woods. The house was definitely out, and the yard seemed kind of risky. Then Matt suggested his truck, but I didn't want to be in such an enclosed space with him, so that's how we ended up sitting next to each other with hard, gray stone underneath us.

"Don't worry, guys, I have a pipe," Matt announces, withdrawing a blue and yellow blown glass implement from his pocket.

I roll my eyes. "Of course you do."

Matt looks at me like he's about to return with a snippy comeback, but Jackson elbows him in the ribs and he stays silent. Taking the bowl from Matt, Jackson packs the off-green weed into the end.

Matt hands him a lighter. "All yours, dude."

I'm trying to decide if it's odd that Matt just called him "dude" when Jackson flicks his thumb down and the flame springs to life. He inhales, drawing the droplet of fire into the pipe. A moment later, the flame winks out, but Jackson keeps breathing in, persuading the glowing embers to endure.

When his chest is puffed all the way out, he passes the pipe to Matt but doesn't exhale. He starts to cough but suppresses it, and only a little puff of smoke escapes from his nose. Finally he expels a stream of hazy gray, coughing a few times but for the most part keeping himself together.

"Nice work," Matt tells him, touching him on the back in something between a sportsmanlike slap and an affectionate rub. I ignore this action, but I'm actually impressed too, even though I'm not sure if I should be.

Matt goes next, taking a hit with more practiced ease than Jackson, which doesn't surprise me at all. When he hands the pipe and lighter to me, I do the same, inhaling a bit less than Jackson did before having to cough.

We continue to pass the pipe until the relaxed tingling has diffused through my fingers and time has slowed to a crawl. At last when the pipe is cashed, Matt sets it to the side and leans back, propping himself up on his arms. Jackson's eyes glazed over a few minutes ago – at least what felt like a few minutes ago – and now he's lying on his back, eyes closed.

This was actually kind of fun, and Matt hasn't been that bad. "How you feeling?" Matt asks me.

"Pretty good," I say with a smile. Am I really smiling at him? Oh well.

He reaches over, tapping me in the chest with the back of his hand. "I'm glad we did this."

I look down at his hand. It's still touching my chest. I can't tell if that's weird or if I'm just high. He's staring at me. "Dude," I say, shooting a look at Jackson. He's still lying back, eyes closed. Christ.

"Shh," Matt whispers. Leaning closer, he presses his lips against mine. They're kind of dry and not as soft as I'm used to. It's so unexpected that I can't even react at first. Not until he touches his tongue against mine. My arm flying forward, I shove him backward so hard that his head thuds against the stone.

"You piece of shit," I snap, jumping to the ground.

"Huh?" Jackson looks up for the first time since we finished the bowl. He's got a goofy smile on his face and seems generally content. "What's wrong?"

Matt doesn't appear fazed as I give him the worst look I can muster, hoping that it conveys exactly how mad I am. Then I direct my words to Jackson. "Nothing. Matt is just being stupid. I'm out."

Without turning back, I walk away from him and the clearing. The rage inside me is almost too much to control. How can he be such a shitty boyfriend? And now I either lie to my brother, or tell him the truth and hurt him even more than he already has been this week. I hate Matt, but I feel like he's the only thing keeping Jackson afloat right now. Which means the only way for me to protect him is to keep my mouth shut.

The December sun is warm on my neck, but the day is cool enough that I'm uncomfortable in just my t-shirt. Stepping inside from the balcony off the living room of our condo, I wander into the kitchen and open the fridge. Mom won't be back for hours yet, even though I got home from school a while ago. I hate it when she works so late. Her working hours vary with the time of the year, but around the holidays it's always long days for her. And for me alone at home. Sometimes I'll hang out with my friend Cody after school, but usually I just come home and wait around for something to happen.

My stomach feels empty but I'm not really hungry. Closing the door to the fridge and flopping down on the couch, I grab the remote. My thumb hovers over the power button. Instead of pushing it, I set down the remote and run a finger lightly over the imitation rubber of the channel change buttons. If Jackson and I had never moved apart, would he be here watching TV with me right now? Or would we be somewhere else entirely, sharing a hobby with no one but ourselves?

The last time we spoke was almost a week ago, which feels longer than normal. Usually he calls me, though.

No matter how often we talk, our conversations never feel like enough. Is it the same way for him? Maybe it's time for more than just a phone call. Before I've fully formed the plan in my head, I have my phone out and I'm dialing his home number. I don't think Jackson has a cell phone. At least not one that I know about.

"Hello?"

Crap. "Uh, hi Jeff. It's Ben."

There's a pause. "How are you, son?"

"Good. Is Jackson there?"

"Yeah, just a minute." Was that a hint of disappointment?

I hear shuffling while I wait. My eyes wander over to the huge flat screen across from me, its expansive surface currently matte black.

"Hey," my brother says, breathing like he had to high tail it from somewhere to get to the phone. "Who's this?"

His voice resonates across the line, connecting with some deep part of me. I get such a rush from it that I realize it's been too long since we've talked. More than a week for sure.

"Hey," I say quickly, eager not only to tell him everything that's happened lately, but also to share my idea with him.

"Oh. Hi, Ben." And just like that, he takes it all away. *Ben.* Why would he call me that? I'm not Ben. I'm Benny. I'm his Benny, and he's my Jacks. I feel like I've been punched in the stomach.

I don't know how to recover from the declaration he's just made, especially because I don't understand it. In response to the tightness clamping down on me, I struggle to create a response to fill the silence. "How have you been?"

"Good. What are you up to these days?"

He doesn't sound mad. So why is he doing this? Normally Jacks and I can talk for hours. "Um, good." Afraid of more awkward pauses, I tell him a few things about my year and what I'm looking forward to over summer. But my heart isn't in it.

"Nothing much. I, uh, was just thinking that it would be cool if we... that is to say, I think we should, um..."

"Spit it out, Ben."

"Why don't we get together? Like for a visit. You can get out of that freezing state, and I can take you around L.A. and show you how awesome everything is here. Christmas break is coming up, and you could totally come out here." Half to myself, I add, "I haven't actually asked Mom yet, but of course she'd love to see you. It will be so sweet, we'll be able to–"

"Ben," he interrupts.

I take the opportunity to finally breathe. "What?"

"I don't think Dad can afford to send me out there, especially on short notice."

My shoulders fall and along with them, my hopes to see Jackson again. A moment later, my excitement is revived. "I'll visit you, then. I have no idea how cold it must be there, but I'll fly out to you, and–"

"Ben," he interjects again.

"*What?*"

He doesn't say anything for several seconds, and when he finally does, his voice is low. "I don't think that's a good idea."

My ears feel hot, and a bitter feeling spreads through me. "What do you mean?" I'm afraid of the answer.

"I just don't think it's a good idea, all right?"

"Okay." The word is so heavy it must be made of pure lead. Pain prickles in the back of my throat, and heat grows at the corners of my eyes. "I guess I'll talk to you later then."

"Good talking," he says before hanging up.

I want to be angry. I want to throw my cell phone across the room and smash the TV. I want to rip my hair out and break the windows of the balcony door. But I can't do any of that. Not because I'm afraid of the consequences, but because the pain in my chest is paralyzing every muscle in my body.

Jacks was always the one person I could talk to about anything, the one who made me feel safe and calm, even when nothing else did. *Especially* when nothing else did. So what changed?

I promise myself that next time, I won't be the one to call. I squeeze the remote control so tightly that I expect the plastic to be crushed in my fist, but it endures. Tears drip out of my eyes. I know what that promise means. It means we won't talk again.

Chapter Twenty-nine

Jackson

I roll the silver-colored ring between my fingers, letting the metal chain necklace slide through as it turns. The metal was pressed against my chest before I pulled it out from beneath my shirt, and it's still warmer than the air in my room, even though the weather has been stubbornly stuck back in the high 90s all week.

This is the worst week of my life. Dad is brooding with a silent, corrosive disappointment that eats away at me far more than if he just yelled until he was panting and blue in the face. And while I should be able to rely on Matt, it feels like he's pulling away. The summer is half over, and it feels like he's already half gone. I don't understand why, but I can't pretend like it's not happening.

Ben is trying, he really is, but it's not enough. I'm not sure why it's so hard to let go of everything from the years we were separated, but even when Ben is busting his balls to prove that he's there for me, even when we're actually getting along, I can't distance myself from the resentment that has festered for years. Over time it got in deep, and I willingly let it fill me. Now I can't get rid of it, even though I want to. What scares me the most is that I don't know if I'll ever be free of it. Until I am, I can't let Ben in, not completely anyway.

"Hey," a voice says. Its owner is the subject of my turbulent thoughts. "Are you ready? Matt is waiting outside in his truck. I think he's afraid Dad is going to do something to him if he comes inside."

Ben seems really pleased about that.

If I could avoid coming in this house, I probably would too. "All right, let's go." I grab my board shorts and follow him downstairs and outside. A towel is tucked under his arm.

Ben takes the middle seat in Matt's truck without a fight, so I get shotgun. All the windows are rolled down, but it's still sweltering in here. "AC is broken," Matt says dismally.

"How far is it?" Ben asks as we pull onto the highway.

"About ten minutes," Matt says. Ben seems preoccupied by the scenery outside, but my attention is fixed solely on Matt. On his tank top showcasing the toned muscles of his arms. As our speed increases, the breeze coming in the windows becomes a gale force wind, throwing his hair around and billowing under his shirt. I catch a glimpse of his nipple and the dark circle around it before directing my eyes forward. I would never have checked him out so brazenly in front of Ben, but now that Dad and everyone from my school knows, it doesn't seem like such a big deal to let him see this.

I'm amazed that Ben even agreed to come along. After the three of us got high together, his opinion of Matt didn't seem to improve at all. If anything, it got worse, and I have no idea why.

Accurate to Matt's prediction, just less than ten minutes have passed when he pulls off the highway and onto a narrow dirt road that disappears into thick woods. Ben's curiosity attacks again. "Is this public land?"

"There's a road into it," I point out as we bump over a pair of deep ruts. Matt catches my eye and smirks.

I don't need to turn to know the disapproval plastered across Ben's face. "That doesn't answer my question."

When he realizes he's not going to get a response, he begins to make comments about our presence here, progressing from the fairly innocuous "bad idea" to more pointed words like "illegal" and "trespassing."

"You worry too much," Matt chides.

"And you worry too little," Ben grumbles as we enter a clearing beside a river and hop down from the truck. The woods behind us have given way to a sandy circle, rutted with tire tracks. Clearly we're not the only ones who come out here. I've heard of this place, but it's my first time actually being here.

Under the sun and humidity, we venture toward where the banks have eroded, leaving a steep drop to the spot where the water laps up against the earth. The river is narrow but deep, the water meandering slowly along. About a hundred feet down from us, an ancient railroad trestle spans the distance between the shores.

"Whoa," Ben says the moment he sees it.

Stepping carefully along a path barely better than a deer trail, we reach the end of the ailing bridge. The tracks are long gone, leaving only the wooden trestle. The timbers are thick, but the gaps between them are even wider.

"Welcome to Paradise Bridge," Matt announces, grinning at both of us. "Best river jumping in the county."

Beside me, Ben's mouth drops so fast it's a wonder it doesn't hit the ground. "You're serious? We're not only going to climb out there, but jump in?"

I shrug, trying to silence my own reservations, "It's only like twenty feet."

After several seconds of indecision, Ben's face hardens into a determined look. "Oh, what the hell," he says, tugging off his shirt. He looks around as if trying to identify a safe spot to change into the swim shorts held in my hand. "Um," he says.

Matt's eyes move from Ben to me. None of us are wearing our swim shorts yet. We're in the middle of nowhere, but there's not really any cover nearby. "We're going to end up changing in front of each other anyway," Matt observes, kicking at a clump of unruly grass. "We could just... not bother with the swim shorts."

It would be weird doing that with my brother here, but the idea of skinny-dipping is kind of exhilarating. Something about swimming naked, on top of already trespassing. Except Ben would never go for it. This is the kid who wouldn't shower behind frosted glass with me in the bathroom. Of course he got over that a while ago, but this is different.

Ben confirms my guess. His expression is hard as he says, "I am *not* taking off my clothes in front of him."

Matt examines my brother, his dark eyes glinting in the sunlight. "Why not?"

Pick a reason, any reason. But the most obvious one is that he's uncomfortable getting naked in front of his gay brother and that brother's boyfriend. Likewise turning my gaze to Ben, I wait for his answer.

"Because you're a tool," he says roughly. Holding Matt's eyes, he steps behind the truck and kicks off his flip-flops. I have full view of him, but Matt is blocked by the truck. I look away as Ben pulls down his shorts and changes into the swim trunks, a lopsided smile tugging at the corner of my mouth. Ben has always had a flair for the dramatic.

Pulling off my shoes and socks, I change as Matt does the same. Unlike my aversion to looking too closely at Ben, I allow my eyes to slowly sweep over Matt's body. I saw him naked for the first time last Saturday, but we were tangled up in a heap of sheets on his bed. He returns my stare intently, grinning.

"Come on, guys." He tiptoes through the pokey grass and onto the timbers oozing black creosote. Venturing a look over his shoulder at both of us, he steps farther out onto the trestle. Clearly uninhibited by Ben snapping at him, he asks, "So are you guys identical like *every-where*?" The unabashed interest in his voice is impossible to miss.

Ben looks uncomfortable. We've both seen each other enough times to know that the answer is yes. When we were younger it happened more, but there have definitely been a few times since he moved here too. Modesty can only take you so far when sharing a bedroom and a bathroom. It doesn't matter whether it's true or not though. I glare at the back of Matt's neck. "Keep your eyes where they belong." *On me*, I finish mentally.

Arms held out for balance, we step onto the bridge, moving across the railroad ties. The wind buffets us with humidity, and the trees at the sides of the river whistle with the movement. A drop of sweat slides down my back between my shoulder blades. Just another minute and I'll meet sweet relief in the water below.

Reaching the center of the bridge, the three of us stand in a line. The water is a bluish brown, flowing lazily onward. From up here it looks really far down, but I'm not worried. Ben is, though. I can hear it in his breath. I reach over and give his hand a squeeze before letting go just as quickly. His expression rises, but not with displeasure.

"Woohoo!" Matt shouts as he jumps. He kicks his legs in the air as he falls, straightening them just before he hits the water. As he goes under, the cool darkness of the surface is destroyed by an explosion of white. He reappears, shaking his head and spraying droplets everywhere. "Come on, guys! The water feels great." His hands and feet propel him smoothly away from the spot directly below us.

I risk a glance at Ben. "You ready?" I whisper. He nods. I hold out my hand again, and he takes it. His skin is sweaty from the day, maybe nervousness too.

We jump together. There's no need to count off or say go. We just know. Ben's fingers tighten around mine as the water rushes toward us. He's scared, but I'm here for him, and he knows he'll be okay because of that. We each take a deep breath just before the surging sound of water roars in our ears.

I don't kick for the surface, and neither does he. The liquid between us is almost clear as his eyes stare back into mine, his fingers still intertwined with my own. I want to stay here with him and preserve the fleeting seconds. Our buoyancy is already dragging us toward the surface, but until then, this moment is ours, and I don't want it to end. For the first time since he moved here, I think it might be possible to get back what we had.

We break the surface and take in gulps of air. I almost forget to let go of Ben's hand. The sun is bright in my eyes, but everything else about this day is perfect. What a stark contrast to how shitty the rest of the week has been. All it took was hiding away in the woods with my brother and… my boyfriend. The word still feels strange.

"What was that?" Matt asks, giving me a puzzled look.

"What was what?"

He paddles toward us. "You guys stayed underwater. It was weird."

I shrug but don't answer him. He wouldn't understand, so I don't even want to bother trying to explain.

We clamber back up the abandoned railroad trestle again and again, our jumping positions becoming steadily more ridiculous. After Matt has gone under with his hand on his heart and reciting the pledge of allegiance, and Ben has flailed through his third botched back flip, we finally dry off and pile into Matt's truck.

When we drop Ben off at the house, I expect him to be upset that I'm going home with Matt for the rest of the day, but it doesn't seem to bother him. Maybe he's warming up to Matt after all.

"Have fun, guys," he calls after us, but it sounds a little forced.

Matt sets his arm on the rest between us. "Did you tell him about us?"

"I never told him anything."

An irritated grunt comes from deep in his throat. "Well, he definitely knows."

I watch the fields rush past. "He's my brother."

"Is that supposed to explain it?"

The gaps between the rows of corn whizz by, forming a kind of geometric optical illusion. It's mesmerizing. "Yeah," I say, not looking away from the corn. The field ends, replaced by tall grasses, and my attention strays from the window, coming to a rest on the line of white skin on the back of my hand. No matter how long it's been and as much as I've tried to forget, it still brings me back to that day whenever I see the scar. The clean-cut scar that could never have been made by a mishandled saw blade.

It was two summers ago. I'd just gotten my driver's license, and I was pissed at Dad for making me work at the store so much. I wanted to be out with my friends. Instead I was slaving away my summer five days a week for his business.

It was Sunday afternoon, and I'd already made plans for the next day to go to the mall with my friend Jeremy, even though I knew Dad wanted me to work.

He was sitting at the kitchen table drinking a coke. He'd spent most of the day tinkering around with his stupid plants and had just gotten home. He leveled his gaze on me and told me I didn't have a choice about working.

There was no room in his tone for debate, but I was mad. I told him it was a load of shit and that I was sick of working for him all the fucking time. It was the first time I'd ever sworn at him before. I had no idea what was coming.

In half a second he was up out of his chair, knocking over the coke can in the process. His fist closed around my shirt collar so tight it threatened to rip the fabric, and his eyes were so fierce I almost pissed myself. Yanking me close, the words he said next are ones that I can never forget. His whole body shaking with rage as he shouted, he told me that I was an entitled brat and an insolent little shit. Then he threw me. The cabinets on the opposite side of the kitchen ended my flight. My head cracked against the edge of the counter. I thought that was the worst of it, but the impact to the cupboards knocked Dad's favorite chef's knife off the counter. It landed on my hand, slicing the skin open all the way across the top. Drop forged German steel holds an edge for years, it turns out.

I can forget the pain in the back of my skull. I can forget all the blood from my hand. But I can never forget that the rage in Dad's eyes didn't diminish at seeing me hurt. Not right away at least. He took me to the hospital after wrapping my hand up in a dishcloth. There wasn't any discussion of what I should say about it. He didn't threaten me with anything, because he knew he didn't have to. He knew I wouldn't tell the doctor what had really happened, just like he knew I wouldn't disobey him again.

I remember tears welling up in my eyes as I fabricated the story about the bucksaw. The doctor thought it was from the pain.

"Jackson?" Matt's voice pulls me back to the present. We're parked in the street in front of his house.

"Sorry," I say, hopping out and slamming the aging door shut with a clunk. I follow him up the front steps and inside the house, kicking off my shoes next to his.

"Oh look," he says, smiling innocently. "My parents aren't home."

"What a surprise." I give him a deadpan stare, but it's really hard not to smile back.

He grabs my hand and tugs me up the stairs. Practically dragging me into his room, he locks the door as I sit down on the bed. In an instant he's next to me, pulling me into a kiss. His tongue nudging mine, I'm met by the familiar taste of mint and vanilla, which I discovered last weekend is the flavor of his toothpaste. My body is already responding to his, even before he takes off my shirt.

"What's the rush?" I ask, already feeling unfairly exposed.

His response is his hot breath and tongue on my nipple, focusing there for a moment before working his way down my stomach. My hands roam over his chest, the front, the sides, onto his back. Stifling a moan as his lips cross my navel and continue down toward the top of my shorts, the sound in my throat comes out like a growl. He glances up, his grin a combination of charm and seduction.

His hands struggle with the knot on the front of my canvas shorts. We didn't move this fast last time. It's a little scary, but also intoxicating. I don't want him to stop. The knot gives way under his fingers, but he pauses long enough to let me pull off his shirt. He kisses me again, our chests now touching skin to skin. It's only a temporary distraction before he sits back on his heels and slides my shorts off, leaving me wearing nothing but a pair of neon blue camouflage boxer briefs. They're tight and leave nothing to the imagination.

Matt traces a finger from my belly button down along the sparse hairs just below. At the waistband of my briefs, he detours to the side, sending a wave of anticipation through my entire body. I wriggle under his touch. He smiles, and then he pulls down my briefs too. I feel my face growing red. Now I really feel exposed.

"These have to go too," he says, pulling off my socks. The only thing I'm still wearing is the necklace with Ben's ring on it. Matt seems to realize that at the same moment I do. "And this," he whispers, hooking a finger underneath the chain.

I catch his wrist. "No, that stays." As a compromise, I slide the ring off to the side, so only the chain hanging loosely around my neck is visible.

He inspects me, his familiar grin taking over. "You're so fucking sexy, Jackson."

"This isn't fair," I complain. "You still have most of your clothes on."

He shrugs. "So take them off." I do as he says, and soon we're both naked, his desire just as apparent as mine. Instead of taking me in his mouth like last time, he nestles his hips down toward mine, until we're touching in what feels like all the right places. He wraps his fingers around both of us, and his hand glides up and down as he leans in to kiss me again.

He moves his hand away, and I'm not sure why, because it was feeling so good. Leaning on one arm, he lowers himself to grab something from under the bed. It's a small, clear bottle. Squeezing several drops of lube onto his fingers, he takes me in his hand. My eyes roll backward as I groan with satisfaction. Next he lubes up himself.

If his brief touch was any indication, I'm really looking forward to him going back to what he was doing. Except he doesn't. Nudging the inside of my thigh with his knee, he gets me to move my leg to the side. Shifting his position, he does the same with his other knee. I frown. This is a different kind of exposure that I wasn't anticipating. We just went swimming, so I'm not really concerned about not being clean, but it's just…

His fingers bring the cool, slippery liquid to where I was afraid of, slowly massaging. I try not to squirm. I'm not afraid of sex. It's going to happen sooner or later, and I wouldn't mind it with Matt. Maybe not right *now*, but in general, I've considered that he might be my first. I don't even expect it to be all romantically done up. A humid afternoon like this is perfect.

But I'm not a bottom. I've known that for a long time. Sometimes when I jerk off, I'll touch myself down there, but I have no interest in anything actually going inside. My fantasies about guys have always been quite clear about where I am during sex.

His fingers are still moving around. It's supposed to feel good, but the gnawing feeling in the pit of my stomach overrides any enjoyment. I have to say something. "Um," I venture, cautiously pushing his hand away, "I'm not really, you know..."

Matt's eyes flicker with impatience. "What? You want me to use a condom? I've only ever been with one other guy, and I used one then, so I promise there's nothing to worry about."

I wasn't even *thinking* about that. Who was the other guy? Someone from this last year? I swallow nervously. He's not making this easy. "No, not that."

"Then what?" His eyebrows pull together, his forehead furrowing toward the center.

"I'm not a... a bottom. I don't want to do this."

"Oh." He chuckles like it's no big deal. "It's your first time, right?"

"Yeah."

"Then how can you really know? You'll be fine." He slides his hand up and down his own dick, trying to get the rest of the lube off his fingers. He wipes what's left on the sheets.

"No, you don't get it. I don't want to," I say. Matt looks at me like I'm joking, or being childish, I don't know. "What?"

He shrugs, continuing to touch himself. I'm starting to go a little soft. "It's just a little silly is all. Come on, just try it. I'll go slow. You'll enjoy it, I promise."

I grit my teeth. "All right." I wish we could go back to what we were doing before, but I don't want to disappoint him. Who knows, maybe he's right and this will feel good.

He's grinning again, and his cock seems to stand a little straighter. He's about my size, a bit bigger than what I'd consider average, and a lot bigger than what Wikipedia considers average. "You're going to have to relax if this is going to work," he says.

"What do you mean?"

His finger traces a line along the side of my stomach. "You're tensing. All those muscles are connected."

It takes a conscious effort to relax as I exhale, willing *all* the muscles in my abdomen to relax. Suspended over me with outstretched arms, he scoots a little closer. I close my eyes as he presses into me. He's going slow, just like he said, but holy mother of hell it hurts. He pushes in deeper. I want him to stop. But I agreed to this, right? I said he could do it.

"Relax," he whispers, completely still. His lack of movement is the only thing preventing me from screaming with agony. I force my breaths in and out. Slow as a glacier creeping across a continent, his hips begin to move. Out, and the pressure and pain lessen. In, and they increase. My eyes brim with wetness.

A blissful expression settles across his face as he continues, his eyes half closed. But I have to tell him to stop. The pain is getting worse, gradually turning from intense discomfort to an acidic burning. I think I'm supposed to be touching myself, but I've long since gone limp. His speed increases, and my mouth opens slightly. I. Can't. Do. This.

I want to shout, but my voice is a whisper. "You're really hurting me."

Matt's eyes open but only partly focus on me. "It's okay, just relax." He slows his pace but keeps moving.

I shake my head, drops of liquid forcing their way out of my eyes. "No, please stop."

"Shh, Jackson, it's okay." He slows more.

Why won't he listen to me? It hurts too much to force myself away from him. I don't want it to get any worse. The back of my throat feels raw and the tears falling down my cheeks aren't because of the physical pain anymore. "Stop, just stop," I beg him.

What he finally sees in my face makes his eyes widen. "Dude, stop freaking out. You really want me to pull out?"

When I nod, he sighs with frustration and finally withdraws. Glancing down at himself, he makes a face. "Figures," he says under his breath. "I'm going to shower quick."

I curl into a ball, dragging the sheets around me to cover myself. My heart feels like it's on the verge of being crushed by a black hole, struggling to break free but failing.

Flinching when I hear the bathroom door shut, I pull the sheets tighter around me. My hand gropes for the chain around my neck, following it along until my fingers close around the ring.

It's almost impossible to find the strength to move, but I need to get out of here, *now*. I can't bear to look at Matt right now, much less talk to him. The moment I hear the water turn on, I throw off the blankets and yank on my shorts and t-shirt. *Forget the fucking socks.* Risking one last glance toward the bathroom, I tiptoe down the stairs and jam my bare feet into my shoes. Once I'm out the door, I run.

"It wasn't Matt's truck that dropped you off. Who brought you home?" Ben asks me absently as I pass his room on the way to mine. "And why aren't you wearing any socks?"

I forget that his window looks out across the road past our house. "Another friend drove me home." I don't want to explain anything to him. Not because he doesn't deserve to know, but because I'm... I don't want to think the word, but my mind won't even grant me that reprieve. I'm *ashamed*, and I'm not even sure why.

Shutting my door behind me, I curl up on my bed. My fingers again find their way to the ring hanging around my neck. I cling to it like a talisman that can ward away the darkness. Things were going so well with Matt. Why didn't he listen to me? Was I not assertive enough? And does that make it my fault? I don't think it should be my fault, but if that's true, then why do I feel so much embarrassment and shame?

I'd prefer to stay lying here forever, until time itself withers up and fades away, but eventually I have to pee so bad that I can't hold it any longer. Staring at the toilet, it takes a few seconds to start going. The sickly sweet scent of the lube Matt used hits me a second later and I wince. I want to get it all off me, every disgusting molecule. Locking the door, I turn the water to hot and step inside the shower. Normally I wouldn't dream of using Ben's Axe body wash, but for once, an overpowering, cloying scent is exactly what I want.

Cupping my hand, I squirt out a glob the size of a golf ball and go to work scrubbing it over every inch of myself. Except when I get to my backside. It feels like a knife has hollowed out the area to be twice what it should be. I'm afraid to go anywhere near it with the Axe, so instead I turn down the temperature and let the water do the work. Even so, it stings.

Back in my room, I resume my position on the bed. It's too hot up here to cover myself with any blankets, and I've already banished my sweaty t-shirt to the corner of the room. My arms are squeezing the life out of my pillow when there's a knock on the door. I know it's Ben. Something about the knock. I wait but don't answer.

He opens the door slowly. "Hey Jackson, you're not sleeping, are you?"

"Nope."

"Okay, good. Can I borrow your phone quick?"

I still haven't turned to actually look at him. "It's on the desk." I don't have the strength to ask why he wants it.

"Great, thanks." He crosses the room and into my field of vision as he picks it up. He sniffs and stares at me. "You got into my Axe, huh? I thought you hated that stuff."

"Changed my mind," I mumble.

He raises an eyebrow. "Seriously? As I recall you said it smells like 'horse piss and maple syrup,'" he quotes me perfectly. His smile falls when that doesn't get any reaction out of me. "You okay?"

"I'm fine." He doesn't look like he believes me. I try again. "I'm just tired."

"Huh, okay... I'll be back with your phone in a minute."

He walks into the hallway, and I can hear the sound of the floor creaking under his weight. His voice carries around the corner, even though I'm not really listening. "Hey Matt, I left my towel in your truck."

The words douse me like a bucket of ice water. Like watching a train wreck and being powerless to stop it, I tighten my grip on the pillow and listen to the unfolding disaster. "Uh, what do you mean, you're sorry?" Pause. Creak of shifting weight on the hardwood. "Sorry for *hurting me*?" Another pause. "Whoa, whoa, this is Ben, I'm just using his phone, but what the fuck are you talking about? What did you do to Jackson?" He's shouting into the phone now. Silence, then muttering. "Son of a bitch hung up on me."

I want to disappear. I close my eyes, wishing that the next few minutes didn't have to happen. When I open them, Ben is standing in front of me. "I knew something was wrong."

"Just go," I plead. I don't have the energy to keep myself from imploding and fend off Ben's curiosity as well. I know I'm not being fair. He really does care, but he can't fix me right now.

He sits on the edge of the bed. "No way am I leaving you. Tell me what he did." His expression is determined. Why does he have to pick this moment to dig his heels in? Not that he ever *doesn't* dig his heels in, but still. I can't deal with him right now. "Tell me or I'm going over to Matt's house and I'll beat it out of him, I swear to God."

"I..." Whatever I'm planning on saying – which is nothing because there is no plan – gets caught in my throat.

"Well? Spit it out," he prompts, adding as an afterthought, "I'm not leaving until you do."

If I don't tell him, he'll drive to Matt's and get the information out of him one way or another. Ben might seem like a softy, but he's one hundred and seventy pounds of pissed off, and he'll use it if he really wants to. But if I do tell him, he'll go over there anyway. I don't have much of a choice.

Not that I care about protecting Matt. This is about protecting myself. I don't want my shame paraded in front of my brother, much less Matt's parents or God knows who else will get involved if he goes over there with his fists out. It should make me feel good that he's so willing to defend me, but it just... doesn't. I want to hide away until I can forget what happened, how it made me feel so small and worthless.

"Please go away," I whisper.

Ben looks at me for a long time. Finally he says, "If I do, I'm going straight to Matt's."

"Don't."

"Sorry, can't do that." He pauses, meeting my eyes as his voice quiets. "Someone has to watch out for you too, big brother." Ben always hates it when I call him little brother, and he's certainly never validated my frequent assertion of being a few minutes older. He stands up to leave. "Have it your way."

Goddamn him for forcing me to do this right now. Leaping off the bed, I tackle him. We both go down, hitting the floor with an impact strong enough to knock shit off the walls.

"Jesus, Jackson, what the hell," he shouts, clocking me in the jaw with his elbow as he tries to push me off him. I don't care if it was an accident or not.

Suddenly I'm pissed. More than pissed. I'm enraged. I hate that he came here for the summer. I hate that he caught me jerking off to a gay magazine. I hate that I got outed because of him. I hate that he keeps trying so fucking hard to bring us together again, when it was his choice to leave. Mostly I hate that he left in the first place.

Balling up my fist, I hit him in the chin. Pure shock spreads across his face. Eyes wide, mouth open, jaw slack. He fights harder to push me away, but I don't let him escape. My left hand gripping his shirt below the armpit, I punch him again, this time near his temple. He winces but doesn't relent in his efforts to get away. Angry as I am, a part of me is impressed. We continue to roll across the floor, me pummeling him in the face and chest as often as I can while continuing to hold him close, him working furiously to get free of me.

We're an even match, but not for the obvious reason. We're only even because he's not fighting back and I'm so emotionally depleted that I might as well be half my size for the punches I'm throwing. Some strength must still be left inside me, I think darkly, because blood oozes from the corner of his lip and he's becoming more sluggish in fending me off.

With an unexpected shove, he pins me between the bed and himself. I might have seen it coming if I were less crazed, but what comes next I couldn't have warded off even at my best. Maneuvering himself with uncanny speed, he grabs my arms and tucks them behind me, pulling my back toward his chest. Just like that, I'm completely restrained. After a few weak attempts to free myself, I give up.

Rotating me around so he can lean against the foot of the bed, Ben spreads his legs apart just enough so I can stretch mine out as well. When we were younger, our parents took us to a water park once, and we would go down all the slides in this position, just like we were riding in a sled. Except of course Ben wasn't restraining me then.

Our chests rise and fall with labored breathing, and I can smell the sour scent of sweat on him. With every ounce of my strength spent, I let him hold me for several more seconds without making any attempt to move. As my breathing calms, so does my anger.

His voice is quiet in my ear. "If I let you go, you won't attack me again?"

"I won't. I promise."

"All right." He slowly disentangles his arms from mine. I reach a hand up to massage my shoulder, sore from where he held me. "Why did you do that?" he asks, wincing as he breathes. His chin and jaw are red, and a hint of blood is hiding in the corner of his lips. As if seeing through my eyes, he slides his tongue straight to the spot and licks it away.

I look away. "I didn't want you to go to Matt's."

"Bullshit. I wouldn't have gone after you jumped me. Everything that came after that was for something else, wasn't it?"

He's right, but I refuse to let his eyes lock onto mine. "I can't deal with this right now, Ben. I don't even feel like I can talk to you about any of this. I know you don't really want to hear it." I feel bad, because that's a lie, but I need to give him a reason why I won't let him in. I push myself to my feet, risking another look at him. "Just don't go over to Matt's, okay?"

He seems upset, but he doesn't fight me on it. "I won't." He pauses, continuing to look at me. "Jackson, I *really* don't care that you're gay."

I give him a dirty look. He's just saying this now so I'll open up. "You freaked out the second you found out and then you moved the hell out of my room, because you couldn't stand being that close to your queer brother. Now you expect me to believe that you don't care?"

His face glows red. "I'm serious, Jackson. It doesn't bother me. How many times do I have to tell you before you believe me? You're my brother and that's never going to change, regardless of who you like to sleep with." Apparently unable to help himself, the earnest edge drops from his voice, and he grins. "Or jack off to."

Dad picks that moment to bust into my room. "What the hell was all that goddamn noise for?" His hawk eyes snap between Ben and me.

"We were just messing around," Ben says, abandoning his pissed off look. He's trying to sound nonchalant, but his voice wavers ever so slightly. He's still trying to suppress pain from somewhere. I can see it in his face.

"Liar," Dad growls, focusing his attention solely on Ben. Snapping his fingers, he points at the floor in front of him. Ben flinches, but he holds it together as he approaches Dad, coming to a stop at the indicated spot.

Dad inspects Ben's face but doesn't seem to find what he's looking for. "Take off your shirt," he demands. Ben does as he's told. His ribs look red and battered. I must have laid into him harder than I thought. Moving down from his collarbone, Dad's fingers press into my brother's ribs one by one. When Dad touches a spot even with the top of Ben's abs, he gives a muffled cry through clenched teeth. *Shit.* No wonder he looked in pain when he was talking. Dad's seething eyes drill into me. I look away, unable to withstand the onslaught. "You did this," he states. Even if it weren't true, I couldn't bring myself to argue with him.

"Put your shirt back on. I told you boys not to break any bones." His voice is cold. He closes his eyes, and for a moment I think he's going to drop the bullshit and become Dad again. But then he opens them, and when he speaks, he sounds just as angry as before. "Get in the truck. We're going to the hospital."

*　*　*　*

"Bruised, not broken," the doctor says. He's an older man with gray hair circling his bald head in a horseshoe shape, but the moment he says that, I could kiss him. Ben, again shirtless on the examination table, gives an audible sigh of relief, but I'd bet money that he wasn't worried about the longer recovery time associated with a break.

"You're sure?" Dad asks the doctor.

The man nods. "Yes, absolutely. Ben should be pain-free in just a few days."

Ben and I look expectantly at Dad. As mad as he might be, and as much as he might have been hoping that Ben's rib actually *was* broken, he's a man of the rules. Technically we didn't break them. We know it, and so does he.

"That's a... relief," he says, forcing the words out.

What a fucking lie. What would he have done if it really had been broken? Did he have a punishment already cooked up? Would it have been for both of us, or just for me?

None of us says a thing as we cross the parking lot back to the truck. Dad's ringing phone is the first to speak. "Who's this?" He answers it not particularly politely.

"Oh, I'm sorry." Pause. Listening. "Yes, I understand." Ben and I are still waiting for him to unlock the doors. "Absolutely. Thank you for letting me know. Yes, you too, Ms. Baker." He taps the screen on his phone and shoves it back in his pocket.

Neither of us dare to ask him what that was about, but thankfully we don't have to. "Cherie Dodd passed away yesterday. Funeral is the day after tomorrow." He doesn't sound particularly surprised, but then, she was pretty far gone, even if she wasn't on her deathbed.

Chapter Thirty

Jackson

An overcast afternoon with low hanging clouds presides over the reception, sending waves of mist rolling across Cherie's lawn. The gardens outside her home are getting overrun with weeds, and the vines have migrated past the trellises and are crawling along the exterior walls.

The unkempt appearance is a stark contrast to the manicured lawn and flowerbeds that I remember from when I was here with Dad last year. I wonder if it looked like this when Ben came to help with her raspberries that first time, or if everything went to hell in just the last few weeks. He wouldn't have known the difference, not then, but I can certainly tell. Was it just in her last weeks that she was really slipping, or did it go on far longer than that and I just never noticed?

For some reason, Dad didn't want to bring Ben and me to the funeral. So he left the two of us at Roanoke Gardens, picking us up afterward for the reception. Ben and I both thought it was weird, but after ending up at the hospital the other day for not-broken bones, we didn't dare push Dad on this one. It's never been worth it to push, but especially not now.

And the last few days? Fucking miserable. I'm holding myself together, if only barely. Ben has backed off at least, but I sort of wish he hadn't. I know I told him to, and then practically beat the shit out of him, but I really need him right now. I haven't talked to Matt at all.

And neither has Ben, at least not that I know of.

I stare down at the matte black of my dress shoes as Dad knocks on the front door. Unlike at any other social gathering, not a single sound can be heard from within. I get that everyone is sad at a funeral, but sometimes I wonder if all that gloominess in one place might just attract Death for a second round.

A heavy, middle-aged woman opens the door, examining us. The lines around her face are vaguely familiar, even though they reflect a weariness that isn't. I assume she's related to Cherie. Her piercing eyes skewer Dad and his charcoal gray suit first. Then me and my pure black one. Finally Ben in his khakis and dark blue polo. Is she actually considering whether or not to let us in? Or is she just super nosy?

"Come in," the woman says, holding the door for us. Ben shifts beside me, and I feel bad for him. He got stuck with what I used to wear to choir concerts before I quit in tenth grade. I don't have to look to know that the bottoms of the khakis are hovering around his ankles.

Dad steps forward and we follow him in. Inside it's just as depressing as I imagined. There are maybe fifteen people here, making we wonder how few were at the funeral. Isn't the reception supposed to fetch a bigger crowd? Maybe that's just at weddings.

"Food?" Ben asks under his breath.

I survey the spread in the kitchen. "Uh, sure."

Ben grabs a plate and just stares. "What is this?"

"Tater tot hotdish."

His expression empties of all understanding. "Huh?"

I lower my voice. "Damn, Ben, it's a fucking casserole." Minnesotans love their hotdish. It shows up at every social gathering from grad parties to bake sales, whether it's welcome or not.

"Why don't you just call it that, then?" Ben quips.

Resisting the urge to smack him as I grab my plate, I explain, "Because they're different. Casserole is slightly classier than hotdish. I mean, casserole is still pretty salt-of-the-earth, but it's no hotdish."

He slops a scoop of gooey beef mixture topped with half burnt tater tots onto his plate.

Not wanting to mingle with anyone else here, we retreat to a spare bedroom with our food and take seats on the bed.

Between mouthfuls, Ben points to a plant on the dresser. "That's the snapdragon I gave her."

I wait to swallow before I speak. "Cool." Beside me, Ben drags his fork across the plate, guiding a piece of tater tot from one end to the other. "What is it?" I ask.

He looks up, biting the corner of his lip. "Cherie had me pick it out for her. She said she wanted something that wouldn't die before she did. I guess she got her wish." As I watch him, his vision blurs as his eyes drift across the emptiness of this room.

I wonder why Ben is so upset. "Cherie was a really nice lady, but she was old. It was her time to go."

"Yeah," he says. "I guess so."

In a way, I'm grateful for the distraction. The distraction from what happened with Matt, and from Ben always watching me from afar. If I could just forget that it ever happened, maybe Matt and I could move on.

"I have to go to the bathroom," I announce.

"Right now?"

"No, next week." My eyebrows twist together in irritation. "Damn, Ben. Yes, right now." I get up, leaving him sitting on the bed. In the kitchen, I set my plate in the sink. The tater tot hotdish is all gone. Go figure.

Avoiding eye contact with anyone who looks like they might want to talk to me, I find the bathroom down a short hallway and thankfully away from the action, if it could even be called that.

When I'm finished, I make sure the fan is on and the door cracked just a little so at least the next person to enter will do so with caution.

I check in the guest room, but Ben is gone. Where did he scamper off to?

Leaning over to peek out the kitchen window, I see Matt standing beside his truck talking to Ben. He's wearing a suit and actually looks rather dashing. I keep staring out the window. They're deep in conversation. Matt has an oddly smug look on his face, but Ben is turned away from me. I don't know how I feel about Matt anymore, and I sure as hell don't want to talk to him right now.

The moment I hear the shout, I know it's them. I'm out the front door in less than five seconds, not giving a shit about the librarian-looking lady I bump into on my way out.

Matt is pinned against the passenger side of his truck, the black of his suit contrasting against the red paint as Ben's arm jams into his collarbone.

As if stepping away from reality, I consider that Matt's suit looks a lot like mine – a stark difference to Ben's highwater khakis and ugly polo, which you'd think he'd picked up at a thrift store just before we came here. I almost laugh, but Ben's snarling voice drags me back to the moment. "Stay away from my brother, you son of a bitch!"

"Dude, get off me!" Matt tries to shove him away, but Ben has his neck pinned now. *You go, Ben,* I think as I race toward them.

I would never have expected Ben to actually throw a punch, but the first blow makes contact with Matt's jaw. His eyes widen just before Ben hits him again. This time he drops to the ground. Ben is on him in less than a second, punching him mostly in the face, again and again. Matt tries to push him off, even knee him in the crotch, but he's not fast enough to get my brother off him.

Ben's storm of rage is so fierce that he doesn't seem to notice me yelling at him until I grab him around the chest and yank him back. "Jesus Christ, Ben, *stop!*"

Ben doesn't make me fight him, but where his fists left off, his mouth picks up the slack. "You miserable piece of shit," Ben screams at him. "You couldn't leave my brother alone for what, three days?"

Blood trickles from Matt's lip, and he's going to have at least one black eye. His features are tainted by fear as he tries to brush the dust and drops of blood off the front of his suit jacket.

I drag Ben farther from Matt and the elderly pickup truck, aware of several adults now gathered in front of the house. "Let's walk," I tell him, pushing him roughly along the street. I can feel the stares of a dozen or more people on us, but I refuse to look back.

From Ben's rising and falling shoulders to the set of his eyes, his determination doesn't abate as we continue down the block. "Where are we going?"

I glare at him. "We'll call Dad for a ride later, but I don't want you to get arrested. You were beating the shit out of him."

The misty evening covers us in droplets of moisture, making the air feel unnaturally heavy between us as we walk at the side of the street. "Why was Matt even there?" Ben asks.

A car approaches us, and for a second I think it's going to stop. When it passes, I exhale in relief. "Cherie was like his great aunt or something. He mentioned it one day at the greenhouse when he saw her leaving," I explain.

He shakes his head. "Weird coincidence, huh?"

"Not really," I say with a shrug. "Northfield is small. Lots of people are related."

I feel like I'm on the verge of freaking out, just going crazy, destroying everything in my path, and tearing down the walls of the world itself. Instead I take a deep breath, closing my eyes and shutting out everything, letting my gradually slowing heartbeat and the sound of my footsteps become my entire consciousness. I can't believe Ben attacked him like that.

"You said you'd let this go," I finally say.

Ben reaches across the distance between us to bring me to a stop. His hand comes to a rest on my chest before sliding up to my shoulder and giving it a squeeze. My fuzzy vision focuses briefly on his fingers and the blood, not his own, streaked across his knuckles.

Ben looks sympathetic for a moment. "I couldn't," he says before dropping his hand and continuing walking.

"Hey, wait," I call after him. Jogging a few steps to catch up, I fall into step with him again. "Why did you do it? What did he say to you?" When Ben doesn't answer, I add, "If I hadn't come outside when I did, you might have put him in the hospital. You owe me an explanation for that."

His voice is soft. "Are you going to keep seeing him?"

"I don't know. Probably not. You made a damn fine mess of things." We're both quiet again, longer than I want. "Why did you do it?"

The expression he's wearing is so full of agony that I'm afraid he's going to start crying. "Please just trust me that he deserved it. He's no good for you. I know that you're going to have all kinds of questions, but please, Jackson, if you're ever going to trust me on anything, it should be this."

What choice do I have? I could grill him about it until he finally explained what the hell he means, but... Ben has never asked me something like this before. "Okay, I trust you."

It's another hour before Dad picks us up. He looks pissed off, but the ride home is a quiet one. For the first time today, the mist rallies together and it starts to rain. The windshield wipers swoop back and forth, but none of us says a word, not even after we pull off the dirt road and into the driveway.

Chapter Thirty-one

Jackson

"I'm going for a run before I shower," Ben says, waiting until I nod before he pulls on a pair of basketball shorts and leaves me sitting silently on the bed. I listen as he patters down the stairs. He still wears my shoes every time he runs, but it doesn't really bother me anymore. Definitely not as much as the wretched screech of the screen door slamming behind him. It must be the worst sound on the planet.

Restlessness steals over me. I don't want to go for a run or anything, God forbid. That's Ben's thing anyway. But I do want to get out of the house.

Matt's truck is pulling into the driveway just as I let myself outside. I stare as he gets out. "Hi, Jackson," he says, strings of nervousness pulling at his voice as though it were controlled by an amateur puppeteer.

Any remaining indecision of how I should feel at seeing him is obliterated by his unease. He's worried about what I'm going to say. "Haven't heard from you in a while," he says, revealing the edge of his lip that still has a dark red slit where Ben hit him the other day.

"I haven't heard from you, either."

Matt looks uncomfortable. "I was going to call, but I figured I'd do this in person. I don't know if we're really together or not, but in case you think we are, I'm breaking up with you."

I feel like he's just punched me in the stomach. It's not like I didn't know this was coming or that it didn't need to happen, but I expected it to be less, well, unexpected. "Just like that? You realized that you can't fuck me, so now you're out?"

"Look, Jackson," he says, gesturing like he's trying to let me down easy. "You're really nice, and you're cute, but we're not a good match."

Cold determination emboldens me as I glare at him. "I hate the way you treated me, but that's the biggest load of lies I've heard in a long time. We had a great time together, and you know it. At least man up and tell the truth."

He looks conflicted, then he just shrugs. "Oh, what the hell. You're right. I had a great time, but it can't work. I should never have gone along with this, because I've got a great guy waiting for me back East."

Rage seeps into my blood like poison to a well, pushing me to seek answers when I shouldn't. "You what?" I ask, my voice barely above a whisper.

"Sorry, man. I tried to keep my distance in the beginning, but you're persistent. And hot. I was hoping that after we fooled around a few times, it would fizzle out. But it just got more intense." He sighs. "I figured if we had sex and you didn't have a good time that you'd decide we weren't compatible and want to break it off."

I wish Ben were here. Then he could do what I don't have the strength to. It's not really Matt I'm looking at. It's not the guy that Ben and I hung out with this summer. Definitely not the guy who came after me the night of the Fourth. Instead, it's just some punk who hurt me. Hurt me in a way that can't just be forgotten. The kind of hurt that doesn't heal cleanly but scars.

"Just go," I breathe, turning back toward the house. My footsteps feel heavy as I move away from him. Still heavy as my fingers grapple with the latch on the screen door. Heavier yet as I stumble into the kitchen, thankful at least that Dad isn't here.

Legs crossed, I'm sitting on the stone in the woods. The place that always used to bring me comfort now only stares in silence at the shattered pieces of my insides. With the funeral and Ben attacking Matt, it was almost possible to forget what happened last week. But even if Matt hadn't shown up tonight, the minutes and the quiet of this place would have brought it all back.

I'm still sore – both from what Matt did and when Ben held on to me so tight that day. By far though, the agony inside far outdoes my physical pains.

I made only one stop before fleeing the house. Across my palm I roll the mostly-full bottle of Glenlivet 21-year-old stolen from Dad's private stash. I've never taken anything like this before. I was always too scared.

The one time I really defied him, he threw me across the kitchen and my hand almost got sliced off. The second time was last week, when I told him I liked guys. That one has yet to come back to me in full, but I figure it will. Taking us to the hospital for Ben's bruised ribs wasn't about me or Ben at all. It was about him. About his need to punish me for what I've done. He's too smart to just – I don't know – hit me. But that doesn't mean that he isn't waiting for an opportunity, because I don't believe for a second that he's letting this slide. If he waits long enough, eventually he'll find one.

So why steal the whiskey? Especially this bottle. It's probably the most expensive of all of them. I have no idea what he's been saving it for. It was already opened, but I know it's being saved. Whiskey doesn't go bad. I roll the bottle back across my palm. I didn't actually mean to pick this one in particular, but I do know why I brought it here.

Something about choosing the impetus that finally brings Dad's wrath down on me makes me feel like I can still control something. It's not much, but for a summer that has wrenched itself away from me, it's something at least.

I twist off the top of the whiskey. Catching a whiff of the intense, spicy scent, I raise the bottle and take a drink. A stitch of revulsion touches the back of my throat as the liquid slides down. Breathing out through my nose, I feel the warm coolness of evaporating alcohol in my sinuses. I take another swig, leaving the bottle to my lips a little longer this time.

I know that what I'm doing is fucked up. Drinking by myself... and why? Just because I need a distraction right now? Maybe, but it's more than that too. The last couple weeks have been such a mess, and all I really want right now is *not* to feel.

I don't see Ben walking toward me until he's almost right next to me. Adrenaline hits my veins the moment our eyes meet. Feeling more exposed now than when he caught me jerking off, I set down the bottle beside me, hoping to God that he won't lecture me. Not that I don't deserve one, but I just don't want to think about Ben right now, which is a hell of a lot easier when he's not standing in front of me.

He hops up onto the rock and sits down. He's still wearing the clothes he ran in, including my shoes. "Jackson," he says, concern filling his voice. "What are you doing?"

Sweat mingles with the fine hairs on the back of his neck, giving him an air of athleticism that I admire. Looking away, I take another drink and he makes no move to stop me. Instead, he puts his hand on my knee. I want to tell him how much I need him, but all I have is pent up anger, undiminished by all those times I hit him. I shift my leg so his hand falls.

I lift the bottle again, but this time he sets his hand on top of mine. "Jackson, tell me what's wrong."

"Take your pick," I say bitterly. Ben gives me a helpless look, probably because he has no idea what to say. "Matt stopped by while you were running," I state. "He told me he has a boyfriend back at college and I was just his summer fuck or whatever."

Without even a hint of surprise, Ben whispers icily, "I'm going to kill him."

"You knew?" The weakness in my voice warns of tears like distant storm clouds herald the rain.

Following a long sigh, he admits, "He told me at Cherie's funeral. That's why I started beating his face in." Scooting closer, he puts his arm around my shoulder. "You're going to get through this," he whispers.

Am I really? It makes sense in theory, but I don't know what that could actually look like. I feel like between Matt, Dad, and Ben, a huge crater has been blown in my life. And yeah, Ben is responsible too. "You left," I say. The words are simple, but saying them gives me a sense of power. My fingers tingle with the rush of alcohol. "You left me."

"That's what this is about?" He releases his grip on my hand and the bottle. "I mean," he clarifies, "not like this moment, but this whole summer. The reason you never let me get close was because Mom and I moved away?"

Anger flares within me once more. "How can you act like it wasn't a big deal? Like it wasn't the biggest deal of our entire lives?" I try to glare, but I'm pretty sure it just comes out soaked with sadness. "I missed you so much. I never wanted you to leave, but you left anyway."

Ben shakes his head quickly. "That's not what I meant. I know it was the biggest thing that ever happened to us." His voice lowers. "The *worst* thing that ever happened to us. But that's exactly what it was. It happened *to* us. I didn't choose to leave any more than you chose to stay."

"That's not true," I shoot back, tasting the whiskey on my tongue in more ways than one. "You chose to leave. I know you did because Dad *told* me years ago. God I wish he wouldn't have, but I know and I can't change that. But you know what? After all this time, it was almost okay. Except now that you're back, everything has gone to shit. Dad won't even look at me anymore, everything is fucked up with Matt, and most of the time I feel like we're not even brothers anymore." I take a deep breath. "You left me, and I wish you had just stayed away." My voice breaks.

Ben takes a deep breath. "I don't know what Dad told you, but there's more to it than that."

"What do you mean?" He would have to be pretty ballsy to lie to me right now.

"Before I knew about the divorce, Mom asked me what I thought about if she and I went on a trip, a longer trip for just the two of us. She asked if I'd like that." He pauses. "And I told her yes."

Above us, the leaves tap against one another, rustling to tell us of a change in the air. High summer has just shifted into late summer. I've always loved the way the wind rushes through the trees here. It's reliable, and it's strong, and it always has something to say.

"Jackson," he says. "Say something."

If only the wind could speak for me. "What do you want me to say? You left."

His eyes drop to the hard stone beneath us. "It wasn't like that. I didn't realize what I was agreeing to. Their divorce was really fucked up. I don't know exactly what happened, but by the end, Mom was ready to do anything to get out of here. She wanted to take both of us with her, but Dad threatened to drag everything out in court if he didn't get to keep one of us. She didn't have the money for that, and she was set on getting the hell out of Minnesota. So she gave in."

I swallow hard. That story sounds a lot different than what Dad told me, but I'm afraid of what that means. Everything he told me about Mom and the divorce… was it really all a lie? My voice is tight as I ask, "Why did you agree to leave at all? You could have said no."

He's quiet for several seconds, and silence consumes the space between us. "Because of you," he says softly, the corner of his mouth turning upward. "Because you were always so confident and independent. Everything you did was cooler and better than what I could do. I wanted to have a chance to see what I could be without you. For once I wanted to be able to come back and impress *you* with something."

He sucks in a breath to continue his monologue, "But hell no did I ever think it was going to be permanent. By the time I figured it out, we were already living on the other side of the country. Once I knew, I hated it just as much as you did. I *begged* Mom to let me come back, but she didn't want to lose me, just as much as I didn't want to lose you." An irritated look appears on his face. "I wanted to stay in contact. I called you, I tried to get you to visit, or to visit you, but you never wanted that. If you were so hung up about me leaving, why did you push me away?"

"I was so angry that you left. Even more so when I found out that you'd done it voluntarily. I've been mad for so long that I couldn't stop feeling that way." My eyes wander away from Ben, getting lost in the sprawling acres of wheat. "I guess I wanted you to feel abandoned like I did."

"That's really shitty, Jackson."

Wringing my hands together, I whisper, "I know."

"Don't ever do that again."

I meet his gaze. "I won't."

We stare at each other for a long time. Finally Ben breaks the silence. "Now tell me what the hell you're doing out here with a bottle of Dad's…" He picks up the bottle. "Oh shit, Jackson, this stuff is expensive. Do you know what this is?"

I nod. "I know."

"What were you thinking?" he asks in disbelief. "Dad's going to… damn, I don't know what he'll do."

"Kick me out? Because that wouldn't be the worst thing. I hate it here."

Ben laughs nervously. "Don't joke about that."

I scan the edge of the trees ringing the clearing. The leaves catch the wind a few seconds before it blows over us, bringing a welcome relief from the day's heat. Evening is already pressing down on us, and it'll be dark soon. "It would be so easy," I whisper. "I could run, just run away and never come back. Leave him and everyone else behind."

"You're scaring me, Jackson." Ben's tone dips into uncertainty. "I can't tell if you're serious, but it seems like you've actually thought about this." In my peripheral vision, I see him pick up the bottle and roll it across his hands, just like I did earlier. My heart tap-dances against my ribs as he turns his full attention back to me. "Would you really leave like that?"

"I don't know," I mumble. "Sometimes living here is really tough."

Ben looks at me like he's really seeing me. "I don't know if I could lose you again," he says softly.

"Are you mad?" I'm not sure why I'm asking.

Shaking his head slowly, he says, "No, not mad. Worried, though." He speaks slowly, like he's afraid I'm fragile. Maybe I am.

"Will you be back out here again?" he asks, sounding like he already knows the answer.

"No. Yes. I don't know," I shrug. "More often these days I feel like I don't have control over anything anymore. Usually I just sit here and think."

"And today?"

"Some days are different."

He lets out a long sigh, dropping his face into his hands. "I want to talk about this, Jackson, but I want to make sure Dad doesn't catch you with that bottle."

"I'll bring it back to the house. Then we can talk if you want."

"I want to," he affirms. "I have to take care of something quick, but I'll be right behind you. Promise you won't do anything rash?"

I nod.

"All right, then get that stuff back to the house and into his cabinet before he gets home. I'll meet you in your room in like twenty minutes, okay?"

I nod again and get to my feet, leaving Ben on the rock, phone in hand. Maybe I should be worried about who he's calling and what he might say, but I'm not. I trust him.

Inside the house, my arm reaches over the crowd of bottles in the cabinet beside the refrigerator, trying to sneak the Glenlivet 21 into its resting place at the back. The bottom clunks against two other bottles as I stretch. I'm about to replace it, good as new with no one the wiser when a voice stops me. "What are you doing?" I close my eyes, bracing for what's coming.

"I didn't drink any," I say shakily, hoping I can sound convincing. "I was just being stupid."

"At least you're being honest about one thing." Dad sets a hand on my neck and I shiver despite the sultry heat in the kitchen. When he squeezes, I scrunch up my shoulders and tilt my head back to lessen the discomfort. He's warning me. But a warning against what? Will he throw me across the kitchen again? Not at this exact moment with my arm hovering over a dozen bottles of expensive whiskey, that's for sure.

He lets go, but I don't relax. Beneath his words is a river of contempt. "The one you're holding, let me see it." I do as he says. "The 21?"

I flinch at his tone. "I didn't know which one I grabbed. I didn't drink any."

His eyes examine first the bottle, then me. In a swift movement, he grabs my jaw. "Breathe," he commands.

I bite my lower lip. His fingers tighten on my chin, giving it a shake. I exhale like he says. "Hmph," he shakes his head. "A thief and a liar." I turn my head away slightly, preemptively squinting my eyelids half closed and expecting the blow at any second, but it doesn't come. The pressure on my jaw disappears.

"So you want to drink whiskey, huh?" he asks. Looking up, I see he's moved to the table. He sets the bottle in the center. "Sit." When I don't move, he snaps his fingers and points at the chair. "*Sit.*" I pull out the chair and do as he says. Dad takes two shot glasses from the cabinet and sits across from me. Setting one down in front of me, he keeps the other for himself.

I don't get it. I've obviously shown that I don't mind the taste, so why is he going to make me take a shot? Has he given up on punishment altogether?

Removing the cap, he pours a shot for each of us. Any doubt I had as to whether he was still angry disappears when he speaks. "Drink," he commands. The tiny glass is cool against my fingers. I put back the shot. So does he. Thanks to my sips earlier, my throat is already numb to the worst of the burn.

Without pausing, he pours another shot for each of us. The chill in his voice is the furthest thing from the heat permeating the air. "Drink," he says. I put back the shot. So does he. I gaze uneasily at the bottle. It's still three-fourths full.

On the third shot, my fingers hesitate to touch the glass. His steely glare cuts into me like the knife across my hand when I was sixteen. Swallowing my apprehension, I close my fingers around the tiny glass. I put back the shot. So does he.

I'm not ready for it when the strength of the alcohol hits me. My stomach has been humming warmly for a few minutes already, but now the feeling surges through my hands, my face, my feet, my tongue.

The level in the bottle steadily drops as he pours round four, five and six for us. I don't need another of his looks to know that I don't want to know what will happen if I refuse to play this game. I put back the shots. One. After. Another. So does he.

Round seven empties the bottle. Well, almost. There is still a little left in the bottom. He tips the bottle over my glass, waiting for the last drops to glide along the inside of the bottle before dripping into my share. My torso decides to lean forward a bit. I catch myself and straighten, reaching my hand out to take the shot. What's one more going to matter? At the thought, my throat constricts and my tongue feels heavy. I'm not used to feeling this way. I never gag or feel sick when I drink. But then, I also never drink like this. I glance at Dad. Hasn't he made his point already? His cold gaze answers my question with an unequivocal "no."

I put back the shot. The kitchen sways back and forth without any movement from me. I clench my teeth as the liquid falls down my throat. I'm not used to gagging at all. Once it's down, the feeling disappears. I'm thankful for that. My head lolls to the side, but it doesn't bother me. It's more comfortable that way. Across from me, Dad's features are suffused with disappointment, but I can't tell if he's disappointed in himself or me. As if on cue, he gets up without a word. Like always, it's his silence that hurts the most.

Chapter Thirty-two

Ben

I tried calling Mom three times. And then I left messages. On our landline's answering machine, on her cell phone, and her work cell phone. Then I left a message on her secretary's voicemail. It seems like weeks since I've talked to her, and I need her now. Jackson is going through some serious shit that I can't solve on my own.

Finally giving up on reaching her, I cross the yard and walk inside, passing Dad on his way out. He doesn't say anything to me, which strikes me as odd. At least he doesn't seem angry, so Jackson must have successfully stashed the bottle.

Jackson is sitting at the kitchen table. But something is off about him, because he's leaning awkwardly to the side. My attention snaps to the object in the center of the table. My heart sinks. It's the empty bottle of Glenlivet 21.

"Jackson," I say cautiously. "What happened?"

Instead of answering, he falls out of his chair onto the floor. *Fucking hell.* Kicking the chair of the way so he can lie on his back, I kneel beside him. His eyes open slowly, and his lips form into a lazy grin. "Ben." His smile grows wider for a moment. It's not a true expression of happiness though, instead it's tainted by something dark. He touches the side of my face, the tips of his fingers dipping into my hair.

"What the hell did you do?"

He frowns, looking away. "Don't yell at me."

I grunt. "You promised you wouldn't do anything stupid."

He winces when I say the word *stupid*. "Don't say that." He assumes an air of lucidity. "Dad calls me that enough." Then seeming to forget what he just said, he rolls onto his side, hitting his head on the table leg. "Ow." His voice is muffled because he's talking into the floor.

I raise my head enough to see the top of the table. Two shot glasses. Then it all clicks. "Did Dad make you do this?" Jackson doesn't respond, so I drag him onto his back again. Shaking his shoulder, I repeat my question.

He lets out a long breath, and I'm forced to turn my head away. It smells like he soaked himself overnight in a bath of booze. "I didn't want to," he whines. "I didn't want to, but he made me."

A swell of rage rises within me. *Goddamn it, Dad. How can you treat Jackson like this?* Leaving Jackson lying on the floor, I run out of the house, throwing the screen door open as I go.

Dad is already in his truck and turning the key. As it rumbles awake, his eyes catch mine, flooded with a disappointment so deep I'm afraid I might drown in it. Then the engine roars and he pulls out of the driveway, tires kicking gravel.

I'm so mad I can barely think, but Dad is gone. Jackson is the one who needs help. With a parting wish that Dad crashes himself into a tree, I turn back toward the house and the person half passed out on the kitchen floor.

"Hey, big brother," I say, crouching beside him again. "You and Dad split the bottle, right?" I pat his cheek to get his attention, doing it lightly so as not to cause further injury to my damaged brother.

Jackson's eyes have been fuzzed out, but they focus on me now for just a second. I think he's trying to nod as he slurs his words together. "I took a shot, he took a shot. I took a shot, he took a shot. I took a shot, he took a–"

"Okay, I get it," I interrupt him. The bottle is a 750 milliliter. If I remember right, that's seventeen or eighteen regular shots when it's full. It wasn't quite full when they started. So if there were, say, fifteen shots left in it, then each one would get seven, maybe a bit more. Shit, that's a lot. But it's not too much. I know, because I know I can handle that much. It'll be rough for him tomorrow, but he'll live.

It would be easier if I could get him to throw up, but that's pretty much impossible for either of us. It's why we can put down so much food. Or alcohol. Little gag reflex, even less weakness to nausea. Roanoke-No-Puke is a nickname I sometimes got called back home. It's a

dumb one, because it doesn't rhyme and it's not particularly imagina-
tive, but it is accurate.

Heaving his arm up over my shoulder, I give him a second to get
his feet under him before beginning the task of getting him up the
stairs. He sways unstably, so I sling my arm around his waist. He lets
his head drop onto my shoulder but still makes an effort to walk up the
stairs along with me.

We're halfway up the stairs when he says, "Ben." His voice is clearer now, as if the alcohol has given his brain a temporary respite. Standing up might have helped, for the moment anyway.

"What is it, Jackson?" I ask, pausing in my efforts to heave him up
the stairs.

We sway back and forth, finally coming to a rest against the wall.
The words are difficult for him to get out. "I hate him." He burps, wincing as he exhales. *Yeah, I bet that burns.* I lean away from the cloud of
whiskey vapor.

His head braced against the wall, he lets his eyes rest.

"It's wrong what he did," I say. "It would be child abuse if you
weren't eighteen."

He barks a laugh. "So it suddenly stopped being abuse when I had
my last birthday?" He's trying to keep his words clear but they're still
tripping over each other.

My heart breaks for what our dad has put him through. But his admission makes me wonder if there's more I don't know about. "What
else has he done?"

Jackson burps again, smaller this time. "Does it really matter?"
He pushes himself away from the wall. "Help me up to the bathroom,
'kay?"

"Sure."

He stumbles at the top of the stairs, but with my help, we make it
to the bathroom. I position him in front of the toilet, his arm still slung
around my shoulder. "Um, you need to take a piss or what?" I'm not
convinced he can stand up by himself right now, but I'll stay and hold
him up while he does his business if he wants me to.

His fingers fumble at his zipper. "Don't look," he mumbles.

Like he even needs to tell me that. "I won't," I assure him.

Leaning forward just a bit, he starts peeing. Except the sound I
hear is the dull, muted one of liquid striking plastic. *Really, Jackson?* I
have to break my promise not to look. He's aiming way too high and

would be hitting the front of the tank if the seat weren't up. Making sure not to touch something I shouldn't, I push down with one finger on the back of his hand until he's actually peeing into the bowl. For fear of him straying again, I maintain the pressure on his hand until he's finished. He doesn't say anything.

I can't imagine what Dad would think if he saw *this*. But I also don't really care. He can go fuck himself. He lost the right to have an opinion when he forced Jackson to drink all that booze, but really it was probably long before that. The thought digs into my throat like barbed wire as Jackson zips up and I flush the toilet for him. The water swirls. I wish we could flush our lives, to let the water sweep through and take away all the bad things we don't want to see or think about.

Instead of turning to wash his hands or leave, he pulls away from me and drops purposefully to his knees, his hands grabbing the edge of the toilet bowl. "You're trying to puke?" I ask, incredulous. We don't throw up. We just don't.

A year ago, I was at a party and went overboard. After I woke up at the hospital, Mom started asking questions and eventually figured out that I hadn't thrown up since I had the flu in fifth grade. No matter how much I drank, it didn't come up. My friends were jealous and assumed it was a blessing. It isn't.

A sickening heaving sound from Jackson's throat brings me back to the moment. He has two fingers stuffed into his mouth past his knuckles. He heaves again, but it's just the hollow echo of gagging. I can see the tendons moving faintly in his hand, so he must really be giving that muscle in the back of his throat a hard time, but as he gags for a third and then fourth time, it's clear he isn't getting anywhere.

Removing his fingers, which now have a glistening layer of saliva covering them, he lets his head hang. *"Fuck,"* he growls through gritted teeth. I kneel next to him and rest my hand on the middle of his back. The look he gives me can't be described as anything but despair. I try to reassure myself that the redness in his face and the tears in his eyes are probably from trying to make himself throw up.

"Ben," he says. "Don't let this happen."

I'm not exactly sure what he means, but when he sticks his fingers back into his mouth, I remember the one time I *was* able to throw up. It was less than three months after I was in the hospital. I knew I'd had too much, and I didn't want to disappoint Mom again, so I tried *everything*. Eventually something worked.

Jackson is facing down into the toilet, the first of the inevitable waves of gagging resonating out of the toilet bowl, when I put my arm around his waist.

"I'm going to try something that worked for me once," I whisper. He doesn't respond, so I proceed by slipping my hand under his shirt and placing my palm against his stomach. His skin is warm. Hot, really. He dry heaves again. Sliding my hand down an inch or two under the waistband of his boxer briefs, I press up and in on his abdomen, bringing my hand up past his belly button. The next retch sounds like there's more substance behind it, but it's hard to tell. It all sounds terrible. Pushing away my own embarrassment at touching my brother this way, I move my hand down to its original position and press again, a little firmer now. This time the empty heave is replaced by the disgusting sound of liquid traveling up his throat.

I exhale in relief and quickly remove my hand from his stomach as he begins to vomit. Now that he's started, there's no stopping him. When he finally finishes, his left hand is covered in a caramel-colored slime of mucus and stomach acid and his face is even brighter red than before. He spits one last time into the toilet before pushing himself to his feet. I step around him to flush the toilet while he washes his hands and face. From the way he's leaning on the vanity while he does this, I can tell he's intoxicated. He saved himself from a horrible hangover, but he's still drunk for the time being.

"Drink water," I say, holding out the empty glass we always keep by the sink. He fills it and drinks. Then he refills it and drains the second glass as well. It's unclear if he still needs help to keep his balance but I give it anyway.

The twilight of evening paints shadows into the hallway as we move along it. When we reach his room, I relax my grip on him and he falls face first onto the bed. He groans but doesn't move. What do I do with him now? In case he does throw up again, I want to be here. I've heard too many horror stories of drunk teens choking on their own vomit. I shudder at the thought.

Holding his arms, I heave him over onto his back. "Ben," he says. "Don't go." His words are partly coated with the syrupy insincerity of intoxication that still lingers in his voice, but hidden underneath is something more substantial. He needs me now. "Don't go," he repeats, wrapping his arms around his chest like he's warding off a chill. Ironic considering how hot it is in here.

"Okay," I whisper. He rocks from side to side. I don't think he heard me. I want to fetch him more water and some ibuprofen, but I might as well get him ready for bed before he gets comfortable. Not that comfortable means anything to him right now.

Again being careful not to touch anything I shouldn't, I undo the tie on the front of his shorts and tug them down. I go slow and try my best to preserve his modesty, but the friction is a bit too much and his boxer briefs get pulled down a few inches before I get the shorts off. His briefs today are fuchsia with bright yellow stripes. Turning my gaze away from his partial exposure, I quickly pull his underwear back up.

Jackson tilts his head to the side, but he's not really looking at me. "What are you doing?" he mumbles.

"Just getting you ready for bed," I say. Sitting beside him, I get him to sit up and then I remove his t-shirt too. He flops backward the moment I let go.

Despite his request not to leave him, I tiptoe out of the room and downstairs to the kitchen, returning with a tall glass of water and a pair of pink ibuprofen tablets. Setting them down on the nightstand, I take a seat on the edge of the bed beside my brother.

My eyes focus on his chest, narrowing in on the simple necklace with the ring on it. Picking up the small round object resting on his breastbone, I roll it between my thumb and forefinger. What significance does this have to him? Was it a gift from Matt, or was there someone else? A bolt of jealousy strikes me. Not jealousy over some love affair. I don't care about that. No, the idea that bothers me is that Jackson has someone so close to his heart that he needs this physical reminder always with him. In our years apart, did he try to replace me, and did that someone give him this ring?

It's hard to see in the semi-darkness, but a faintly glassy reflection tells me that Jackson's eyes are open and fixed on me. I don't let go of the ring, but I don't move either. I wasn't expecting him to be anything but completely passed out, but I guess purging all that alcohol from his stomach must be speeding him toward sobriety.

"You promised," he whispers.

"Promised what?"

"The day you gave me this."

My eyes shift to the ring, and I realize what's in my hand. I'm not sure how I know, but I do. It was so long ago, but I remember opening it before I gave it to him, so I would always know what was inside. The one-dollar plastic bubble that I gave him. The ring was indeed meant as a physical reminder of someone close to him. But it wasn't for anyone else. It was to remember me.

Despite the dimness in the room, I examine the ring just as I did years ago. The metal is covered in scratches, some deeper than others, but overall the abrasions bring out a dull shine. Did he wear it until his fingers grew too big? From the weight and how it's taken scratches, it must be some kind of low grade steel, which is surprising since it came from a vending machine. Then again, it was almost ten years ago that I gave it to him, back when everything wasn't made quite so cheap.

And I remember my promise. My promise to come back to him.

His stomach rises and falls with steady breathing, but his eyes don't move from mine. Despite his even breaths, despite his intoxication, despite everything that's happened today, I can sense the tension contained within every cell of his body as he awaits my response. The trillions of cells that have the same blueprint as every one of mine. A wave of regret crashes over me. I don't know what he's gone through over the years, but whatever it was, he didn't deserve it. He's my twin brother, my other half, and we should have been together.

"I won't ever leave you again, Jacks," I say quietly, using his childhood nickname for the first time in years. The word feels simultaneously light and heavy.

Glistening liquid wells up in his eyes. "How can I know you really mean that this time?"

I set the ring back onto his bare chest, letting my hand rest on top of it. His skin is hot under my fingers as tears pool up in my eyes as well, threatening to drip at any moment. My voice is husky when I tell him. "I always meant it."

"Did you really?" His voice is tense, but underneath it I hear... hope.

Instead of answering with words, I strip to my boxers and lie down next to him. Pushing lightly on his shoulder, I get him to roll over onto his side. Moving behind him so his back is just a few inches from me, I reach over and sling my arm around his chest, holding him like he always used to hold me when we were kids. I pull us together, feeling his timid heartbeat as he relaxes into me, and for the first time in weeks, I'm able to breathe freely.

"I'm never letting you go," I whisper in his ear.

* * * *

When Jackson's breathing – always steady even when awake – deepens to a heavier note, I extricate myself from him as carefully as I can. I'm pretty sure that he managed to expel the majority of the alcohol he consumed, but whatever was left must be working in my favor, because he doesn't awake as I slip out of bed and get dressed.

It's completely dark now as I steal down the stairs and out of the house. I'm not sure what time it is, but the moon and the stars shine down through a clear sky. Dad's truck is nowhere in sight. Wherever he went, he hasn't come home yet.

Reaching the clearing, I take a seat on the stone where I sat beside Jackson several hours earlier. Lying back, I gaze up into the night sky. The stars glitter above just as they always have. Why am I even out here?

A midnight breeze caresses my cheek, carrying with it a green poplar leaf. Taken before its prime, the leaf flutters down, landing beside me. Sitting up, I reach out to touch it, but at the last moment my hand detours, distracted by the leather of my shoe. Running the tips of my fingers over the sueded leather, I stop at the torn section from when Jackson kicked a hole in the wall while wearing my shoes. In that piece of leather, I find the answer I've been looking for.

I have to go back to California soon. I'm not sure exactly when Mom comes back, but her trip wasn't supposed to last *all* summer. She's coming back soon, and when she does, I'll be on a flight home. But that doesn't mean I'll be leaving Jackson again. Even if I wasn't honestly scared to leave him here alone, he doesn't deserve this life here. He needs me now – maybe more than all those times I needed him – and I'm not going to abandon him. Not again. And that starts tonight.

Back inside the house, I peek into his room to make sure he's still okay. Peacefully asleep, his chest moves with his breaths, lifting and lowering the ring I gave him. As much as I'd love to get my own rest, I'm still worried about Dad and what he might do when he comes home. Closing the door once more, I sit down in the hallway, blocking passage to the room. Leaning against the wall, I cross my legs. This night might be a long one, but it's better than the alternative. I won't let anyone hurt my brother again.

I'm awoken the next morning when the bedroom door opens. Jackson is staring at me. Pushing myself up to a sitting position, I exhale a groggy breath and wipe the sleep from my eyes.

"Benny?" His voice has always been able to pull me out of my own thoughts faster than anything else, but his use of my childhood name brings a warmth into my chest and causes my eyes to snap to his within a fraction of a second. "Jacks," I answer. The syllable glides across my tongue, tasting foreign yet at the same time deeply familiar, like welcoming an old friend home. He smiles.

The two words we've just exchanged are so much more than that. They contain more information than an encyclopedia and are more heartfelt than a romance novel. They're a declaration, an affirmation, and an oath – of our brotherhood, and our twinship.

I pull my knees up to my chest and simply look at him. Sitting down beside me, back against the wall, he looks right back at me. And then we talk. For the first time since I moved here for the summer, we really talk.

I tell him about how I've gotten to know Katie and how much I actually enjoy working with the plants. I tell him about the friends I left back home. About how no matter how hard I tried to make a friendship that emulated our relationship as children, it never came close. I tell him how much I missed him. How much it hurt every day that we were apart.

He tells me about how our dad's discipline slowly changed over the years to become punishment just for the sake of it, occasionally crossing a line. He tells me about first realizing he was gay, how he felt so alone, how he wondered if I was the same way. He tells me how he always blamed me for leaving, and couldn't bring himself to accept my offers throughout high school to reconnect, even as it killed him inside to turn me down. He tells me about getting to know Matt, and he tells me what happened the day they had sex. He tells me how it hurt.

I bristle, more so than I have at any point through all of his painful confessions. Jacks must be able to detect the change in me too, because he says, "I'll get past it. It will just take some time, I think."

Clenching my teeth as if that will help stifle the rage inside, I lean over and wrap my arms around him. He melts into me, his muscles relaxing.

I don't understand how someone could hurt him like that. It makes me want to scream and break shit. It makes me want to hurt that fucker back. More than anything, it makes me wish I could protect Jackson from the world. But that won't help. The only thing I can do right now is to be here for him, to hold him through the hurt.

I continue to hold him as tears drip from his eyes, through his whimpers and mumbled words. I hold him until he's quiet and my white-hot rage has mostly burned itself out.

"What do you want to do about Dad?"

"What is there to do?" he says, shifting his eyes to the window and the early morning sun stretching its warm fingers toward us. "We both leave here at the end of the summer, then it won't matter anymore. I'll survive until then."

"You can't stay here, you know."

In an instant, fury overtakes his expression. "Where the fuck am I going to go? I can't run away to California like you. I'm *stuck* here. I've always been stuck here. Don't you get that?"

I don't respond right away. Jacks is right to be angry, but that doesn't mean he's right about the rest of it. The gears click together in my mind, systematically bringing me closer to a solution.

"What are you thinking about?"

I look up, still mentally hammering out the details. "What if you came to live with Mom and me for the summers? You would never have to see Dad if you didn't want."

"Dad wouldn't allow it." Then after a pause, he says, "You think she would be okay with that?"

"I'm sure she would, and it doesn't matter what Dad thinks."

Jacks rubs the side of his thumb over his knee. "I don't know."

Without responding to him, I withdraw my phone and call one of the numbers I attempted yesterday. On the third ring, it gets answered. "Hello, this is Marjorie Speerman. Can I help you?"

"Hi Marjorie, it's Ben," I say quickly. "I left a voicemail on your line yesterday. I'm trying to get a hold of my mom." Jacks shoots a questioning look at me. I shrug and make an impatient gesture. Marjorie is Mom's secretary, and she's always been nice to me, so I don't want to be rude.

"Oh, I see," she says, using an overly happy office voice. "Unfortunately, she isn't back in the office yet and won't be for another week."

"Thanks," I say, my hopes disappearing. If Jacks and I could have flown out now, there would have been half a chance to get away from this place. But if Mom is still overseas and we have to stay here, I'm afraid Jackson will never be able to come with me.

"You're welcome." She hangs up.

Chapter Thirty-three

Jackson

"Benny, talk to me," I say, gripping his shoulders. "Benny," I repeat. His eyes slowly rise. The hollow look I find there scares me. I'm the one whose insides have just been scraped clean, but the vacant expression staring back at me looks exactly how I feel.

"I thought we could leave," he says, his earlier hopes fading into darkness. "What are we going to do now?"

"What do you mean? We're going to be fine." I watch him, noting the changes in his expression. For the most part, I've been able to suppress my feelings regarding all the fucked up shit happening over the last week, but it's only because I've had Benny. His support and daring cheerfulness have kept me afloat through the storm, even as the waves and wind and lightning have pummeled me into near submission. Without him, nothing would be left to hold me up. Which is why it's so damn scary seeing him like this.

"Benny," I plead. "What's wrong?"

His jaw clenches, his lips pressing into a line. "I can't let you stay here. I can't do that to you. But we can't just up and leave, not at least without one of our parents knowing what we're doing."

My fingers dig into his biceps, I pull him to me. He leans in awkwardly, practically falling into my lap. I hold him and wait. It's always been impossible to force anything out of Benny.

One by one, his muscles soften, and he accepts my embrace. I exhale slowly, banishing every last molecule of air from my chest. I squeeze extra tightly for just a second, and then I release him. "Why not?" I breathe the words like a confessed secret.

"Why not what?" Benny asks.

"Why can't we just go to Mom's place? You have the keys right?" I say, speaking faster now. "We'll leave a note telling Dad where we went, so he doesn't report us as missing persons or whatever. And then we go. We're eighteen, no one can stop us."

The hope in his eyes is reflected in my own. After all these years it finally feels like we're charting our own course instead of having it done for us. The thought is exciting, and terrifying. Standing up, I pull him to his feet as well. *Are we really going to do this?*

Benny's arms tighten around my chest as we merge onto the freeway and get blasted by a gust of wind from a passing semi truck. It's one of the few times since leaving the house that I'm glad there are two of us on the bike. We are *so* going to get pulled over. And when we do, we're screwed. The bike is street legal, but with only a conditional motorcycle permit, I'm not supposed to have passengers, and I'm definitely not supposed to be on the freeway with one. We took back roads most of the way here, but there was no avoiding this highway if we want to get to the airport. Benny doesn't even have a helmet.

With the two of us, this thing can barely do sixty-five with the throttle wide open. As irritating as it is to have cars whizzing past us, I slowed down to sixty a while ago so the engine doesn't overheat or anything. Driving to work is one thing, but taking the freeway toward Minneapolis is a whole different game. I flick my eyes to the side mirror as we pass an onramp. *Please let us not get pulled over.*

We get lucky. In the ten miles of freeway to the airport, we don't pass a single cop. As we pull into the long-term parking ramp and into one of the motorcycle spots, I exhale in relief. My palms and forehead are covered in sweat. Behind me, Benny slips off the bike so I can drop the kickstand.

Slung over his shoulder is the small backpack with our stuff. Considering how fast I packed, even the minimalist in me was surprised at how little we managed to bring. Our passports, two pairs of boxers, two pairs of socks, a bottle of Gatorade. That's it. I would have brought more, but we couldn't really carry much more without a car. Most of his stuff is back in L.A. anyway, and I know on good authority that it all fits me. His clothes are probably a lot more trendy than any of my stuff anyway. And he was surprised when I assumed he was gay, too.

With Benny in tow, we enter the Lindberg terminal. I've been to the Minneapolis-St. Paul International Airport a few times, but always with Dad or a school group or something, never by myself. And I sure as hell have never bought a ticket at the airport before, but I know it's possible. The ticket and check-in counters stretch for what looks like a half mile. *Damn this place is huge.* I glance at Benny and his eyes glazed with exhaustion. He looks despondent, his attention wandering across the expansive terminal.

His current physical state is a reminder that he spent the entire night outside my door, watching over me just in case Dad came home. He stayed up all night. For me. At that moment, my heart seems to double in weight, as if it can't hold all my feelings for Benny on its own.

Approaching the nearest information counter, I wait behind an older man with a rolling black suitcase. When the lady points him off toward the far end of the terminal, I tug on Benny's arm to get him to stay with me as I move up to the counter. "Hi," I say.

The lady smiles at me. She's chewing gum but not being unprofessional about it. "How can I help you?"

I feel like an idiot, but there's no other choice than just to ask how this works. "We need to fly to L.A., but we don't have tickets or anything. We can just buy them at a counter, right?"

She smacks her gum. Okay, now it's irritating. "Look at the outgoing departures and then go to the airline counter and ask if you can still get a ticket." She glances at Ben behind me, her widening smile indicating that only now is she realizing that we're identical. "Or two tickets."

"Uh, thanks." I tug on the hem of Benny's shirt to pull his gaze back from whatever he's staring at. He follows me to the displays with all of the departures. A few are going to L.A., but they're leaving too soon to even try to catch them. Most of the flights on the screen are for Delta, though, so I figure that might be a good place to start.

The line isn't too long for the ticketing and check-in counter, but my eyes keep darting glances at the other passengers. Everyone already has tickets of course, brandishing them as proof that they're in the right place. We get a few looks from people in the line, so I try to keep my gaze fixed on the floor as much as possible. I'm not sure if the curiosity is because of the bruises still on Benny's face and his exhausted expression or just because we're identical. It's probably no help that we're both wearing plain white t-shirts. Whenever we match in public – always by accident, of course – it attracts even more attention than normal, like we're the locus of some mystic magnetic field.

The last passengers in front of us finish checking in a monstrous bag that must have been over the weight limit, because the man is stuffing a credit card back into his wallet. The woman at the counter in her crisp dark blue uniform waves us forward. A glance over my shoulder confirms that my brother is following without me having to nudge him.

"Identification and tickets, please" she says.

My cheeks grow hot as I struggle with the zipper on the backpack. Benny is standing just behind me. I'm worried he won't snap out of this until he has a chance to sleep, but it's impossible to tell with him.

I lay our passports in front of her. "We don't have tickets yet," I admit.

"No problem," she says. "Where would you like to go?"

"Los Angeles."

"Sure," she says, squinting at her computer. She taps away at the keyboard. "The next flight I can get you on leaves at 5:15 p.m., arriving at 7:12 p.m. local time. Tickets are $698.00 each."

Holy hell. "Are you serious?" I suspected I might not be able to afford for both of us to fly, but I can't even send Benny. I would pay it if I could, but I definitely can't. The card I got to start building credit only has a $750 limit. I pay it off every month, but it has like a hundred bucks or so already on it this month.

The woman gives me a small smile. "Prices to fly day-of are quite expensive I'm afraid. Any flight to LAX today will be the same price."

"Um, never mind then I guess," I say, my cheeks swelling with embarrassment.

"Wait, what?" Benny interrupts me. "Jacks, we have to go," he says, his voice imploring.

I flush, lowering my voice. "I can't pay for both of us. I would if I could, but I can't drop fourteen hundred bucks on this if I don't *have* it."

He looks confused, like I'm speaking a foreign language to him, before the cloud of tiredness around him clears just a bit. Then he pulls out his wallet and hands me a silver American Express card. "Use this."

Raising my eyebrows, I take the card from him and hand it to the woman. "Try this, I guess."

"Two tickets?"

"Yeah."

Benny remains coherent enough that we're able to get through security and to our gate without any awkward questions, but once we sit down on the waiting bench, I can see his gaze fade away again as he stares across the tarmac. I wish there was something I could do to help him, but he really just needs a good night's sleep.

Our flight leaves in an hour, but after the trip here and the ordeal of getting our tickets, I'm okay with having a moment to catch my breath. My phone starts ringing. I slide it out of my pocket and look at the screen. The muscles in my chest constrict and suddenly it's hard to breathe. It's Dad calling. Dragging my finger across the red phone icon, I send him to voicemail. Benny doesn't shift his eyes away from the endless stretches of runway.

I have to piss, but I don't want to leave him here alone. "Come to the bathroom with me," I tell him. He doesn't respond, so I give his arm a squeeze. At my touch, he stands up and follows me.

He hovers behind me as I walk up the farthest urinal. I aim an irritated look back at him. "You going to pee or just stand there? I'm not going to hold it for you."

For the first time since pulling out his Am Ex card at the ticket counter, he really looks at me. Then he approaches the next urinal over and unzips. I let out a long sigh. I'm going to be so glad when this day is done.

The moment Benny gets the deadbolt retracted, he rushes through the door and into the condo he shares with Mom. Lights flick on as he passes the rooms, destroying the darkness. I stifle a yawn and lean against the doorframe, unable to move another inch. I'm utterly exhausted, so I have no idea how Benny is still going. A moment later he reappears. "She's not here," he says. He managed to nap a little on the plane, which was fortunate, because I've been hopelessly lost since we left the airport. The cab ride was over a half hour, but all it took was another flash of that silver credit card and the driver gladly took us.

"What now?" I ask. Ever since we've gotten here, he's been running the show. He's not back to normal, but he's functional at least.

Benny looks around the entryway like he's expecting to find instructions. "I don't know. If she's going to start work again in a week, she must be getting back soon. They won't send her back without at least a day off."

I check the time on my phone, ignoring the notification about my still unopened voicemail. "It's almost eleven," I inform him.

"I guess we sleep then."

Neither of us has eaten since having a quick snack on the plane, but for once I'm actually more tired than I am hungry. He must feel the same way too, because after sharing a glass of water, he leads me to his bedroom. Their condo is really nice, way more spacious than I would have imagined. Then again, since Mom is apparently a hot shot VP at her company, it's not that much of a surprise I suppose.

The room is immaculately clean. I wonder if he sanitized before he left, or if he always keeps it like this. Letting the backpack drop from my shoulders onto the floor, I strip down to my underwear as Benny does the same. I watch as he climbs into bed.

I know we slept next to each other for part of last night, but I don't want to make any assumptions. Benny has always been more reserved about that kind of thing. "Should I sleep on the couch?" I ask.

He stifles a yawn and flicks off the bedside lamp. "If that's what you want," he says, his words alluding to another half of the sentence left unspoken – *but I'd rather you stay here.* I slide under the covers beside him. Neither of us moves for almost a minute. He sniffles beside me. It's the first time today that either has had a chance to let our guard down.

"I'm scared, Jacks," he whispers.

"Of what?" Somehow I feel like the big brother again. He did what was needed to get us out of Minnesota, but now that we're here...

"Of losing you."

"It's going to be okay." I hope to God that I'm not lying to him. Or to myself.

His arm sneaks across the gap between us and takes hold of my wrist. Turning onto his side, he pulls me with him, draping my arm across his chest. Drawing us close together, I hold him, just like he held me last night.

Is it weird that we're doing this? To any outsider, it might look really fucked up. But it's not, and I can't explain why. It's like after so many years apart, we're starving for a closeness that no one else can provide. It's the same sort of thing when someone wraps their arms around themselves trying to find comfort in a time of need. Except when we do that, it doesn't really help unless someone else is tucked into those arms too. We're different people, but we're also the same.

Then I realize I don't really care what anyone would think of this. Like so many things that we share, it doesn't matter if it makes sense to anyone else. What Benny and I have isn't something that can be explained or reasoned with or judged. Our connection is visible, and it's invisible. And it's exasperating, and it's amazing, and it's sometimes painful, but it has always been ours alone.

Chapter Thirty-four

Jackson

Broken. The word never meant as much as it does now. It encapsulates and quantifies and defines how I feel. Shattered pieces that I can't fit back together, no matter how hard I try. Yesterday I held it together, because Benny needed my help to get us here. I can't do it anymore, though. Benny still needs me to be strong, but I can barely hold myself up. How can I possibly be there for him?

I set the phone down on the table. My father's voice echoes crystal clear in my mind. *Only a coward would have left like that.* His words now hurt more than all the times he raised a hand against me. *Just up and left, like your mom did.* Or ignored me. *She should have taken you, not Ben.* Or forced me to split a fifth of whiskey with him. My eyes close, willing the world to wink out of existence right along with my vision.

"What's wrong?" Benny sounds tired, even though we both slept over eight hours.

Without opening my eyes, I push the phone across the table in his direction. "Dad left a voicemail," I say quietly.

I hear a soft scrape of plastic on wood as he picks up the phone. I don't move, nor do I make any effort to bring back the image of the room around me. Finally the sound of the phone being set back on the table indicates that Benny has heard everything. All the worst things that could possibly be said to someone.

He wraps his arms around me, involuntarily including the back of the wooden chair I'm sitting in. "Oh my God, Jacks, I'm so sorry," he whispers, his voice close. "I don't even know what to say. I don't understand how he can be so horrible to you. And it was my idea to leave anyway." He bites his lip, his eyes rising to touch mine. "You're not a coward... and definitely none of that other stuff he said."

I sigh, finally looking at my brother. "It's not your fault. This was building for years."

"You can stay here for the summer, so don't worry about that." He rests a hand on my shoulder and kneels beside me. "We're going to figure everything out. I promise."

I nod. It's the best I can give him right now. I got him here, but now it's his turn to take over.

"What is *that*?" The massive silver sedan parked in the underground lot is, well, massive.

Despite everything, Benny grins as he pushes a button on the key fob and the taillights flash once. "It's an Infiniti M56. The new model came out in March, and I convinced Mom to get one."

I raise my eyebrows. "You're serious?"

"Yeah, why wouldn't I be?" He shrugs and opens the door. "She needs a nice car for work."

I get in across from him and sink into the luxurious leather. "This is *way* more than a nice car. This is–" I don't finish, because I don't know what I'm trying to say.

He taps the engine start button and a rumble of understated power emanates from under the hood. Backing up, he slowly pilots us out of the underground parking garage and onto the street. Once we're outside, he guns it and I'm thrown back in my seat. *Holy hell, Benny.* I've never ridden passenger with him before, but he clearly enjoys driving.

"Damn, dude," I snap as we careen – tires screeching – through a ninety-degree turn at nearly thirty miles per hour.

"What?" He aims a look in my direction and tosses me back into the seat again. My stomach starts to gurgle. No one drives like this back in Northfield, and I'm pretty darn sure that not very many people around here do either.

"How fast is this thing?"

"Not sure," he says. "It's governed at bit over one fifty, though."

"I hope you had to look that up."

He gives me an unreadable look as he pulls onto the freeway and mashes me into the seat again.

Thanks to Benny's driving, we get to the grocery store in less than ten minutes. The kitchen was barren, but if Mom really hasn't been home for almost two months, it makes sense.

As we walk up and down the aisles and Benny throws stuff in the cart, I try to remember how long it's been since I've seen Mom. What will it be like? Will she look way older, or just a little more weathered? If she asks how I've been, do I tell her the truth?

"This way, Jacks," Benny calls from several feet back.

My head snaps to his voice. He took a left at the last junction but I kept going straight. I jog back to him, not wanting to be responsible for any delay to breakfast. "Sorry," I mutter.

"Don't worry," he says.

"Worry about what?"

"Seeing Mom again."

I manage a weak smile. Good old Benny.

We're back in the car and heading home when my stomach really starts to protest. Thanks to Benny's recklessness, we make even better time on the way back.

Leaning against the wall, I wait while he opens the door to the condo. Before he even has it all the way open, he freezes in place. "Mom," he says.

A brief pause follows. Then a woman's voice, resonating with notes of deep familiarity. "Oh my goodness, Ben, it's you."

Two rushed footsteps, and then silence. The door hangs open, just as the plastic grocery bags do from my hands. Shifting away from the wall, I stand back enough so they can't see me.

Eventually my brother speaks again. "I've missed you." The longing in his voice makes me worried. Now that he's home, will I get sent back to Minnesota?

"I'm so sorry, Ben. I kept hoping I would finish sooner. How did you end up back here?"

"It's a long story, but actually, there's something more important than that right now."

"Oh?" she asks, curious. "What's that?"

"Someone else is here to see you." My heart thuds. "Jacks, come on."

Like always, I do as Benny wants. He's standing just beside our mom. She does look older, and weathered too. But she's still beautiful. Her hair is long and blond, the same color as Benny's and mine. When she smiles at me, the years fall away and I'm staring at the same woman who picked me up from elementary school and took me to swimming lessons all those times.

I don't mean to cry, especially since it's the first time she's seen me in so long, but I can't help it as I close the distance between us. She holds open her arms and I fall into them. Her embrace is warm and it feels like home in a way I never thought I would feel again. Her grip around me not loosening a single bit, she says, "Jackson, oh, Jackson. I have missed you so much." Her breath is hot in my hair. The tears keep coming.

Amidst this, another hand comes to a rest on the middle of my back. "You're safe now, Jacks," Benny says.

Mom shifts to look at him, but she doesn't release me from the hug. What secret looks must they be exchanging right now? With a sigh, I push the worry out of my mind. Benny will tell her about everything eventually. For the moment, though, I want to savor feeling exactly the way my brother described – *safe*.

Chapter Thirty-five

Jackson

Movement nearby nudges me out of my slumber. Not wanting to open my eyes quite yet, I pull the covers closer and roll onto my side. It's been a week. A quiet, relaxing, restorative week. At least as far as my sleep is concerned.

Benny and I have slept in his bed every night since we arrived in L.A., even though a guest bedroom is just across the hall. We haven't fallen asleep in each other's arms since those two nights, but I'm not ashamed of it or anything. We just haven't felt the need, I guess.

Mom accepted the sleeping arrangements without any question. She did, however, have quite a few questions about what went down at our dad's place. Benny assured me that she would stick by us no matter what we told her, but I asked him to let me pick the time to come out. He insisted that she wouldn't care, and I believe him, but I just want this time to not be about that. Especially after what happened with Matt, I don't know if I'm ready to even think about that part of my life.

I don't know how long it's going to last, what we have going on here. It's understood all around that I can't return to Northfield and live with our dad anymore, and I doubt that Mom would let me go back even if I wanted to – which I absolutely do not. Even the thought of it makes me feel empty inside.

After what happened, Mom took off the rest of the month before she returns to work, so she's been spending a lot of time with us. It feels good not to be working all the time, but more than that, it feels good to spend time with her and Benny. In a way, it almost seems like we're a family again, albeit one with big underlying issues. Not least of all because the last few days Mom has been treating me like I'm a highly breakable object. Benny must have told her more than what we all discussed that first day. It pisses me off that he did that, but he did it because he cares about me, so whatever.

"Morning, Jacks," Benny says over a yawn. His arms stretch above his head, his knuckles whacking the wall as he arches his back.

"Morning."

"I hope you're excited for the day. I have something special planned."

Special, huh? "Oh really?"

"Yeah, really." He sits up, eyeing my chest.

I look up at him. "What?"

Instead of answering, he traces a line down my neck. I'm not sure what he's doing until he hooks his finger under my necklace. Gently tugging on it, he rotates the chain around my neck until the ring appears from beneath the covers. "You always wore this?"

An uncomfortable heat spreads in my chest and my face. I never feel embarrassment when I'm with Benny, so why now? Pushing past the emotion, I admit, "I never took it off."

"Why not?"

Sitting up beside him so our arms are touching, I tell him the truth, even though it makes me feel stupid. "I was afraid if I lost the ring, that I'd lose you too. It was the reassurance I always had that you'd come back. Without it..." I don't want to finish the thought.

For the thousandth time, a shard of agitation slices into me. *What if Benny hadn't come to live with me this summer?* Everything would have just continued along, the same as it had always been. And it would have been completely my fault that Benny and I never reconnected before we went away to college. Colleges across the country from one another. I suppress the thought, because I don't want our impending separation to contaminate the rest of our time together.

Benny shifts, the fine hairs on his arm grazing against mine, but he stays silent. A feeling reverberates across the invisible connection between us, and I get the impression that he's thinking along the same lines. Can he honestly reassure me that if it weren't for this summer, that we would have eventually found each other again and rebuilt our relationship? I don't think he can, and that scares him just as much as it does me.

We were given a chance at becoming brothers again, but what now? Sure, we'll see each other on breaks and holidays, but otherwise? Bitterness dances around the inside of my mouth. I don't want to leave him.

Benny and I have just demolished two cheeseburgers and fries. Each. Damn it feels good to pig out with my brother again. Benny stifles a burp and rubs his belly. Yeah, he's satisfied too. Being a guy under twenty with a high metabolism has to be one of the best things in the world.

The waitress thought we were joking when we ordered. Then she asked if she should bring out extra plates for friends coming to join us. Shit like that makes us feel a little guilty, but we love stuffing our faces too much to care. We might not eat for a day. We certainly won't *need* to, but Mom will probably cook tonight. *If we're lucky.* I grin to myself. My mirror image catches my eye and grins back.

Mom wanted to come with us, but the moment she suggested it, we both gave her the same look, the one that said this was time we needed to ourselves. Benny drove us to a burger joint that he claimed was the "best in town" and conveniently near the ocean. Near enough that now when he suggests we walk to the beach, I'm not entirely opposed. More than a few blocks though, and my stomach will get angry. It's still trying to organize right now.

One of the best things about having Benny is that it's not awkward if we don't talk. If something is on our minds, we'll discuss it. And if there's nothing, we're just as content to spend the time together in silence.

So it doesn't feel strange that we haven't spoken since leaving the restaurant. With the sun bright overhead, we plop down onto the sand, propping ourselves up with our arms behind us.

"I really love living here," he says.

"It's nice. Way too many people, though. Every-fricking-where. But you'll be in San Francisco when you go to Stanford."

"San Francisco is good too," he says. Something is off about his tone.

I shuffle through the various things that could be bothering him. "Have you talked to Katie since you left?"

"Nah. It was pretty much over after the Fourth of July."

"Really? I thought you guys were hitting it off pretty well. What happened?" Guilt clings to my words. If I'd paid any attention to him at all in the last month, I would already know the answer.

Thankfully he doesn't sound upset. "She was mad that I didn't make her enough of a priority."

"Why didn't you? It's summer and you even worked together, what the heck were you doing instead?" It seems odd to be casting judgment on Benny's relationship with her, especially after everything that happened with Matt, but that's what brothers are for, right?

When he doesn't answer right away, I worry that I might have offended him. Finally he speaks, his voice soft, "She needed my time, and you needed my time. You got it, she didn't."

I swallow quickly and take a deep breath, focusing instead on the waves crashing onto the beach, transforming the smooth blue water into white chaos. Something about the vast and endless makes me uncomfortable. After living so long in a place where the land rolls on without ending, being so close to all that water is unsettling.

"I think," Benny starts again cautiously, his voice snapping me back to our conversation. "I think I don't want us to split up again."

I glance away, concentrating on the heat of the sun on the bridge of my nose. Apparently he's been thinking about that just like I have, except now he's doing it out loud. I turn back to him and toss a handful of sand at his feet. "Don't talk like that," I snap. "I don't want us to split up either, but there's nothing we can do about it."

A touch on my shoulder brings my eyes to his. "I'm not going to let you go again," he says, his tone coated with the steely armor of conviction.

"What are you saying?"

"I'm going to decline the offer at Stanford. I'll go to school in Minneapolis with you."

"Then you'd be an idiot." I wish I could prevent my voice from seething with regret. I want him to go to his dream school, not be held back by me. But I also don't want to let him go.

He nods. "Then I'm going to be an idiot." The certainty in his gaze leaves no doubt that he's serious.

"You talk to Mom about this?"

"She doesn't like the idea of passing up on Stanford, but she knows it's my choice."

"I see." I want to jump up and hug him and scream for joy. And I want to tell him he's being stupid. I don't do either of those things. I'm caught somewhere between apprehension that he's going to change his mind, and guilt that I'm not trying to convince him to do exactly that.

"You don't sound excited." He bites his lip. "Do you not want me around after this summer?"

It occurs to me that I could lie to him now and he would go to Stanford like he's supposed to. But against his insecurity, his vulnerability, I have no choice but to tell him the truth. "Goddamn, Benny, how could you think that? I never want you to leave again. I love you more than anything in the world, and I don't want to be away from you. Ever."

A thin line of liquid glistens along his lower eyelids, catching the sun's light. "Then what is it?"

"I don't want you to give up your dream just because of me."

He shakes his head. "Now who's the idiot? Between you and Stanford, it's not even a choice. You'd win every time." His voice growing quiet, he admits, "Between you and *anything*, you'd win every time."

I smile, and a heaviness I didn't even know was there lifts off my entire body. I would feel ten pounds lighter, but I just devoured like five pounds of burgers and fries, so maybe five pounds lighter is more accurate.

"So what now?" I ask.

"We start over," he says. "Just you and me."

Chapter Thirty-six

Jackson

Mom has given me plenty of space in the days since Benny and I showed up unannounced at her condo, but I know she's been waiting to have some real one-on-one time with me. So when Benny tells me that he's going to spend the morning catching up with a friend from high school, Mom jumps on the chance and invites me to go to a little indie coffee shop near their condo.

I don't know what she wants to talk about, or if it's anything specific at all, but as we walk down the street lined with towering condo buildings, I come to a decision about what *I* want to say today. Pulling out my phone as we walk, I tap out a text to Benny. *I'm going to come out to Mom.*

Almost instantly, I get a response. *Don't worry, you'll be fine. She loves you no matter what.*

Thanks. I message him back, feeling bolstered by his words.

And so do I.

You what?

Love you no matter what. Thinking of you bro!

I smile after I read that, checking quickly to make sure that Mom isn't annoyed that I'm texting. She smiles back but doesn't ask me to put my phone away, seeming content to enjoy the morning sun in silence. *Love you broseph.*

Again his response is immediate. *Love you brohan.* Grinning, I think quickly to keep this going, watching the messages pop up one after another.

Me: *Love you bromigo.*

Ben: *Love you brofessor.*

Me: *Love you broseidon.*

Ben: *Love you brometheus.*

Me: *Love you bromeo.*

Ben: *Love you my little brony.*

It takes me a second to get that before I burst out laughing. Getting a look from Mom, I finally put away my phone. I can't believe how lucky we are to have found each other again. It seems like the slightest thing at any point this summer could have ruined our chances, but we made it. And now we have something that I wouldn't trade the world for.

Mom and I have just sat down with our iced coffees at a tiny round table near the window, but neither of us has taken a sip yet. Across from me, her eyes shine blue just like mine and Benny's. It's just one of a slew of features that the three of us share, making me wonder how much Benny and I actually inherited from our dad. Even the hands clutching her plastic cup are like ours too, except they carry years that we haven't yet seen.

"I've missed you," she says.

Looking up from her hands, I echo her words. "I missed you too." Deep resentment prickles in my chest, despite my words. She should never have left in the first place.

Instead of the thing I wanted to talk to her about, this new feeling muscles its way into my mind. No matter how much I might enjoy having Mom back in my life, it can never be real unless I understand why she did what she did. Emotion coils up in my throat until I can't bear it any longer. "Why did you choose Ben?" The sounds feel so much sharper when I say them out loud.

"Oh, Jackson." Her voice rings with regret. Reaching across the table, she grips my hand. Her fingers fade toward white as she squeezes. "It was the hardest thing I have ever done." Her lips tremble as she speaks, but her fingers hold tight to mine. "I hated myself for it. Every single day that passed, I promised myself that once I was back on my feet, I would fight to get you too. You have to understand that it could have taken months to get full custody of you both. I didn't have the resources for a protracted divorce case. At least not while working a part-time job and being a mother to two ten-year-old boys–" She stops abruptly, trying to swallow away the tears gleaming around her eyes.

Taking a deep breath, she forges on. "I took the job out here, because it was the fastest way to get ahead. It took three long years, but I wanted to be sure. I had enough saved to hire the best lawyer in the state to get you back. But after I started the process, you just stopped talking to me–"

I cut her off, speaking quickly, "I shouldn't have done that."

Her smile is weak. "Maybe not, but you were right. You were so right, Jackson. I should have found another way."

It feels good to hear that, but something is still bothering me. My jaw clenches. I shouldn't ask this, but I'm more afraid of not knowing than I am of what she might say. "You haven't said why you took Benny and not me."

Releasing my hand, she runs her fingers gently through my hair, finally bringing them to a rest on my cheek. "Because you were stronger than Ben." The words sink in for a moment before she continues. "But you went through more than you ever should have had to. Living with your father was very challenging for me, but he never, ever hit or abused any of us. At least not physically. I would never have left you there if I thought even for a second that he would hurt you in any way."

Before she can say anything more, I stand up and pull her into a hug. Her warmth cascades over me. Comforting, and healing. I still hate that she left, but at least now I understand. I think people are watching us, but I don't care. She holds me for a full minute, her cheek pressed so close against mine that I feel her eyelashes whisk against my skin when she blinks.

After we take our seats again, Mom says softly, "Ben told me a lot of things that happened when you were at your dad's. Do you want to talk about that?"

"What can I say?" I shrug and finally take my first drink of coffee, letting the chilled liquid glide over my tongue. "It sucked, and toward the end it got pretty bad, but I'm not there anymore. Now I just want to move on."

"You might be able to press charges against him, if you wanted," she says, her face reflecting compassion. "But it doesn't sound like that's what you want."

I shake my head. "I just want to go to college. As long as I don't have to go back there, I don't care."

"You never have to go back. Not for the summers, not for winter break, not even for a visit if you don't want."

Would she say that if she knew everything? "There was something that Ben didn't tell you."

"Oh?" Her eyebrows rise in piqued curiosity. "And what would that be?"

Memories come tumbling back from the summer and the times I got outed. Getting caught jerking off, an overheard conversation, and small town gossip. But this time it's up to me to share this message with someone, in my own way.

"Benny and I... are different," I say, unsure how to say this without actually saying it. Mom's smile encourages me to go on, even though I'm not sure how. "The reason that Dad freaked out so much at the end, it's because he found out that I–" My voice stops. Why am I so afraid to admit this?

Mom's hand tightens around her coffee, forcing the plastic cup to bend inward and the beads of condensation to grapple with her fingers. "You can tell me anything," she says.

"I... prefer to be with guys."

"Like for your friends?" She sounds confused.

Oh, Christ. In that moment, I decide that if I'm going to do this, I might as well go the whole way, because I don't want any part of my life to be just tolerated. I want acceptance, or nothing at all. "No, Mom. I *like* guys."

Her eyes grow wide. "Are you sure?"

Frowning, I consider how best to make it clear. "Yes, I am absolutely sure that I like dick." I give her a look.

"I'm sorry, I shouldn't have asked that," she says, blushing. "Of course you know what you like, I'm just a little surprised."

"What do you think about that?" I ask, staring her down.

Chuckling, she gives me a big smile. "You're my son, Jackson, and I want you to be happy. Whoever you end up with is going to be one lucky guy."

With this simple statement, the tension across my chest dissipates, leaving me smiling back at her and ultimately glad that I decided to share this part of myself with her. Thankfully, she doesn't ask any uncomfortable questions about relationships, instead steering us back toward safer topics like college plans and what I like to do in my free time. And all the while, time sneaks past, watching over our conversation like an invisible conductor counting out the beats. It makes me sad that my relationship with her was put on hold for years just like mine and Benny's. I want to move forward, and I think Mom does too.

Chapter Thirty-seven

Jackson

Four Weeks Later

"Just take it. I've hated that car since the day I bought it. It's like driving a tank with a turbo-whatever," Mom complains.

Benny looks annoyed. "No, Mom, that engine is naturally aspirated."

"Huh?" She sounds confused.

"He means there's no turbocharger," I clarify with a snicker.

"Oh, whatever. It has a bigger engine than anyone ought to have. I shouldn't even let you take it, come to think of it."

My brother speaks fast, like he's trying to ward off impending disaster. "We'll drive it safe. And you know that car has like a forty-star crash rating."

"Good thing too, because you'll probably crash it. I know how you drive," she huffs.

"I won't crash it, I promise," he whines. "Besides, Jacks will drive half the time too. He drives like a grandma, so it will all even out."

"I don't drive like a grandma," I snap. He returns a warning look that says, *don't mess this up.*

Mom sighs. "Please don't make me regret this."

Benny grins because he knows he's won her over. Soon it's going to be just the two of us on our own.

I don't know how she did it, but after numerous phone calls and emails, Mom managed to secure a late entry spot for Benny to the

University of Minnesota. We still don't have a place to live, since the dorms are already booked to over capacity, but it's official, Benny and I will be going to the same school! It feels surreal. The whole *summer* has felt surreal. Especially the last month with just Mom and the two of us.

Looking back, our relationship began to rebuild itself from the moment Benny first stepped through the front door, but I never could have seen it at the time. It wasn't until the very end, when he held me despite Dad's threats and guarded the door through the night, that I realized how this summer gave us a chance to reclaim what we had. Part of me is sad about leaving Dad after all the years we lived together, even though he deserves a lot worse than that for what he put me through. Another part of me is done feeling bad about things I can't change. I don't know if Benny taught me that, or if just being around him helped me see the truth that was there all along.

Tossing the last duffel bag into the trunk, I pull it closed with a solid thunk. The sky is so overcast that it would be impossible to tell if it was morning or evening if I didn't already know. But the weather is the last thing that can dampen my spirits today. Benny and I are about to begin our adventure.

The semester doesn't start for ten days, but I'm not in any rush. Mom wanted us to fly, but Benny convinced her to let us road trip back to Minnesota. Somehow he managed to get her to let us *keep* the car, too. There must be some parts to their mother-son relationship that I still don't understand, because it doesn't make a lick of sense to me. If she didn't like the car, she could have traded it in. At a loss, sure, but a hell of a lot less of one than watching it drive away across the country. Benny went so far as to joke that this car cost about the same as four years of college. I hope he was kidding.

As I sink into the luxurious seat across from him, I make a conscious effort to let go of my reservations about the financial sense of us having the car. We have it, because we do, and that's good enough for me.

Benny starts the engine and we wave to Mom as he pulls away from the curb. I roll down the window just a tidge as he drives calmly down the street. He must be channeling my grandma-driving. For once the air outside isn't too hot, which makes the breeze actually feel good.

Coming up to the end of the street, he brings the car to a halt even though there's no stop sign here. Nearly two thousand miles of cityscape, desert, mountains, plains and forests lie between us and Minnesota. We got the go ahead to splurge on hotels if we want, courtesy of the silver American Express card, of course, but we have a tent tucked into the trunk alongside the rest of our stuff, just in case.

"Ready, big brother?" Benny asks.

I flash a look at him and the eager grin on his face. The next ten days are all ours. And a hell of a lot more time after that too, I hope. "Just you and me?"

"Just you and me."

Half an hour later, the muted buzz of the tattoo iron is the only sound in the small shop. The air is cool in here, especially with my shirt off. The side of the artist's hand brushes my nipple as she adjusts her position, continuing her work on my chest a few inches below where my collarbone slides up toward my shoulder.

Dragging my eyes away from the point where her iron meets my skin, branding me forever, I look up at my brother sitting across the room from me. The moment he said he wanted a tattoo, I insisted that we both get them.

Benny actually came up with the idea weeks ago, but we didn't want to do it while still living with Mom. "Does it hurt?" The curiosity and concern in his voice make me smile.

"Stings a little bit, but not too bad."

"I still think it's dumb that you're going first. It was my idea after all," he says with a played up scowl. He's not really mad.

"I'm older, which means I get to go first." I grin. The woman working on my chest chuckles.

As soon as she's all finished with me, she starts right away on Benny. I watch him just as he watched me, our communication entirely nonverbal. He doesn't need to say anything to let me know how much he likes the idea of us doing this.

From the moment we were born, our physical resemblance was always there – whether we liked it or not. No one ever *asked* us if we wanted to be identical, if we wanted to be given this rare and special and exasperating connection.

What we're doing now has a much deeper significance. Marking ourselves in this way is entirely our choice. It's an affirmation of our absolute acceptance of one another.

When the woman finishes, Benny sits up on the tattooing bed as I cross the short space between us. Stretching my fingers out, I run them across the right side of his chest, over the contour of his pectoral muscle. Five characters in a sloping script are inscribed there. *Jacks*.

Likewise he touches the still exposed skin of my chest. It's hard to see at this angle, but in the same spot on my own body, I now bear my brother's name. *Benny*.

Our eyes connect, and his lips pull upward in a subtle smile. I can't help but return the expression, knowing that what we've imprinted on ourselves today will stay with us for all our lives. It will be there for everyone to see when we're at the beach, it will be there every morning when we look in the mirror, and it will be there whenever either of us is intimate with anyone – for the first time and every single time after that. And whoever that is will know that no matter the connection they may have with us, someone else was there first. That name burned into our skin and our hearts. A brotherhood shared, forever.

Did you enjoy this book?

If you did, please consider leaving a review on Amazon, Goodreads, or even a forum or blog. Word of mouth is important to any book's success, but especially for Indie books that don't have the hefty resources of a publishing company behind them!

Chase Potter lives in St. Paul, Minnesota with his husband Mitchell and their dog Alex in an aging duplex they're slowly working to rehabilitate. Remember My Name is his second novel. Growing up in rural Minnesota, Chase has also lived in Germany and Austria. The feelings of isolation growing up in a small town and his struggles to adapt to foreign culture and language have served as inspiration in his writing.

Made in the USA
Middletown, DE
04 April 2015